Pitch It

Evie Blum

To N, *for giving me a love so steady and true*
that it inspires me to write love stories.

To all the aspiring and accomplished authors out there imagining worlds
and stories and inviting readers along for the ride.

And to readers who support art and creativity.
Without you, there's nothing.

Contents

"If I had to give one piece of advice to startup founders, it would be to accept early on that hard things take hard work. But you have to believe in yourself and stay the course. There will, without a doubt, be times that you'll wonder whether you're smart enough or tough enough to accomplish your goal. But if you believe it's a worthwhile endeavor, you've got to have the patience and the determination to see it through. The best things in life—building an innovative technology, closing a huge deal, or winning over the love of your life—well, those life-changing things take time and hard work."

EXCERPT FROM "STARTING UP"
PODCAST DISCUSSION WITH KEVIN WONG,
FOUNDER/CEO OF INSTINQT,
SERIES B STARTUP ACQUIRED BY
LIGHTVERSE IN 2022

DECEMBER 2022

Staging Environment

SARAH

As I sit at my mom's kitchen counter, my hands wrapped around a hot cup of coffee, I stare out the window and wonder whether the fog will lift or if I'm destined to be a cold, soggy bride today. I haven't looked in the mirror this morning, but if the way I feel is any indication, Camila—my best friend since high school and my makeup artist for the day—will have her work cut out for her. I didn't sleep well last night, and it's too early to be awake, even for me.

While I wait for Camila to finish her beauty sleep, last night's dreams float through my mind. My heart tightens as a long-forgotten scene from my childhood surfaces—me holding onto my father's hand on the shore of the Pacific as a wave threatens to drag me out to sea, but knowing it won't since he's holding me tightly. *If only he were here now.*

I sip the too-hot coffee and wince as it burns my tongue. The image of my father's face is replaced by that of another man, another memory: the night Nathan broke up with me. I blow on my coffee and watch the small ripples on its milky surface, considering the inner workings of my mind, seemingly hell-bent on drumming up all the emotions on my big day.

I'm wondering what my husband-to-be is thinking about this morning when I hear Camila roll out of bed and trudge to the bathroom upstairs. A few minutes later, she joins me in the kitchen.

"Good morning," she says in a melodic voice. I take in her flawless brown skin and long, silky dark hair. Her deep brown eyes look sleepy, but in no way take away from her natural beauty. A cursory glance in my direction and one perfectly shaped eyebrow raise later, she ponders—directly, but not unkindly—"I wonder what foundation color cancels out green."

"Is it that bad?" I ask her, grimacing. She doesn't notice, though, since she's busy making herself a cup of coffee.

"No, I'm trying to make you laugh." She turns and smiles at me. "You look beautiful, and even if you didn't, I'm a makeup miracle worker. I've been doing this since my quinceañera."

I remember. We've been friends since our freshman year of high school, and if I turn out half as beautiful today as she did at her quinceañera, I'll be in great shape.

"He's gonna swoon when he sees you," she reassures me.

"He's not exactly the type to swoon."

"Actually, he's totally the type to swoon."

She's right. He is.

"It hasn't been that long since he fell in love with you the first time, but you'll look so great, he'll do it all over again."

"Maybe," I concede.

"You know it's all gonna be alright, don't you? I know you didn't expect things to turn out quite like this, but what you have—who you have—is good."

She's always been the wiser of the two of us. And I've always been able to trust her, her judgment. I nod in response.

"Now, I need something to eat," she says, opening the refrigerator to scan its contents. "Then we can get started. Hair first, okay?"

***

Camila, as usual, was right. When I joined my handsome groom in the vestibule, only fifty feet from where all our friends and family sat waiting for us to walk down the aisle, he didn't even try to hide the emotion that seemed on the brink of overwhelming him. I willed myself not to cry and simply mouthed, "I love you." He leaned in to tell me how beautiful I was and almost kissed me before stopping himself millimeters from my cheek.

"We should probably wait. It's only a few more minutes, right?" he said, grinning. In lieu of a kiss, he reached out and touched my hair. "Ready?"

"So ready," I told him, and though the ceremony had one or two unexpected moments, we promised to spend the rest of our lives loving and supporting each other, and I felt . . . whole.

Only now, on the dance floor, am I able to finally relax. Things are going fine until the slow song transitions into something with more energy. It's a song I know well, but something about it feels wrong.

The music is too loud—jarring and out of place, here and now. And it's not the acoustic version. More than anything, though, I'm dancing to it with the wrong person. The man holding me close, this isn't *our* song. It's mine and Nathan's song, the one he first played for me when we spent the night together in Seattle. He told me then it was his favorite song because it reminded him of me. And now I'm dancing to it with someone else, and who knows where Nathan is.

I glance up and look into the handsome face of someone I never expected to meet, someone who has been at the center of so many of the good things I've experienced this year. He smiles down at me warmly. I can feel his warm, sure hands on my waist through the fabric of my dress. He narrows his eyes, asking me a wordless question, trying to discern what I'm thinking. To avoid the intensity of his gaze, I glance down and notice the skirts of my off-white silk wedding dress swirling. I begin to feel a little "swirly" myself, but his hands steady me as he feels me go off-balance.

"Are you okay?" he asks. I nod and tell him I'm fine. His brow wrinkles, doubtful.

"Just a little too much celebratory champagne," I say.

Why am I dancing with him to this song? All of a sudden, I'm on the edge of a mild panic attack. Overwhelming guilt about everything that has happened descends upon me like a freak storm that could capsize a small boat. It comes out of nowhere and feels like it might crush me here, in front of everyone I know and love.

I try in vain to do box-breathing, hoping that even here—in the middle of a song, in the middle of a dance floor—the ordered breathing might have some effect in calming me.

He notices and tries to pull me back above water by telling me how beautiful I look. "Like an angel."

Not realizing, it seems, just how unsteady I already am, he twirls me around, keeping a close eye on my balance, never letting his strong hand veer far from my waist. And we both notice it—him—at the same time. Nathan. Standing off on the side, dressed casually, leaning up against the wall with his arms crossed and looking as if this whole wedding and the dance I'm sharing with Carter—the man he despises—is of no importance. He catches my eye and raises his eyebrows.

"I'll go," Carter says. "He looks . . . annoyed. Brides are only allowed to be happy on their wedding day."

I stop dancing. A few wedding guests have noticed Nathan, too, and are staring at him—at me—waiting to see what happens now.

"No, that'll only make things worse," I say. "It's me he wants to talk to."

Before Carter can stop me, I stride over to Nathan and get tripped up in the silk fabric, flowing beautifully but trickily around my legs. As I fall, only a few feet from Nathan, I hear Carter call out, concerned, "Sarah," and see Nathan rush forward to catch me.

Faintly, as if he's somewhere far away, I hear Nathan's voice, "I told you I wouldn't let you fall." Then I'm out.

EIGHT MONTHS EARLIER - APRIL 2022

WIREFRAME

SARAH

With LightVerse's acquisition of Instinqt a few weeks ago, Nathan left the company, and I miss seeing him at work, chatting in the office kitchen, or sending him funny GIFs while he's in a meeting to see if I can break his concentration. My consolation prize, though, is spending almost every evening with him after work. No longer worried about people at work discovering our feelings for one another, we've been playing catch up for the months we held back.

When I wake in the mornings now and see him lying in bed, still asleep, I'm reminded of the first time I ever woke up next to him. I'd snuck out of his place, thinking I'd never see him again. Fate obviously had other things in store since it took less than two weeks into my first job in high-tech to discover that the newest executive at Instinqt was none other than the sweet and sexy Nathan from the one-and-only one-night stand of my life.

It's been a dramatic few months, but since we've become official, we've fallen into a comfortable pattern. We spend a few nights at my place, then a few nights at his. At first, I brought an overnight bag packed with extra clothes and my toothbrush, but a week or two into our new arrangement, I saw that he had quietly, unceremoniously made space in his closet for my clothes. And he'd bought me a new toothbrush.

"A thinly-veiled comment on my dental health?" I'd asked him one evening before bed, holding it up to examine it.

"If your dental health was questionable in the least, I wouldn't kiss you so much," he replied tartly. To prove his point, he placed one of the aforementioned kisses directly on my mouth.

He left the bathroom but popped his head back in to smugly add, "Although, I did notice you don't floss daily."

I'd rushed out of the bathroom and tackled him, pushing him down onto his bed and sitting on top of him. He'd gone willingly, of course, and a short-but-lively make-out session—in an effort to prove that my flossing frequency might not be ideal but was not sub-par by any means—had ensued.

God, kissing him is the best, I think to myself now as I pack up my bag and get ready to leave the Instinqt office in downtown San Jose. On the elevator ride downstairs, I check my phone. It's been on silent for the last few hours, and I've missed a few text messages. Nathan's usual text game ranges from silly to romantic to downright perverted. Today's batch includes a GIF of a cat holding a "You're cute" sign and then simply, "You're beautiful." The last one brings a wide smile to my face:

Nathan: You're so sexy. And I'm thinking about you. And I can't wait for you to come over so I can put my mouth on your ???

Me: On my WHAT?! Don't leave me hanging!

On my way to meet him at a nearby coffee shop, I get stuck at a corner, at the mercy of the crosswalk light. While I wait to cross the street, I study him, in profile, sitting at a circular table near a large window in the coffee shop. He's wearing one of my favorite outfits—nothing objectively special, but the way his soft t-shirt fits him just right, highlighting his broad shoulders and strong arms, is enough to make me think about the feel of those arms around me. Knowing him, he probably picked up any old pair of shorts without giving the slightest thought to the way they hug his muscular legs and other attractive assets.

When I discover him in moments like these, when he doesn't immedi- ately notice me, and I'm free to just watch him, I catch the corners of my mouth turning up. My stomach does a little flip, like the first night I met him when I noticed him approaching me in the bar, embodying tall, dark, and handsome but bucking the cliché by adding in a dash of shyness.

The afternoon sun is shining brightly—it looks like it's directly in his eyes—but he's focused on his screen and doesn't seem to notice. His brow is scrunched, mouth twisted to one side. Then his face relaxes. He takes a sip of his drink and begins typing something, then turns toward the window and notices me looking at him. A warm, broad smile crosses his face, and his eyes crinkle. He closes his MacBook and slips it into the backpack sitting on the empty chair across from him.

The traffic light changes, and I cross the street and go inside the coffee shop to join him. He stands to greet me, and I lift up on tip-toes to give him a peck on the cheek. "You don't have to pack up if you're in the middle of something. I can read on my phone while you work."

"I'll work on it later tonight. Unless you want coffee now?"

"No, I've had enough today."

"In that case, let's go back to my place. Or we could go for a walk first?" He takes in my outfit, checking if my footwear is suitable for an afternoon stroll. His glance lingers on the curve of my hips and butt, and he runs his fingers lightly over the object of his affection.

I smirk. "You've been caught."

"Doing what?" he asks innocently.

"Trying to guess which underwear I'm wearing."

He sniffs out in amusement.

"I could use some exercise," I tell him suggestively.

He grins mischievously. "My place, then. That type of exercise requires some privacy."

I actually *have* worn comfortable shoes today, so our walk to his apartment—five blocks away and in one of the few skyrise apartment buildings in downtown San Jose—doesn't take long. We're slowed only momentarily when I stop to dig a couple dollars out of my backpack for a homeless woman on the corner. After I hand her the money and a pack of unopened tissues, we continue on our way.

"When did you start carrying small bills and tissues?" Nathan asks.

"When I started dating Mother Teresa," I reply with a wink. One of the first times I hung out with Nathan, he'd given away his dinner to a homeless man. "Hanging out with you must be having a good influence on me."

He rolls his eyes good-naturedly. I've embarrassed him, but he just pulls me in for a quick side hug, and we continue on our way. When we reach his building, the elevator is already on the ground floor, and as we step on and the doors close, he looks at me, a playful glint in his eye.

"What?" I ask.

A faint but noticeable guilty look crosses his face.

"Nothing."

"What's going on with you today?" I ask.

He hesitates but answers. "I was just wondering if you've ever had sex on an elevator."

"A couple of times," I reply immediately.

His mouth drops. But I can't hold the serious face I'm giving him.

He closes the distance between us and puts his arms around me as the elevator ascends to the tenth floor. "I'm not suggesting we do it now, but you know, just want to evaluate the options."

"Always good to have options, right?"

The elevator dings as it arrives at his floor, and the doors open.

"So," he replies, "you're saying you *would* do it. Duly noted." He shoots me a wink and exits the elevator before I can respond.

Entering his apartment is like entering another world—Nathan's world. The giant picture window on one side showcases the view of the mountains on the east side of San Jose. Having spent a good amount of time here over the last month or so, and being an early riser, I know that the view at the end of the day, as beautiful as it is, pales in comparison to the sunrise coming over those mountains. I've watched it a few times, a full cup of coffee warming my hands and my sleepy soul while I wait for Nathan to wake up.

His apartment, simply but tastefully decorated, always smells good, too, due to his love of cooking. I come in and take a seat on his couch and prop my feet up.

"Want something to eat?" he calls from the kitchen.

I get up and join him at the kitchen sink, where he's washing his hands. I thread my arms through his from behind and stick my hands under the running water. He looks back at me, a questioning expression on his face. He's quite a bit taller than I am, and I can barely see around his broad back to reach the faucet.

"Come here," he says, switching places with me—taking his place as the big spoon to my little one. He leans into my neck, kissing me behind my ear. I feel a sudden burst of heat and wonder if he can see the blush that I feel crawling up my neck and into my cheeks.

"What's going on with *you* today?" he asks, amused. "Is hand-washing an unknown aphrodisiac?"

"No. Just–" I begin to say, but I can't go on, too embarrassed to share the real reason I'm blushing—my sudden recollection of a very hot dream I once had about him. One that took place in this very kitchen, in this very same position, with Nathan behind me, rubbing my hands the same way he is now.

He turns off the water, spins me around to face him, and pushes me gently up against the counter with his hips, blocking me in.

"What are you not telling me, Sarah?" He takes my jaw in one of his still-damp hands, and he's close enough for me to see the mischief dancing in his eyes, playing on his lips.

"Dream Nathan was teaching Dream Sarah how to make pasta, and then . . ."

"Yes?"

"Then," I say, "we began to make out. You hoisted me up onto the counter, and I got super turned on by you wearing an apron."

"Shame I'm not wearing an apron now," he replies. "Maybe I should put one on now? So you can rip it off . . . with your teeth?"

He's grinning ear-to-ear, displaying his straight, white teeth, and I can easily imagine what articles of my own clothing I might like them to rip off in the very near future. I recently shared with him that I like some dirty talk in the bedroom, and I can tell he's trying—his texts earlier today, his playful suggestions now. I wish he'd do it more—go a little further—but

I've come to understand that he has his limits, so I encourage him by putting my own damp hands around his neck and pulling him down into a deep kiss.

He *thinks* he has the upper hand now, but he's also more than turned on by the description of my dream. Right now, I'm pinned between the hard counter and something else that's getting harder.

"This is the part where you lift me up onto the counter," I whisper in his ear. "At least, that's what Dream Nathan did."

"Sounds like that horny bastard has some good ideas." He lifts me roughly and sets me down on the cold marble. Now we're eye-to-eye, something that doesn't happen very often when we're vertical.

"I missed you today," he says, slipping back into his naturally sweet mode.

"I missed you, too."

He slowly unbuttons my shirt and traces kisses down my neck to my collarbone and then further down.

"I missed these, too," he says, slipping a hand in between the silky fabric of my shirt and my sheer bra to gently cup one of my breasts. He's eye-level with the current objects of his affection and tilts his head back up momentarily to check my expression, I think, but I'm distracted by his thumb, lightly rubbing across one of my nipples.

"When you put on this shirt this morning," he says, pausing and coming back to my mouth for a thorough kiss, "it was cold in the room, and I could see your nipples poking through it. All day long, I've just been imagining them rubbing up against it and thinking about how much I want to kiss them and put them in my mouth."

"So those are the question marks you mentioned in the text," I reply, and close my eyes while he kisses my neck. My skin is heated from his hands caressing me, from his words, but then I truly absorb what he just said. "Wait, can you really see my nipples through this shirt?"

"Not too much. But a guy's allowed to imagine. No wonder I couldn't focus on work today." His low laugh feels like a soft, warm blanket enveloping me.

While he's been talking and kissing me, he's managed to unbutton the rest of the buttons, and my silky shirt slides off of me and onto the floor as if blown by a breeze.

"Not fair," I chastise him. "You know the rules." The "rules" we somehow came up with a couple of weeks ago are that if I take off a piece of clothing, he must follow suit.

"Fine. Shirt or pants?" he asks.

"Both."

"But then we're uneven."

"So take it all off. Then," I pause, building the suspense, "put on *only* your apron."

My attempt at "smoldering eyes" is sending him into meltdown mode.

"You always have original ideas," he says, shaking his head at me as he begins to shed his clothes. In short order, he's down to his socks, and while I really do want to see him in *just* an apron, today will not be the day. I'm too impatient—all of this is too new. We'll save the sexy chef role-play for some other time.

While he bends down to rid himself of his last shred of clothing, I hop down from the counter and begin taking off my own clothes. I'm down to my bra and underwear. He's standing—stark naked—in his kitchen, examining me with his head tilted to the side.

"You don't really want me to wear an apron, do you?" he asks doubtfully, moving closer to me to wrap his arms around me. We're skin-to-skin in enough places that the last thing I want him to do is put another layer between us.

"No," I say, shaking my head. "The only thing I want on you . . . is me." And I pull him down to the floor.

***

"So, you guys just did it on the kitchen floor?" Camila asks me the next day, a dubious look on her face.

I nod, just a bit shamefacedly. "I know, right? I'm out of control around him. It's ridiculous."

"Ah, young love. Ryan and I used to do crazy stuff like that," Erin says wistfully. "If we tried to do it on the kitchen floor now, I'd probably come up with Cheerios stuck to my back."

I giggle. "You're a great advertisement for life with kids, Erin."

"Well, you know, Zoey's cute, but she's a three-year-old who won't stay in her bed, so no hot kitchen sex for me in the near future."

We're sitting outside, having lunch in the park. Since Erin and I work together and Camila's office is also downtown, we've formed a lunch club on Fridays. Usually, we get takeout, but today, Erin brought Korean food for us.

"I went overboard at Super Kyopo last night. My mom's coming for the weekend, and I had to stock up," she told us as she unloaded a full picnic basket of food onto the table.

Between bites of delicious *japchae*, I tell them the remainder of the evening—not all the details of course—but just enough to keep up my reputation as a sex goddess. Never in my life have I been the friend in the group to have a hot boyfriend and a great sex life, but it seems that I'm all we've got, so I'm on the hook for bringing the goods.

"Well, after we finished up, it was definitely dinner time. We were already near the fridge, so he just got up, opened it up, and asked if I want a sandwich. I thought I was going to pull a muscle laughing."

"That doesn't sound hygienic," Camila says.

"He was joking. I mean, he *did* make us sandwiches, but he washed his hands and put on boxers first. Don't worry, Cam. We're not animals."

She gives me her second highly skeptical look of the conversation and pops a piece of *gimbap* in her mouth.

"Anyways, what's happening with you?"

"Well, I didn't have kitchen sex last night," she tells me. "I did go out on a date. It was . . . interesting."

"And?" I ask.

"Not what I was looking for, I guess," she replies.

"What was wrong with him exactly?" I ask.

She presses her lips together as if she's trying to think of what to say when her phone pings with a text message. In lieu of an answer, she just shrugs and opens her phone. She snorts then quickly recovers, and I wonder if maybe the date didn't go as badly as she thought.

"What?" I ask her again and glance at Erin.

"Nothing. Shut up. Leave me alone," Camila says, rolling her eyes, before getting up and stalking away to text something back.

"Is it just me, or doth the lady protest too much?" Erin says in a bad British accent, looking positively mirthful.

While Cam's on her phone about ten feet away from us, Erin asks if Nathan's making progress on his startup idea.

"I mean, it's only been a few weeks, but he's got some direction. He said he's not ready to hash it all out with me yet. I think he's still processing everything that happened with the exit."

Everyone who worked at Instinqt has gone through changes since the LightVerse acquisition last month. A few, some of the startup's earliest employees, became actual millionaires. They had taken a gamble and joined the company when it was first founded a few years earlier, back when all the founders had to offer was a low salary and equity that might one day be worth a fortune—or might turn out to be worthless.

Then there are others who are currently wondering if they'll even have a job in a month. As the short-lived Chief Product Officer at Instinqt—brought over less than a year ago by his best friend and Instinqt's founder and CEO, Kevin Wong—Nathan's situation was closer to this second group. Given his short tenure, LightVerse gave him the option to continue with the new company as a technical lead or quit with a nice severance package. He'd chosen the latter.

"He's still doing meetings a few days a week to pass off information to the LightVerse guy who'll handle the product vision from their side," I tell Erin.

"Oh, yeah. I think I met him on a Zoom," Erin says. "Carter?"

"Maybe."

Cam has rejoined us, but before I grill her on her little text-break, she asks me, "You think you'll see Danica once everything's more settled?"

I snort. "I certainly hope not."

The last person I want to think about is Danica, Nathan's ex from college who helped connect Kevin and Nathan to LightVerse's CEO. The suggestive texts and half-naked selfies she sent Nathan's way almost led to the downfall of my budding relationship with him earlier this year. Not seeing her again is probably too much to hope for considering we now work at the same company, but as long as we don't end up in adjoining cubicles, I'll consider myself lucky.

A meeting reminder sounds on my phone.

"Ladies, I gotta go. Meeting with Kevin in ten minutes," I say.

Camila raises her eyebrows.

"I know, right? Me, meeting regularly with the CEO. Who could've imagined it when I started?"

"Me. Like, *literally* me. I could've imagined it," Camila replies, giving Erin an exasperated look. "I told you you'd be running the place in a year."

Erin smirks at her.

"You did. Right, as usual, Cam. But not exactly running the place yet."

Camila rolls her eyes at me and winks. "Soon," she says as we begin to pack up. She heads off in the direction of the consulting firm where she works, and Erin and I make our way back toward Instinqt. Kevin is coming up the sidewalk when we arrive.

"Coming back from lunch?" he asks. He has his bag slung over his shoulder. It looks like he might've worked from home this morning and is just making it into the office for the day.

"Yeah. Just got back from our Friday 'ladies' lunch,'" I reply.

"Nice," he replies distractedly. "Um, Sarah, do you mind if we meet at the coffee shop instead of the office today?"

"Sure, but I need to run up and get my computer. I'll be right back."

He nods. "I'll wait for you here."

As the elevator rises to the third floor, Erin leans back against the wall and toys with a lock of her chin-length black hair, recently highlighted with blue and teal streaks.

"You think something major's going on?" she asks.

I shrug. I'm not at liberty to share the details, but as Kevin's new unofficial merger and acquisition assistant, I was cc'd on an email earlier in the week about the budget for the Instinqt staff compensation for the next year. It looked like with our current employees we were way over what LightVerse wanted to allocate. I have a hunch our meeting outside the office might concern that.

The elevator doors open, and I tell Erin "bye" as I quickly head to my desk and grab my laptop and bag. When I return to the lobby downstairs, Kevin slips his phone into his pocket.

"Ready?" he says, smiling at me.

"Yep. What's going on, though? Why not at the office?" I ask, heading outside with him.

"I just don't feel like being in the office today. Being the CEO has its perks, you know?"

"I thought you had a new title now," I reply.

"I guess you're right," he admits. "Anyways, I need some good coffee. Like, *not*-coffee-machine coffee."

I note his appearance. His tall frame is clad in his usual trendy-but-casual style—nice jeans and an expensive white t-shirt. But his recent shave and fresh haircut—his short black hair, spiked up with gel—can't hide the fact he's tired.

"Rough night?" I ask.

"It was okay. I was up late, though. Just busy . . . with all this LightVerse stuff going on."

We enter the same coffee shop where I met Nathan yesterday afternoon, order some drinks—double espresso for Kevin, latte for me—and grab a table near the back. The barista calls our names as we get settled.

"I'll get the drinks," I tell Kevin.

When I return from collecting our coffees, he's already opened up his laptop, and we jump right in. We spend the next hour going over the budget I saw in the email a couple days ago, and it's what I suspected. Not everyone from Instinqt will have a place at LightVerse. Kevin tells me that LightVerse HR has been combing through our employee roster and figuring out who is essential and who isn't.

"This sucks so much," I say. "People have given so much to make the company a success, and now they're gonna get laid off."

"It does suck," he agrees, a strained expression on his face. He was probably up late worrying about the new budget and the seemingly inevitable layoffs. "The only thing I can do is make sure they get nice severance packages, which is what I'm trying to do. Don't worry."

"Don't worry, as in I'll get severance, or don't worry—I'll still have a job?" I ask him.

"*You* definitely have a job. I wouldn't be asking for your help on all of this if you didn't. I've told them that you're essential. Way too valuable to lose."

I hesitate, but decide to ask, "It's not because of Nathan, is it? The fact that we're dating, and you guys are best friends?"

"Definitely not," he reassures me. "If anything, the fact you're dating that jackass is a strike against you."

I snicker, and he winks at me.

"Seriously, though. You're great, Sarah. I'm happy we're getting a chance to work together more closely."

It's unexpected—him being this open and personal with me. He usually guards himself more.

"Me, too, Kevin."

"You can call me 'Kev' if you want. We're colleagues, but we're also friends." He gives me a questioning look that seems to require a response.

"Yeah, I think so . . . Kev," I say, trying it out.

He graces me with a small, uncharacteristically shy smile just as an email notification pops up on his screen. The computer dings for the fiftieth time during our discussion.

"Someone from LightVerse," he says. "I should take care of it."

"I'll head back. Let me know if you need my help on anything, okay?"

"You'll come to regret that offer," he jokes as he turns back to his laptop to check his email.

PROOF OF CONCEPT

NATHAN

Nathan's more than aware he should be working on something at least tangentially related to his startup idea instead of slouching in his desk chair, distracted by memories from the past year. Was it a good year or a bad one? On his mental scorecard, there are plenty of tally marks in the "good" column—getting to know Sarah and helping Kevin secure Instinqt's acquisition both rank pretty high. But the memory of his father's illness—the long weeks Noah spent in the hospital, his family by his bedside, not knowing whether he would recover or not—lingers, like a morning fog, unwilling to dissipate and allow the sun in. Nathan still feels the weight in his chest some mornings, especially when he's alone at home working—*supposed* to be working.

His father's prostate cancer diagnosis late last fall and subsequent auto-immune issues had left him feeling powerless. *What if they had known sooner?* That question plagued him while his dad was in the hospital. And this tiny seed of a question—Nathan's inability to let it go, to do nothing—led him to his current situation. An out-of-work software engineer either ambitious or naive enough to think he has the brains to solve this kind of complex problem. His goal? Create a tool that brings together the right personal health data—blood tests, scans, genetic data, and more—in a clear user interface to help healthcare professionals diagnose correctly and earlier.

God, I should have been a video game designer.

A honk from the street ten floors below drags him back to the present, and he's grateful for it. He shifts his gaze toward the mountains—currently green with smatterings of color from the spring flowers. He'll take Sarah to see the super-bloom on the other side of the ridge this weekend. Thinking of her, he smiles, despite himself, fully aware that he's a dopey guy in love. Things are going well with her and, thankfully, with his father's health. His mom texted him on Tuesday that his dad is feeling strong after last week's radiation treatment, and he allows himself a cautious hope that his family's hard times are behind them.

Returning his attention to his laptop, he tries to remember where he left off and wonders whether he jumped into the technical side of things too early on this startup idea. He'll eventually have to pitch all of this to a venture capital firm, and just thinking about it makes his heart race. He checks his Garmin watch, which confirms his heart rate is indeed higher than normal for this time of day, and sees it's almost 2:00 p.m. His meeting is starting soon, but he can spare a minute to check in with Sarah.

Nathan: Hey, hottie. <kiss emoji>

A few minutes later, she responds with a selfie. *Taken in the stairwell?* The angle is *very* complimentary. A few tendrils of her long brown hair have come loose from her ponytail and are resting on the top curve of her breast, drawing his attention away from her full lips. Her raised arm—presumably to snap the selfie—seems to have caused just the tiniest gap in her blouse, and he might be imagining it, but he *thinks* he sees the trim of a white lace bra.

Nathan: Why'd you sneak out to the stairs?
Sarah: I can't take a cleavage pic at my desk, now can I?
Nathan: <flame emoji> How's your day going?
Sarah: Reviewing customer contracts for Kevin. I'm his new M&A assistant now. <spiral eyes emoji>

Nathan: Good to know I'm not the only one he's torturing
with paperwork.

Nathan has reviewed his own share of legal documents the past few
weeks, and he can just imagine what Kevin is dumping on Sarah.

Sarah: Definitely torture. Is it 5 o'clock yet?

No, but it is time for his meeting with Carter Michaels, LightVerse's
Head of M&A Product Strategy. Kevin asked Nathan to work with him
as part of the company transition processes. Carter is—put simply—not
his favorite person. In their recent meetings, Carter has asked insightful
questions about the Instinqt product, but he's a little too sure of himself.
The fact that Carter has essentially taken over Nathan's job doesn't help
matters. It *was* Nathan's choice to leave the company after the exit, but
it still stings.

He sends Sarah one last message.

Nathan: Getting on a meeting with an LV person myself. Will
I see you tonight?
Sarah: As if you have a choice. <wink emoji> I'll text you
when I'm on my way home.

Her place tonight. Good. They've spent a few nights this week at his
apartment, but he loves being at her place. He heads to his bedroom to
change his shirt, then sits back down at his computer to start the call.
Carter signs in to the meeting, and Nathan turns on his camera.

"Hey, Nate," Carter says.

"Hey, what's up?" Nathan replies, forcing the tight muscles in his jaw
to relax enough to smile.

"Lots going on," Carter answers. He's wearing a button-down shirt.
Who does that for a Zoom call and on a Friday, no less? Carter's mil-
lion-dollar smile doesn't quite reach his eyes. "I just have a few more

questions after our last call. Thanks for jumping on a call on a Friday afternoon."

So he does know it's Friday.

"Yeah, sure." Nathan tries to sound friendly, but he's not feeling it.

"So, I just talked to Kevin, and he still has a lot of stuff to go through, but he said he'd pulled in one of the project managers to help out."

"I heard," he replies, thinking of his recent text with Sarah.

"You guys are tight, huh?"

"Best friends since college."

"And you're sure you don't want to stay on with the company? As an engineer?"

"Yeah, I'm working on my own thing."

"Kevin mentioned that. VC money is drying up with this bad economy, though."

As accurate as Carter's insight is, Nathan doesn't like his tone.

"So, what questions did you have?" Nathan replies abruptly.

Carter doesn't seem bothered with the quick shift in the conversation and jumps into a series of questions. They focus mostly on the product roadmap, but some touch on engineering concepts. As Nathan describes some of the more technical aspects of the architecture, he can tell that Carter doesn't entirely understand what he's saying. Nathan usually tries to make technical concepts more accessible to non-engineers, but not today. Not for this guy.

"Well, you're definitely an engineer," Carter says.

I did spend the last ten years of my life becoming one. Jackass.

"Anything else?" he asks Carter, willing himself to remain civil.

"No, I think I have what I need. I'll check with Maya on some of the more technical stuff you described if I need more details."

He considers for a moment what Maya Kapoor, Instinqt's former Chief Technology Officer, must think about this guy. She hates pompous assholes. It brings a smile—a real one—to his face, and he signs off.

***

A couple hours later, he's hunched over his computer—intermittently staring at his laptop screen and staring out the window, trying to figure something out—when he gets a text from Sarah.

> **Sarah:** Buying ingredients for dinner. You're coming over, right?
> **Me:** Yep. What should I bring?
> **Sarah:** Just yourself. I'm cooking.
> **Me:** Gonna wear an apron? <wink emoji>
> **Sarah:** Guess you'll have to come and find out.
> **Me:** What time?
> **Sarah:** Not a pro like you. It'll take me some time. 7?
> **Me:** See you then <kiss emoji>

He showers, dresses quickly, and grabs his AirPods on his way out. As he leaves the building, he notices the sun setting over the Santa Cruz Mountains in an array of oranges and pinks. The warm day is starting to cool down, and he tries to imagine his own mind—full of code, questions, and doubts from the day—doing the same.

Desperate to clear his head, he pulls his phone out of his pocket and uncharacteristically chooses music, instead of his usual podcast or audiobook, for the walk to Sarah's. He taps on a slightly girly and upbeat playlist Sarah made for him and smiles as he heads into Trader Joe's to the sounds of BTS and Lil Nas X.

He arrives at her building, and when he knocks on her door, she opens it quickly. It's been less than twenty-four hours since he last saw her, but just the sight of her—freshly showered and in a dark blue, soft-to-the-touch sweater that hugs her shape perfectly—lifts his spirits. He offers her the tulips he brought.

"Oooh, beautiful."

"Like you."

She comes close to place a kiss directly on his mouth. As she backs away, he sees her quick survey of his outfit.

"You're looking cheery this evening. Have I seen this shirt?" she asks.

"I'm pretty sure you could see this shirt from ten miles away," he replies. "But I'm not sure if I've ever worn it around you. I was probably trying to make a good impression."

She snickers.

"Now you know. I like yellow," he says, stepping inside and shutting the door. He leans down to remove his shoes and places them on the rack near the door.

When he straightens back up, she's looking at him carefully. "I take it back. You actually seem a little . . . down?"

"No, not down."

"Fine. Contemplative?"

How does she do that?

"Maybe. I *was* thinking on the way over. Wondering if I made the right decision not joining LightVerse. You know, with the economy and everything. Wouldn't have been the worst idea to have a steady income while I work on the startup idea."

"Everyone misses you—especially me—but I think you made the right decision." She lifts up on her tiptoes and kisses him on the cheek. He pulls her close and angles his head down to kiss her more fully, but before their lips connect, she pulls away and turns to go into the kitchen.

"Give me a second to go put these in some water, okay?"

She returns a minute later to join him on the couch. She lays back against the armrest and rests her legs on his lap. As she recounts her day, including a conversation she had with Kevin earlier, he feels a small, unexplainable pang of jealousy. During their overlapping time at Instinqt, he and Sarah didn't collaborate much at work, but at least they were part of the same professional world. Now, well, he's only a part of his own professional world. And it's starting to be a damn lonely one.

It's not like working on a PhD in computer science didn't require a lot of heads-down time. He spent plenty of quiet hours banging out code and writing academic articles to cross the finish line of his studies. Moving out to California last year, only to find himself in a pandemic lockdown wasn't exactly a breeze either. He was able to meet people here and there, but even a natural introvert has his limits, and he was more than ready to get back in the office. Now that he's been working at home by himself the past few weeks, with no set schedule or specific work demands, he's had the free time to calculate that he only got three months of face-to-face time in the work world before finding himself right back in his quiet—very quiet—apartment again.

He traces his fingers up Sarah's smooth calf and focuses on what she's saying.

"—and then he shares this spreadsheet from hell with me. I swear, Nathan, there were like a thousand rows, and each of them refers to some different document or spreadsheet. It was just . . ." She exhales in a huff.

"He's lucky he has you on board to help him, but I'm a little bit jealous," he admits.

"Of my spreadsheet?"

He snickers. "No, of Kevin. I miss working with you."

Kevin must be benefiting from Sarah's help—she's smart and extremely versatile. There's also sensitive information about the merger and acquisition, and he knows he can trust her. Kevin told him so explicitly. Still, Nathan loved seeing her at work, being there to witness and celebrate her successes with her real time.

"Yeah, you and I did a lot of 'work' together," she jokes, using quote fingers. He smiles, thinking of the countless hours of Zoom meetings they spent flirting instead of talking about anything work-related.

"Maybe one day we'll work together again."

She clears her throat meaningfully.

"I mean, *actual* work," he clarifies.

"Oh," she says, laughing. "Yeah, that *would* be nice. So, how are things going? Any new directions? Moving forward on the original one?"

"It's hard. I mean, I jumped into the code quickly. I kinda wanted to see if I could get lucky and crank out a proof of concept, but I'm still not sure how it's going to make money. That's the part the venture capitals will want to see."

"Well, you've only been doing it for a few weeks. Good things take time."

"Right." She is right, but he can't shake the feeling that it won't be enough—that *he* won't be enough.

"Kev mentioned today that he was connecting you with a venture capital friend of his, right?"

"Kev?"

"Yes, Kevin, your bestie?"

"It's just the first time I've heard you call him 'Kev.'"

"Oh, yeah, he told me I could call him that," she says. "Thought I'd try it out."

Relax. Everything is bothering him today. He's hungry. He had an annoying meeting with Carter. He's taking everything too seriously.

"Yeah," he says, letting it go. He doesn't want to ruin their evening over something dumb. "I'll probably schedule it for a few weeks from now. It's just grabbing a cup of coffee with a contact of his to get a sense of what's going on in the market. Get some general advice. Kev thought it'd be a good idea, even if I don't have things built out much yet."

"You're lucky he's got your back."

He nods and tries to let his earlier annoyance go.

She stands up and holds out her hand. "Want some dinner?"

"Definitely."

"Come, then." She pulls him off the couch toward the kitchen. "I know it might not be as good as something you've made, but I think you'll like it."

The table is set with colorful dinner plates, wine glasses, and several dishes she must have been working on the last couple of hours: *shakshuka*, chopped vegetable salad, and flatbread that's a tad black around the edges. She probably forgot it in the oven—she's been known to do that. But he doesn't say a word. She's self-conscious about her cooking, and he would never make her feel bad about it.

"It smells amazing. Let's eat."

After they sit, he opens the bottle of red wine on the table with the corkscrew and pours each of them a glass.

"To Friday night dinners," he toasts.

"To yellow t-shirts," she responds.

"To smart, hot girlfriends."

"And boyfriends."

They clink glasses, and each takes a sip.

"So, I was having lunch with Cam and Erin today," Sarah tells him, as she begins to serve them both food, "and Cam mentioned she went on a date last night."

"Good for her."

"Well, she said it actually wasn't all that good, but I suspect it went better than she was letting on."

"Hmmm, okay."

"Anyways, I saw her, like, super-suspiciously texting someone and was wondering what it was all about."

He furrows his brow. "What does super-suspicious texting look like?"

"Like this," she says, grabbing her phone and mimicking someone getting a flirty text from someone, putting her hand over her mouth in mock-shock. She continues the charade and shoots a furtive look around to see if anyone's noticed her pleased reaction, then pretends to text back something even flirtier, all while dancing gleefully in her seat.

"That does look suspicious." He laughs. "What kind of text did you get now?"

"Too scandalous. Can't share."

"Was it an unsolicited—" he begins to say.

"Dick pic?" she asks, interrupting him. "Yes, yes, it was. *How* did you know?"

He leans in close and whispers in her ear, "Because I sent it." She gasps in mock surprise, then gives him an amused smile.

"Come here," he says. He pulls her to a standing position, then twists her just right, so she falls into his lap.

Close to her, he feels better than he has all day. He rubs his hands down her arms. "You know how I told you, like a month or two ago, that I'm starting to love you?"

"Yes?"

"And then it kind of scared you, so I didn't really say it again?"

She nods, a sheepish look on her face.

"How are you feeling now?"

"I'm feeling—"

"I love you, Sarah," he says before she can finish her sentence.

No self-restraint whatsoever.

She locks eyes with him and touches his face. He realizes he hasn't shaved since yesterday—and so does she, judging by the expression on her face. But then she leans closer, touching her forehead to his, eyes open, staring at him. He waits. She's being just the slightest bit weird. She does this when she's either nervous and trying to cover it or just so completely comfortable that there's no reason to hide her little quirks. He loves it so much it hurts because he knows how she felt in her last relationship—uncertain, not good enough.

Her opening up and sharing her silly side with him makes him want to wrap his arms around her—love her, protect her from all harm. He waits, giving her a minute to figure out for herself how she feels and then to clue him in.

"Nathan?"

"Yes?"

"I love you, too."

He kisses her softly on the lips in response. "Can I make love *to you?*" he asks, beginning to nuzzle her neck with his nose.

Sarah likes him to be bold and gets turned on by him telling her directly and descriptively what he wants to do with her—to her—but his natural setting is "sweet." He can't help it. But now that she's also said that she loves him, he's feeling more at ease and he wants to feel close to her. The weight from before—from the annoying call with Carter, from his own self-doubt, from being the tiniest bit jealous of his best friend—is gone.

"Yes. But this time, totally normal, in-a-bed sex. I pulled a muscle from doing it on the kitchen floor last night," she jokes.

"Sounds like you need a massage." He moves his hand up to her breast.

"*That's* supposed to make my back feel better?"

"I can do lots of things to make you feel better." He picks her up and carries her with ease to her bedroom. He carefully places her on the bed, and she lies on her side, propped up on her elbow, watching him as he calmly and methodically begins to remove his clothes—sun-yellow shirt first and dark blue jeans until he's down to his boxers.

"You know the rules," he says to her as he lies down next to her and spoons her. "Let me help."

He gently rolls her to her back and begins to remove her sweater. He prefaces every movement of his fingers with a kiss, and he can tell she's enjoying the attention he's lavishing on her. Her eyes are closed, and when he slips her last article of clothing—her sexy underwear—down her legs, and she's completely naked, she opens her eyes.

"When did you take off your underwear?" she asks, surprised.

He winks at her. "I'm a magician. Wanna see a few more of my tricks?"

"Mmmm, yes," she replies.

He kisses her softly, slowly at first. Then their kisses, the touches they share with one another—his hands on her back, pressing her into him, her hands splayed on his hard chest—become faster, more urgent. She moans softly as he takes her nipples in his mouth. He caresses her lower, and she's wet, aroused, and ready for him. Reaching out, she touches his hard cock—asking how it can be so hard but so soft and silky at the same time, and he smiles into her mouth. She talks—questions here, insights there—when they make love. And at first, it surprised him, but it quickly became one of the things he loved the most about her during sex. That and her ass. Well, maybe her breasts and the warmth he feels when he's inside of her. Well, *every part of her is amazing.*

She rolls to her side and pushes him onto his back.

"I want you—"

"You have me—" he starts to say.

"I want *you* . . . in my mouth," she says, cutting him off and straddling him. Then she begins to move down his body, kissing him on her journey south.

"It's not going to hurt your back?"

"What exactly do you think I plan to do?" she asks, laughing. "Should I stretch first?"

"Come here," he says, laughing. "You don't have to do that."

"I think you need to just listen to me and enjoy yourself for a minute. Got it?"

God, I love when she's bossy in bed. But that's battling his desire to make sure she's getting what she needs out of this. He pulls gently on her arms, trying to get her to come up higher, so he can kiss her more, do something for her.

But she pulls back and shakes her head. She parts her lips just enough and runs her tongue gently over her teeth while shooting him a naughty expression. Imagining what's about to happen thirty seconds from now, he simply nods.

"Just let me kiss your breasts first," he almost begs, propping himself up on his elbows.

She pushes him back down on his back and slides up his body, allowing him to take one of her nipples in his mouth. He licks and plays with her until she moans.

"That feels good . . . Oh!" she says, as he bites her softly. "It feels . . . Ohhh—No! I said it's *my* turn."

Before he can protest, she slides back down his body. As she sinks lower, she licks her lips and parts them. He almost comes undone at the sight. Bracing herself on his hip bones, she winks at him before gently placing him in her mouth. When she begins to move her mouth up and down on him, he moans in pleasure. He has to concentrate not to come right away. It feels *that* good.

"You want me to keep going?" she asks, pausing for a second with her mouth but continuing to move her hands up and down his shaft.

"No," he says, breathless. "Come here."

She pouts at him.

"I think you need to just listen to me and enjoy yourself for a minute. Got it?" he says, mimicking her.

She smirks at him but joins him on the pillow, and he pulls her hips toward his, so she's facing him. He grabs her thigh to wrap her leg around his back, and in this position, his hard cock is rubbing up against all sorts of wonderful places on her body. Suddenly, she shivers.

"I'll warm you up," he says. He jumps up, so he can turn down the blanket, and she scoots under it, holding it open for him to join her.

Once he's there, things proceed quickly. She's on her back, legs parted, inviting him in, and he accepts the invitation wholeheartedly. He rocks his hips back and forth, creating a rhythm that could send him into a coma with its intensity. Her eyes are closed, and he takes a second to lean down and kiss her on her temple.

She opens her eyes for a second to smile at him and say, "Keep going." And then, "I love you."

Her words give him even more purpose, and he moves in and out of her, speeding up until she dissolves. Then he, too, melts into her.

When he can talk again, breathe again, without panting, he says, "Sarah?"

"Hmmm?" She looks at him with a slightly glazed expression.

"I'm glad you're my girlfriend." He feels good now—good *with her*—and he wants her to know it.

"Well, it certainly has its perks, doesn't it?"

"Hell, yeah."

She sits up, gathering the sheet around her upper half. "We didn't really finish dinner before. Should we have dessert now?" she asks.

"There's more?"

"Of course. I was planning on eating strawberries and whipped cream before you whisked me off to bed."

He sits up with a start and snatches the sheet off her upper half, eyeing what he's revealed. Gently squeezing one of her breasts, he whispers, "Whipped cream, huh?"

"You're insatiable," she says, giggling and pushing him back down on the bed. "I'll be back in a second. Don't leave."

"I'll never leave you," he whispers. But she's already out of earshot.

Agile

SARAH

I'm sitting at my desk in the office, half-working, half-contemplating going in search of a snack in the kitchen when the "new email" sound pings on my laptop. "Updates," the subject line reads.

Uh-oh.

Recent emails with that subject line have brought all sorts of news, ranging from more information on LightVerse's onboarding and HR processes to announcements of budget cuts and layoffs. I click to open the email and quickly scan it.

"*We're moving?*" I say to Erin, who's sitting in the row of connected desks about six feet away from me. I knew it was a possibility, but I didn't think it would happen this soon.

While an open office has its downsides—no privacy and limited quiet spaces to work—it's extremely effective for group conversations, especially one of this nature. Moments after I've finished reading the email, I can already hear murmurs of surprise coming from every direction.

"To Mountain View?" Erin says. "Castro Street? This is going to be so much fun, Sarah. So many good restaurants!"

Mountain View is nice, definitely nicer than downtown San Jose, but my five-minute commute to the current office has always been a great job perk. I'm already envisioning the horrendous commute north on Highway 101 when I need to work from the office. I'm expressing exactly this sentiment when Erin reminds me that I can work from home most days.

"We'll coordinate our days in the office, so we can have lunch together," she continues.

She opens Google Maps on her browser and begins to check out the address.

"Look at this building," she says, clicking on the street view.

I go to her desk and peer over her shoulder at the screen. It *is* beautiful—modern architecture with tons of glass windows and a stylish LightVerse sign near the entrance. I've always liked our Instinqt offices, but the new building seems like a major upgrade. Erin clicks back over to her email, and we skim through it again.

"We'll be moving in a couple weeks," I say, noticing a detail I missed on my first read-through.

Just then, Kevin exits the elevator with a man I've never seen before and tips his chin at me. The man with him—an attractive, dark blond guy who looks to be in his midthirties—notices Kevin's greeting and smiles in a friendly way, almost as if he knows me. I don't know *him*, but I smile back. I can't help it. He exudes confidence. It's something about his gait, the set of his shoulders, broad but relaxed just enough. I bet he's used to getting that reaction from people.

No, from women.

On their way across the office toward the conference room, Kevin and his companion, the Chris Hemsworth doppelgänger, stop to say hello to us where we're standing at Erin's desk, and Kevin introduces us.

"Carter, this is Sarah Hoffman, the technical program manager I was telling you about, and you know Erin Park already from our Zoom meeting last week. Ladies, this is Carter Michaels. He'll be leading some important product strategy initiatives for Instinqt in addition to a couple of other product lines under LightVerse."

"Carter, so nice to meet you in person," Erin says politely, extending her hand. Then she turns my direction so only I can see her face, and her eyes dance with, well, glee. She's waggling her eyebrows at me. I can't shoot her a look back because both Kevin's and Carter's eyes are on me. So I send her a mental message—"Will you chill out?"—and hope it pings into her addled brain.

Distracted as I am by Erin's behavior, it takes me a minute to notice that Carter is now holding out his hand to me. I look up—he's tall, almost the same height as Nathan—and his eyes meet mine.

"Um, yes, nice to meet you, Carter," I say, holding out my hand. He has a firm handshake that lasts a second too long.

Carter glances at Erin's computer screen and finally drops my hand. "Checking out photos of the new office? It's really nice."

She glances up at Carter and replies in a dreamy voice, "The view is amazing," and I will myself not to laugh.

"I'm sure you'll love it. There are a lot of new things you'll like about LightVerse," he says, looking directly at me.

"Shall we?" Kevin asks Carter, gesturing in the direction of the conference room.

"Let's do it," he replies but leans into me to say quietly, "Your reputation precedes you, Sarah. I look forward to working together."

Have I gone crazy, or did he actually just compliment me after knowing me for approximately sixty seconds? I swirl around to check if Erin heard him and find her up to her usual antics, fanning herself with the black Moleskine notebook we got in our LightVerse swag bags.

"That guy . . . is *hot*," she says, angling the notebook in my direction to fan my face.

Swatting it away, I reply drily, "I didn't notice."

"Sure," she says, laughing and rolling her eyes at me.

"Did something seem different about him?" I ask her.

"I mean, he looks exactly like Liam Hemsworth–"

"Oh my god, I was going to say Chris Hemsworth, but yeah," I say, interrupting her. "But, like, besides that?"

"He seems like the type of guy who's used to getting what he wants," she replies thoughtfully.

She's hit the nail on the head. *Used to getting what he wants.* It'll be interesting to see just what Carter Michaels wants.

Due Diligence

SARAH

On Sunday morning, I open my eyes and stretch my body like a cat waking up from a long nap. Sun rays are already streaming through the window. I roll over to the side of the bed Nathan sleeps on—taking a second to appreciate the fact that we've already established our respective sides of the bed—and find it empty.

Why's he up so early?

Then, I hear his low voice, talking quietly in the other room, and his parents' voices as well. He must be on FaceTime with them.

"How are things going? You and Sarah doing okay?" his mother, Claire, asks.

"Yeah," he says. Am I imagining a wistful tone? Likely. "Things are good. Really good. We spend a lot of time together. I'm hardly ever at my place anymore."

"*Good. Really good.*" I concur.

"I'm happy for you, sweetheart," his mom replies.

"Where's Dad? I want to tell him Happy Father's Day."

Right. That's why he woke up early to talk to his dad.

I take a deep breath. It's been a few years since I've had someone to wish a Happy Father's Day. I hear Nathan's dad join the call, and I get up to go to the bathroom and splash some water on my face, hoping it freshens it up enough that the few tears that slipped out won't be noticeable. I come out of the bathroom to find Nathan standing in the bedroom doorway, still on the call with his parents.

Nathan glances at me, and his eyes narrow.

"Dad, I'll call you back later, okay?"

"No, just enjoy your day. Tell Sarah 'hi' for us," his father says.

He ends the call and comes over to me, walking gingerly, different from his usual carefree way of traversing the world. Placing his hand lightly on my arm, he examines my face and rubs the soft pad of his thumb lightly under the corner of my eye. He knows I've been crying.

"You heard me?" he asks.

"It's okay. I mean, the whole world can't stop just because my dad died, right?"

"I didn't want you to hear. I should've gone outside."

"No."

"No, what?"

"You don't have to hide the fact that you have a dad. If anything, you should be celebrating it after the past year," I reply. I mean it. His father dealt with numerous complications following his biopsy—an unexplained fever and vitals all over the place. There were times when they didn't know if he would pull through.

"Doesn't mean it can't still be hard for you." He comes closer and pulls me into a bear hug.

"Neck," I tell him.

"Neck" is short for "You're breaking my neck." He's taller than me, and when he hugs me tightly, my neck is pushed backward at an awkward angle.

"Oooh, right." He spreads his legs and squats down so he can hug me at my height. "It's like a hug and a quad workout all in one," he says, laughing.

"Perfect for you."

"You are," he says and kisses me sweetly on the mouth.

"So, what should we do today?" I ask.

"Make breakfast together and go on a hike?"

"Yeah, I'd like that," I say.

He's still squatting—his legs are probably getting tired—and then he surprises me by saying, "Sarah, even though you're kinda short, I love you."

"You should love me *because* I'm short," I retort.

He goes down on his knees now and hugs me around the waist, his head nuzzling my chest and his hands cupping the bottom of my breasts. "Would you still love me if I only came up to here?"

"I can see the advantages of dating a short guy," I reply with a giggle. I run my hands through his hair, which is still sticking up from sleeping.

"Sarah, I do love you. You know that, right?"

"Nathan, you know that I love you, right?"

"Yeah," he says, looking up at me with a bashful smile. "I do."

***

It's late morning by the time we're ready to leave for the hike.

Nathan checks the weather on his phone. "It's supposed to be hot today," he says.

"Where should we go?" I ask.

"Sanborn?" he suggests, and I groan. He loves that hike. I guess I do, too, and it *does* have shade, which is essential since we're starting out midday. It also has an uphill start that I don't quite feel ready for this morning.

"I guess that's a 'no,' then."

He opens his phone again and checks the map. After tapping around, he says, "We could drive to Aptos and do that hike you told me about."

"Forest of Nisene Marks? Perfect. I can't believe you haven't been there yet."

The Forest of Nisene Marks is about ten minutes from where I grew up, and I've been there too many times to count. In the winter months, the creeks overflow. More than once, I've come out muddy and numb at the toes after somehow managing to land in all the puddles. It's nothing short of paradise in the summer, too. The gurgling creeks are less full, but banana slugs abound. The misty air in the cool, shaded areas under the giant redwoods—ten degrees cooler than out in the sun—transport you to an almost fantasy-like world, especially if you're lucky enough to find yourself away from other hikers. I can't wait to take Nathan there today.

I zip up my backpack and stand. "We can also stop at Soul Salad on the way back," I say in a sing-songy voice. He pulls me in for a kiss on the cheek and chuckles at my weird relationship with salads.

Despite the rocky start, it's going to be a perfect Sunday.

We head out to Nathan's new car, a hybrid SUV he bought with some of his Instinqt severance package cash. He wanted a vehicle that could more easily carry his mountain bike and had treated himself.

"You wanna drive?" he asks.

"Nah, I'll be DJ," I say, hopping in the passenger seat.

"Twenty One Pilots?" he asks as we head up into the mountains on Highway 17.

"Yeah. I never really listened to them that much, but Kevin—"

"It's Kevin's favorite band," he replies. "He used to play it all the time in college."

"Oh, really? He's been playing music while we do contract review. Says it makes it less painful." I smile, but when I glance over at him, he has an odd look on his face. "You okay?"

"Oh, uh, yeah," he replies, realizing I caught him. "I was just . . . You're working a lot with Kevin these days."

His tone is mildly curious, but am I also hearing a hint of jealousy? That's not like Nathan. What does he think Kevin and I talk about? It's either work or, well, Nathan. I rub his leg, and he squeezes my hand. We drive for twenty minutes, mostly in silence—each of us lost in our own thoughts—when suddenly, I turn to him.

"I have an idea," I say suddenly.

He glances at me. "What's that?"

"Would you . . . want to meet my mom?"

We'll pass Santa Cruz on the way to Aptos, and today feels like the right day for them to meet. It's been a few weeks since I've seen her, and it's

Father's Day, which likely hasn't escaped her notice. Maybe a visit from me—from us—will raise her spirits. Maybe it'll raise mine.

"Um," he says, glancing at me quickly but also trying to keep his eyes on the road. "Yeah, I mean, I guess you've met my family, but I haven't met yours."

"True."

"Let's do it," he says, in a decisive tone. "I'd love to."

"I'll call her and make sure she's at home. Just get off at the first exit for Santa Cruz in a couple miles, okay?"

I catch her on her way home from the grocery store when I call, and she says she'd love for us to come visit. Nathan taps on the steering wheel and keeps glancing my direction, then out the window while we sit in the traffic exiting the highway.

"You okay?" I ask him, touching his arm.

"Yeah. I was just thinking, though, that if I'd known I was going to meet your mom, I probably would've dressed nicer." He looks amazing in the navy-blue V-neck t-shirt he chose this morning.

"Oh my god," I say, laughing. "She'll love you."

He exhales and nods. When I met Nathan's parents, I was so concerned with other things—trying to figure out what was going on between Nathan and me, worrying about him, worrying about his father—that I didn't even have time to feel nervous.

"If you say so," he says.

"She'll loudly declare that you're drop-dead gorgeous, and you're finally going to understand why I'm so weird."

"You're not weird."

"Ehhh, I am. A little bit."

"Yeah, okay, you *are*, a little bit," he admits and laughs.

When we pull off the highway, I give him directions to my mom's house in Westside. As we drive through the streets toward the neighborhood I grew up in, he notes the rainbow flags decorating the lampposts for Pride month.

"I bet it was nice growing up here," Nathan comments thoughtfully.

"It really was." I'm unexpectedly excited about showing him where I'm from and about him meeting my mom.

We pull up in front of my mom's house just as she's coming out the front door.

"Oh, man," Nathan says, in a surprised tone, as he notices her standing on the front porch. "You're like her twin, except thirty years younger."

As I get out of the car, I take a moment to admire my mom—her chestnut brown hair with strands of gray falling beautifully around her smiling face—and hope that I look as good as she does when I'm in my sixties.

"Hey, Mom!" I call out.

Nathan comes around to the passenger side, next to the curb.

"Ready?" I ask, taking his hand and looking up at him.

He kisses the back of my hand and nods.

***

Twenty minutes later, we're sitting in the backyard, under the shade of our oak tree, with fresh mint lemonade and the beginnings of a light lunch on the table in front of us.

"Lynn, how did you make all this with no notice whatsoever?"

My mom and I exchange knowing looks. She's not a fancy cook, but she loves to have people over and has some staples that she can prepare almost on the spot when company arrives. Currently sitting on the table is a platter with a variety of dips and snacks.

"Nathan, you're so sweet. This is nothing, dear. Please, eat up."

She touches his shoulder, much the way I do, and heads inside to bring out another serving spoon.

"Sarah," he says, looking at me wide-eyed. "You're *just* like her."

"How I look?"

"Not only that. Your sense of humor, too."

"I guess we are pretty similar. Not something I would've admitted ten years ago." I smile but then feel a weight settle in my stomach. "But . . ." I sigh.

"What?" he says, eyes trained on mine.

"Well, I'm also a lot like my dad. It's just . . . you'll never meet him."

"I wish I could have," he says, looking at our joined hands. "But you'll tell me more about him."

I trace my thumb over his thumb joint. His hands are bigger than mine, a bit rougher, but still pleasant to hold. I meet his eye. "I will. Not while we're around my mom, though."

He nods, and, as if on cue, she returns, plops a serving spoon in the guacamole, and crosses her arms.

"So, tell me Nate. Are your intentions with my daughter honorable?" she deadpans.

He swallows visibly, then searches my face for some indication of how he should respond. I start to crack up, and then so does my mom.

"I'm just kidding!" she says, almost cackling. "Nathan, don't take me so seriously, dear."

I blush. I mouth "I'm sorry" to him, but he surprises her by responding, "Ma'am, you know your daughter better than I do. My intentions are honorable, but hers . . . likely are not."

My eyes widen, and my mom starts to laugh harder than I've heard her laugh in a *very* long time. In a split second, I imagine the recap conversation she would have with my dad after meeting Nathan if he were still here.

"Did you see his face, Jake? You think he can handle our Sarah?" my mom would ask as they did the dishes together later that afternoon.

"I think he seems like a nice young man, Claire. And you heard his answer. He knows just how to handle the women in this family," my dad would have said before playfully snapping a towel at her.

"You're handsome *and* funny," my mom tells him. "Oops, I almost forgot the veggie quiche I put in the oven. Sarah, come help me."

I follow her to the back door and glance back at him before going inside. He shoots me a mischievous smile, and I shake my head at him. Seems like he fits right in around here. When I join my mom in the kitchen a minute later, she's just closing the oven door.

"The quiche isn't ready, but I just . . . I wanted to tell you I'm glad you came today. I was thinking about your dad. . ."

I pull her in for a hug, and she hugs me back tightly, oven mitts still on her hands. I let myself linger in her arms for a moment before pulling away.

"How are things going at work, honey?" she asks, tossing the mitts onto the counter.

"I'm managing. Things are still up in the air since LightVerse bought us, but . . ."

"You still like your role?" she asks.

"Um, yeah. I mean, it's been fun working with the engineers, but I'm starting to think that there are other things I could do."

"Like what?"

"Well, I've been helping Kevin—you know, Nathan's friend—with the merger and acquisition stuff, so I'm learning more about the business side of things. Might be interesting to work on something like that." I shrug.

"Hmmm, like business strategy?"

I smile. My mom retired from her full-time job a few years ago and consults businesses on setting and meeting their revenue goals.

"Yeah, maybe I'll follow in your footsteps."

"Well, I never worked in high-tech, but you seem pretty at home, and I know you can swim in any water."

"Well, you and Dad raised me to be independent."

A thoughtful look crosses her face. "Indeed, we did." She hands me a water pitcher to fill and leans back on the counter to watch me. "You are independent, but it's not just that. You don't shy away from challenges, and you're creative. I bet Kevin and all those other people at LightVerse see that, too."

Awww. Mom's in proud parent mode.

"I'm not sure yet," I say, "but now that I understand more about how they develop products in high-tech, I think . . ." I pause as I set the pitcher on the counter and take the sliced lemons from the cutting board to add them to the pitcher.

"What?"

I turn to face her. "Well, I have some good ideas about what we could build, things that could grow the business." I bite my lip and scrunch my shoulders.

"What?" she asks, taking in my stance.

"I think that's the first time I've said that out loud to someone. Who knows what's next? It feels like maybe everything's coming together for me."

My mom beams at me. "Well, I believe in you, and I bet Nathan does, too. He is . . ." she pauses. She seems to consider her words before continuing. "I like him a lot, sweetheart."

"So do I."

"And, let's just say that if things work out? Beautiful children." I can almost see the visions of cute grandchildren dancing behind her eyes, now crinkled at the corners from the huge smile on her face.

"Don't get ahead of yourself, Mom."

"Well, he's smart and respectful, and there's something about him that seems very . . . genuine."

She's right.

"Don't let that one go."

"I'll try not to," I say. I come closer and give her another hug. "Did you really need help with the quiche?"

"Of course not. What do you think I am? An old lady?"

"Never," I say as I turn and playfully bump my hip with hers.

I head back outside and sit on Nathan's lap, wrapping my arms around him. I lean into him and kiss his neck.

He glances up toward the house.

"You don't want my mom to catch us making out?" I tease.

"Uh, no."

"In that case . . ." I grab his hand and place it on my butt the second my mom walks out the door.

"Sarah!" he says, snatching his hand back and almost dumping me off his lap. He keeps me from hitting the ground at the last minute.

"Don't worry, Nathan," my mom says as she places the now fully baked quiche on the table. "I know my daughter's a handful."

Nathan turns beet red, maybe thinking about what his hands were full of a mere second ago.

"Would you like some quiche, dear?"

He clears his throat and takes a deep breath.

"I'd love some. Thank you, Lynn," he says in a strained voice. *Is he embarrassed or trying not to laugh?*

"Oh, I forgot to turn off the oven," she says and heads toward the house, leaving us alone once again.

"You arc a handful," he says, pinching my butt while my mom is inside.

"You know it," I say, pecking him on the nose.

Integration Testing

NATHAN

While they eat lunch, Lynn regales him with hilarious stories about Sarah as a kid. The time she rode her bike into a ditch filled with water to see if it would float since "the tires were filled with air," the time she insisted on doing her own dance routine—very different from the routine the other children performed—on stage at her ballet recital, and even her valedictorian speech at her high school graduation in which she quoted *Star Wars*.

"I didn't know you liked *Star Wars*."

"I do," Sarah admits.

"And you were valedictorian of your class?"

"I was, and I love that you asked me about *Star Wars* first and that second," she replies, laughing.

"Now I *know* you can learn to code Python," he comments.

"It always comes back to coding, doesn't it?"

He bumps her knee with his and smiles. "I love learning new things about you."

Later that afternoon, after promising Lynn to visit again soon, they drive to the state park and set out on their hike, heading down the first trail they see. Only a few minutes into the woods, it feels like they're in another world. They walk, hand-in-hand, quietly—a break from the energetic conversations earlier in the day—and simply absorb the sights and the sounds of the forest around them. The sense of peace in the woods is palpable.

After an hour or so of walking, the creek, with its calming flow, beckons them, and they sit to rest. Nathan leans back against a tree, and Sarah turns to sit cross-legged, perpendicular to him and props her arms and head on one of his knees.

"What's the story with all the felled trees?" he asks.

"As your tour guide, I should've told you. This used to be a logging area, but in the 1960s, the family that owned the land donated it to be a nature preserve," Sarah explains. "I never get tired of this place."

She turns his direction, and a small ray of sunlight, peeking through the trees, shines off her hair. It's a beautiful brown, and after a few weekends of being outdoors this summer, he notices that strands of it are starting to lighten up as if they've been dipped in gold. *The seasons of Sarah.*

"I can see why," he says, reaching his fingertips out to touch the golden bits.

She snuggles up against him. Despite the heat earlier, as the sun shifts to the west, blocked by the thick trees, a slight chill enters the air, but he feels her warm body through his t-shirt. After a few minutes of comfortable silence, he finally builds up the courage to ask her something.

"Whose apartment do you like more? Yours or mine?"

"Let's see. Yours has a great view," she says. "But I do feel safer walking around at night on the Alameda than I do downtown. Then again, your apartment always smells better than mine since someone is always cooking yummy food there. And, well, *you're* there."

"I could say a lot of the same things about your apartment. It smells amazing there, especially in your room. And *you're* there."

"What are you really asking?"

Is it too early? Maybe. But he's been thinking about this for a few weeks, even admitting to his brother David on a recent call that he wanted to talk to Sarah about moving in together.

"She told me she made a mistake moving in too soon with her ex," he explains to David. *"He ended up being an asshole."*

"Well, are you planning on being an asshole?" David jokes.

"I mean, I'm doing my best not to," Nathan replies.

"I think when you're with the right person, you just know," David advises. *"I say go for it."*

"Go for it, huh?"

"Yeah, go for it. Sarah's awesome, and you love her."

And that's how he ended up here today, his heart pounding and barely able to breathe as he looks at the woman he loves. "So, I need to renew my lease in a month or two, and . . ." He pauses.

"Yes?" She looks up at him expectantly. He suspects she already knows where he's going with this. Half the time, she seems to know what he's thinking before he can even put it into words.

He takes a deep breath and exhales slowly. "I know you felt like you rushed into living with your ex, so maybe it's not a good idea. I mean, maybe you won't *think* it's a good idea, or you'll be worried."

"You want me to move in?" She slants her head, waiting for him to answer.

"Well, um, I think I'd want to come live with you," he says. He pauses, and when she doesn't say anything, he begins to rush his words, over-explaining. "But only if you want me to. We spend the night at each other's places all the time anyways and—"

"Yes," she interrupts him, nodding.

"Yes? Just like that?"

"Yeah. Just like that. When does your lease end?" she asks him.

"About a month and a half from now?"

"We could do a trial run. Like, you could move in soon. With me . . ." she says and pauses, her lips curling into the world's most adorable smile. "And if it turns out to be a terrible idea—"

"Like I'm a serial killer or something?"

"I was thinking more like you never wash your socks or you enjoy making pickles at midnight—"

"I wash my socks regularly," he scoffs. "And I don't make pickles at midnight. Though I might bother you at midnight with . . . other things," he says, running his hand down her side and patting her ass playfully.

"Sounds like a feature, not a bug," she quips.

He leans in and kisses her softly, and parts her lips with his tongue. He takes her free hand—the one she's not using to prop herself up—and encourages her to explore some of the other "features" he has to offer.

"Yeah, you should definitely move in. Maybe even tonight," she says, nibbling his ear lobe.

And, since they haven't seen anybody for half an hour, they allow themselves some time to relax and explore each other in the cool air.

His mind is mostly on the feel of Sarah's tongue in his mouth, but he can still hear the sounds of the creek and the birds as he enjoys the light trace of her fingers on his neck and jawline. He lifts the hem of her shirt, wanting to feel her bare skin, and realizes he must be inadvertently tickling her when she emits a small half-sigh half-giggle.

They stop for a breather and begin to plan their trial "Nathan moves in with Sarah." Now that she's had a moment to digest the idea, she has more questions. He's grateful for it. Nathan doesn't want to talk her into anything. He wants her to feel safe and heard—things she lacked in her last relationship.

They discuss finances—rent and utilities—as well as the practical aspects of living together, like who will cook (him), who will wash dishes (her), and who will be responsible for laundry, including washing socks (both). Happy with their plans, they get up, and Nathan dusts off the seat of her pants.

"Any chance to grab my butt, huh?" she teases.

"Yep," he says, leaning down to steal one more kiss for the road.

As they head back to the car, he contemplates what turned out to be a pretty eventful day. He woke up this morning expecting a run-of-the-mill Sunday. Now, he met her mom, and he and Sarah are moving in together.

On the drive back, he catches Sarah smiling to herself. "What?"

She turns to him. "Nothing. I'm just . . . happy, hopeful. This is going to be good, isn't it?"

He nods. It *is* going to be good.

RELOCATION

NATHAN

The following weekend Nathan officially moves into Sarah's apartment, and they enlist Kevin and Camila's help to pack up. Nathan's just returned from taking a suitcase downstairs to the parking garage, and he opens up the drawer of the TV console, checking for any cables he might have missed. From the sounds of things being thrown into a box, he surmises Sarah must be packing up some of his things in the bathroom. Then he hears Camila's melodic voice and realizes she's in his bedroom keeping Sarah company.

"This is really exciting," Camila says.

A pause, then Sarah's voice. "Yeah . . . it feels kind of fast, though." And then in a lower voice, "I'm not making a mistake, right?"

Oh.

"I don't think so," Camila replies confidently. "You know how I felt about Blake. Nate's really different. He's a good guy."

Thank you, Cam.

"Yeah," she agrees after a moment, "you're right."

"I am right," Cam replies. "Now, are you taking this lamp from the nightstand? I can take it down with the cooler we packed."

Shit, they're coming to the kitchen. He quickly calls out, "Hey, ladies, I'm back. What else should I take down?"

Sarah comes into the living room holding a small box, presumably full of his toiletries. "This one? Don't worry. I packed *lots* of dental floss."

He snickers.

"I'm going to head down," Cam says from the kitchen and heads out the door with the cooler and lamp.

He takes the box from Sarah, sets it down on the coffee table, and pulls her into him, hands on her waist. "Hey, you feeling okay about all this?" he asks. He's going into this with a full heart, and he wants to be sure she is, too. "I can bring all my stuff back upstairs if you're not ready. I won't be angry or upset." He needs her to understand he's different than her last boyfriend, the guy who gaslighted her and made her question her actions.

She meets his eyes and takes a deep breath. "Thank you for saying that, but don't worry. I feel ready. I feel good . . . because I'm with a good guy."

He brushes a strand of hair out of her eyes. "I'm glad because I have a good feeling about this." He smiles, pecks her on the forehead, and turns toward the couch. He lets out a dramatic sigh.

"What?"

"I feel bad leaving that couch behind. It's seen some things." He slides his hands from her waist up her torso, resting them just under her breasts. The first time they hooked up it was on this couch, and it's seen a fair amount of play in the meantime.

"Then, we'll just have to test out *my* couch," she replies, "with similar activities." She turns to walk away, then turns back to smack him sharply on the butt. "May the best couch win."

***

When the elevator opens, Camila is standing there.

"I forgot my sweater in your apartment, Nate. Can you let me in?" she asks, stepping into the hallway.

"Yeah, sure." He digs in his pocket for his keys. "Sarah, can you take this box? We'll meet you and Kev downstairs in a minute."

"No problem," she says.

He opens the apartment door for Camila and follows her inside. While she searches for her sweater, he checks the kitchen one last time and notices his favorite frying pan forgotten on the counter. He quickly grabs it up and is holding it in one hand when he walks into the living room.

Camila smiles at him. "You look like a very serious chef or an old lady about to knock out a burglar."

"I never really thought about using this pan in self-defense, but thanks for the idea," he says, laughing.

"Nate?" she says.

"Yeah?"

"I like you," she says.

His eyes widen, and she starts to laugh.

"Not like that. Don't worry. I think you and Sarah have had enough issues with third wheels."

Okay. So this isn't that type of situation. He settles down.

"I mean that . . . I think you're a good guy, but I feel like it's my responsibility to take care of Sarah. She can take care of herself, of course, but I don't want to see her get hurt again."

He's not sure how to respond.

"You're going to do the right thing?" she asks.

He studies her expression. He's noticed she uses her dark eyes and striking features to good effect when communicating, and now is no exception. Physically, she's on the small side, pretty close to Sarah's size, in fact. But she gives off powerful energy. *Like a mother wolf.*

"Cam," he says. "I love Sarah, too, and I also don't want to see her get hurt. I'll do the right thing. Don't worry."

She looks at him for one moment longer and nods at him.

"Are we good?" he asks.

"We're good."

They head down to the parking garage in the elevator, and while it could be awkward—following their little tête-à-tête—it's not. Any doubts Camila might have had seem to have dissipated, if her joking manner is any indication, and knowing that Sarah has Camila watching out for her reassures him.

When they arrive downstairs, Kevin and Sarah are both sitting on the cooler next to his car, watching something on Kevin's phone. Something about the scene—the two of them sitting close together, laughing together—rubs him the wrong way. Kevin suddenly looks up and stands quickly, causing Sarah to almost slide off her side of the cooler.

"Dang, Kev. Give a girl some notice, huh?" she says, laughing.

Kevin glances in Nathan's direction like he's trying to figure out if he's in trouble or something.

"What took you guys so long?" Kevin asks.

"Oh, Nate was saying his goodbyes to some of his favorite spatulas. Right, Nate?" Camila answers.

"Something like that," he says, giving her a conspiratorial glance.

He's not really in the mood right now for Kevin and would love to get back to Sarah's—no, to their—place and relax before unpacking.

"Thanks for the help, guys, but I think we can take it from here." Nathan turns to Camila, "Do you need a ride home?"

She doesn't have a car—she lives, studies, and works all within a few-mile radius of downtown. It's not that far, but he wants to make sure she's sorted for a ride.

"I'll take her," Kevin offers.

"That works," Camila replies.

"Thank you so much for your help," Sarah tells them. "We'll have you both over for dinner one night soon."

"Is Nathan going to cook?" Camila asks, and Nathan smothers a laugh.

Sarah shoots him a mock-warning glance. "Well, I'm good at *other* things . . . in the kitchen."

Camila's mouth twists in amusement.

What does she know?

"Sarah, should we head out?" he asks in a tight, slightly embarrassed voice. "Lots of things to unpack at your—*our*—place."

"Especially in the kitchen," Cam adds.

"You sure you guys don't need help with anything? In the kitchen?" Kevin asks, oblivious to the joke.

"They'll be just fine, Kev. I've heard Nate's a real expert in that room of the house," Camila comments and shoots him a devilish smile as the falcon-wing door lowers on Kevin's car.

He stands there, shaking his head as Kevin speeds out of the parking garage.

***

Nathan can barely move, exhausted from carrying all the boxes earlier. He's lying on the couch, legs propped up on the coffee table, and she's resting her head on a pillow on his lap.

"I'm sorry for telling her we had, well, you know, in the kitchen."

"Oh, it's okay. I mean, it's a little embarrassing, but she's your friend. Mine, too, I guess."

"Yeah, yours, too," she agrees.

"And she means well," he comments off-handedly.

"What do you mean?"

"Oh, uh, nothing," he replies. He glances away, but Sarah reaches up and adjusts his head back in her direction.

"What are you not telling me?" she asks, sitting up. She traces her hand down his chest, over his abs, and even lower. "Will I be forced to convince you with my womanly wiles?" She knows how to get her way. That's for sure.

"Well, you're more than welcome to do that," he says. "But I'll tell you now, and if you want to do that afterward, I won't object."

"So?"

"Well, when we were upstairs alone, she wanted to ensure my intentions with you were good. That I'm gonna treat you the way you deserve to be treated. Be here for you when you need me."

She huffs out a small breath and smiles. "That girl."

"I was holding a frying pan at the time. And since she mentioned it could be used as a weapon–"

She raises her eyebrows.

"Against a burglar," he clarifies. "I thought it best not to test my luck, and I confirmed that I do indeed intend to be a good boyfriend. To support you, help you when I can, feed you, keep you warm at night, and love you."

Her eyes crinkle as a sweet smile comes to her face. "I know you do." She scoots up and kisses him on his jaw. "Do you think I'll be a good girlfriend?" She moves to kiss him on his neck, then pulls the collar of his t-shirt aside to nip his collarbone.

He gasps. "Careful, there."

"Mmmm," she replies, nipping again.

Her hands begin to explore lower, and his ab muscles tense.

"Ah," he says.

"You didn't answer me," she teases as she nibbles a toned muscle on the side of his stomach.

Fuck.

"Sarah," he says breathlessly, "I *already* think you're a good girlfriend."

She tries to untie the stubborn knot in his pajama pants, but before she succeeds in loosening it all together, he tips her chin up to look at him and cradles her face in his hand.

"I was hoping I might get a promotion to *great* girlfriend tonight," she says and slides his pants down below his hips, revealing that he's ready for what she's offering. He watches her part her lips to take him in her mouth and leans his head back, closing his eyes. He runs his fingers gently through her hair, and unable to stay silent while an intense feeling of pleasure pulses through him, he agrees, "Yes. Great, for sure. Oh my god, great." *Fuck.* "The . . . absolute . . . ah . . . best."

WYSIWYG

SARAH

"To what do I owe the pleasure?" I ask Nathan when I step out of the shower and see him awake at least an hour earlier than usual. I dry my hair with a towel as he stands from the bed and stretches.

"It's your first day at the new office, and I wanted to see you off," he replies, yawning. His hair is sticking up, and he looks adorably sleepy. I have half a mind to push him back into bed and ask for a quickie. But I don't want to get stuck in traffic on the way to Mountain View, so I drag my eyes away from him and begin to choose my clothes.

"When are you leaving?" he says, grabbing a sweatshirt from the chair near the window and pulling it over his head.

"In about twenty minutes?"

"Good. I'll pack a lunch for you."

"You don't have to do that."

"But I want to," he says, coming closer and wrapping me in a warm hug. I've only just gotten my bra and underwear on, and he rubs his hands up and down my mostly bare skin. I hug him back and run my hands through his wild morning hair.

"I can't let you go hungry," he says. He leans down to kiss my neck before letting me go and heading off to the kitchen.

After a moment's consideration, I choose a nice button-down shirt paired with a sleek pair of dress pants, then quickly brush my hair and teeth. Makeup will have to be done on the way. I'm due at the office at

9:00 a.m. for a group tour of our new working space, and traffic is getting heavier according to Google Maps.

I pop my head into the kitchen, and Nathan hands me a bento box full of lentils and rice left over from last night's dinner with some sliced vegetables added in for color.

"Drive safely," he says, leaning down and kissing me on the mouth—warm but chaste.

"Are you going back to bed? Weren't you up late last night?"

"Nah, I'll have some coffee and get to work. I have a problem I'm trying to crack, and I think I might've dreamt of a solution."

"Well, good luck," I tell him. He's been running into some roadblocks recently, and things don't seem to be gelling yet.

When I arrive at the office, I get signed in and grab my new work badge at the front desk. After a quick introduction, a woman from LightVerse's people team begins our tour of the building on the fifth floor. There's a stylishly landscaped rooftop patio from which you can see the surrounding area. Mountains lie in one direction, with the Caltrain tracks in the other.

Erin leans in to whisper in my ear, "This is nice. Like, ten times better than the old Instinqt office."

"Yeah, it is pretty nice," I begrudgingly agree with her, feeling a strange inclination to defend Instinqt's smaller, less flashy office. It was my first job in tech, and it's where I met Nathan—at least where we got to know each other—and it holds a special place in my heart.

We head down to the fourth floor, where the Instinqt team will be located. Natural light pours through the huge windows onto a sea of white desks. The place is filled with glass walls, separating the space into meeting rooms of all sizes, and high-end flat-screen TVs and other electronic devices.

Our LightVerse tour guide directs us to the area designated for us. "Feel free to take any open seat in this area," she tells us.

Erin's eyes skim the area, and she chooses a desk one row over from where I'm standing near the window. It's exactly the same orientation we used to sit in at the Instinqt office.

"Creatures of habit, I guess," she remarks.

Setting my bag down, I open my laptop on the height-adjustable, modern desk and jump back into a project I paused on Friday afternoon. About half an hour in, I'm concentrating and listening to one of my regular work playlists when I sense someone peering over my shoulder. I take out my AirPods and look over my shoulder to find Carter—the guy Kevin introduced me to a couple of weeks ago—smiling at me. I startle, one of my AirPods dropping to the floor. He leans down at exactly the same time I do, and we crash into each other.

"Ouch," I blurt out.

"I'm so sorry," he says. He straightens up, rubbing a presumably sore spot on his head. "Are you okay?"

"Yeah, um, I'm fine, but you should really wear, like, a bell or something," I say, also rubbing my head and looking up at him.

"Sorry, I've been accused of being lurky before." He shrugs, then leans in to peer at the spot on my head I've just been rubbing. I glance up at him, but it seems really close. Now *he* startles and quickly steps back.

Is he blushing? But he composes himself quickly and holds out the fallen AirPod for me to take.

"So, what's up?" *Why were you hanging out behind my desk?*

"Would you like to join me for lunch? I mean, with some other people. I know it's your first day, and I wasn't sure if you knew the area or had brought something."

"Oh, actually, I did bring something—"

"Maybe you could have it for dinner instead?" He shoots me a charming smile. "We're all gonna grab some pho. It'd be a good chance to meet some of the LightVerse people you don't know yet," he says in a slightly questioning manner. I can tell he wants me to come but doesn't want to sound pushy.

"Yeah, that would be nice," I agree, realizing that now that we're part of a large company, I should get to know new people.

I turn around and see Erin doing her best spy impression—watching without looking like she's watching. "I'll invite Erin, too, if that's okay. She's my usual lunch buddy."

"Of course," he says. "We'll leave around twelve o'clock. Just meet us downstairs."

Erin's all in—she loves pho—and we meet the small group of LightVerse people downstairs at noon sharp. Besides Carter, there are a few engineers and product people, and everyone is friendly.

On the walk over, Erin talks to one of the engineers who, it turns out, knows her partner Ryan from a company they used to work at together.

I end up walking with Carter, who asks me tons of questions—some work-related and some personal. I tell him I'm from Santa Cruz originally, that I studied political science in college, and that I lived abroad—Europe, the Middle East, and Asia—for a couple of years, volunteering and teaching English.

"That's so cool. I love to travel," he tells me.

"Oh, really? Where've you been?"

"Well, after college, I backpacked in South America for about three months. That was a while ago, I guess," he admits. "My friends and I really like rock climbing, so we visited a ton of places we could hike and climb. Ever since we get together once a year and go somewhere together. It's been hard the last couple of years, but I want to get back to it."

I notice the muscles in his arms on full display in a heather gray t-shirt with the LightVerse logo and the name of some product they're known for, and I can imagine this guy rock climbing.

At lunch, I sit next to some of my new colleagues. I can see Erin chatting up Carter and a few other people at the other end of the table. As we head back to the office after lunch, Erin joins me and hangs onto my arm, slowing us down so we can talk away from the group.

"Have a nice lunch date with C.H.?" I joke, using the not-so-clever code name we invented for Carter.

"I did actually but, well, I noticed him noticing *you* earlier, and I just wanted to let you know that he's kind of important. I looked him up and talked to Kevin. He's Eden's right-hand man for when LightVerse acquires new companies. He comes in, evaluates the product, determines what's going to happen, as well as who stays and who goes."

I press my lips together and try to think. "Okay, what exactly does that mean in non-corporate professional speak?"

"It just means be careful what you tell him. About Instinqt, Kevin, and . . . yourself." She shoots me a meaningful look.

"Is this what big companies are like?" I ask her, deferring to her experience. She's been in tech much longer than I have.

"Sometimes, yes. But don't worry too much. He seems to like you," she says, winking at me. "I saw your little AirPod incident."

"Ugh, no. Maybe I should let it slip that I have a boyfriend?"

"Yeah, maybe," she says thoughtfully. "Anyways, just . . . watch yourself."

I nod, glancing quickly at Carter, laughing with some of the engineers. Erin and I scan our badges and head inside the building.

RAMPING UP

"I hate to admit it, but the LightVerse office has been a major upgrade," I admit to Nathan on our early afternoon walk. I have a break from meetings, and I need some fresh air. "On-site, free lunches and an unlimited supply of gummy bears are perks I didn't know I was missing."

"Hey, I offer you on-site, free lunches, too," he jokes, referring to the fact there is almost always something waiting for me in the kitchen around lunchtime.

"You do. And yours taste better, of course," I reassure him.

"I noticed you've been going into the office more," he comments as we cross the street to find shade.

"Yeah, I only planned on going in once or twice a week, but sometimes it's just more effective to be there in person." Last week, I ended up driving into the office for four days.

"Well, I'm glad you stayed home today," he says.

"Really? I thought I might be driving you crazy with all the sprint kickoffs and daily standups."

"Not at all," he replies. "I love hearing you boss *other* engineers around."

I narrow my eyes at him and swat at his arm. *Is he hinting that I boss him around?*

"You just miss me," I tease.

Surprising me, he admits in a quiet voice, "I do."

Oh. Here I was, thinking he might need a break from me when maybe it's me who needs the space.

"I like your company," he says.

"I like your company, too." *Damn. He's lonely.* Who wouldn't be, working at home by themselves?

I'm not sure what to say. Should I work from home more? No, I enjoy going in. So, I change the subject, knowing before I've even finished my sentence, he might give me a one- or two-word response as he's wont to do lately when I bring it up. "How are things with the startup?"

He surprises me, and instead of the usual "fine" or "I'll get there" response, he opens up.

"Actually, I feel . . . blocked."

"Tell me about it."

He meets my eyes and seems to consider sharing more but then decides not to. "It's a nice afternoon, and I enjoy not thinking about it for a little while. I like just . . . being with you."

I take his arm and look up at him. He smiles, but his eyes are clouded by a million thoughts.

"Then, let's walk together," I reply, "and just be."

***

Kevin has connected Nathan with a venture capital contact of his up in Redwood City, and the day has arrived. He took the Caltrain there and will meet me in Mountain View after work. There's a LightVerse happy hour on the roof, and he's planning to join me after his meeting. That way, we can drive home together.

It's almost five-thirty, and I take the elevator to the roof to see what's going on. There are at least twenty-five people already there, enjoying snacks from a fully-laden buffet. I choose a glass of white wine from a drink table and go in search of someone I know. Not finding anyone immediately, I head over to a couple of chairs under a pergola. Though it's the middle of summer and the sun won't set for at least two hours, the sun is starting to dip lower in the sky, and I could get lost in the fiery colors on the horizon.

I'm thinking about my day and enjoying the surprisingly good taste of the wine when I hear a familiar voice say, "Hey, there."

Carter heads in my direction. He sets his drink down on the small table near us and puts both hands on the balcony railing, leaning against it. I get a weird sense he's trying to seem nonchalant. Cool even? *Is he flexing on purpose? Stop. You're being weird.* I avert my eyes from his very nice arms and notice he's enjoying the same view I was a minute ago.

"It's a beautiful time of day, isn't it?" I remark.

"Personally, I prefer sunrise," he says.

"Early riser?"

He nods.

"Yeah, me, too, actually. The day holds such potential when everything is quiet, and you have a hot cup of coffee in your hand."

"Completely agree," he says, the corners of his mouth curling up.

I take a sip of my wine, and in the pause, he sits next to me.

"You like white?" he asks, referring to my drink.

"Well, I won't say 'no' to white—which is how I got this, I guess—but red's my favorite."

"Good to know," he replies. "So, I wanted to talk to you about something. I need someone who can guide me through some of the product and engineering stuff related to Instinqt, and Kevin said you might be interested."

"What kind of stuff?" I ask.

"I'm trying to figure out feature roadmaps for some of the different product lines we've acquired recently, and he said that it's a specialty of yours."

"I wouldn't exactly call it a specialty, but I guess I know it."

"You're too humble. Women in tech need to boast about their abilities from the rooftops. You don't know that yet?"

"How do you know so much about women in tech?"

"Well, I had a girlfriend who was pretty outspoken about it, and I guess it just stuck with me . . . even though she didn't."

I set my wine glass down and try to think of a suitable response, but as I move my hand away, I accidentally knock the glass over, spilling half its contents on the table.

"Oh, shit," I mutter as it drips onto the stone floor.

He rights the glass and hands me the napkin from under his drink. "It's not all that bad," he says, shooting me a slightly crooked and surprisingly sexy grin. "Bad breakup, but I've recovered."

Why is he sharing all this with me?

"I know about bad breakups," I say, for some reason sharing more than I should as well. "But you do eventually recover, don't you?"

"Yeah, you do," he says. "It always helps if you find someone new, someone better." Again, unsure of what to say, I give a noncommittal "Hmm."

"I'll set up some time with you soon, okay? Maybe you can come into the office that day so we can meet in person. Kevin said you have a knack for strategy, and you might want to learn more about the business and not just herd cats all day long with the developers."

I laugh at the reference. "Herding cats sounds about right."

He shoots me a smile that is somehow extremely confident yet warm.

"Keep an eye out for the invite," he says as he turns to go.

"I will."

My first instinct is to feel proud of myself—and happy that new opportunities are opening up. But in the back of my mind is Erin's advice about being careful with Carter.

He turns back. "Sarah?"

"Hmm?"

He glances at the view of the mountains, then back at me. "Hope you catch the sunrise tomorrow."

I watch him go and notice Kevin looking in my direction, but he quickly turns back to the other people he's talking to and takes a sip of his drink. Before I can give it any more thought, I feel my phone vibrate:

Nathan: Hey, I'm downstairs. Can you let me in?
Me: Yes, coming now.

I slip my phone into my pocket and walk quickly over to the elevator. The door is closing as I approach it, but then it stops and opens again. I step on and find Carter going down.

"You again?"

"Yeah, I'm heading home. Need to work on a few things. Leaving already?"

"Just going downstairs to let someone in."

"Same floor, then," he says, pressing the button for the first floor. "I need to check if I left my charger in the conference room downstairs."

It only takes a minute for us to reach the first floor. I exit the elevator to meet Nathan, and Carter heads in the same direction toward the conference room.

The entire entrance is glass doors and windows, and Nathan notices me and smiles. He looks handsome in a pale green polo shirt, but even from here, his eyes look tired. Carter scans his badge to enter the conference room but then turns back and glances toward the front windows.

As I let Nathan in, Carter calls, "Nate? Hey, what're you doing here?"

Nathan acknowledges Carter with the tip of his head. His smile looks more like a grimace to me, but maybe it's enough to fool Carter.

"Hey, Carter, what's up, man?" he says, extending his hand.

Watching them shake hands, both of them large, broad, and muscular, is like witnessing some sort of superhero matchup. Their hands grip each other—friendly enough, but there's something a little stiff, even a little intimidating—and I'm not clear from which side it's stronger.

"Are you here for a meeting or something?" Carter asks, looking confused. The workday is over.

"No, just meeting my girlfriend," he says. Up until this moment, I stood back, letting them exchange their pleasantries—or not-so-pleasantries—but now I come closer. As I do, Nathan leans in to kiss me on the cheek.

Carter's expression—surprise mixed with the slightest bit of disappointment—is unmistakable. I notice it, and I wonder if Nathan does, too. But Carter is nothing if not professional and smiles broadly to cover his slip.

"Oh, I didn't realize you guys were together," he says. "Cool. Well, I gotta run. We'll be in touch."

Maybe Nathan thinks Carter's addressing him since he says, under his breath, as Carter walks away, "Rather not."

Netflix and Chill

NATHAN

Yeah, asshole. Sarah's my girlfriend.

Nathan doesn't know if Sarah saw Carter's expression when he learned that little bit of information, but *he* definitely did. He's not usually the type to be possessive, but with Carter, any win feels good.

They head up in the elevator to grab Sarah's belongings. She asks if he wants to say "hi" to Kevin at the happy hour.

"I'd rather just go, okay?"

On the ride home, he's quiet, even for himself. Sarah seems to understand he's not in the mood for a full-on conversation, but she does ask a few questions.

"Did he have any helpful advice?" she asks, trying to get him to share more about his meeting with the VC contact. Her tone is noticeably gentle.

"Not anything I couldn't have learned from Kevin. It was sort of a waste of time."

"I'm sorry."

"I mean, he did say if I send him my work-in-progress slide deck, he'll check it out and give me some pointers."

"Well, that sounds promising," she says, reaching across the console to take one of his hands in hers. Her touch seems to thaw the tight, frozen feeling he's had in his chest this afternoon since the meeting. Maybe he *is* in the mood to talk.

"I dunno," he says. "I'm beginning to wonder whether I'm cut out for this. Founding a startup."

"Of course you are," she says, taking her hand back so he can use both hands to drive. "You're a great programmer. My god, Nathan, how many articles have you published? You have a PhD in computer science."

"So do half of the people in Silicon Valley."

"Yeah, I guess you're right."

"I didn't tell you, but on the way up to Redwood City, I stopped and had lunch with Eli at Google."

"How was it?"

"It was cool. The campus is really nice, and he invited his manager to join us. We got to talking. He basically said all I have to do is say the word, and they've got a place for me on one of their machine learning teams."

"Oh, wow. Would you be interested in that? Like, not doing the startup now and going the FAANG route?"

He sighs. "I don't know. I feel like I peaked too early."

"What do you mean?"

"My first job out of college, I became an executive of a startup that succeeded within my first year there. But I'm totally inexperienced in leadership. I can't jump into some senior position in a corporate environment. I love to code, but it's also hard to imagine just becoming some individual contributor in a big company with other people telling me exactly what to work on."

He's not exactly a rule follower. Sarah probably doesn't know that about him yet.

"So, corporate's not your jam?"

"Not really. I mean, one day, when we're married—"

Oops. Way to play it cool, bro. "When *I'm* married," he corrects himself, "You know, I'll have more responsibilities, like kids, and be busier. That's the time to work in one of the big tech companies. I feel like maybe now's the last chance I'll have to do something like found a startup."

"That . . . makes sense."

He can see her glancing over at him from under her eyelashes and trying not to look too pleased at his slip-up.

He takes a breath and continues. "And I know I can do the technical parts, but maybe I don't know enough about productizing stuff. Maybe I'm *just* a good programmer or engineer, but—"

"No, I don't buy it," she says, cutting him off. "I know I'm a broken record: 'You'll figure it out.' But that's because you will. You're so smart, and . . . I'll help you."

"You already have a full-time job. I don't want to bother you with this after hours."

"But it's *not* a bother. You're my boyfriend," she tells him mat-ter-of-factly.

"I love it when you call me that," he admits.

"Well, you *are*. I mean, what else would you be? My clean, orderly roommate? My personal chef?"

"Also, both true," he says. Her comical way of describing things is beginning to lift his spirits.

"My favorite Netflix buddy?" she suggests.

"Maybe 'Favorite Netflix *and chill* buddy?'"

"Also an accurate label." She reaches out to massage the back of his neck, then lets her hand slide down to his bicep. "Maybe we'll Netflix and chill when we get home."

"Definitely a good way to turn around a bad day," he agrees, squeezing her thigh. "Want to put some music on?"

"Yeah."

While she searches for just the right song, he glances over at her, admiring her profile lit up by the phone screen.

"Sarah?"

She smiles, looking up at him, waiting for him to continue.

"Thanks for being you," he says.

She reaches out to caress his face. "Thanks for being you, too."

Downward Trend

NATHAN

"*What* is going on with you?" Sarah asks in a flustered tone as he pushes his food around his plate at dinner.

His mood has left a lot to be desired in the last couple of days. He's been quiet—withdrawn—and Sarah has definitely noticed.

Since the meeting with Kevin's VC contact, he has tried to double down on the question of how to productize his currently bare-bones software. The architecture is sound, but he's hitting a wall trying to define the business model of his startup idea.

"Nothing. I'm fine," he replies.

"Nathan."

"What?"

"I'm trying to communicate with you. To connect. Can you *please* be real with me?"

He sets his fork down—harder than he expected—and it pings on the ceramic plate. "I am 'being real' with you. You just ask me—all the time—and I don't have anything new to report. Yesterday, I programmed and worried about the business model. Today, in a big turn of events, I programmed some more and worried about the business model. I wonder if I even know what I'm doing—"

"Well, it's early days," she says, interrupting him. "You have to start somewhere, but . . ."

"But what?"

She hesitates before continuing. "Do you think you should be spending time working on a proof of concept before you've defined your product requirements? I mean, don't you first need to understand *what* to build?"

He knows she's right. She does this every day at work—deals with the product managers and designers who conceptualize products, then coordinates with the engineers who build them. Starting to build before you've nailed down requirements isn't best practice for building a product—in fact, it's a waste of time—but doing what he does best, programming, makes him feel like he's not spinning his wheels. He's spent at least fifty hours talking to doctors and nurses, trying to understand what kinds of data they use in patient diagnoses. Yet, the more he learns, the more he realizes how much he doesn't know.

He exhales his pent-up frustration in a huff of breath, then draws in some air, bringing his eyes to her. "You just . . . ask a lot of questions. I already feel like I don't know what I'm doing, and you just make it that much more explicit by asking me questions I can't answer."

She takes a measured breath. "Did it ever occur to you that the reason I ask you so many questions is that maybe I'd like you to ask *me* some? You know, I also have a career I'm trying to grow after some false starts. Having my boyfriend be interested in that would feel . . . I don't know, encouraging?"

Shit. He begins to wrap his fingers around her forearm, but she pulls away and stands.

"Sarah—"

"I need some fresh air," she utters in a shaky voice and slips on some sandals before walking out the apartment door without a backward glance.

He cleans up the dinner dishes and tries to keep himself busy for a couple of hours, wondering where she's gone. When he finally breaks and checks her location on his phone—just to make sure she's alright—he discovers she's hunkered down at Cam's. *Probably telling her how much of a jerk I am.*

When she finally comes home, he's already in bed, awake but with the lights off. He's been trying to read an article about how to create satisfying user experiences but hasn't made much progress. After getting ready for bed, she slips in beside him but turns to face the window, pulling the sheets up to her chin.

"Hey," he says, gently cupping her shoulder and urging her to turn over to face him.

"Hey," she responds, falling onto her back and looking up at him.

He pulls her closer, and she hesitantly sinks into him, wrapping an arm around his waist.

"Are you angry with me?" she asks in a quiet voice, and he feels her breath on his neck, where she's settled.

His chest tightens with guilt. He closes his eyes and hugs her tightly, trying to communicate through his closeness just how much he loves her, how he wants to be her refuge in the world, not the cause of her uncertainty or pain.

"*Tell her how you feel, sweetheart,*" his mom's voice says in his head. It's the seemingly obvious yet hard to implement advice she imparted last week when he confided in her his doubts about his communication abilities.

"I'm not angry with you," he says, surprising himself with his openness. *What does Sarah need to hear? What do I want her to know?* "I'm sorry. It's no excuse, but I think . . . I think it's the stress talking."

At least, that's what Kevin had diagnosed when Nathan had pulled his moody asshole routine on him during what was supposed to be a chill dinner. "I get it, man," Kevin had told him. "Back in the early days of Instinqt when I felt like it would all come crashing down on my head, I was moody, too. I didn't have a girlfriend at the time, though, so it was mostly me losing it on co-founders."

Nathan strokes Sarah's hair and kisses her on the forehead.

"I thought maybe I did something," she says.

"It's not you. You're . . . you're great." He twirls the ends of her hair around his finger and pulls a lock of hair across her face like a mustache, and he feels her lips curl up into a smile on the backs of his fingers. "Want to tell me how things are going at work?"

She takes a deep breath and exhales slowly—her reset button in stressful situations. "I would, actually. So, I have this new project that might be starting up, something that's more on the business and strategy side than I've been doing. I'd be working with . . . a new business partner, and I think it could be a real learning opportunity."

"I know you'll do great," he says. "Everybody loves you." He traces her brow bone with his thumb, cups her jaw, and looks directly into her eyes, trying to evaluate where they stand by her barely visible expression. "Are we okay now?"

"We're okay. You can get up and go work in the living room now. I know you were probably laying here, waffling back and forth between worrying I'm upset with you and trying to crack some problem."

He sniffs out in amusement. *How does she know?*

He laughs softly and pulls the blanket up to her shoulders. She always gets cold during the night. "I won't stay up too late. Sweet dreams."

***

The squeak of the shower faucet being turned on awakens him in the morning, and he jumps out of bed to go prepare breakfast for Sarah.

"Good morning," he says when a freshly showered Sarah walks into the kitchen ten minutes later.

"Why are you up so early?" she asks.

"To apologize for being in such a bad mood lately."

"You woke up early to tell me you're sorry *again*?" An amused smile crosses her face, and he marvels at how his heart still jumps at the sight of it.

"I woke up early to tell you that I love you and to make you breakfast," he replies, handing her a mug of freshly poured coffee. "And also to say I'm sorry."

She sips the coffee and looks him up and down. Sporting the wrinkled t-shirt and boxers he slept in, he must not look like much, but she chews on her lip in that cute lopsided way, the tell-tale sign she finds him adorable. She admitted as much a few weeks ago, and he wills his expression to remain neutral. *I'm forgiven.*

She sets the coffee mug on the counter. Starting at his shoulders, then moving slowly down, she smooths the soft fabric of his shirt with her warm hands, letting them trace over his pec muscles. One hand over his heart, she tilts her head to look up at him, "Is everything okay? Inside?"

I'm not sure. He considers the open tabs on his computer browser right now: "Python Decorators for Memorization," "Average VC Investments 2022," and "Signs of Depression and/or Anxiety in Men." A real parade of lighthearted subjects.

He exhales, enjoying her touch—feeling, at least for the moment, that if she's here with him, touching him and talking to him, that he'll be okay—and replies, as convincingly as possible, "Yeah, I'm okay."

"I'm here for you," she says.

He nods. *But I shouldn't need you to hold me up.*

Changing the subject, he asks, "Do you have time to eat here?"

"Would you mind if I take it to go? I need to get to work and prep for a meeting this morning."

He wishes she had time to stay. "No problem. I'll pack it for you," he says and pecks her on the cheek.

HOTFIX

It's Wednesday, and we're having a team social event tonight with drinks and apps at Stein's, a pub near the office. I told Nathan about it last night, and he suggested I take the train, so I can have a few drinks.

"You can take an Uber home, or I could come pick you up if you want," he'd suggested.

"You could join us?" I replied.

"I don't know. I don't really feel a part of that world anymore."

"What do you mean? It's only been a couple months."

"I feel like I'm on some desert island, where somehow there's coffee and Wi-Fi, and all I do is code my fingers to the bone."

"So, maybe it's a chance for you to get reconnected. Please?"

He hesitated, then gave me a small smile. "Okay, I'll come."

"Great," I said. "Come around six? Kevin will be there, and some of the other Instinqt people, too."

I'm glad he agreed. He needs something to lift his spirits.

My work day is just a regular Wednesday filled with meetings. When five o'clock comes, a few of us walk to the restaurant, where I find Kevin and Carter hanging out on the patio reserved for our group. Kevin has a beer in his hand, and Carter's drinking a cocktail.

Kevin notices me and invites me over. "How's it going, Sarah?" he asks, giving me a hug. "I didn't see you around the office today."

"Probably because I was in the office the *whole* day, unlike you," I joke with him. "I had a few meetings with marketing, so I was down on the second floor. Where were *you*?"

"Ah, just holed up in some e-staff meetings with this asshole," he says, gesturing toward Carter. Carter rolls his eyes good-naturedly at Kevin and grins at me. *When did they become such good friends?*

Maya joins us, and while Kevin starts a conversation with her, Carter leans in and whispers in my ear that I look like I've had a long day.

"Still beautiful, just a little tired," he says. "Everything going okay?"

He's close, so I have to crane my neck to look at him. "Yeah, everything's fine."

He's close enough for me to note his scent—a mix of what I'd guess is a pleasant-smelling laundry detergent and manly deodorant—and then he puts his hand on the small of my back.

"Did you have a chance to read through the materials I emailed you end of last week?" he asks.

"Yeah, I actually have a list of questions and a couple of ideas I could share . . . you know, just to get your thoughts?"

"Definitely. I mean, we *could* discuss now, but we're supposed to be socializing," he says, winking. "Send me a calendar invite for this week?"

"No problem," I say, hoping my words turn out to be true.

After seeing Carter's disappointed reaction to finding out Nathan and I are together, I haven't gone out of my way to initiate any one-on-ones with him. Since that night, I've put together some clues—Nathan's past remarks about dealing with Carter during the Instinqt transition as well as the interested vibe Carter puts off when he's around me—and I've been hesitant to accept his offer to work together. But working directly with someone in such a strategic role is quite an opportunity, something I can't afford to say "no" to as I try to build up my career.

It'll be fine. I'll make sure things stay professional. And I won't have to tell Nathan that Carter's the senior business strategy person showing me the ropes, at least not for now. I chew on the inside of my lip as an uneasy feeling—the faintest shadow of a memory—takes hold in my chest. *It's what I used to do with Blake.* Not lie, not *really*. Just . . . not share everything, to avoid arguments, judgmental glances, harsh words.

Nathan is not Blake, a voice in my head informs me. *But your relationship with him is still new*, a second voice argues back. *And he won't like you being around Carter so much.* As I war with myself on whether my actions are justifiably self-preserving or simply self-serving, Carter leans in and asks, "What are you so deep in thought about?"

I look up at him, then my eyes flick to the door leading out to the patio, and the familiar man standing there looking at me. Nathan's eyes are narrowed, and he's paused there. *Watching my conversation with Carter?*

I consider the situation from his point of view. I'm almost certain he picked up on Carter's interest in me, and here I am, having a cocktail and a friendly conversation with the man. I quickly turn and walk over to greet Nathan with a hug. He's a bit stiff but returns my hug. I can feel his head still turned in Carter's direction.

"Hey," I say to him, "over here." I gently pull his chin and gaze toward me. He tilts his head down, and I kiss him directly on the mouth. Maybe nobody's watching, but I have a feeling at least one person is, and he—along with Nathan, of course—is who it's for. *Don't mess this up for me.*

Nathan slides his hand further down my back and pulls my hips in close to his body, sending his own message. *Oh, so that's how it is.* He bites my lower lip gently right before he breaks away from our kiss, and when I look at his face again, he gives me a quick wink. Good, he understands. What he saw between Carter and me wasn't from my side.

Kevin joins us and greets Nathan. "Wanna drink, dude?" He puts his arm around him and leads him over to say "hi" to Maya and some other engineers, leaving me standing there by myself.

Thanks, Kev.

I listen in on Kevin introducing Nathan. "Hey, guys, meet my bro from back in the day, Nate. This guy is a smart mofo. He passed on coming to LightVerse, but he's working on his own startup now." And just like that—with Kevin's stamp of approval—and his upbeat introduction, Nathan is accepted and in his element.

The group Kevin and Nathan are talking to drift over to the food tables and look like they're settling in for a long conversation, so I head over to talk to some of my teammates and a couple of people from IT, including an IT staffer I've become friendly with recently, Alyssa.

She glances over at the table Nathan's sitting at and asks me who he is.

"Boyfriend?"

"Yeah, my boyfriend, Nathan," I reply.

"He's cute."

"Thank you."

"I thought maybe you and Carter had something going on, but—"

"Oh. No, no, no. Nothing going on," I clarify. *Shit.* So, his being into me is obvious enough that even the IT people have noticed.

"Well, Nathan's cute. Good for you."

Exactly. Good for me. Nathan is good for me.

I mingle some more, and after another hour or so, things wind down. I slip over to where Nathan and Kevin are sitting at a patio table, deep in conversation with a couple of LightVerse engineers.

"Hey," I lean down to whisper in his ear, "you ready to go, or need some more time?"

I'm pretty sure he hears the tone of my voice—my "I'm-three-drinks-in-and-if-you-come-with-me-now-there's-a-good-chance-you'll-come-with-me-later" voice—because he tells the guys he's talking to he'll connect with them on LinkedIn and stay in touch.

As we leave, I inadvertently meet eyes with Carter, who's talking to a woman from marketing. To anyone watching, he's engrossed in the conversation, but to anyone watching *closely*, it's clear his eyes are following me and Nathan.

As we leave the restaurant, I ask where Nathan parked.

"Over near the train tracks," he says. He offers to carry my backpack for me and takes my hand to pull me in the right direction. "Wow," he says, sensing my slight delay in following. He leans in and tries to sniff me unobtrusively. "How many did *you* have tonight?"

I scrunch my nose, trying to remember. "I don't know. Two . . . maybe three. I lost count. You were deep in conversation with your brogrammers, and I was trying to avoid—" I stop short.

"Yeah, I can guess what, or *whom*, you were trying to avoid."

I catch his eyes.

"I guess getting my job wasn't enough. Now he'd like my girlfriend, too." The seemingly nonchalant tone of his voice fails to mask the vulnerability floating just beneath the surface. He exhales loudly and unlocks the car with the remote key.

Before he can get in, I snuggle up to him and pin him gently up against it. "Hey, I want us to have a good night."

He leans down and kisses me on the forehead. "Me, too. Just . . . I can tell he's into you. Please try to keep your distance from him?"

"I will," I tell him.

I back up, and he turns to open the driver's door and gets in, probably assuming I'll walk around to the other side to get in the front passenger seat. But I'm feeling playful—maybe it's the drinks, maybe I just want to coax Nathan into a better mood—and hop into the back seat instead. I scoot over to the other side so he has to look back at me diagonally.

"What are you doing?" he asks. "Am I your Uber driver now?"

"I wanna ride back here."

"You want to ride back there?"

"In a manner of speaking," I say. "I want *a ride* back here . . . with you."

He has an incredulous smile on his face. "Sarah, we are, like, fifty feet from your office and a hundred feet from a police station."

"Good, we won't get robbed while we're doing it."

"It's summer. It's barely dark out," he protests.

"Nobody's here, and there are lots of trees. We'll be discreet." I pout my lips theatrically. "I promise it'll be worth it."

He narrows his eyes at me. Then he turns back to the steering wheel and runs his hands through his hair before hopping out of the car and opening the back door to join me.

"I knew you couldn't resist," I say, laughing. "Lock the doors."

He clicks the lock shut and turns toward me. "What now?"

"Now," I say sidling up close to him, my legs curled up under me, and leaning my breasts into his side, "you get to see why you don't need to worry about who I spend time with at work because you are the one I come home to." I take his hand and slide it up my skirt, along my inner thigh.

"Mmmm," he says in a low voice.

"Do you know how much you turn me on? That jealous look you got in your eyes earlier got me hot and bothered."

He's moving closer to me, trying to figure out the best position since this will be our first chance to make out in the backseat of his new car. As he moves closer, his fingertips get even closer to the sheer panties I wore today. I'm radiating heat from my core.

"Yeah, I can tell you're 'hot and bothered,'" he says.

"What should we do first?" I ask him, reaching out my own hand, and caressing his muscular thigh. "Remember what the salesman said when you bought the car? 'Think of all the possibilities.'" I giggle.

He had likely meant a bike rack on the back for his mountain bike, but Nathan and I had exchanged glances when he said it.

"So many possibilities," he replies, amused, but I can tell he's beginning to get turned on. His eyes are closed, and his thumb is lightly rubbing me, tracing over my wetness, over my clit. I can almost sense his concentration, considering his next step in the cramped space.

"Come closer," he says and pulls me toward him. He helps position me just right, laying me back onto the seat now. One of my legs is bent, propped on the back of the seat, and the other is on the car floor. I'm open—legs spread wide to him—giving him access to wherever he chooses to go next. It's gotten darker outside, and a part of me is grateful for the diminishing light and that his back windows are tinted. But it's a small part, and a much bigger part simply wants him inside of me.

He continues to touch me through my underwear as he begins to kiss the inside of my legs. I like where this is going. I run my fingers through his hair as he works his way toward my center, kissing every few inches starting from my knee and continuing up my inner thigh. Every so often, instead of a kiss, he bites me softly, and my leg muscles tense under his teeth. Between the warmth of his breath, now closing in on its target, and his fingers, which have found their way inside my underwear, I'm beginning to make little noises that seem to spur him on.

"Please, Nathan."

"What do you want, Sarah?"

"I want you."

"Which part of me do you want first, though?"

"Mmmm, I want your cock," I say. I feel his smile against my skin, just above my mound. "No, no, I take it back."

He laughs softly, and small breaths flicker across my lower abdomen, where my skirt has ridden up, exposing the skin. "First," I clarify, "I want your mouth..." I take a deep breath and try to calm myself enough to speak intelligibly—in full sentences—but it's hard to concentrate with his skillful fingers gently toying with me in my most sensitive spots.

He looks up at me, and says in a pleased tone, "I was hoping you'd say that."

Within seconds, he's pulled down my underwear to my knees, pulled my skirt further up, around my hips, and his tongue is on me—in me—and it is pure magic.

The man knows his way around at least two things in life: C++ and, well, something else that starts with C. And I'm begging for him to give me a break, but he doesn't. I feel as if waves are crashing down over me as he uses his mouth and fingers in a diabolical combination to bring me to completion.

Between the strong orgasm and the drinks I had earlier, I feel like a ragdoll thrown across the backseat of his car. He's come up for air and has turned me on my side, resting his head on the curve of my butt.

"You sure you don't want a better pillow?" I ask.

"What are my options?" he asks, and gently massaging my breast. Somehow, they've yet to come into play this evening, and with all my nerve endings firing from our playtime, my nipples perk up immediately at his touch.

I pull myself together and sit up, forcing him to sit up as well since his "pillow" has disappeared.

"That was. . . whew . . . *very* good," I say. "But I think you'll recall I said I wanted a ride."

Before he has a chance to inquire what I mean, I crawl onto his lap. My underwear is already on the floor somewhere, and I am well-positioned right over his cock, which is already hard and ready for me. He slides his hands up under my skirt, massages my bare ass, and moans.

"It doesn't take much for you to lose all your inhibitions, huh?" he asks, his voice strained.

I kiss his mouth greedily while I rub myself against him rhythmically, getting him even more turned on.

"It's all . . ."

Kiss.

"Your . . ."

Bite.

"Fault."

"Fuck, I'll take the blame if *this* is the punishment I get," he says in a husky voice. He begins to unbuckle his belt, quickly. "I have to be inside of you."

I murmur in agreement.

"Tell me you want me inside of you."

"Nathan," I whisper in his ear, my voice thick with desire. "I want you inside of me."

He slides down his pants and boxers to reveal an impressive erection. He holds himself, and I replace his hands with my own over his hard shaft and begin to stroke him up and down while kissing him deeply, entangling my tongue with his.

He pulls away from our kiss long enough to say, "Tell me again."

I lean in close to his ear. "I want you to fuck me, lover."

He moans.

"Here. Now."

And he does. He slides into me and fucks me. Or I fuck him. Or we fuck each other. At some point, a train goes by, and the noise of it drowns out any sound he makes while he comes. But I know he's peaking because he grips my ass tighter as it happens. I lean into his neck, and I can feel the vibration of his vocal cords and his breath catching in his throat, then one long, almost-exhausted exhalation.

"Oh . . . my . . . god," he says, breathing hard.

The train passes, and it's quiet again. Nathan's grip on me loosens. I kiss him fully, deeply, and he kisses me back almost lazily.

When we're both able to breathe normally again, I slide off of him, pull my skirt down, and sit next to him. Out of the side of his eye, he looks at me, and I look back at him—and we exchange tired but sated smiles.

Just then, we hear a small pop, and we both jump. Something must've fallen on the windshield, and all of a sudden, a squirrel lands on the car and scurries away.

"Oh my god, I almost had a heart attack," I say, my heart pounding. "I thought that was someone. Can you imagine if, like, Kevin found us here? In this state?"

"He'd probably hop in the front seat and ask if we had a good time," Nathan says, and we both crack up.

"Make sure you send me a status update on that tomorrow, Sarah," I say, impersonating Kevin.

"You do a good 'Kev,'" Nathan says, kissing me on the temple.

I laugh softly.

"You always know how to cheer me up," he observes.

"Well, sex isn't the most original idea."

"And yet, it works, doesn't it?" He gives me a serious look, one that I can barely see in the almost-dark.

"I hope you'll always be mine," he says.

"I think you're stuck with me."

"Speaking of sticky," he says, laughing and grabbing some tissues from the front seat and offering me one.

"Oh my god," I reply, dissolving into laughter, as I start to get ready for the ride home.

RUNTIME ERROR

NATHAN

Nathan's on his way to Kevin's now and glances in the backseat of his car to make sure he brought his laptop. It reminds him of what he and Sarah were doing last night in the back, and he snorts. *That woman is a bit unpredictable. But amazing.*

He has more important things to think about right now, though. He's been replaying his conversation with Peter, the venture capital contact he met in Redwood City last week. As pieces of their conversation come back to him, his grip on the steering wheel tightens.

"Nate, I can see that you stayed up some late nights coding, and yeah, it works. But what I'm not understanding is your pitch to a VC. How are you going to make money on this?"

Nathan knows what venture capitals want to hear, and yet somehow, he's not quite able to articulate some of the ideas he has brainstormed for the business model.

"I know it'll be hard to prove ourselves to health care providers, institutions—"

"They are very skeptical," Peter says. "I mean, the clowns from Theranos are still going through trial."

"I know, I know."

"And you're a technical guy. You don't have a business person on board with you yet as a co-founder. You don't have medical expertise. There are a lot of things you don't have."

"I know that," Nathan manages to say through gritted teeth. He's not upset with this guy, Peter, but all his fears are being played out in front of him in this one conversation.

You can't do this, a negative voice in his head says.

But a calmer voice, one that sounds a lot like Sarah, says, I know you can. You'll figure it out. And he gets a second wind.

"I have connections in the medical community. Someone really knowledgeable—Dr. Thompson, she's well-known in Seattle—is consulting me and has agreed to be on the board if . . . when this becomes a reality. And Silicon Valley is full of business people looking for technical co-founders. I'm sure I can find someone to support me on that side."

"Maybe," Peter says in a doubtful tone. "Listen, I'm not saying you should give up, but I think you should take some time to really dig in on the financial potential. If you want, you can send me your deck. I can review it and give you my thoughts."

"Thank you. That would be great," Nathan tells him. Peter advised Kevin early on, back when Instinqt was just an idea. Maybe he'll be able to help Nathan, too.

As Nathan waits for the traffic light to turn green, he tries to brainstorm something that will lead him in the right direction. That's why he's headed over to Kevin's now. Since they were college roommates, there hasn't been a week they haven't caught up by email, text, or phone. And since Nathan moved out to the Bay Area last year, they've revived their long-distance friendship, meeting up at least once a week for a beer or just to walk and talk about life, tech, or—when it's needed—women.

Nathan's swallowing his pride and finally taking Kevin up on his numerous offers to help. As he pulls into the driveway of the fancy new home Kevin bought in Los Gatos after Instinqt's exit, he feels relieved. Kevin has always had his back, and he can admit now that he's been stupid not to have asked for more of Kevin's advice earlier. Nathan gets out of his car and heads to the front door. Before he has a chance to ring the bell, Kevin opens the door.

"How'd you know I'm here?"

"Security camera."

"So fancy."

"Damn, right," Kevin replies without missing a beat. "How's it going? You want to sit inside or out near the pool?"

"I bet it feels nice to be able to ask that, huh?"

Kevin cocks his head. "It does. Can you believe that you and I used to live in a room the size of my bathroom together?"

"Let's just say I'm glad these days I share a room with Sarah, instead."

"Ouchhhh. Okay, okay," Kevin says. "Beer?"

"Yeah, sure."

They sit out near the pool, but Nathan brings his laptop so they can look over a preliminary pitch deck he's been building.

Kevin peruses the presentation while Nathan leans back on the lounge chair and enjoys the view of the mountains and the sound of the fountain flowing into the pool.

"You bring any girls here yet?" he asks.

Kevin laughs. "Nah, man. Maybe someday soon. I want to make sure they like me for my charming personality and wit—not my money."

"You're not that charming," Nathan replies, laughing. "Wait, someday soon? Someone specific?"

"We'll see," Kevin says.

Nathan narrows his eyes. "Okay."

He's not sure why Kevin's being so secretive, but he also knows that Kevin is like a lockbox. When he doesn't want to share something, he can't be persuaded otherwise.

"So, the way I see it," Kevin says, gesturing at the screen, "you've locked in on B2B, which is fine, but some sectors are harder to get into than others. This is medical shit. You're going to have to deal with HIPAA and all sorts of other regulations with anything that requires releasing medical info. Doctor-patient privilege and all that stuff. I think that can be *one* of your potential lines of business, but VCs will want to see some proof that this info is even valuable to people—"

"Of course it'll be valuable to people," Nathan interrupts.

"I know that. At least, I believe that, but they're going to want early proof points. I think you should consider adding a B2C offering. Something that you don't need to sign a half-a-million-dollar contract to prove. 'Hey, this makes money.' You got something like that?"

Nathan considers what Kevin's saying. "Yeah, I think I do. Sarah actually had a similar idea the other day."

"Well, you've obviously surrounded yourself with highly intelligent people."

Nathan sniffs out. "You think that strengthens the pitch?"

Kevin nods. "Have I ever led you astray?"

"Only like forty-seven times in the decade I've known you."

"Dude, you're driving a new car and can take off work for six months to work on a startup. I think I helped at least a bit with that."

"Yeah, you're right."

"You want something stronger?" Kevin asks, noticing Nathan has barely touched his beer.

"What're you thinking?"

"I dunno. Bourbon?"

"Sure, why not?" He needs to relax, and he's feeling bummed out. "Sarah's working late tonight anyways."

"She is?" Kevin asks, a confused expression on his face.

"She told me it was some project *you* recommended her for."

"Oh, right. Must be the one Carter's leading. He wants to pitch Instinqt's machine learning tech as the sole solution at LightVerse for user content recommendations."

"What does Sarah have to do with that?"

"Well, he likes her ideas—how she thinks about things. He's as impressed with her as you and I are."

I'm sure he is.

"Anything I should know about this 'working' relationship?" Nathan asks him, uncharacteristically direct.

"Something making you suspicious of your girl all of a sudden?"

"I'm not suspicious of Sarah. I'm suspicious of that . . . smug jerk," he spits out.

It's not the whole truth, but he's not able—or willing—to share everything weighing on his mind. *Why has Sarah been going into the office so much? Is it to avoid dealing with my moodiness?* He can't admit to his best friend, or to himself, that the honeymoon period with her is officially over. The easy comfort they've felt with one another the last couple of months is waning, and he doesn't quite know how to keep it from slipping away.

Kevin sighs. "Dude—"

"I just know how easy it is for things to happen sometimes, okay?"

"Ah, there it is. So, in this situation, Carter is Danica, and Sarah is . . . *you?*"

Nathan clenches his jaw. "Carter can help Sarah accomplish her dreams, and he's . . . successful in a way I'm not."

He, embarrassingly, spent an afternoon going down an internet rabbit hole this week. Starting with some innocent curiosity, when LinkedIn suggested he add Carter as a connection, it went downhill from there. Scrolling through Instagram posts of Carter doing extreme sports and hanging out with beautiful women turned into an hour reading articles highlighting Carter's contributions to a myriad of business ventures. Where the former failed to ignite a spark of jealousy, the latter, Carter's success in the same world in which Nathan himself is trying to succeed—technology, business—was enough to awaken his competitive nature.

"Did you know Carter managed the IPO for Z-Nova?" Nathan asks.

"Yeah."

"Is there anything he *doesn't* do well?"

Kevin levels an impatient stare at him. "Is there anything *you* don't do well? Let's list *your* annoyingly successful characteristics and accomplishments: PhD in computer science, a startup exit, you can bench your body weight, and you have a smart, hot girlfriend."

"And up until this point in my life, everything technical I touched turned to gold. And now, I'm bashing my head against the wall, trying to see a way forward on this startup idea."

"Well, if you expect it all to happen easily, then you're dumber than I thought," Kevin says acerbically. He leans back on the patio sofa, props his legs on the table, and looks at Nathan for a moment before continuing.

"Bro, try to quit moving the goalpost on yourself all the time. Take a minute to enjoy all the shit you've accomplished early in life, and then maybe you'll have the confidence to keep making it happen."

Maybe he's right.

"Anyway," he continues, "you don't have anything to worry about with Carter and Sarah. I mean, some women at work—come to think of it, a guy, too—talk about how 'hot' he is, so maybe he has *that* in common with Danica, but Sarah's a hell of a lot smarter than you." Kevin leans back, hands behind his head, and smiles smugly.

He stands before Nathan can respond and goes inside to grab the bourbon and turn on the patio lights. While he's gone, Nathan texts Sarah.

Nathan: Going okay?

Sarah: Yeah, I'll head home soon.

Nathan: No rush. Just drive carefully.

Sarah: Okay, we'll finish up here in a few.

She doesn't say who "we" is.

Kevin returns and pours him a drink, offering up his usual toast of *"Ganbei"* to which Nathan responds, *"L'chaim."*

"You wanna brainstorm some more?" Kevin asks.

Nathan sighs. "Sure. Someone told me recently that working with you always leads to greatness."

Kevin laughs. "Exactly." He sets his glass on the table and opens the laptop. "Now, give me all your best ideas."

***

Nathan returns home late that night. Kevin sent him in an Uber with a promise to drive his car downtown tomorrow to a meeting he has scheduled. He's searching for the right key when Sarah opens the front door, a curious look on her face.

"How's it going there?"

He leans on the door frame, and for a second, he remembers the first time he visited her place. It was the night of the Instinqt partner event, a few hours after they had been forced to go their separate ways. A few eventful hours during which he and Kevin had met the LightVerse CEO, and Danica had made a move on him. But he had made it back to Sarah in the middle of the night, and she had welcomed him in and allowed him to spend the night. He remembers falling asleep with his arms around her. *Simpler times.*

"I'm doing fine." He goes inside, sets his backpack on the floor, and takes off his shoes. When he stands back up, she's standing close to him.

"Where have you been?" she asks.

"I was out with a Mr. Kevin Wong. Your boss, or something like that. The guy who sets you up for success and recommends you for new projects with . . . *new people.*"

She looks at him like he's lost it. He's drunk, and he knows he's not making any sense. *Why am I trying to start a fight?*

"Okayyy," she says. She seems confused, but then a flicker of understanding crosses her face. "I need to tell you something."

"Go ahead."

"I was working on something tonight with Carter, something he asked me to do for the new project I told you about."

"You didn't tell me he's the . . . what did you call it? 'New business partner?'"

She takes a deep breath. "I'm sorry."

He scoffs.

"What? I know you don't like him, and you asked me to keep my distance. But I can't exactly do that if we're working on the same project, now can I?"

It might be true, reasonable, but that doesn't mean he has to like it. "Sarah, he obviously wants more than just a professional relationship with you."

She looks away. *What does she know? Has something happened?*

He touches her arm lightly, his tone softer now. "I don't like the way he looks at you. Or the way he touches you."

"He didn't *do* anything, Nathan," she says, pulling her arm away.

"Yet."

"You do understand that he's a key for me?" she says, her voice rising.

"A key for you?"

"Yes, a key to open doors for me, professionally."

That's not the only thing he's trying to open, he thinks bitterly. But he's smart enough to keep that particular thought to himself. He takes a deep breath, trying to calm his nerves, but even he can hear in his ragged exhalation how much frustration he's pushing down.

"What is it?" she spits out, her annoyance finally bubbling over. "You obviously have something to say."

"I think . . . you're ignoring the obvious, and I thought . . ."

"What?"

"I thought that honesty was an important part of . . . us—what we're trying to build here. You're risking that by spending more time with him than you need to."

Her mouth drops open, and it takes her a moment to regroup. "So, I'm risking our relationship by working for the company that pays me a salary? You need to trust me, Nathan. I'm not going to do anything to jeopardize what we have. Carter simply asked me to work on a special project."

"Fuck Carter and fuck his 'special project,'" he says in a bitter tone that surprises even him with its intensity.

"Excuse me?" Sarah says in a tone rivaling his own.

He should let it go or try to say something conciliatory, but now he's warmed up. There are a few more F-bombs he needs to drop after a doubt-filled, frustrating week.

"And fuck LightVerse. And fuck—"

"Stop. Right. There. If you say 'fuck my job' or 'fuck me,' I'm leaving." Her voice sounds thin, hurt. He recognizes the tone because he feels the same way.

"You don't have to because *I'm* leaving." Nathan slips his feet back into his shoes and opens the apartment door.

"You just got here."

He turns back to answer her. "I'll go to my own place. Spend the night there."

"Nathan, it's late," she says, reaching out to touch his arm.

"I don't want to be here right now," he says and turns, walking out the door.

***

It's past midnight, and despite his size, as he walks under a darkened railroad overpass, he's doubting the wisdom of walking to his place late at night in downtown San Jose. He pulls out his phone to use as a flashlight and begins to walk faster, but then notices the bright headlights of a car driving slowly behind him. *What the hell is going on? Am I going to get picked up by a cop for drunken behavior? Will my career end before it's even started?*

The car passes him, then stops, and the passenger window rolls down.

"Nathan Levi Goldman, get your ass in the car."

"Uh-oh," he says dumbly.

"'Uh-oh' is right. Get in the car and quit behaving like a toddler."

He doesn't want to. He really doesn't want to. He's still angry, but the more he hears Sarah berate him like a mother who's finally lost it on a misbehaving child, the more he's forgetting why he was mad.

"Nathan, please," she pleads, her voice suddenly softer. "It's late. You're acting . . . You're tired, and you've had too much to drink. Get in, please. We'll go home and talk in the morning."

He's annoyed, but his mind is beginning to clear. Spending the night at home—the one he shares with Sarah, not the almost-empty, cold one in his skyrise building—sounds infinitely better than the mile-long-walk and whoever he might encounter along the way.

"Fine," he relents.

"Wonderful," she says, unexpectedly lapsing back into the tone one uses with a petulant child.

He opens the door and gets in. She locks the doors, then floors it and pulls a sharp U-turn, like she's in an action movie. He didn't know she knew how to drive like that, and, honestly, it's kind of hot. Considering the current situation, though, it's probably not the best time to mention it. He sits in silence while she drives the few minutes back home.

She puts the car in park when they reach the parking lot and unexpectedly grabs one of his hands and squeezes it. Without saying a word, she leaves him in the car and goes inside the building.

He doesn't know what else to do, so he gets out and follows her. She glances up when he comes into the small lobby and presses the "up" button on the elevator. She waits, arms folded. She's cold. It's a chilly night, and she left without a sweater.

He closes the distance between them and stands silently next to her. When she doesn't move away, he reaches out tentatively and gently wraps his hand around her bicep on the arm closest to him, untangling the fold of her crossed arms. She hesitates but lets him pull her hand into his. He intertwines his fingers into hers, his large hand dwarfing her smaller one.

She takes a deep breath and exhales. The breath that leaves her body is eerily calm, even. He has seen her truly mad—the night Danica sent him that thirst trap of a selfie and Sarah thought he'd slept with her comes to mind. She's annoyed now, but she's not as mad as then, not by half. When the elevator doors open, she steps on, ahead of him, loosening her hand in his, but he holds on. In his imagination, he sees himself letting go and her floating away from him, like a rudderless boat on the sea. She could be gone forever. It startles him, and he grips her hand tightly in his own.

As the elevator rises, his own clarity follows suit. *What is going on with me?* He accused her of lying to him, but more than that, lying to him for the purpose of covering up . . . what? An affair? Her last boyfriend cheated on her. Physically? Maybe. Emotionally, for sure. Nathan didn't cheat on her, but he wasn't completely straightforward with her at the time about what was going on with Danica. She knows what it feels like to be on the other side, to have someone be dishonest—purposefully or through a lie of omission—and she wouldn't do that. And here he was, accusing her of doing *exactly* that.

When the elevator doors open again. Sarah shuffles toward their shared apartment. She worked long hours today—she's exhausted—and now she's out in the middle of the night chasing down his dumb ass. She flips through the keys, searching for the right one.

"Here, let me do it," he says, taking the keys from her hands. He unlocks the door and holds it open for her. It's insignificant, but it's a start to show her he's not mad—at least not really, and not with her—and he wants things to go back to normal. She looks at him, and a worried smile ghosts her lips before she heads inside.

"Are you going to make me sleep on the couch?" he asks, venturing a joke.

"I should," she replies without much emotion. "Go brush your teeth and come to bed."

She walks to the bedroom and collapses into bed. He does as she says, brushes—and flosses—his teeth, then gets undressed and slides into the bed next to her, under the covers.

She's lying on her side, facing away from his side of the bed, toward the window. The curtains are open, and the moon is visible outside. She loves the moon, and it's almost full tonight. He hadn't noticed before when he was outside. Maybe that's why everything broke down.

He lays a hand on her waist. He loves her whole body, but resting his hand on her waist when she's laying on her side might be his favorite goddamn thing in the world. She puts her hand over his, and he understands that he's allowed to come nearer. He spoons her smaller body and leans in to smell her hair.

"I'm sorry. I—I trust you. I don't trust him, but I trust you implicitly."

"I'm tired, Nathan," she says in a small voice.

"I know." He takes a deep breath and goes out on a limb. "But please don't leave me hanging tonight. I feel . . ."

"What?"

"I feel . . . a little bit lost somedays."

He can feel her tense under his touch. She turns over to face him. "Oh, sweetheart. I-I'm sorry, too. I shouldn't have lied to you about who I was working with tonight, but do you—"

"I understand why you did," he says, cutting her off. He looks at her, the worry in her eyes. "I'm sorry you felt like you had to."

He knew that's what she was going to say.

It seems to address what is causing the strain in her eyes, the tension between her eyebrows. He leans in and places a small kiss in that very spot, and he can feel her exhale into the front of his neck. He feels whole here, with her in his arms. Not lost. Not even a little bit.

He smiles. "You went full-on disciplinarian in the car. You used my middle name."

"Oh my god," she says, starting to laugh softly. "I did, didn't I?" She starts to laugh harder, and he joins her. Pretty soon, they both have tears in their eyes and are struggling to catch their breath.

"And where the hell did you learn to drive like that?" he asks.

"Like what?"

"I don't know, like *The Fast and The Furious, Dukes of Hazzard*—"

She's laughing and interrupts his list of high-speed action movies—he had at least a few more to add—by kissing him. But he doesn't mind being interrupted for such things and kisses her back.

"How do you always taste so sweet?" he asks her.

"Because I am sweet, Nathan. Try to remember that," she says. "I'm so tired. I have to sleep, Nathan . . . Levi Goldman."

A small laugh escapes him. "Good night, Sarah Naomi Hoffman."

VERSION CONTROL

Around nine on Saturday morning, Nathan's phone buzzes with a text, and I glance at the screen. Kevin. We've agreed, after the last time there was a misunderstanding via text, that it's probably best for us both not to check each other's messages, even though we trust each other. A wisp of a thought—doubt—floats across my mind as I consider what happened on Thursday night, but we talked for a while last night, and we're determined to move past it, the uneasiness, and have a good weekend.

I leave his phone connected to the charger in the kitchen and head back to the living room, a fresh cup of coffee in hand, to dive back into the book I was reading.

I set my mug down on the coffee table and grab my Kindle when I notice I've also gotten a text from Kevin. So, *it's for both of us.*

> **Kevin:** Wanna come over for a BBQ later today?
> **Sarah:** Oooooh, yes. I'll bring tofu.
> **Kevin:** The vegan masses will be pleased. <winky emoji>
> **Kevin:** I assume Loverboy is still sleeping?
> **Sarah:** How did you know? <smiley emoji>
> **Kevin:** Tell him our friend Chetan from UI is in town, so I invited him. Maybe a couple of Instinqt people, too?
> **Sarah:** Want me to text Erin? She can bring her family.
> **Kevin:** Yeah, that works.

> **Sarah:** Cam, too?
> **Kevin:** Sure. Whoever you want.
> **Sarah:** When?
> **Kevin:** See you at 3?
> **Sarah:** <thumbs up emoji>

Nathan wakes half an hour later and joins me in the living room. Finding me still camped out on the couch in the middle of a spicy scene in *The Kiss Quotient*, he leans over me and gives me a sleepy—and from my vantage point, upside-down—smile.

"Good morning," he says and kisses me on the forehead. He glances at the Kindle. "Enjoying your high-tech porn?"

I giggle. "Computer nerds deserve love, too." I stretch my neck up, indicating he should give me a better kiss. It's a funny angle, kissing someone upside down. "Oh, I hope you don't mind. Kevin texted and asked if we wanted to come over for a barbecue later today. I told him yes. He invited a couple more people, and we'll pick up Cam on the way."

"Sure. Sounds fun." He goes to the kitchen, likely to get a cup of coffee and check his phone.

NATHAN

"Fuck," Nathan says as he checks his phone.

"What?" Sarah calls from the living room.

"Uh, nothing. Burned myself on the coffee pot," he says, lying through his teeth.

"Are you okay?"

"Fine."

His expletive actually has a very good reason behind it. The text thread he's currently reading from Kevin starts at 9:00 a.m. this morning.

> **Kevin:** Wanna come over for a BBQ later today?

And about twenty minutes later:

> **Kevin:** Um, so Sarah said you guys are gonna come. You're
> gonna be pissed, but I accidentally invited Carter, too.
> **Kevin:** I was trying to invite Chetan, who's out here for the
> week, but I must've mistyped and didn't notice until later.

Just how I wanted to spend my Saturday. Nathan takes a sip of his coffee and texts Kevin back.

> **Nathan:** I'll manage.
> **Kevin:** He probably won't come anyways.

And miss a chance to see Sarah? Not likely.

Nathan is reminded of that thought and feels somewhat vindicated—though not really pleased—when they arrive at Kevin's that afternoon and find a Jeep he doesn't recognize parked in the driveway. He makes an educated guess it belongs to Carter. As he, Sarah, and Camila head up the walkway to the house, Carter comes out the front door and walks over to the Jeep. He grabs a bag from the backseat before noticing their arrival.

"Hey, Sarah." Then, as an afterthought, he says, "Hey, Nate, what's up?"

Nathan tips his chin at him. Sarah says, "Hello," then turns in Nathan's direction. "What is *he* doing here?" her confused expression seems to ask. He just shrugs and tries to tell her with his eyes that he'll tell her later. While they try to communicate wordlessly, Carter introduces himself to Camila. Then Sarah jumps in.

"Oh, sorry. Carter, this is my best friend, Camila. Cam."

"Nice to meet you, Cam. I think Sarah's mentioned you before."

"Oh, really? Sarah's never mentioned *you.*"

Nathan's not sure if Camila is telling the truth or not, but he sees the look on Carter's face—disappointment. Not a second later, Camila glances at Nathan, catching his eye, her lip twitching in restrained amusement—and he gets her meaning. So Sarah must have told her at least *something* about Carter—maybe even Nathan's feelings about him. He winks at her, and she winks back.

"I got you," Cam mouths at him.

They find Kevin in the kitchen, preparing some meat to go on the grill.

"Hey guys, welcome," he says.

"Need help?" Sarah asks.

"Um, yes, but I'm pretty sure you don't like touching raw meat so—"

"I'll help," Camila offers.

"Sure. You guys can head outside if you want. There are some drinks in the cooler."

Nathan and Sarah walk out to the patio. Erin, Ryan, and their daughter, Zoey, are already there, embroiled in a struggle. Ryan is tugging some floaties onto Zoey's little arms, Erin is applying sunscreen to her face, and Zoey is trying to escape from both of them.

Sarah kneels down to Zoey's height. "Hey, there, sweetheart!"

"Sarah!" Zoey exclaims, giving Sarah a hug and covering her with sunscreen. Sarah is Zoey's favorite babysitter when Erin and Ryan need some adult-only time. Sarah wipes a few globs of sunscreen from her shirt but seems unbothered. She helps distract Zoey while her parents finish the swimming preparations by singing some kid song about an entire family of sharks.

Zoey's face lights up at Sarah's antics. She's in love. *God, so am I.*

He glances over to where Carter is sitting and sees that he, too, is watching the show. It puts a damper on his mood, but he refuses to let Carter's presence ruin his afternoon. His friend Chetan's arrival serves as a nice distraction.

"Hey, what's up? It's been forever, huh?" Chetan says, slapping his back.

"Yeah, like three years." Chetan hasn't aged a day. Nathan notices his fresh haircut and Gucci brand glasses. He looks ten times more put-together than Nathan does these days. He considers his own t-shirt and shorts and the beat-up sneakers he slipped on before driving to Kevin's.

"So, I heard you got your PhD. Nice," Chetan says.

"Yeah, I finished up last year and then joined that clown," he replies, gesturing with his head to Kevin, who has come outside with Camila. She's laughing at something he's saying.

Chetan surveys the nice pool and expansive backyard and whispers, "You get as rich as him?"

"Nah, man, but I'm doing okay."

Sarah joins the conversation, and Nathan introduces them. "This is Sarah, my girlfriend. Sarah, Chetan."

"Nice to meet you, Sarah."

"You, too," she replies. "So, you two were at school together?"

"Yeah, but it was more like Nathan and Kevin kicking everyone else's asses and us trying not to fail."

Nathan shakes his head at her, indicating that wasn't exactly the case.

"You know, it's not surprising that you're doing your own thing now," Chetan tells him. "I saw the high-performance computing paper you presented last year at Supercomputing. That shit was complex. If you can do half that well with something that makes money, next year, we're gonna be in your mansion having a barbecue."

Sarah has a pleased expression on her face. She seems to enjoy hearing Chetan speak so highly of him. She stands and asks if he wants a drink from the cooler.

"Thanks, but I'll get it myself," Chetan replies. "I think I'll go talk to that cute girl over there."

Nathan and Sarah exchange a look. That's exactly what Camila needs, a nice guy to talk to this afternoon. At least, he's guessing that's what Sarah thinks. On the drive over, Sarah asked Camila if she'd been out on any dates lately. Camila had shut down her line of questioning with one look. He's no expert on women, but he knew that particular look meant "Not now."

"Goldman," Kevin calls. "Let's have a beer, man."

Nathan joins him. Unfortunately, so does Carter.

SARAH

The guys—Nathan, Kevin, Carter, and Ryan—gather around the grill. It's like watching some manly ritual of old—men around the fire, discussing the meat that they've hunted. Except in this case, it likely came from Whole Foods. No matter. They all seem to have an opinion on how to grill it best.

I sit down on a lounge chair and keep Erin company while she plays in the water with Zoey.

Noticing the guys at the guys at the grill, she whispers, "What's Carter doing here?"

"No idea."

"Did you know he has a tattoo?"

I glance over to where her attention is focused. Carter has taken off the open shirt he was wearing over a tank top. His shoulders and biceps are clearly visible. A tattoo on one of his biceps is doing a more-than-adequate job of calling attention to the muscle underneath it.

I lean in and whisper to her, "You might close your mouth, you know."

"Do I have to?" she responds, and I laugh.

Nathan looks up at the sound of my laughter and smiles at me. *If he only knew what we're talking about.*

"So, how's the project with Kevin and Carter going?"

"I'm learning a ton. I mean, Kevin is even smarter than I gave him credit for," I say, laughing. "And Carter. He's . . . wow. He knows his shit. I spoke with him for a long time on Thursday about, well, some ideas I had about how to pitch Instinqt's strengths internally, and he asked me to write a brief for him to share with some LightVerse higher-ups."

"Nice work, girl. What does Nate think?"

"About what?"

"About his girl kicking ass at work, of course?" she replies, smiling broadly.

"I mean, we talk about work some, but," I start to say, but then lower my voice, "he thinks Carter's got a thing for me. So, I've been kind of downplaying anything that involves him." My voice goes up at the end, and I bite my lip.

"I see," she says, flitting her eyes in Nathan's direction, then glancing surreptitiously at Carter. Before I can determine whether her skeptical expression is intended for me, Nathan, Carter—or perhaps all of the above—she moves her sunglasses back down over her eyes and refocuses her attention on Zoey.

"Here, baby," she says, supporting her arms. "Kick your legs."

I admire the birds of paradise in Kevin's backyard and distractedly toy with the frayed end of my jean shorts. Keeping things from your partner isn't a sign of a healthy relationship. I know that because I've had to do it before, but I want things to work with Nathan. I don't want us to fight about something I have under control. Carter *does* seem to have "a thing" for me, but I'm smart, and I won't let things get out of hand. I can make things work at home and also at work. All of a sudden, my wandering thoughts—as well as my clothes—are doused by a splash of water from Zoey's energetic kicking in the pool.

"Oh, sorry. Ready to get wet?" Erin asks, laughing, breaking the tension from our previous discussion.

"Now is as good of a time as any," I say. "I'll go get my swimsuit on."

I grab my swimsuit from my bag and head inside to find a place to change. With Kevin's new giant house and bachelor status, it's not hard to find an empty room.

NATHAN

When Sarah comes back from changing, Nathan takes the extra clothes out of her hands.

"You want to eat something before you swim?" he asks while shoving the rolled-up t-shirt and what he thinks is her underwear hiding inside it into the big bag they brought. "I think there are some tofu-skewer things ready."

Sarah glances over to the grill, then back at him. "No, I'll swim with Erin and Zoey first."

"Want some help with your sunscreen?" he asks.

She looks up at him curiously. "Um, sure."

They sit on some lounge chairs, and he squirts some sunscreen onto his hands. As he begins to rub it onto her back, he notes Kevin and Carter talking near the barbecue. Carter glances in their direction but then averts his eyes when he sees Nathan notice him. Nathan knows he was looking at Sarah, and he knows why. Sarah looks like a goddess in her bikini.

She reaches back to help him rub in some of the cream—telling him to make sure he gets under the string of the bikini top stretched across her back—and he stills her hand.

"I got you, babe," he says and leans in to kiss her neck. He sees goose-bumps spread on her arms and trails a pointer finger down her spine to see her reaction.

"Stop it," she says, turning around. "What's gotten into you?"

"Nothing. Just admiring my beautiful girlfriend." She smiles at him and walks off to slip into the pool with Erin and Zoey.

Chetan makes his way over to Nathan with a veggie burger on his plate and sits. "Sarah seems pretty cool. You guys serious?"

"Getting there," Nathan says. "We're living together, doing a trial run."

"What does that mean?"

"It means that I haven't given up my apartment yet, but if things go well, then I probably will soon."

"And are things going well?"

If you'd have asked him the other night—his fight with Sarah and the reason for it, currently sitting about ten feet away from him, drinking an IPA, and talking to *Nathan's* friends—he would have said "no."

But he doesn't want to say "no," or even that he's not sure, so he takes a sip of his drink to give himself a moment to think. Nathan wants to be happy for Sarah for the opportunities and recognition she's receiving at work. She's smart, and she completely deserves it. It's clear to him, though, even if she or Kevin won't admit it, that it's more than just professional recognition. When he saw Carter's hand on her back at the work happy hour, he knew right away. He doesn't trust him—with Sarah or anything else, for that matter.

He wonders why he's even putting up with this. But he watches Sarah in the pool with Zoey, splashing around and having fun—she's smiling, glowing, and full of life—and he knows why he's putting up with it. Because she doesn't have a clue. No, she *does* have a clue, but it's not her fault. She's trying to succeed in her career, and LightVerse happens to be the environment she's currently in. She's being offered professional opportunities, and Carter—unfortunately for Nathan—is the person they currently hinge on. Kevin says he's keeping an eye out, but Nathan can't help but fault him, too, with this whole situation. He's the one who put Sarah in Carter's sights.

So, what exactly is the answer to Chetan's question? Some things are good, but something doesn't feel right. He looks up and notices Carter glance quickly at Sarah again. He clenches his jaw.

Chetan tilts his head, waiting for an answer.

"Things are fine," he says, finally answering. "We love each other. That's what matters."

BUSINESS OPPORTUNITY

ENCRYPTED

It's late, and he's in bed, thinking back on the day. He didn't mean to find her in such a state, but when an opportunity presents itself, well . . .

"What are you doing in here?" he asks, entering the bedroom.

"What does it look like? I'm changing into my swimsuit," she says, crossing her arms over her chest. The ties on the top are still undone.

"Should I avert my eyes?"

She raises an eyebrow. "I think you know the answer to that."

He shuts the door softly behind him and takes in her half-clad body, his lips curling up involuntarily at the beautiful sight in front of him.

"You Santa Cruz girls know how to choose a swimsuit," he remarks.

Her eyes dart to the side, maybe out of shyness, then she seems to reconsider and meets his gaze directly. He knows she's not meek. That's exactly what he likes about her.

"I'm glad you came today," he says.

"Me, too," she replies in a soft voice. "I'm having fun."

He hesitates for just a second, then takes a step toward her, closing the gap between them. If he reached out his hand, he could touch her easily, but he hasn't yet summoned the courage. Over her bikini bottom, she's wearing ripped jean shorts, currently unbuttoned, and his mind begins to wander, thinking about what he'd do if there weren't ten people on the other side of the frosted sliding glass doors.

She notices where his eyes are and shakes her head.

"*Eyes up here, please.*" *She lifts his chin with the gentle touch of one hand—the other still carefully holding her top in place—and his eyes meet hers.*

"*Need help tying the strings?*" *he asks, finally getting the nerve to raise one of his hands to her bare shoulder.*

"*I don't think that's—*" *She stops abruptly, distracted by the slow swirls of his fingertips on the smooth skin of her shoulder. "A good idea."*

She's just finishing her sentence, but he chooses to interpret it differently. "You're right. It is a good idea."

He's facing her, but instead of walking behind her to tie the top strings from the back, he moves closer to her—they'd be chest-to-chest if she weren't so short—and he leans over her shoulder. The angle provides him a great view: the curve of her waist, her cute ass. And he can smell her hair—clean, floral. Every time he sees her, he wishes he could tell her how he feels and act on it. Maybe now? No. Too many people here now.

While he ties the strings, his fingertips skate over the skin of her neck—her upper back. He feels goosebumps pop up on her skin, and his focus shifts downward to her nipples, hard and poking through the white bikini top she has on.

Fuck. Deep breath.

"All done," *he tells her in a slightly ragged voice.*

She's watching him, trying to puzzle something out, all while biting her bottom lip. He imagines doing the same to her, wishing he could bring imagination that much closer to reality. The last couple months of dancing around what they both obviously feel—attraction, temptation, restraint—has him on edge, and he wants her. The feel of her in his arms, the taste of her on his tongue. But he hasn't completely forgotten there are other people here. In a second of awareness, he hears music playing and realizes they might be missed.

She looks into his eyes and shifts her gaze down to his lips, before she exhales roughly and turns quickly to gather up her things: her shirt, a towel. Double-fuck. Is that black, lacy underwear?

She rushes quickly over to the door, and as she's about to open it, he says bluntly, "More. Later."

She turns back and opens her mouth to say something but then seems to think better of it and slides out the door, leaving him there.

He wipes his hand over his face now and takes a deep breath. He's good at moving things forward at work. He'll have to devote some time and effort to this project as well.

Async

SARAH

On the drive home from work, I feel great but also a tad nervous. I've been invited to a senior leadership meeting this week to present a few slides, and while I won't be talking for more than three minutes, I'm excited nonetheless, and I've already planned out the evening. Nathan and I can go out for a quick dinner somewhere so I can share the news and we can celebrate. We have been out of sync lately, so maybe this can be a "reset," a way to get us back on track.

But when I unlock the door, I find the apartment empty. I text him to ask where he is, but after ten minutes of no response, I check Find My Friends. His little dot is somewhere up in the mountains, about forty-five minutes away from here. He must be on a bike ride. Determining that the celebration will have to wait, I grab a cheese stick and an apple and get to work on my slides.

Around 8:00 p.m., Nathan comes back, streaked with dirt and still sweaty. On his way to the bathroom, he leans down to kiss me on the forehead, and I flinch.

"You're kinda gross."

"Nice to see you, too," he says, sounding hurt. "Guess I'll go shower."

I meant for it to come out as a joke, but I'm disappointed about my plans not playing out the way I'd hoped. I call out, "Sorry, I just . . ."

"It's okay," he says, closing the bathroom door.

When he finishes, he heads into the kitchen, and I join him.

"Where were you? I saw you near Soquel."

"Yeah, I was at the Demo Forest, mountain biking with some guys."

"They don't have work on a Monday?"

"I mean, yeah, but they took a day off."

"Yeah, and I guess you can go whenever you want, huh?"

"I mean, I don't have a nine-to-five anymore like you, but I *do* work."

Ugh. I didn't mean it like that. I take a deep breath and give him an apologetic look, moving closer to give him a kiss, but before I reach him, he opens the refrigerator and starts to rummage around.

"What did you have for dinner?" he asks.

He always asks if I've eaten, and it makes me feel even worse for speaking to him rudely.

"Oh, I just snacked. I wanted to work."

"More work?" he says, going to sit down at the kitchen table with a bowl full of random—all healthy—things. Some cold chicken, leftover roasted broccoli, and, strangely, a washed whole cucumber.

I join him at the table. "I mean, I have this important thing coming up. I wanted to tell you. I was actually planning on trying to celebrate tonight. I thought we could go out together or something."

"Oh, yeah? Sorry. I didn't know. Maybe on the weekend?"

"That's fine," I reply.

"So, what are we celebrating?" he asks, eyes focused on me.

"I was asked to present in a senior leadership meeting."

"Oh, wow," he says, his face breaking into a smile. *That's my Nathan.* "What are you presenting?"

I start to tell him about how I happened to catch an elevator ride today with some engineering director, and when I introduced myself, he made the connection to Kevin and asked if I'd like to talk about Instinqt's latest feature releases for a few minutes in an upcoming meeting. Just as I'm about to tell Nathan the features I'm considering highlighting in my slides, he gets a text message and looks down at his phone.

"Oh, shit. I forgot I was supposed to send something to Kevin to review. He's going to pass my product-market fit draft to someone he knows for feedback."

"Um, yeah, of course," I say, trying not to let my disappointment show on my face. He jumps up to grab his laptop from the couch to sit at the kitchen table, and within a minute, he's in another world.

I consider hanging out to see if he'll be done soon, but when it seems like it might take a while, I head to the bedroom to change into running clothes. I need to get out of here—be active.

On my run, I put on music, but I barely hear it. As I wind my way through the neighborhood streets toward the nearby high school track, I think about all sorts of things: my upcoming presentation, walks I used to go on with my dad, and my last troubled relationship. That last one is especially heavy tonight. You think you know someone well, but living with them *really* lets you get to know them. The same thing happened with Blake, my ex.

Stop. Nathan is not Blake. Sometimes, like tonight, he zeros in on things, and his mind is elsewhere, working out some problem in his head. He's quiet, yes. But he's not manipulative or intentionally hurtful like Blake.

It's dark by the time I reach the track. I run some laps, and when I'm done, I stay and stretch. My phone chimes with a text message.

Nathan: Where are you? Everything okay?

I'm about to respond when the stadium lights begin to turn off, and I realize how late it must be.

Me: On my way back.

I amble my way back to the apartment, choosing streets that have more streetlights, and when I walk in the door, Nathan's exactly where I left him—working on his laptop at the table. He looks up.

"Are you alright?" he asks. "Do you wanna talk?"

"No, I'm just going to shower and go to bed."

"It's cool if I go for a walk with Kevin?"

I'm used to the walks they go on late at night, usually once or twice a week, to talk about—well, I'm not exactly sure, but knowing them, it's probably something nerdy.

"Yeah, sure," I say, and lean down to kiss his forehead.

"You're kinda gross," he says, imitating me from a few hours ago, the hint of a smirk on his face.

"Sorry, I was kinda snarky."

"It's okay. I *was* kinda gross," he admits. "I was thinking we could move the celebration dinner from the weekend to tomorrow night?"

I smile. "That works. Be careful walking, okay? It's late."

"I will. You need anything?"

Just you.

"No, I'll just shower and head to bed."

"Okay, sleep well," he says, standing and pecking me on the lips.

Out of Office

NATHAN

"It's not an emergency, Nathan," his mom says on speakerphone. "Your dad just wasn't feeling well last night, and I probably overreacted taking him in, but—"

"You did the right thing, Mom," Nathan says, interrupting her. "Better safe than sorry."

"But you definitely don't need to come up. He's getting released from the hospital in an hour, and I'll take him home. We'll be fine."

"I'll be fine," his dad says loudly, for his benefit, in the background.

Nathan chuckles. His dad's voice sounds strong—a good sign. But Nathan has already decided he's flying up to Seattle. He can work from anywhere. If nothing else, it will give him a chance to meet with Dr. Thompson face-to-face and discuss the dashboard he's building.

"Mom, I love you. Tell Dad I love him, too."

She sighs in relief, thinking she's won and that he won't fly up now.

"I'll see you tomorrow," he tells her and ends the call.

When Sarah comes home from work, he zips up the suitcase he was packing in the bedroom and pulls it into the living room. "Hey, there."

She eyes the suitcase. "What's going on?"

"Well, my dad went to the hospital last night. I need to fly up and help them out."

"Oh, wow," she says. "Um, of course. You should go."

"I'll miss you," he says, leaving the suitcase near the couch and greeting her properly with a hug.

She seems stiff at first but relaxes into him. "I'll miss you, too. But I'm sure they could use your help."

He slides his hands down to hers and pulls her into the kitchen. "Yeah, but I had a nice dinner planned for us tonight. I know you wanted to go out, but I figured you might also need to prep for your presentation, so I made some of your favorite foods."

"My favorite foods?"

He gestures to the counter. "Quiche, chopped salad, and . . ."

"Brownies?" she asks hopefully, glancing at the oven. She must have caught the scent.

He nods and smiles, pleased with her reaction.

"You're the best. Are you sure you don't have time to eat?" she asks.

He checks his watch. "No, I have to go." He had planned on taking a flight the next day, but he found a last-minute flight this evening for $200 cheaper.

She frowns.

"I wanted us to catch up, have a chance to talk before I left," he says. "I'll be gone for ten days."

"So long?"

"I thought if I'm already going up there, I should stay a little longer to make sure they're sorted."

"I guess that makes sense," she says, sounding disappointed.

"I wish we had time to . . . well, you know, before I left."

"Quickie?" she asks, biting her lip.

"Oh, god," he says, drawing in his breath quickly. "I wish, but if I don't go now, I'll miss the flight." He exhales and looks her in the eyes.

She pops open a button on her shirt, taunting him and pouts her lips invitingly.

"Nooo. Don't do that to me. Send me a sexy selfie later?"

She smiles and nods.

"But like, after I'm on the plane. Otherwise, I might just come right back here and tackle you."

She laughs. He goes to his desk to pack up his laptop and charger. Before he heads out the front door, he turns to her. "Come here," he says.

She comes closer, and he hugs her and gives her one last kiss. He can't seem to leave.

"You need to go," she says quietly, placing her hands on his chest, and then gently pushing herself away from him.

"I do."

"Have a safe trip," she says, and he smiles at her before he walks out the door, all the while wishing he didn't have to.

***

As his flight takes off a couple hours later, he looks down at the sparkling lights of the San Francisco Bay Area. *Am I doing the right thing, leaving now?* Things have felt shaky with Sarah lately, with fights cropping up over the dumbest things sometimes.

He constantly has to search for things she misplaces: phone chargers, the television remote, sometimes even *his* phone. But the one that drives him completely crazy is the keys.

"Why do you even take *my* keys?" he asks her each time it happens. It's a pointless question because he already knows the answer. She takes his because she has lost her own. It always seems to happen when he's in a rush to leave, too. He was seconds from walking out the door on Saturday afternoon only to discover Sarah had struck again.

"Just keep track of things," he says in what he knows is an impatient manner. The moment it leaves his mouth, her face hardens.

"I do keep track of things. I keep track of your laundry when I wash, dry, and fold it for you. I also keep track of paying all the bills and buying groceries, don't I?"

She stomps into the kitchen and, unable to leave without keys, he follows her and finds her half inside the refrigerator, bent over, searching for something to eat. Or so he thinks. She sighs audibly. Then her cute backside begins to shake in what he suspects is laughter.

"What's so funny?" he asks. A cute snort of laughter answers him, then the sound of jingling keys. "What?" he insists. "You put them in the refrigerator?"

She straightens up and closes the refrigerator door, her face fighting a smile. Unbelievable. This intelligent, organized-in-every-other-way woman—his girlfriend—has refrigerated his keys.

Dancing over to him, rubbing the presumably cold keys between her hands, she teases, "I bet you'd like these back so you can go play basketball, huh?"

He nods, unable to prevent a smile from creeping onto his face. And he sees in her expression the moment she realizes he isn't annoyed anymore. She pulls up his t-shirt and presses the cold keys onto the bare skin of his stomach.

"Those are cold, you nut," he says, laughing and pulling her into a hug.

"True, but I found them," she replies. "Now you can go."

Feeling her close, though, wearing short shorts and a tank top, he suddenly isn't so interested in leaving. She turns to walk back to the living room when he catches her from behind and hugs her tightly. Wrestling her playfully, he cups her breast, and she whispers in his ear, "I knew you'd forgive me." He forgives her—twice—and is late to play basketball.

Things had ended well, but he wished they wouldn't argue at all. Combativeness, grudges, tension—none of it is in his nature or hers.

His worry over the startup and Sarah's stress from the increasing demands of her job have been creeping into their interactions. They should be each other's stress *relief*, not the cause of each other getting wound up and exploding. Or worse, going to bed without saying good night after barely talking, like last night.

What if Sarah's relieved he's going up to Seattle? Maybe she's confiding in Camila or Erin right now that she needs the space. Or maybe he's the one running away because *he needs the space. No, that can't be it.* It's only been a couple hours, and he already misses her.

He pauses the audiobook—distracted, he's missed the last ten minutes of it anyways—and opens his Photos app, scrolling through pictures that he and Sarah have taken together. Sarah holding up a peace sign and kissing his cheek. Her curled up on his lap at Kevin's one night, both of them half-asleep, him with a slight smile on his face. The most recent picture? The selfie she texted him right before he boarded the plane of her about to take a bite of one of the brownies he baked with a "#dessert4dinner" sticker she added.

He mindlessly scrolls through all the pictures again. So much good. So much happiness. Even when they have hard times, she makes him so damn happy.

Lately, so many of the things he thought he knew about himself feel like they're slipping through his grasp: who he is, what he wants, what he's capable of. Coming to terms with the fact that you might not be the person you thought you were is not an exercise for the weak, but he could probably survive letting go of many of those things. What—or who—he can't lose? Sarah. Her and what he has with her.

I could lose a lot and still be whole. But I can't lose her.

TEAM SYNC

SARAH

"Hey, I know it's last minute, but I was wondering if you want to go rock climbing?" Carter asks me on Wednesday afternoon. He's caught me just as I'm about to get on the elevator.

"Rock climbing?" I ask doubtfully.

"Yeah," he says. "There's an intro course at the gym I go to, and I've invited a few people from work. It could be nice for us to get to know each other outside of work."

"Who's going?"

"A couple of the Instinqt engineers—Chen and Aleks—and Erin also just Slacked me that she can come."

"Oh, really?"

If Erin is there, that might shift the decision to go rock climbing with Carter from a bad idea to simply a neutral one. She'll run interference. I could just bow out, but with all the talk at LightVerse about "winning together," maybe it'll help Carter to show he's succeeding at integrating the Instinqt team into the larger company.

With Nathan in Seattle, I don't feel like going home to an empty house, and I'm feeling upbeat after my presentation this morning on the senior leadership call.

"You know what? Sure."

"Awesome," he says in a genuinely happy tone. "Have you done it before?"

"Never," I say, laughing nervously.

"Well, a friend of mine teaches the course. I promise it'll be fun. I'll send you the invite with the details. Tonight at seven."

"See you there," I say, pressing the elevator button again as he walks off.

I take my phone out and begin to text Erin:

> **Me:** You like rock climbing?
> **Erin:** Not particularly. But I've always wanted to try it, and I want to get in shape. Maybe this will be my thing.
> **Me:** Okay, so, what do we wear?
> **Erin:** I'm going to wear leggings and a t-shirt. You, on the other hand, should probably wear a bag.
> **Me:** What?

Erin calls me, and I answer. "I just got on the elevator. The call might cut out."

"Sarah, seriously, if you're gonna go, keep your distance from Carter." *Has she been talking to Nathan?* "I wouldn't put it past him to arrange this whole thing just to hang out with you more."

"Don't be ridiculous." My voice drops to a whisper. "I know he's into me, but he invited a lot of people."

"And he made *extra sure* I'm coming."

"So, maybe he likes *you*—"

I'm deflecting. I know that, and she knows that. It's evident from the noise I just heard her emit over the phone.

"To make sure *you* would come," she says drily.

She's right.

"I have a sense for these things," she says. "Listen, just try not to be so damn cute, and we'll have fun."

I laugh. "I'm not that cute, Erin."

"Unfortunately, you are." She sighs. "See you later."

***

We've all gotten our special climbing shoes, and our instructor at Planet Granite, Greg—a guy who looks like he's made of granite—is showing us how to put on our harnesses. Despite Erin's warnings, I wore my usual workout gear, black leggings, and a tank top. It's been in the nineties this week, and I couldn't force myself to wear anything baggy today. I'm glad I dressed the way I did. The gym is warm, and we haven't even begun moving around.

Coach Granite, a.k.a. Greg, demonstrates a figure-eight knot and explains how to tie ourselves into the harnesses. As we all begin to practice, Carter makes a round and helps Greg check that everyone has secured their harnesses correctly. Then he drills a few people on the proper tying and harness checks. "Okay, Erin, what's the harness checklist?"

"Tight waist and double-backed, rope through the tie-in loops, five parallels in the knot and . . . two-fists worth of rope coming out."

"Excellent student, Erin," Carter says, coming closer to me and tugging on my harness. "Sarah, on the other hand, seems to be having trouble with her knot." I glance at Erin, who opens her mouth to say something, but then Greg tells the group of people who have already finished to head to the next station.

Carter notices me watching Erin walk away, tilts his head, and asks if everything is okay.

No, not really.

"Everything's fine," I lie.

"Except your tie-in skills," he jokes.

"Except for those," I agree, smiling sheepishly.

"Here, I'll help you," he says, examining the knot that's supposed to look like an eight but looks more like a six with a bad attitude. He unravels it and takes hold of my hands, guiding me.

This is too close. Close enough that I think I can smell the soap he uses, and every time his arm brushes mine, I make a note of it. I take a deep breath and exhale.

"You okay?" he asks for the second time, looking at me intently.

"It's, uh, hot in here, right?"

"Well, this corner of the room's definitely hotter than the rest," he answers in a low voice.

Is he hitting on me?

My lips part slightly in shock at the suggestive nature of his words.

"See?" he says, glancing up. "The air conditioner vents are all aimed in the other direction since this area has a rock jutting out above. They don't want it to blow directly on people climbing there."

"Oh," I say, gazing upward. "I see."

"Why? What did you think I meant?" he asks with a smirk. He knows *exactly* where my mind is.

We go back to tying me up, I mean *in*—*chill out, brain*—and rejoin the rest of the group.

They've already jumped into how to belay someone. After we've all learned and practiced the PBUS method—punch brake-under-slide—we have to choose a partner and go through the belay checks.

Erin and I partner up, and we're running through them when Carter comes over.

"Ready, ladies?"

"Yes!" Erin answers excitedly.

Her excitement is the polar opposite of my own growing hesitation. Somehow, until this moment, I didn't internalize the fact that I'm going to have to climb to the top of a fifty-foot wall. *Shit.* How exactly I forgot my fear of heights until now? I'm not sure. I try to recall the box-breathing technique I learned from the therapist I saw after my dad passed away and do one round. In-two-three-four, hold-two-three-four, out-two-three-four.

Greg calls us over to a wall with purple rocks. "So, this is a beginner's route. As you can see, the rocks here are closer together and easier to grip than on the more advanced walls."

But it's so tall.

I study my harness and clasp my mildly shaking hands together.

Carter leans in and whispers, "What's wrong?"

My stomach has butterflies in it, but they're not the good kind, or maybe not *only* the good kind. His closeness has me flustered. He touches my arm, I think, in an attempt to calm me, but it has the opposite effect. His fingertips on my bicep feel like they have an electric current running through them.

"You have goosebumps," he says, his mouth curling up.

Yes, I do. And I shouldn't. Not from you.

"I'm . . . a little n-nervous," I manage to stutter out.

"Why? You'll be fine. Greg and I are here to help everyone."

I glance over and see Erin tying in under Greg's watchful eye.

Yes, this is a very "helpful" place.

"Either way, I'll belay you. It looks like Erin is otherwise engaged."

So, Carter is going to be my partner. In that case, it's only fair for me to let him know what he's getting into.

"I'm scared of heights," I blurt out.

"Oh," he says, and his ocean-blue eyes soften. He looks at me carefully. "Why didn't you mention it before?"

"Um, somehow, I didn't think much about it before. But now that I'm looking at that giant wall, it's getting harder to ignore." My voice is more high-pitched than usual.

"You'll be okay. You'll only go as high as you want to," he reassures me.

I nod.

"Listen to me. It's mind over matter. And *you* can do amazing things. There's nothing stopping you from reaching the top—rock climbing or otherwise."

I nod again, feeling bolstered. I'm quite aware that Carter's frequent compliments toward me are, at best, 50 percent due to my professional skills and 50 percent more personally motivated, but I still appreciate the encouragement.

"You ready?" he asks, crouching down so he's eye-level with me.

"Yeah, I'm ready," I say with bravado. "I can definitely do this."

I'm not at all sure I can do this.

"I know you can."

I look up to see that Erin's already a third of her way up the wall. She glances down for a second, looking for a rock to place her left foot, and we catch eyes.

"C'mon, Sarah. See if you can catch me. This is so fun."

So *fun*. Sure.

I approach the wall and take the rope next to her—designated for a second intro route—and begin tying in while Carter gets ready to belay for me. We go through our checks, and when he assesses my knot, he pulls me closer to him—completely unnecessarily. The soft, bouncy floor gives way under his weight, and I find myself leaning into him, almost touching.

He leans down to whisper in my ear, "The knot looks good, and in case I forget to tell you later, so do you."

The look in his eyes is magnetic, and I have to force myself to look away. I abruptly turn to face the wall when he reminds me that I need to check his belay.

Oh, dear god.

The last thing I should do right now is put my hands near this man's body, but I turn and tentatively tug on his waist belt and check the clasp. My fingers, currently shaking from nerves, are between the belt and his skin, where his shirt has ridden up, and I can feel the hard muscle on the outside of my fingers. He seems to notice, too, because I hear his intake of breath when our eyes meet.

He pulls his hand up to slip the material of his t-shirt back into place, and his fingertips brush my hand. He leaves them there for a second and stills my shaking hand.

"You're safe. You can do this," he reminds me.

I pull myself together and move my hand to check his center loop and the carabiner hooked on it. It's waist level—not that close, but too close—and he looks at me with a naughty grin.

"Locked," I say, checking the carabiner on his belt.

"And loaded," he responds, his mouth twisting.

He's enjoying this, the little bastard.

"Rope check?" he asks.

I go through the checklist of four rope checks, knowing that the moment of truth has almost arrived. A ragged breath escapes my mouth. At this point, I can't be sure if it's the fear of climbing up the wall or the knowledge that my behavior might be encouraging Carter in a way I shouldn't be.

Interpreting it as the former, he tells me not to look up. "Or down, either, actually. Just focus on the next step." And he puts his hands on my waist and gently pushes me toward the wall.

I can do this.

"On belay," I say, following Greg's instructions about the proper calls.

"Belay on," I hear Carter respond.

"Climbing," I say, placing my foot on the first rock and trying to determine which rocks to grip with my hands.

"Climb on," he replies. "Sarah, you got this."

I begin to climb. Once I'm fully on the wall, about five feet up, I do what Carter advised and just focus on the next step—not how I'm going to make it to the top or *if* I even need to reach the top. Here and there, I pause, figuring out the next best place to grab onto or rest one of my feet. I like the challenge, and surprisingly, it doesn't take long before I realize I've run out of rocks. I'm at the top, fifty feet off the ground, and I'm not scared. Somehow, I'm not scared. It's likely not the best idea, but I look down over my shoulder and see Carter smiling up at me.

"Ready to come down?" he asks, "or you like it up there on top?"

I *do* like it on top, but I'll have to contemplate that innuendo when I'm back on solid ground.

"Ready to lower," I yell down.

"Lowering," he responds.

And I let go, knowing that Carter's got me.

The whole group gets a couple more chances to climb. At one point, Erin and I are off to the side, watching Greg belay for Carter, who is scaling up one of the harder courses. As he stretches up to reach a hard-to-reach rock, his tattoo peaks out from his short-sleeve shirt.

"That is one lucky wolf," Erin says.

"Phoenix," I correct her since Carter has a tattoo of one on his arm, but then I notice the object of her admiration is actually Greg's bicep, which is tensed as he belays for Carter.

I shoot her an unbelieving look. "Remember Ryan, the love of your life?"

"Of course I do. I'm just acknowledging that Greg has a good body. Honestly, it's nice to know that some random guy still finds me attractive as I approach forty."

I nod.

"Anyways, I don't think *I'm* the one here who's in any danger," she says in a chastising tone, looking at me pointedly and flicking her eyes up to Carter. She gets up and heads to the restroom, and I follow her.

I wash my hands and ask Erin, with a naughty smile, "So, you have any tattoos I don't know about?"

"Yeah. A picture of your cute face . . . on my ass," she deadpans.

I snort and throw the damp paper towel at her. "I'm going to head out, okay?"

"Sure," she responds, still smiling at her own joke.

The final pairs have finished their climbs, and I join the group near some benches at the entrance. Carter steps up. "You did a great job, guys. It's not always easy to try something new." He finds me in the group and locks eyes with me.

I feel my pocket buzz, and I check my phone to find a text from Erin with a picture of me climbing near the top of the wall. I forward it to Nathan.

> **Me:** Can you believe what I did tonight?
> **Nathan:** You made it all the way to the top? That's amazing!
> <heart emoji>

The text exchange makes me feel a little less guilty, a little less uneasy—about the flirting tonight and, well, a lot of things. Our group starts to disperse, but I still need to gather my things and put on my regular shoes. I sit on a bench off to the side. Carter comes over and sits next to me, his leg close but not quite touching mine.

"Have a good time?" he asks.

"Definitely."

"You're a natural climber. Like a mountain goat," he jokes.

"Well, I hope that I, at least, smell better than one."

He leans closer and sniffs theatrically, wrinkling his nose as if the answer is "no." Then, to my surprise, he blushes.

"What?" I ask.

"I was going to say you smell just like a goat, but honestly . . . you smell really good."

There's a short, awkward silence, and to break it, I say, "It was really fun. My hands are a bit red from the ropes, but—"

He takes one of my hands in his own, examining my slightly chafed fingers. His hands are slightly rough, and I can feel the strength in them. All that damn rock climbing, probably.

"Just a sec," he says and leans back to pull one of the bags under the bench closer. As he does, his shirt creeps up, exposing some skin, and I avert my eyes.

He takes a container of cream out of the bag and opens it. "Hold your hand out."

I open my hand, and he takes it in his once again, squirting some of the thick cream onto it. It smells like coconut, and before I can stop him, he begins to massage it into my hand. And god, does it feel good. I train my eyes on his hands massaging my own because I'm pretty sure if I look up, I'll faint from embarrassment.

About thirty seconds in, he finishes, and we meet eyes. "Feel better?"

Gulp. "Yessss." *Smooth.*

His mouth curls into a sexy grin.

"Carter, thanks for pushing me to . . ." *Do things I shouldn't? Risk my relationship with my boyfriend?*

"Do things that scare me," is what comes out, but the pleased look on his face alerts me to my misstep—and the potential double-meaning of my words.

"Well, I like helping people . . . overcome their fears."

"Carter—"

"Listen—"

We both start to talk at once and stop at once.

"You first," I say.

"Okay, um . . ." He almost never hesitates in our work conversations, but the pace—the feel—of our conversations tonight has been different.

I look at him, waiting.

"I was just going to say that I know we work together, which complicates things, but you and I . . ."

This is not happening. This shouldn't be happening.

"Carter—" I start to say.

"Wait," he says, touching my hand, and I look down at it. "We could be really good together, Sarah." He looks into my eyes for a beat, then scans his eyes down my body.

I fake-cough. Knowing he's been caught, his mouth twists in a restrained smile. "Really good," he adds unapologetically.

Fuuuccckk.

I'm speechless, but it seems like some sort of response is required so I nod. Then I realize nodding is definitely the wrong response because it seems to encourage him to go on.

"There's something about you. You're—"

"Carter," I interrupt. *But what do I say?* "Thank you. It's, um, a compliment, but . . . we shouldn't continue this conversation. And this—whatever it is between us—it should stop." *Wow, Pulitzer nomination forthcoming.*

The look in his eyes shifts. He's hiding it well, but it seems like he might've been expecting his pitch to work. And, even though I don't want to admit it, it might have in another time and another place. But this has already gone too far, and . . . *Oh, right, I have a boyfriend.*

After a moment, he looks over at me. He seems to have composed himself. The look of disappointment has been replaced by one a bit more mischievous, a bit more determined.

"Would you say I'm pretty successful?"

Surprised, I answer, "Yeah."

"Well, I didn't get to where I am through luck alone. I set goals and work hard to achieve them. Determination and patience are all you need sometimes."

So damn cocky. I hate to admit it, but it's damn sexy, too.

He leans to whisper in my ear. "You were amazing tonight. Remember how great it feels to be on top. It won't be the last time."

He *did not just say that.*

He stands and saunters away, looking back over his shoulder to deliver a truly wicked smile.

Yep, he definitely did.

Just then, Erin joins me. "What was that all about?"

For the first time in our friendship, I lie to her. "Nothing. Everything's fine."

DISRUPTIVE TECHNOLOGY

SARAH

I drank too much tonight when I went out with Cam, especially considering I have a 9:00 a.m. meeting tomorrow. Without any dinner in my stomach, it hit me hard. But it's been a while since the two of us have had a girls night out, and I wanted to have some fun. Fun—the kind you can only have with someone who has known you forever—was definitely had. I needed a distraction from the week I've had—a delayed feature release at work due to all kinds of bugs cropping up, Nathan rushing off to Seattle, and my still fresh-in-my-mind rock climbing experience with Carter. I'm rummaging through the refrigerator when I get a text from Nathan.

> **Nathan:** Hey, you up?
> **Sarah:** Yeah, just making a sandwich.
> **Nathan:** Really? At almost midnight?
> **Sarah:** Went out with Cam earlier but missed dinner.
> **Nathan:** Okay, text me back when you're done? Wanna talk to you.
> **Sarah:** <kiss emoji>

I eat my sandwich in only a few bites on my way to the shower. I begin to unbutton my top, then decide that this outfit is too hot not to share and stop to take a selfie for Nathan. I pose—drunk-sexy in the mirror, cleavage for miles—and take a few. "Wish you were here tonight," I type, attach the most revealing of the photos, and press "Send."

Under the warm spray of the shower, I let my mind wander. The steamy conditions I've created conjure equally steamy images in my mind, specifically, the last time I was in a hot hotel shower—in Park City with Nathan. It's probably not helpful to let my mind go there. What good can it do when he's a thousand miles away in Seattle? So, I finish up and step out to dry myself off.

As I dry my hair and brush it out, I examine myself in the mirror. I'm feeling... uneasy since he left. Things between us are okay, but only okay. The recent rockiness we've been going through has been unsettling, making me wonder, in my more emotionally fragile moments, whether we rushed into living together. I just wish there was some way to feel *right* again.

Right after moving in together, we had been fine—great, in fact. But emotionally, something hasn't been clicking. Our conversations are censored from both sides. I bite my tongue, not to mention Carter whenever work comes up, and I can tell Nathan's holding back, too. The easy-going, sensitive guy I fell in love with is still there, but he seems to be hiding behind a layer of uncertainty or pain. He's right. Him under stress hasn't been good for us, but I can't deny my own role in our troubles.

I push thoughts of what—or rather whom—is at the center of said troubles and head into the bedroom. I lay on the bed and check my phone. No text back from Nathan on my selfie, but that's okay. I'll FaceTime him, and he can enjoy the real thing.

When I call, he answers immediately in that sexy baritone voice of his. "Hey."

"How was your day?" I ask.

"Really good, actually. I talked through a few things with Dr. Thompson, and I'm feeling more positive about the direction it's going."

"That's awesome."

"How was your date with Cam?" he asks.

"Really fun. We drank a lot. Danced like idiots."

He laughs. "Sounds fun. Sorry, I missed it."

I take in his surroundings. He's sitting in the tan oversized chair in his old bedroom in his parent's house.

"I thought about you a lot today," he says.

"I thought about you, too," I tell him. "In fact, most recently, I was thinking about you . . ."

"Yes?"

"In the shower."

"Continue," he says, giving me a warm laugh. "What were you thinking about exactly? About me? In the shower?"

"Oh, just our first time having shower sex."

"Just that, huh? *Just* the time we almost killed ourselves having sex in the world's most slippery hotel shower?"

"Yeah. That," I reply matter-of-factly.

He smiles broadly and looks down, almost shyly. It's been tough lately, and it feels good to joke around with him.

"What are you thinking?" I ask.

He looks back up now, directly into the phone camera. "I'm thinking that it's not very nice of you to remind me of such things when you're not here to repeat the performance."

Where's he going with this?

"You should probably offer me a rain check or some sort of consolation prize," he throws out, seemingly nonchalantly. "My flight back is over a week from now. A week is a long time ..." he trails off, maybe waiting to see if I'll pick up on his not-so-subtle hints.

"That *is* a long time," I agree. "What do people do when they won't see each other for a while and they're feeling . . . you know?"

He bites his lip, fighting a smile. "You remember that time I was in Seattle, and you were in San Jose, and we FaceTimed? You wanted to see what I was wearing?"

I nod, listening, and he continues. "And then you showed me what *you* were wearing, and—"

"Yeah, I remember," I whisper. "That was . . . hot."

"Well, we never got to finish because the call got interrupted," he says. "I went to bed with lots of dirty thoughts, and I ended up having *very* dirty dreams about you."

"Nooo."

"Yessss," he replies and laughs.

I know what consolation prize I can offer him, but I want him to ask.

"Sarah, can we . . .?"

"Can we *what*, Nathan?"

He takes a deep breath. "Do it here, on FaceTime?"

It's not quite the explicit ask I was hoping for, but I know he's trying.

"I think we can do that. But I need to know one thing first. Where are your hands right now?"

"One of them is holding the phone, and the other one . . ."

"Yessss?"

"Is already on my, well, I think you know. While you were in the shower, thinking about me, I was sitting here, thinking about you."

"Tell me more," I say.

"The last time we had sex on your couch, you bent over the armrest and me behind you, and–"

"Yeah . . . you told me that was in your Top Ten," I say. "You don't have to think back, though, or try to remember. I'm right here."

"You gonna show me?"

"What do you want to see?" I ask him directly. Just talking to him about this is turning me on, and I want him to tell me what and how.

"Take off your shirt. I want to see your breasts."

"I'm not even wearing a shirt. I just got out of the shower."

"What *are* you wearing?"

"Just a towel," I tease.

"Show me, then."

I angle the phone toward my face and my still-covered breasts. Then I slowly move the towel down, exposing them.

He bites his bottom lip, considering what to say or maybe do. "Is it cold there? Your nipples look hard."

"It's not cold. I'm just turned on," I admit. He changes the phone angle—maybe he's propping it up somewhere. I can see his face, but I want to see more.

"I'm calling 'rules.' Take off your shirt."

Without hesitation, he pulls off his t-shirt, the soft navy heather one I love on him—so soft and stretchy. It's tight in all the right places on him, accentuating his pecs, biceps, and broad shoulders, which I'm viewing in all their glory.

"Did you work out today?" I ask.

"Yeah."

"And you showered after?"

"Yes. Why?"

"I bet you smell great now," I reply.

"Are you touching yourself?" he asks. Without waiting for me to answer, he continues, "Touch yourself."

"I am. Tell me what else to do."

"Show me." Then he adds, "Please."

I hesitate, but it's not fair to ask him to venture outside his comfort zone without doing so myself.

Still . . .

"Um . . ."

"I've already had my mouth on every square inch of your body, and now you're getting shy?" he teases.

"It feels different on the phone."

"You don't have to do anything you don't want, beautiful. I just, I miss you, and honestly . . ."

"Yeah?"

"I'm really horny."

I laugh. Just when you think your boyfriend could use communication classes, he tells you he's turned on and asks you to masturbate on camera for him.

"Fine, I'll show you," I say quickly before I can change my mind.

He whispers "Thank you" in such a grateful manner that I almost giggle, but I hold it together. Never have I ever had FaceTime sex with a guy. I have literally no idea what I'm doing, but I hope that any lack of expertise or finesse will be made up for by the fact that my vagina is about to make its film debut. I set the camera on the nightstand and lay on my side, facing it, facing Nathan—so far away from here.

I begin to massage my breasts and trace my fingers around my raised nipples.

"Is this good? What should I do? Tell me."

"Can you hold the camera and get it closer? I want to see you up close."

"Okay," I say and reach out to bring the phone closer to my body. I slip my free hand between my legs, using two fingers to explore what feels good, wishing Nathan was here in person to do the exploring.

"Wait a second, I'm looking at your face," he says. "It's a beautiful face, but I suspect you're doing something else." His tone gets direct. "Show me."

Yes. I angle the camera down, not quite sure what I'm showing him, but his moan indicates it must be something good.

"You are so hot."

"Yes, I am." I'm already getting slick. *How the hell did I not know before now how hot this is?*

I tilt my phone back up for a minute so I can see what is happening on his side, and the angle of his camera is such that I don't have a full view of him stroking himself, but I can see his chest and hard abs and his hand moving up and down rhythmically. Just knowing what he's doing while I play with myself is heating me up.

"Tell me what you want to do to me when you get back," I say in a throaty whisper.

"Mmmm, so many things. First, a long, hot kiss while I slip my hands up the back of your shirt and undo your bra. Then, I'll push you up against the wall and take off your shirt and suck on your sweet nipples while I begin unbuttoning your pants."

"You want to hear what I'm going to do to you?"

He almost moans a "yes." His hand hasn't stopped moving while we've been talking, and I wonder how far along he is.

"While you're kissing my breasts, I'm going to run my hands through your hair and rake my nails down your back, and when you come back up and bite my collarbone the way I love, I'm going to wrap my legs around your waist, and then—"

He jumps in. "Then *I'm* going to carry you over to the couch and throw you down and *keep* taking your pants off, and I hope you have on those tiny, black lace underwear that drive me crazy."

"But I won't be wearing *any* underwear, lover."

He moans in appreciation. "Even better," he says, happy to improvise further. "So I'll go down on you. Until you're begging me to put my cock inside of you—"

"I will so beg. I have no shame when it comes to your cock."

"Are you wet?"

"Yes. I am so fucking turned on right now." I continue to stroke myself and close my eyes to focus—to imagine him naked, on top of me, inside of me—but figure he's right there, on the other side of the camera. *Why not just ask him to show me?*

"I want to see you now. Show me."

I can hear his heavy breaths. Then in a slightly strained voice, he says, "It's a little embarrassing. I'm going to lose it hearing you talk this way."

"Show me your hard-on. I want to imagine it inside of me."

"Okay. Yeah, I can do that," he says, and he shows me. *Wow.*

"Your turn, my love. Angle the camera down. I want to see your—"

"What do *you* want to see?"

"I want to see you touching your p—" he says but stops himself just short of saying it out loud.

I smile. We both feel vulnerable. It's okay not to tear down all the walls at once.

"I'll show you," I say, and angle the camera so he can see where my fingers are, rubbing along my seam, focused on my clit.

"Oh, fuck, Sarah. This is . . . so hot. Can I come?"

"Oh my god. Yes. Tell me what you like."

"I like putting my cock inside of you."

"Nathan, I *want* your cock inside of me."

And through whispered—at times, strained—descriptions of what we like, what we want, what we can't do without, we both finish. We're both quiet for a minute, but I can hear his breathing begin to calm. I turn off my camera and lay the phone next to me on the pillow.

"You there?" I ask quietly.

"I'm here."

I pick up the phone again and see his face, flushed and sporting a hundred-watt smile.

"I love you," I say. "Let's talk tomorrow?"

"I love you, too. I can't wait to see you next week."

I don't know how I'll wait to see him again, either.

We both end the call, and I feel calm—exhausted but happy. We're far away from one another, but I feel closer to him now than I have for the last month. Our first little foray into virtual sex seems to have done more than just help us get off. The emotional gap I've been feeling growing between us feels just a bit narrower. Tonight feels almost like our early days when we were getting to know each other, and we'd text and stay on the phone with each other for hours.

I'm lying in bed, drifting off to sleep—likely with a post-orgasmic grin on my face—when I get a text. I open one eye to see who it is. Maybe Cam is sending me a half-drunk text—she always does that after we go out together. One last thing she forgot to tell me at the bar. Or maybe Nathan, telling me "Good night" one last time. But I'm surprised to see it's Carter.

Why is he texting me after midnight?

I open up the phone and read his message:

Carter: Wishing YOU were here right about now.

What?

Then I realize what he's responding to. And I suddenly understand why Nathan didn't mention the selfie I sent him. Because I didn't send it to *him.*

Oh. Shit. What have I done?

I sent it to Carter.

Carter: Looks like you had a good time tonight. Here's MY good night selfie.

I peek at it, and my mouth drops. Carter is leaning back on what looks like the headboard of a bed. He's unshaven, and his hair is a bit of a mess. I don't know who taught this guy selfie angles, but damn. In a fitted white t-shirt that accentuates his toned upper body, he looks . . . *Don't even finish that thought.* I should definitely clear up that I didn't mean to send *him* my sexy selfie, but before I can focus my thoughts, he texts me:

Carter: Sweet dreams, hottie. See you at 9am.

Fuck. That is going to be one awkward meeting.

VELOCITY

SARAH

My alarm is set for 7:01 a.m. this morning, but I've been awake for at least two hours—tossing, turning, mostly worrying. In light of my moronic text mistake last night, I consider telling Carter I'm sick to avoid our meeting today. Figuring that will only delay the inevitable, I drag myself out of bed when the alarm sounds and trudge to the kitchen.

While I wait for my coffee to brew, I have a mini-panic attack. *Fuck. I have to tell Nathan.* He's going to be so pissed off. He detests Carter, and I sent him a hot selfie. *How could I have been so stupid?* I wrap my hands around the hot mug, and it smarts but grounds me. It gives me something to focus on besides my racing heartbeat. When the pain becomes too much, I pull my hands away and examine my red fingertips, then place them over my eyelids and breathe deeply. *In, out. One emergency at a time.* And the first one on today's list is dealing with Carter.

I stand in front of my closet, pondering what exactly one wears to try to convey professionalism after a royal fuck-up like the one I executed last night. Nathan's button downs stare at me accusingly from his half of the closet, so I snatch a pinstripe blouse and some wide-leg dress pants and shut the door. After dressing, I evaluate the combo, attractive but modest. No skin showing here. *Lord knows he saw enough last night.*

When I arrive at the office, I find a small Post-it Note on my desk:

Meet me at Alyzee? -C

I leave my backpack on and walk like a condemned prisoner down Castro Street in the direction of the French bakery Erin and I treat ourselves to once a week. Today's visit will be anything but a treat. Carter is sitting outside at a small table talking on his phone when I arrive. He's wearing a fitted heather gray t-shirt that I suspect he knows looks quite good on him.

When I sit, he gestures to one of the two coffee mugs on the table, indicating that it's for me. As I wait for him to finish his conversation, I will my racing heartbeat to slow. He stands, mouthing "sorry" to me about the phone call and holding up his pointer finger. He walks away to wrap up.

"Yeah, actually, I'm just about to talk to her about it. I'll confirm in half an hour," I hear him say.

He ends the call and joins me at the table. "Good morning, Sunshine." He's not quite smiling, but I can see the mischief dancing in his eyes.

"Is that a reference to my early wakeups?" I ask, hoping I can keep the blush I feel creeping up my neck under control.

"Well, I thought after last night, you might have slept in."

His blue eyes are locked on mine. I can't be sure, but it feels like he's trying not to look elsewhere. I force myself to meet his eyes, but I don't respond. I'm not really sure *how* to even respond. This meeting was set earlier in the week, so I assume he's not planning to fire me, but I suppose he might want to re-purpose the time to take care of some HR issues he recently encountered.

When he realizes I'm not going to respond, he leans back in his chair, crosses his arms, and continues. "I just assumed that . . . you might have had a few drinks . . . I mean, in order to send that selfie—"

"Yes," I jump in. "That was a mistake. I apologize, and I really hope you won't let that affect your impression of my skills—my *professional* skills."

"I'll keep it between us," he assures me. "And honestly?"

"Yes?"

He leans forward and whispers conspiratorially, "A selfie like that can only help my impression of you . . ." *Oh, god.* "And your . . . *skills.*"

Failing to find any words that fit this train wreck of a situation, I take a sip of my coffee to buy some time. The foam rests on my upper lip, and while I'd usually just lick it off and keep going, I'm overly aware of my lips, or more specifically, Carter's focus on them.

I reach for the napkin on the table, but he grabs it first and holds it out to me. While I wipe my mouth as nonchalantly as one can, he cocks his head and observes me, an amused grin plastered on his face. I fold the napkin into small squares, avoiding his eye, and wonder how often meteors strike people dead during conversations as uncomfortable as this one.

Who knows? Maybe today will be my lucky day.

Apparently deciding this episode of "See Sarah Squirm" has gone on long enough, Carter sits back up and opens his laptop. "So, the reason I wanted to meet today—I know I *could* have done this on Zoom, but just thought it might be nicer if you're here—is that I'd like you to go to Austin next week with Kevin and me to present what we've been working on to some people on the board."

"What?" The embarrassment I was feeling just seconds ago is replaced by surprise.

"That reaction is the one I wanted to see in person," he says, grinning. "You've been working with me and Kev, and you have good insights. I want you to present your ideas. Getting this type of face time with company leaders is something that can set you up for your next big jump, professionally."

"Say less."

"Huh?" he asks.

"I just mean, I'm in. Definitely."

"I'm happy to hear that," he says. "So, let's talk details."

He moves his chair to my side of the table, so I can see his laptop screen. While he runs through the presentation outline, he leans in to talk to me. I try to focus on his words, but I'm still trying to process the quick shift in our conversation—from an awkward, even flirtatious, start to a fast-paced tactical discussion about the largest opportunity of my career. I take a deep breath and look down at the ground.

"Am I boring you already?" he teases.

I look up. "Of course not. I'm just . . . thinking."

"About?"

"Are you *sure* I'm ready?" I ask. And here I was, just starting to feel confident about work, when my old friend, Impostor Syndrome, shows up. *Sneaky bitch.*

He looks at me for a moment, then replies calmly, "Why not?"

"Lots of why nots . . . There's a lot of technical information in the deck. You or Kevin will do those parts, right?"

"If it makes sense and works with the flow of the presentation, then yes, but if it's part of your section, you should present it."

"I'm not an engineer."

"Neither am I."

"Yeah, but you were a programmer—"

"A long time ago," he interjects.

"But you've worked in this space a while, and I just—"

"You just *what*?" he asks, studying me carefully.

I shrug. "I'm just a program manager."

"There's no 'just' about it," he says. "You understand this stuff well enough to present it. I've been listening to you talk knowledgeably about it for weeks. Just play to your strengths."

"Which are?" I ask, still not sure.

"Well," he says, hesitating, "they're too many to name."

Again, we seem to have veered into dangerous territory.

"But the ones I mean now—in the *professional* realm—are your knack for explaining difficult concepts in a clear way and your genuine personality."

My mouth curls up as I consider what this all means. Presenting to a huge high-tech company's board. *Wow.*

"And, uh, maybe keep the selfies to a minimum," he teases.

I look down. His gaze is too piercing on a good day, let alone today.

"It's true," he says.

I look up. "What is?"

"Before I ever met you, Kevin told me that you have a way with people," he says. "He was right."

He opens his mouth to say something, but I look away before he can continue. He must sense that I need a change of subject and asks about Nathan. *Strange.* "So, how are things going with Nate's startup? It's dealing with medical data, right?"

"Yeah. It has to do with pulling in medical test data from lots of sources and using it to improve early diagnosis of diseases. He's got some crazy mathematical model run by . . . I don't know . . . some code. I don't entirely understand it, but Kevin says it's, and I quote, 'fucking genius,' and Nathan's going to change the world."

Carter's eyes narrow. Hours and hours spent in discussion with him have taught me that he's taking in information and analyzing it.

"It's going okay for him," I continue, not wanting to divulge too much and realizing I might've already said too much. "He's actually up in Seattle meeting with one of his advisers right now. Things are moving along . . . fine."

"Oh, good," he says, sounding skeptical. He likely knows as well as I do that trying to get a startup funded in the current economy will be a huge challenge. "He might be wasting his time with a startup right now, but I . . . hope it works out for him."

Carter might be right. Nathan has expressed that same sentiment more than once himself, but it's disheartening to hear someone confirm his suspicions.

"I should probably go. I've got another meeting soon," I say, not wanting to share anything more about myself—but especially about Nathan—with Carter. It feels wrong admitting, or even hinting, that Nathan might have a weakness to someone I know he actively dislikes. "I'll send you the first draft slides by the end of today."

"Great," he says. "I'll message you the link to the company travel portal, so you can book the flights and hotel. You should fly to Austin on Wednesday, so you can be there for some important meetings on Thursday. And on Friday, we present. You can either fly home on Friday night or leave on Saturday."

My cousin Jordan is studying at the University of Texas at Austin, and I tell him that I'll probably stay on Friday night to hang out with her. Nathan is scheduled to come home that Saturday, so it'll be perfect timing. Maybe we'll even meet each other at the airport.

I pack up my bag and start to walk away but turn back. "Thanks for everything, Carter."

"Of course," he says. "We'll talk soon?"

I nod, and walk away, feeling conflicted. I would feel so much better if this offer was coming from Kevin or basically anybody besides Carter. Things between us are complicated. *Did his personal feelings for me play a part in his decision to offer me this opportunity?* It's hard to imagine they wouldn't.

I reach the end of the block, and while I wait at the corner for a car to pass, I turn my head to check if he's still there. He's on the phone, and he's looking at me with an expression I can't quite parse.

***

When I get back to the office, I head to my desk and see Erin hard at work on something.

"Hey, I heard you're going to Austin next week," she says, looking up with a bright smile on her face.

Word travels fast.

"Um, yeah. I guess so."

"You're going to kick ass, Sarah. What a great opportunity."

A *great opportunity*. It is. Professionally, it's a great opportunity. In other realms, it feels more like a trap or, at the very least, a risk.

I bite my lip. She shoots me her best mom expression, so I come right out and say it, knowing I'll end up telling her anyway. "I'm just worried about being there with Carter, knowing our, uh, situation. Nathan and I got into a fight the last time I stayed late to work with him on something and wasn't exactly . . . forthcoming."

"Nate will understand. He wants what's best for you. Anyways, Kev will be there. You just do what you're there to do, and it'll be fine."

Maybe she's right. I grab my phone from my bag on the floor and text Nathan.

> **Me:** Guess who's flying to Austin next week?
> **Nathan:** For what?
> **Me:** They want me to present something to the LV board, in person.
> **Nathan:** That's amazing. You're such a badass!

His positivity bolsters me. He's proud of me. I should be proud of myself, too. I'll try to focus on the good, and I'll tell Nathan what happened last night once he's back home. Mistakes happen sometimes. *He'll understand.*

Never Release on a Friday

NATHAN

Nathan's dad has been feeling fine. In fact, even a recent hospital visit couldn't keep him from challenging Nathan to a push-up competition, a Noah Goldman ritual any time one or both of his sons come for a visit. Though, Nathan did make him stop at twenty-five. *Maybe they really didn't need my help.* Then again, his mom hasn't stopped smiling since he arrived.

"I love cooking with you, sweetheart. I know I told you not to come, but I'm glad you did," she says, as they prepare lunch together while his dad takes a work call upstairs. She passes him a plate to serve some of the salad he's been mixing. "It's nice having someone else to bounce decisions off of. You know, to take some of the weight off my shoulders."

He leans in to give her a hug and squeezes said shoulders. "I'm glad I came, too."

"How's Sarah?" she asks.

"She's good."

"She's good and . . .?"

"She's good and . . . I love her?"

His mom smiles widely and caresses his face like he's a little kid. "I'm so proud of you."

"You're proud of me for loving someone?"

"I'm proud of you for many reasons. And, yes, finding someone to share your life with and being open to that, I'm also proud of you for that. It's not easy to let yourself be vulnerable."

Vulnerable. That's exactly how he feels with Sarah. In love, wanting to build a life with her, but all the while, incredibly vulnerable. Exposed.

"What's wrong, though?" his mom asks. "Why'd you come home now?" She takes their plates, adds some of the garlic chicken she's been sautéing on the stove, and sits down at the kitchen island, inviting Nathan to do the same.

He joins her and smiles to reassure her—maybe himself—but it feels forced. Her brow furrows in concern, and she takes his hand.

"I guess . . . things are just harder than I thought they would be with the startup. I'm at home by myself a lot, and sometimes, I feel like it's the Covid lockdown all over again. And every day, Sarah's going off to work and killing it. I'm happy for her, but I guess I just wish I was a part of it, too. Like, maybe I missed my chance, and this wasn't a good time to try to get startup funding, you know?"

"Is that all?" she asks, looking him directly in the eye.

Am I such an emotional simpleton that every woman in my life can read my mind?

He takes a deep breath and exhales in a huff. "There's also this guy at Sarah's work. I had to work with him right after LightVerse bought Instinqt, and I can just *feel* he's not a good guy. I can feel it, like in my gut. And now he's helping Sarah move up in the company, but it feels like it's for the wrong reasons."

His mom nods and waits for him to elaborate.

"Mom, you know me. I'm not some misogynist asshole."

"You're not," she agrees. "We raised you right."

"And she's really awesome at work. She deserves *every* opportunity, but it's clear he has an ulterior motive."

"Which is?"

"Let's just say he appreciates her brains, but he appreciates her other assets just as much."

"I see," she replies. "And it's causing problems between the two of you?"

He nods. "Mom, I *hate* that she's working with him. I want her to be in a place where she's valued for the right things. But . . . I also understand why she's staying the course at the same time."

She furrows her brow. "I know the men in our family are not always the most talkative or forthcoming, but you have to push past that when you're in a relationship. You have to be open with her. Communicate."

"I know. I *do* listen to you."

She smiles. "I know you do. Just try to keep sharing your feelings with her without backing her into a corner, and give it some time. It's amazing what a little time can do to solve a situation."

Time? Given time, Carter would simply swoop in, and through offers of promotions and who-knows-what-else, Sarah would be gone.

He thinks of their conversation from last night. He let down his guard, and she did, too, and the results were good. More than good. Ever since he set out on his own, trying to build this big idea, he has felt exposed. *Is Sarah feeling the same?* She's shared with him how out of her element she feels in her job sometimes, working in a highly technical environment and almost everything new to her. She's told him, but was he really listening? He'll do better. He has to.

****

On Wednesday morning, he worked with his mom's friend, Marcy, a corporate lawyer, to submit a provisional patent application for his startup idea. He doesn't know whether it was a good idea or a bad one—he still feels like he's making it all up as he goes. But his mom had invited Marcy over for coffee, and twenty minutes later, upon learning of his startup plans, she had insisted he sit down with her at the Goldman family kitchen table with his laptop to complete the application online.

"It puts a little more pressure on you to get your ducks in a row more quickly," she told him, "but trust me, you want it on the record that you came up with this idea."

A few hours and one plate of banana-nut muffins later, he clicked Apply, and that's when shit got real, at least in his head. Ever since submitting the application, he keeps asking himself, *What if it all amounts to nothing? Even scarier, what if it actually works out?*

Last night on the phone with Sarah was a welcome break from his worries, but as soon as he woke up this morning, his brain resumed its racing. He worked in semi-productive spurts all day until he finally gave up and went for a long run in Lincoln Park this evening. It seems to have done the trick. He feels a bit more relaxed now, and he's looking forward to a long, hot shower when he gets a text from Kevin.

Kevin: Have you seen this?

He clicks on the link in the text, and it opens to an article about a LightVerse press release from the day before. "LightVerse to enter medical data field; Diagnoses faster, better." He skims the article, trying to understand if it's related at all to what he's working on. There aren't too many details beyond LightVerse entering the same space he is.

He reads the article again, to make sure he hasn't missed anything, and stops when he sees a name he knows. *Carter.*

"Carter Michaels, a head product strategist at LightVerse, says this field is the next logical progression for LightVerse: 'LightVerse has decided to put its data-analysis expertise into the important, life-changing field of helping medical professionals and people around the world find earlier, more accurate diagnoses.'" Apparently, he did miss something on first-pass. That's Nathan's startup idea in a nutshell. *What the fuck?*

That's exactly what he texts back to Kevin.

Kevin: This is the first I heard of it. Did you tell anybody?
Nathan: Just you, Sarah . . . I mean, my parents, Dr. Thompson. Nobody who would say anything.
Kevin: So weird. I'll try to find out more.
Nathan: Yeah, do that.

Nathan rubs his hand up and down his face and undresses. While he waits for the water to heat up in the shower, he leans his hands on the bathroom counter and just stares at himself in the mirror, trying to figure out how the hell LightVerse—Carter, specifically—would know the details of what he's doing. He *just* filed the provisional patent a couple days ago.

He knows both Kevin and Sarah work with him, but they wouldn't leak any information about his idea. At least not on purpose. As he steps in the shower, his thoughts are on Sarah's ability to make conversation with just about anybody. *Did she accidentally let something slip to Carter?*

No. She wouldn't do that. She's friendly, but she's also smart. She would know how important his idea and his specific implementation of it is to the success of his business, to him personally.

After drying off and getting dressed, he sees he missed a text from her while he was showering.

Sarah: Wanna talk?

Not really.

But he calls her anyway.

"Hey," she says in a cheerful voice. "How are you?"

Awful. He's still processing the news Kevin broke to him. Maybe it's something, but maybe it's not. Large companies have all sorts of research and development projects that never get off the ground. They have deep pockets, but the people working on those things don't always have the flexibility—or the pressure—to move quickly the same way startups do.

"I'm okay," he says. "How's it going?"

"Well, I mean, I got good news. I'm excited."

The trip to Austin. Presenting to the LightVerse board. "Right, I'm so proud of you," he says, trying to sound happy for her. His mind is spinning right now, but he doesn't want to dump the issue with LightVerse and whatever Carter's involvement might be on her right now. "So, what's the presentation on exactly? Want to run me through some of your slides?"

"That would be great. You have all the context since you know Instinqt. You want to jump on Zoom so I can share my screen?" she asks.

"Sure, email me the link."

He opens his laptop and checks his email, where he finds the Zoom link from Sarah waiting in his inbox. She's leaning down under her desk when he signs on—probably untangling her charging cord, as usual—and when she pops back up, she smiles upon seeing him.

He musters a smile despite his bad mood. "Like old times, huh?" he says, thinking of their Zoom calls when they both worked at Instinqt and were getting to know each other.

"Exactly," she says. She shares her screen, and it's on a slide with a bar graph that seems to show Instinqt's potential contribution to Light-Verse's revenue in the coming years. "Can you see my screen?"

"Yep, I can," he replies.

"Are you okay? Your voice sounds . . . different."

"I'm okay," he answers. It's a lie. His thoughts are all over the place, and it's no surprise his voice has betrayed him. "Go ahead. Let's hear it."

"Okay." She clicks to the title slide of the presentation, which lists three presenters: Kevin Wong, Sarah Hoffman, and . . . Carter Michaels.

"Carter's presenting, too?" he asks, his tone less friendly than before.

"Yes," she says quietly. "He's the one running the whole thing."

"So, he'll be in Austin?"

"That's the plan. I mean, me, Kev, and Carter are the ones presenting, and they asked us to come do it in person."

"Sarah . . ."

"What?"

He breathes deeply and exhales. "You know what I'm going to say."

"That you want me to keep my distance from Carter?" she asks. "Listen, I know how you feel about this. I do. But I have twelve slides to present, and I was invited to talk to the LightVerse board. I have to be there."

"Maybe you could present remotely or—"

"Why should I?" she interrupts, a sudden edge to her voice.

"Because—"

"Because what?"

"It's the same thing I've been saying for the last month. I don't like him. Or trust him. He doesn't respect our relationship . . . or me."

She narrows her eyes at him. "Or *you*?"

How can he explain to her that it's not just Carter but everything he represents? It's like he's living Nathan's life, the life he could've had, but doing it even better. And Carter—and that life—is what she's choosing. By choosing Austin, by following him there and the "opportunities" he's offering her—something Nathan can't give her—it feels like she's giving up on him, on them.

Then there's the simple fact that Carter is talking about some new project that sounds suspiciously like Nathan's startup idea. That alone is enough to have him on edge—over the edge. But he can't tell her. Why?

Because he's been trying to talk to her for months, and he doesn't feel like she's listening anymore, at least not the way she used to. She asks about his work, but is she hearing just how hard it is to be doing everything he's doing all alone? Or is it just easier to tell him, "It'll be fine," and keep going?

"I just—" he starts to say.

"What?" she says impatiently.

"Sarah," he says, more softly, hoping she'll hear, if not the words he's saying, then his intention, his worry that this could be the thing that breaks them. "I just . . . I don't want you to go. Please."

He considers telling her what Kevin just shared with him, but he's not yet sure what it is or how she might or might not be related to it. So, he sticks to the personal—very personal—reasons he dislikes Carter.

"I've *seen* the way he looks at you. Like he just can't wait to . . ." He pauses.

"Just say it, Nathan. I know you're dying to. I get it. He has a crush on me."

That's too much.

"'A *crush*'? That's putting it lightly, don't you think? I'm a guy, and I can tell when another guy wants to . . . fuck a girl."

"He wants to fuck me?" she says in an odd tone. She's not questioning the accuracy of his statement but rather that he said it so bluntly. He waits a moment for her response. *Is she even going to deny it?*

But what comes out of her mouth is not a denial of Carter's intentions—nor her awareness of what they might be. No, just a barrage of harsh words. "Because that's the only reason I might get invited to present to the board of a billion-dollar company, huh? Because I'm fuck-able?"

She slams her hands down on the desk, stands up, and starts to pace.

"That's not what I said," Nathan says in as even a tone as he can. He's trying to calm her, but it's impossible because he doesn't feel that way himself. He's pissed off, and he's worried about the bad news Kevin shared with him and Sarah not understanding just how much of a prick Carter is.

"Well, that's what I heard," she says in a bitter tone.

"Sarah, you're talented—"

"*Enough.* Talented enough," she spits out. "But boy, do I become a much more attractive candidate when you consider my body, huh? Worth taking to Texas. Go big or go home."

"You're not listening to me."

"I've heard enough."

"Sarah, this isn't in my head. Carter—"

"Carter has opened so many doors for me. He's helped me accomplish more in two months than I have in my entire professional life. So, I'm going to Austin."

"You're not even listening to me," Nathan says, losing any calm he had managed to maintain up until now. "You just get it in your head what you're going to do and do it. Without consideration for me, for us."

"*Kevin* believes in me."

"So do I." *But do you* believe in *us?*

"You don't even know what I do anymore at work," she says, her tone a bitter mix of accusation and hurt. "Two days ago, I was on a call with the Chief Marketing Officer of LightVerse. She said I was a rock star. I'm not giving up a chance like this to save *your* ego." Her voice is different, harsher than he's used to hearing her.

"It's not about my ego. I've *always* wanted you to succeed."

"Good, then you can understand that I'm just doing whatever it takes."

Whatever it takes, huh?

"You know what? Do whatever the hell you want. It doesn't matter to me."

"It doesn't?"

"No, it doesn't," he says, point-blank. "While I've been up here, I've made good progress. *You're* focusing on your career, and maybe the reason the startup hasn't been going well is because I should've been more focused on mine. I was distracted."

She stops her pacing. "Distracted?" she asks in an almost-whisper.

"Yeah, by drama, you, your work, your 'friends' at work," he says, making little quote fingers.

She sits back down—arms crossed, eyes narrowed—and she looks like she would strangle him if she could come through the screen. He knows he just should shut up, but he can't hold in his irritation anymore.

"You know why I didn't hesitate to come up here? I thought I could use a break."

"A break from *what*?" she asks.

"From you and your priorities. You've made it clear what's important to you and what you'll do to get it."

He can see the confusion in her eyes. But there's nothing here to be confused about. She's just been closing her eyes—or worse, knowing what the situation is with Carter and walking willingly toward it.

She's made her choice. And I've made mine.

"I think our trial is over. I'll come back next week and get my stuff," he says and slams his laptop shut.

He folds his arms, lays his head down, and closes his eyes. His head feels like it's going to explode. *What the hell just happened? Why did I say those things?*

There's no reality in which Sarah would have responded calmly to what he said about Carter's intentions toward her. That asshole does like her, and Nathan knows he wouldn't hesitate to sleep with her given the chance. *But why did I say it?*

He's angry—no, livid—with Carter for being the guy in the article talking about *his* idea. He's also pissed off at Sarah. Maybe she *did* say something to Carter. Where else would he have heard it? Nathan should have held his cards closer to his chest. But it was Sarah—*his* Sarah. He trusted her, not just with his startup idea, but with everything.

He paces around the room, kicking some shoes out of the way and snatching up a pillow, then slinging it into the door. He huffs out his frustration, falls onto the bed face-up, and stares at the ceiling.

His phone pings. *Sarah?* No, Kevin.

Kevin: Wanna talk?

He stares at the phone. As much as he wants to jump into problem-solving mode and understand how his idea ended up on LightVerse's product roadmap, he can't focus right now. The last "Wanna talk?" text he received set off a chain of events he wishes he could erase. He turns off his phone and curls into himself, pulling the blanket over his head to block the overhead light he's too exhausted to turn off. Despite the early hour, he falls asleep quickly, his body apparently in self-preservation mode after its meltdown.

Around midnight, he wakes and realizes with a start that the distressing dream in which he ended things with Sarah wasn't just a dream. He *actually* broke up with the only woman he's ever been able to picture spending the rest of his life with. *What am I supposed to do now?* The thought plays on repeat in his head as he tosses and turns for hours and finally collapses into sleep as the dawn begins to break.

SFO-AUS

SARAH

Things are awful, to say the least. A few days have passed since my fight with Nathan, and I'm still confused about what happened. It had been an amazing day up until that point, and I still don't understand how I'd set out to present my slides to Nathan and how the conversation had ended, how *we* had ended. Remembering it now, my throat tightens. Nathan and I were having a few problems, but at no point did I think we wouldn't be able to sort it out.

After a sleepless night, I text Cam on Saturday morning, giving her a basic rundown of what happened.

> **Sarah:** N and I had a fight last night.
> **Camila:** What happened?
> **Sarah:** He was upset about me going to Austin with Carter and Kev.
> **Camila:** Guessing Kev is not the issue?
> **Sarah:** Kev's not the issue.
> **Camila:** He'll come to his senses. He's just feeling unsure.
> **Me:** Yeah, maybe.

Probably not.

Camila: When does he come back?

Me: A week from today.

Camila: Okay. You'll both take a little breather, and when he gets back, you'll work it out.

A *little breather. Not quite.* Nathan's words—"I think our trial is over"—echo in my head. We are over. I don't tell Camila that, though. Admitting it to someone else means it's real, and I'm not prepared to do that right now.

I stuff reality and my feelings about Nathan into a small box somewhere deep inside of me. It's the same murky corner where my last few months living with Blake reside and the bleak place where the dark period after my father died swirls into a ball of nothingness. One more thing to add to that Pandora's box of sadness, self-doubt, and guilt.

Despite feeling like a shadow of myself, I try to pull myself together on Sunday afternoon. A small part of me must realize I have to focus on my trip to Austin, my big opportunity. I force myself to work, taking small breaks to eat—just enough to get by. The food has no taste anyway. Then I comb through my closet, avoiding Nathan's side like the plague. What does one wear for a presentation to the board of a major company? It's likely not flowered sundresses or jeans and t-shirts.

On Tuesday morning, realizing I have less than twenty-four hours left before the trip, I recruit Camila and Erin for a last-minute shopping spree. We meet at Nordstrom Rack that evening and get lucky, finding the essentials for a board-room-worthy outfit pretty quickly.

"You are going to look and do great, girl," Camila says, as we sit outside the mall later, drinking our iced coffees. "I'm really proud of you." She keeps giving me careful looks like I might break if she talks too loudly.

"Me, too. You did really well during the run-through yesterday," Erin adds. She won't be in Austin, but she listened and gave feedback while we practiced our presentation. "Your part, added to the middle section that Carter's presenting, is really going to impress the board."

"Carter's just doing the intro. Kevin's doing the middle section," I correct her.

"Kev didn't tell you?" Erin asks, confused. "He's on his way home to Seattle right now. Some sort of family emergency. Carter's going to be there anyway, so he'll just present Kevin's part. He asked me to check a couple metrics for him this afternoon."

I look at her. She looks at me. Then we both look at Camila, whose lips are pursed. "So, you're not only headed out on a business trip with Mr. Hottie, but now it's with him alone? Something like that?"

"Or, you know, exactly like that," I say, sighing. "I was counting on Kev being there. He's Nathan's best friend, so I just felt like it gives it all more legitimacy."

"Legitimacy?" Camila asks. "This business trip *is* legit. *You* are legit, and you didn't get invited to present to the fucking board of LightVerse for, well, for the reasons Nathan said."

Erin and I exchange surprised looks. Cam has an amazing ability to stay calm and almost never curses.

She notices our expressions. "What?" she asks. "Sarah, I really like Nate–"

I narrow my eyes at her.

"Fine, I *liked* Nate before he acted like an ass. He was being unfair and dismissive. You were invited to do this because you're intelligent and lovable. And you'd never flirt with someone or use the fact that you're pretty to move ahead at work."

I wouldn't, at least not on purpose. Cam's trying to make me feel better, but she's giving me more credit than I deserve, considering my recent behavior.

"She's right, Sarah," Erin adds, pulling me into a side hug. "You got this chance because you're talented, and you rock. I've seen you in action."

I start to tear up—my regret, my worry, and my guilt suddenly welling up in physical form.

"Thank you both for just . . . being here for me. I *do* love you."

"I know we're great, but I don't think that's why you're starting to cry," Erin says, exchanging a look with Camila.

"You're right," I admit. "I've been trying not to think about Nathan, but it's really hard. I love him, and I just don't know how what happened . . . happened."

Erin asks whether we've talked since that night.

"No, he said he needed a break," I say, feeling a swell of unexpected courage. "He can have his stupid break, and I'm going to fly to Austin to kick some ass with Carter or whoever else is there."

"That's my girl," Camila says, winking. "And I assume, since *you* just learned about this, that Nathan also doesn't know that Kevin's not going to be there?"

"I don't give a shit what Nathan thinks right now," I say with bravado.

They both likely know I do, in fact, have plenty of shits to give, but they don't call me on it. The only reason I've been even halfway holding it together since he broke up with me is that I don't have any other choice. I refuse to be some sad, sorry excuse for a woman, crying my eyes out over a man and giving up a great opportunity.

"But, no," I clarify. "There'd be no way for him to know that I'll be there with *only* Carter."

"It'll be fine," Erin reassures me. "You'll probably barely see him. He said he's flying out this evening, so you won't even be on the same flight. Just do work stuff, then go out on your own after hours. Didn't you say you have some friends there?"

"Yeah, my cousin," I reply distractedly.

Ugh. I was banking on Kevin acting as a buffer against anything Carter might be considering. But *only* Carter? This makes things more . . . complex.

"So, you're not interested in Carter at all, right?" Camila asks, narrowing her eyes at me.

"No, of course not," I reply too quickly.

Erin flicks her eyes over to me. "Really?" they seem to say. She's seen me around Carter more than Camila has. I press my lips together and silently plead with her not to bring it up—I *can't handle this right now*—and she lets it go.

"In any case, it's problematic," Camila says.

"What is?"

"The fact that he's hot as hell. Like, if he were a complete dork and so skinny Nate could bench press the guy—or pound him in the ground if circumstances called for it—there wouldn't be anything to worry about."

"He's also *very* charming," Erin adds, completely unhelpfully.

"I don't find him charming," I reply, maybe in an effort to convince myself because I'm surely not convincing either of my best friends.

"Well," Camila says in a measured tone, "then you shouldn't have a problem."

"Be careful, Sarah," Erin says. "Like I said before."

***

I settle into my first-ever business class seat on a direct flight from SJC to AUS. LightVerse is paying for the ticket. Otherwise, I'd be back in economy with all the other peasants. Not sleeping well the past few days has been wreaking havoc on my head and neck, so I close my eyes and roll my head from side to side to loosen it up, then dip my chin toward my chest and use my fingers to massage the tight muscles.

"Is this seat available?" I hear a deep voice say.

My head snaps up. My eyes snap open. *Carter.* I had assumed that since Kevin wasn't coming to Austin—and since he and I were supposed to sit next to each other on the flight—that the seat next to me would be empty, or at the very least occupied by someone other than Carter "Mr. Hottie" Michaels.

Guess I was wrong.

"Good morning. Um, what are you doing here? I thought you'd already be in Austin," I say, trying to cover my surprise with some fake cheer.

"I had some stuff I needed to take care of here yesterday, so I postponed my flight. Looks like I got lucky with the seating arrangement. Kevin got in touch with you?"

I sigh. "Yeah. He texted me last night. His sister was in a car accident, and his parents need his help dealing with everything while she's at the hospital."

"I told him to take all the time he needs. Family comes first," Carter says.

I nod, and a memory flits through my mind of another family, another hospital. *Has Nathan told his parents about us?*

Carter's voice brings me back to the present. "—do fine. You and I are great together."

Wait. What?

"Sorry. What were you saying?" I ask.

"That we'll do fine on the presentation."

I reach down into my bag to retrieve my headphones. My head still hurts, and I was planning to listen to some calm music and rest during the flight. Instead, Carter peppers me with questions. I want to feel annoyed at him, but I find myself enjoying our conversation. When I first met him, I assumed he was a somewhat smart guy, mostly getting by on his looks and charm, but I've learned a lot from working with him the last month. He's smart. Full stop.

"So, how long have you been in the Bay Area?" I ask in a perhaps poorly masked attempt to pin down his age.

"Forever, Sarah. And before you ask, I'm ancient—pushing thirty-five."

"That's not *super* old," I joke.

"Oh, good. So, you won't mind helping me pick up my walker and dentures at baggage claim?"

I laugh, and it feels light and happy—a welcome change from the last few days.

Carter's energy today is different than usual. The cocky guy I've gotten used to—the one who has unapologetically inserted himself into my work calendar, my physical space, and my thoughts—has been replaced by an easy-going alter-ego whose lopsided smile, dimples, and blue eyes are reeling me into a place of familiarity and comfort.

He presses his lips together, and I try not to stare, imagining the few times we've been alone together and where things might have led had I let them.

Chill the fuck out, Sarah.

"I need to stretch my legs," I say, unbuckling my seatbelt. He stands to let me out, and I walk to the back of the plane, putting some space between us. I need fresh air, but that's not an option on a sealed metal tube hurtling toward Austin. I feel like *I'm* hurtling toward some other unknown yet clearly dangerous destination.

When I get back to my seat, I scoot in and quickly realize I should have waited for Carter to stand up first. I'm sure my butt is at his eye level. *Good god.* As I edge past him, the heel of my boot snags on the backpack I left on the floorboard, and I half-fall into my seat—one of my legs tangled in the bag and now resting over his lap.

Heat spreads rapidly up my neck. *Am I just destined to put myself in ridiculous situations around this man?*

He doesn't even try to conceal his amusement at my predicament and grins at me. "Need some help?"

"No, no," I say, but his nimble fingers are already deftly untangling my purse strap from around my ankle. The warmth of his fingers on my bare skin, where my jeans have ridden up, leaves an impression. The second he's done, I yank my foot to the floor and face forward, but I can see him studying me out of the corner of my eye.

"I'm kind of a mess, huh?" I catch his eyes quickly, then notice his full lips, which seem to be fighting a pleased smile.

Bad idea. Back up to the eyes.

"You seem to take care of yourself quite well," he says.

"I do?" I squeak out.

"Yeah. You're not afraid to go after what you want. But I do wonder sometimes," he says, leaning in, "what does Sarah Hoffman *really* want?" His raised eyebrow is a challenge.

Unsure what to say, I'm saved by the flight attendant, who stops next to our row and asks if we'd like a drink. "We have mimosas if that interests you."

"I'll just have sparkling water, please," I tell her.

"You sure?" Carter asks. "It's on LightVerse."

"I don't think it's a good—"

"Believe me. It's a good idea," he replies and winks. He turns to the flight attendant. "We'll have two mimosas, please."

Ah, cocky Carter is back.

He leans in. "Relax, Sarah," he whispers. The flight attendant places our drinks in front of us, and he holds his cup up for a toast. "We're going to have a good time the next few days."

"To business trips?" I suggest, perhaps lingering on the word "business."

"To getting to know special people even better," he replies and takes a drink.

***

We arrive in Austin, and there's no good reason for me to tell Carter that we shouldn't share a ride to the Fairmont Hotel downtown, which is how I find myself in the backseat of an Uber with him. While Carter checks messages on his phone, I do the same, except I'm really looking at him out of the side of my eye. He catches me, and instead of calling me on it, he simply looks out the window. I see his smile in the reflection.

We arrive at the hotel and check in. Luckily, we're on different floors. "315," I say, and he presses the three on the elevator. "I'm 1024," he says, and I press the ten for him. As we head up in the elevator, he asks if I want to grab some dinner.

"It's two hours later here," he reminds me.

"I just want to get settled and rest up for tomorrow."

"Okay," he says. "Text me if you change your mind."

When I get to my room, I take a cool shower—the Austin summer is sizzling. After drying off, I pull on some leggings and a tank top, plop down on the bed, and open up my laptop. Realizing it's a long time until morning, I break down and order some Thai takeout to the hotel lobby, then open my calendar to check the meeting schedule for tomorrow. We have an 8:00 a.m. meeting, which will feel like 6:00 a.m. California time. *Ouch.* I check the location of the LightVerse office on Google Maps, and as I try to determine if the distance is walkable or I'll need to take a taxi, a Slack message comes in from Carter.

> **CMichaels (he/him):** Working?
>
> **SHoffman (she/her):** I could ask you the same :) Just checking when we have meetings tomorrow.
>
> **CMichaels (he/him):** You sure you're not hungry? I ordered some food.
>
> **SHoffman (she/her):** I did get hungry. <smiley emoji> I ordered some, too. It'll be here in 20 min.
>
> **CMichaels (he/him):** Wanna have a hotel lobby picnic?

I shouldn't. It would be easy to make an excuse—"I have some work I need to do in my room"—but I figure not much harm can come from having a take-out dinner with him in the hotel lobby.

> **SHoffman (she/her):** Sure. I'll be down soon.

I slip my key into the side pocket of my leggings and head downstairs to meet my food delivery person. When I get off the elevator, Carter is already downstairs with two bags of food in his hands.

"I guess we both like Thai?" he says. "The delivery guy didn't want to give me yours, but I gave him a good tip and promised him we're together."

His words unnerve me, but he doesn't seem to notice.

"So, we can stay down here, or I thought we might want to go up to the pool. The receptionist told me there's a nice area to sit up there."

"Sure," I agree. The hotel lobby is pretty packed right now, and after the noise and chaos of traveling today, a less crowded spot will be good for my nerves. The closer we get to the presentation on Friday, the more tension I'm beginning to feel in my neck and jaw.

We take the elevator up and step out into a resort-worthy pool area. How something like this can exist in the midst of the concrete jungle outside is almost unfathomable, but here we are. Here I am. Here Carter is. Attractive, successful, and very-into-me Carter.

"Wow," we both say as we take in the multiple pools, cabanas, and palm trees. There are only a few people swimming in one of the pools. It's still light out. The sun is setting but not quite down, and small lights accent the beautiful greenery.

"Shall we?" he says, gesturing toward a small grassy area with stylish patio furniture—some comfortable outdoor-type sofas and a few low tables.

We settle in and begin to eat, talking about unimportant things. How we still have something to say to one another after four hours on a plane together, I don't know.

The conversation slows, and I look up to see him watching me. He has set his food down on the table and is drinking some lime-flavored sparkling water from a bottle. When he notices I've caught him in the act, he smiles, a bit embarrassed.

"Sorry," he says. "Um, I was just noticing you look different than you did earlier today than you do usually."

"Oh," I say, understanding at once. "Yeah, I took a shower. I guess I don't have any makeup on. Avert your eyes."

"Not at all," he says. "I mean, don't get me wrong. You usually look nice, but you look very . . . natural now."

"Natural?" I ask and laugh. "What does that mean?"

"Natural and . . . pretty. Like that day at Kevin's."

Yeah, I remember you noticing me that day, too.

"I should go," he says. "I need to prep some stuff for tomorrow morning. So, the LightVerse offices are about a twenty-minute ride, so we could share an Uber or—"

"Let's meet there," I interrupt. "Does 7:45 work?"

He nods. "Sounds good. Have a good night."

"You, too," I say as he gathers up his things and heads toward the elevator.

I take off my shoes and dip my feet into the pool. The calming sound of the small waterfall reminds me of one of the last hikes I went on with my dad at Big Basin. It was one of his favorites.

I should have gone there with Nathan, I think. I should have told him about that hike. We could have done it together. I stand, shake the water off my feet, and feeling dejected, I head back to my room.

Value Proposition

SARAH

On Thursday morning, I arrive at the LightVerse offices and discover that it's actually a campus consisting of nine separate buildings. I check in at Building One and walk to the elevator bank to head up to the eleventh floor. While I wait, Carter surprises me, placing his hand on the small of my back and leaning down to tell me quietly, "Good morning."

Dressed this morning in tailored dress pants and a checked white button-down shirt, he could be a model. My surprised expression must betray my thoughts, and he gives me a pleased smile.

"Good morning to you," I say.

"Hope you're not too tired. It's *almost* 6:00 a.m. Pacific."

"I *am* an early riser, but not usually this early. I'll get a coffee and hope for the best."

He casually appraises the dress-to-impress ensemble I've chosen, including heels taller than I'd ever wear to work back at home.

"You've never worn *those* in Mountain View," he remarks, biting his bottom lip.

"Well, jeans and a hoodie don't work everywhere, now, do they?"

"You look . . . good," he says, his eyes tracking down for a split second before meeting mine again.

When we reach the eleventh floor, I follow Carter's lead. I try to exude confidence as I clack down the marble-tiled corridor in my new heels. I think I might even be doing a good job until I we reach the huge, modernly furnished conference room. *I'd know that perfectly styled head of blond hair anywhere.* Danica.

I slow my pace, and Carter turns back and gives me a questioning look.

"I'm going to . . ." I say, gesturing with my head toward a side table laden with drinks and food. I focus my attention fully on preparing a cup of coffee before taking my seat and opening my laptop.

Today's agenda includes presentations from finance, legal, sales, and marketing. Tomorrow's focus will be on the product and engineering side of things. My goal today, Carter and Kevin have informed me, is to listen carefully and identify any important items we need to address in our presentation tomorrow.

It's a long day—session after session with a break for a catered lunch—and when 4:00 p.m. rolls around, I hide a yawn behind my hand. Carter, of course, catches me and winks. We wrap up, and I want nothing more than to head back to the hotel to let my eyes, ears, and feet rest. As I pack my laptop in my bag, Carter asks if I have plans for the evening.

"Yeah, I'm meeting my cousin for dinner later," I tell him.

"If you finish early, let me know?"

I nod.

I am *not* letting him know if I finish early. We've already spent too much time together, considering the lingering looks he's been giving me all day and the fact that I'm still reeling from Nathan breaking up with me.

***

Jordan and I choose a place called Swift's Attic for dinner—my treat since she's a student. The last time I saw her was at my dad's funeral, a fact I try to push from my mind. She's grown up a lot in the past few years, and with new blond highlights in her chestnut brown hair and casual but stylish summer dress, she looks at least twenty-five.

Over dinner, we discuss her major and her plans for when she finishes school next year.

"I was thinking of coming out to California, but it really depends on where I find a job," she tells me.

"Well, if you end up in the Bay Area, you can always crash at my place until you get settled. It's small, but, well . . . I guess I have more room now."

She gives me a worried look, but I smile quickly. "Don't look at me like that. My eyeliner's way too perfect to shed a tear tonight. We're going to smile and laugh. A lot. I need it."

She follows my orders and smiles, propping her chin on her hands. "You're my hero, Sarah."

"Me?" I ask, cracking up. "Why?"

"Well, first, because I'm an only child like you, and I need a role model, but also, because you're strong. You've overcome a lot already, and you'll overcome this, too."

I nod and force my mouth into a tight smile. "Want to go somewhere else?"

"Cocktails?" she suggests.

"Yeah, let's find a place with good music."

We stroll around and end up at a rooftop bar called Zanzibar.

"It has a pool," Jordan tells me.

"Damn, I left my swimsuit in my other purse," I say as I exit the elevator to enter the bar. I look back and laugh at her and run directly into . . . Carter.

"Um, hi," he says, stepping to the side to allow a few people to get into the elevator.

"Are you following me?" I ask. My glass of wine at dinner seems to have loosened my tongue.

"I could ask you the same thing. We were just leaving, but uh . . ."

A guy on the elevator calls to him, "You coming, Michaels?"

He glances at them, then back at me. "I'll catch up with you guys later," he tells them.

"Whatever," one of his friends says and laughs, rolling his eyes. "See you next time you're in Austin, man."

"You should join them. You probably don't get to see them much, and you see me every day," I say.

"You're a lot better company than they are," he admits. He takes a step closer and whispers in my ear, "I'd rather stay. Does that work for you?"

His warm breath on my neck makes my skin prickle in all sorts of good ways. *Yeah, that does seem to work for me.*

I smile up at him and introduce him to Jordan, who has been standing next to me wordlessly for the last minute.

"This is my cousin, Jordan," I say.

"Carter," he says, jumping in to introduce himself. "So, can I get you ladies a drink? You told me you like red wine . . . but they actually have these really good cocktails here with giant flowers inside."

Jordan peers up at him adoringly—the hazel eyes she, too, was gifted courtesy of the Hoffman family genes wide and sparkling—and replies in a dreamy voice, "I'd love a cocktail with a giant flower, Carter."

I try to hide my amusement. He certainly has a way with women, and it's entertaining to see his charm working on someone else.

"Me, too," I say.

Carter heads to the bar while we find a seat, and Jordan spits out every thought she's been holding in for the last three minutes. "Who the hell is that, and does he have a brother?"

"Jordan, you can have *him*. You don't need his brother."

"He's obviously into you."

"And I literally just got dumped," I whisper loudly into her ear.

"In that case, you might want to skip that flower cocktail because homeboy is definitely gonna look even better after a few drinks."

"Homeboy?"

She shrugs. We sit, and I position myself in the booth in a way that leaves more space on the side next to Jordan, but when Carter returns with our drinks, she scoots closer to the edge, forcing me to move closer to her and make room for him on my side.

We both thank him for the drinks and do a toast. "L'chaim," she and I say without hesitation, reprising our earlier toast.

"Cheers," Carter says, raising his glass to clink it with mine.

"So, Carter. Tell me something interesting about yourself," Jordan says. She has apparently warmed up enough to speak.

"I don't want to bore Sarah. She's probably already heard all my good stories," he says, glancing sideways at me.

"No, please, go ahead," I say, hoping they'll get into a conversation and I won't be the center of his attention.

"Maybe I'll tell you about Sarah at work and how awesome she is," he replies.

"Maybe I can share embarrassing stories about her when we were growing up," Jordan offers.

I shoot her a warning look.

"Remember that time you came to visit us in Florida, and we were at the beach?" She holds up her hand as if to whisper to Carter without me hearing. "We were trying to get a tan, laying on the sand, and we had our bikini tops untied and—"

"We're changing the topic now," I say.

I glance at him, and he's pressing his lips together—I'm guessing to avoid smiling. Jordan gets a text message, and while she's focused on her phone, he says in a low voice only I can hear, "The one and only time I saw you in a bikini—"

"Don't finish that sentence," I warn him.

In lieu of a reply, he winks at me.

Jordan looks up from her phone. "I'm really sorry, Sarah, but my friend is stranded outside her dorm room, and I have her spare key. I gotta run."

"Oh, yeah, of course. Go help your friend." *And leave me here to fend for myself.*

"Have a great night, you two," she says, leaning in to whisper in my ear that he looks like Chris Hemsworth. "Not a bad option for a rebound."

She walks to the elevator, turns her head in a cute twenty-one-year-old kind of way, and winks at me, like an exclamation point to what she just whispered in my ear.

Carter smiles at me. "She's cute, huh?"

Does he mean "sexy-cute" or "cute-cute?" My consternation must be showing on my face, so he clarifies.

"I don't mean that in a 'dirty old man' way. I have a baby sister. Well, not so much a baby anymore. She's twenty-two. Sometimes, it's like she's from a different planet, but she's cute. Like your cousin. Young, a little naive, goofy."

I relax. Up until now, we've spoken mostly about work and a bit about personal things, but not too many details about family. He's inviting me into his life.

"So, what did you think about today?" he asks.

"I thought . . ." I begin to say, but it's hard for me to collect my thoughts. He's staring at me, too intently, and waiting for me to continue.

Now that Jordan's gone, we have more room in the booth, but if anything, he's moved even closer to me. One of his hands rests on the table, and the other is braced on the seat right next to where I'm sitting. Out of the corner of my eye, his hand twitches as if he's considering moving it.

Then, he touches the tips of my hair, resting on my bare shoulder. The brush of his fingertips on my skin gives me goosebumps despite the hot summer night.

"Your hair's longer than your Slack profile photo. Are you growing it out?"

It takes me a millisecond longer than it should for me to respond, distracted as I am by his unexpected touch.

"Uh, yeah," I stammer. "I mean, Nathan liked it long, and—"

At the mention of Nathan, his eyes narrow the tiniest bit.

"Liked?"

Yeah, past tense.

"Liked," I confirm. "We're . . . on a break right now."

"Oh," he says. I have to give him credit. He doesn't betray even the slightest emotion. No surprise, no satisfaction, nothing.

"Did you always do what he said?"

It's not aggressive, but I don't miss the hint of criticism in his tone. I bristle.

"I don't *do* what Nathan tells me to," I reply. "In fact, that's why I'm here. In Austin." *In this bar. With you.*

"I'm sorry. I'm not trying to get in your business. I just . . . Well, I heard about him from someone—"

"What did you hear about him?"

"Just that he, maybe, plays games?" He has an uncomfortable expression on his face.

And like that, the penny drops. "Danica."

"You know Danica?" he asks.

"Yeah." I sigh. "I know Danica."

How long must I contend with that beautiful, blond villainess?

"We used to date," he says.

He takes in my expression. I've managed to keep my mouth shut, but I'm almost certain my eyebrows are touching my hairline at this point. He begins to laugh.

"You dated Danica?"

"Yeah."

"Wow."

He blushes. "I know."

"I guess it makes sense."

"What do you mean?"

"You're both successful, good-looking," I begin to say but abruptly stop.

His mouth curves up in an amused—also, very sexy—smile.

"Yeah, it didn't really work out," he says. "She's a bit . . ."

"Intense?"

"That's a good word for it," he says, agreeing with my assessment.

"So, what happened?"

"Well, last fall, things began to fall apart—not that we'd been together that long—and who knows if they would've worked out anyway. Her attention seemed to . . . stray."

I'd say. I know exactly where it strayed. To Nathan, right about the time he and Kevin connected with her to get her help with LightVerse. *Oh, what a tangled web we weave.* I wonder if Carter knows what happened—*who* happened—to their relationship.

"And this morning, what was it like seeing her?"

"It was .... affirming."

"Affirming?" I ask.

"Yeah, that she's not what I'm looking for." Our eyes meet.

"And what exactly are you looking for?" The moment the words leave my mouth, I regret asking the question. *Nathan.* A voice in my head—a responsible, sober one reminds me that we *just* broke up. *He broke up with* you, another voice argues back, the voice that is just as obviously charmed by Carter's blue eyes and confidence as I am.

"You already know the answer to that question, so why are you asking it?"

I look down at his hand resting on the table, inches away from my own. He follows my gaze. "It's getting late," he says, "and we have an early start tomorrow." Instead of reaching for my hand, he touches my hair again.

"Getting tired, old man?" I tease.

"Thirty-four isn't that old, Ms. Hoffman."

"I know," I admit.

"And you know, men mature a lot in their late twenties and early thirties. There's time for them to learn things. Things that can . . . benefit a woman, if you know what I mean?"

Well, that took a very hot turn. I knock back what's left of my fruity cocktail to cover my nervousness, and the flower topples from my glass to the table. He picks it up and rubs one of the petals between his thumb and his forefinger. I'm entranced by the motion. Unchaste thoughts spring to my mind as I momentarily imagine the feel of those same fingers tracing my skin. This might just be the first time in my life I'm jealous of a flower.

"Should we head back?" he asks. "We could continue this conversation somewhere more . . . private?"

There's a question in his eyes, and suddenly, it feels as if I'm witnessing the scene from somewhere outside of myself. I'm on the edge of a cliff, but I'm ready to jump, feeling pulled to do so by some invisible force. Oh, right, Carter's sex appeal. It's intoxicating, this euphoria he induces in me when he's close. It wouldn't be the first time I've been tempted by him and let things go too far. He twirls the petals of the flower over my open palm, and goosebumps crop up on my arms. He glances at my lips, seems to draw courage from the small smile playing on them, and scoots closer to me. I don't move away, and I'm one-thousand percent sure that I'm barreling toward a stupid fucking mistake when . . .

"Hey, guys! Glad you're still here," Jordan suddenly chirps.

I run my hand through my hair and look up at her. "Hey, you're . . . back."

"I ended up meeting my friend nearby and didn't have to go all the way to her dorm. You up for another drink?" she asks.

"Oh, um, no, J. I think I should go. Big presentation tomorrow, right, Carter?"

Carter—always cool, always calm—nods. "Yep, Sarah's the star of the show tomorrow."

"Okay, I'll walk you back then," Jordan says to me.

Carter's already getting up and says he'll catch up with his friends before heading back.

"Are you sure?" I ask him, trying to interpret the expression on his face. But it's unreadable.

"Yeah, it's for the best," he says. "Be careful walking back, okay?"

And with that, he's gone.

"What did I walk in on?" Jordan asks after Carter leaves the bar. "Oh my god. I interrupted something, didn't I?"

"Only a potential mistake." I rub my hands together, trying to calm my still-buzzing nerves. "Let's get out of here."

As we walk back to my hotel in the warm night air, I try to focus on Jordan's story about the internship keeping her in Austin this summer, but my thoughts drift. *What would have happened if she hadn't interrupted our conversation? Would I be walking back to the hotel with him now? Would I have done something—something else—to feel guilty about?*

I remind myself, though, that nothing happened tonight. *Breathe.*

***

When I get back to my hotel room, Nathan is on my mind, and I'm a tornado of emotions, ranging from guilt and anger all the way to longing and regret. But eventually, the storm dies down, and my thoughts switch to Carter and the flicker I thought I saw in his eyes when I told him that

Nathan and I are on a break. He certainly didn't waste any time reacting to that new information.

After a quick shower to save time in the morning, I change into a tank top and some shorts. There's a light knock on the door, and I walk over to peek through the peephole to find Carter standing outside. Scantily clad as I am, I open the door just enough to stick my head out.

"Hey," he says. "I just wanted to see that you got back okay."

"I didn't. I'm a figment of your imagination," I say and immediately feel self-conscious. *Why am I always so nervous around him?* Dumb question. I'm nervous because I'm standing here in my pajamas, late at night, in a hotel far from home, with a movie-star lookalike in front of me.

"Well, you *are* dream-worthy," he says boldly, delivering a charming smile. It's a bit cheesy but, much to my dismay, I feel my pulse speed up. "And, um, I also just wanted to tell you that . . . it'll be alright. I mean, you guys breaking up. Sometimes, well, one thing has to end for something else—something, um, good—to begin, you know?" Polished, well-spoken Carter is tripping over his words. He runs his hand through his wavy blond hair, rests it on the back of his neck, and tilts his head to look up at me. It's the most adorable expression I've ever seen on his face, and I might just melt onto the floor.

We've been talking for a minute, and I've sort of forgotten that I'm wearing very little clothing. I'm not standing behind the door any-more, and his eyes glance down and take in my body—my somewhat see-through shirt, the gap where it ends above my belly button, and my shorts slung low on my hips. He comes closer to me and touches my wet hair, currently making a wet spot on my shirt over a very sensitive place.

He bites his lip and looks like he's about to say—or, oh my god, do—something, and I know I should say, or do, something to stop him, but I'm standing there frozen and mute, unable to utter a word.

Then, words come to my mouth. "I'm wet," I say, meaning my hair. Time stops, and I realize just what I've said. *Fuuuccckk.*

He starts to laugh, and then I start to laugh because if I don't vent some of the pressure from embarrassment in my body right now, I will explode.

We're cracking up. I'm sweating from nervousness when he surprises me by pulling me into a surprisingly cozy hug.

Then he holds me at arm's length and shakes his head. "You should definitely let your humor come out tomorrow in the presentation. But maybe not that particular joke."

I attempt to smile.

"We have a big day tomorrow. Sweet dreams," he whispers, trailing his hand down my arm until he's holding my hand. He lets go and walks down the hall.

I close the door slowly and finally exhale, just staring at my left hand, still feeling those slightly rough fingertips of his on the center of my palm. I try to recall what Nathan's hand felt like in my own, but I can't, and I slam my hands against the back of the door. *Why can't I remember? Why did he do this to us? Why did I?*

Before the sob that's building in my throat can escape, I force myself to take some deep breaths and rub both of my hands up and down my bare thighs until I feel fully here in the present. Settling my nerves now is like trying to meditate while a marching band plays outside the window. The pleasant scent of Carter's cologne is still in my nose, and the disquiet—the guilt—I feel from that hug is heavy. The feel of Carter's strong arms around me, the sensation of my breasts pressed up against his hard chest—yeah, guilt is definitely the word. It wasn't that long ago that Nathan would fold me into *his* arms while whispering sweet nothings into my ear.

I turn off the lights, slip into bed, and pull the covers up over my head, trying to block out the light coming in the window. I'm all mixed up inside—a cocktail of shame, nervousness, and just wanting to be held. Unable to settle down, I snake my hand out from under the covers and open the meditation app on my phone. The sounds of ocean waves crashing onto a shore lull me into a calmer state, and sleep eventually welcomes me into its embrace.

I wake in the middle of the night confused, but the numbers on the nightstand clock, though blurry, seem familiar. Nathan's steady breathing behind me imbues me with a sense of comfort, and I close my eyes, ready to fall into slumber once more, when I feel him kiss my neck.

My love.

I'm lying on my side, and I note the dark sky through the slit in my curtains. The moon must be covered by clouds.

Strong, capable hands glide over my waist and my hips, and I hear his whisper in my ear, "It's okay to let go, you know. To try." What does he mean?

But before I can contemplate it too deeply, my body begins to respond to his, and I slide my hand over his and bring it to my bare breast.

"Here, like this," I explain, massaging myself but with his touch, his hand under my own. His hands are a bit rough but warm. Gentle, but just firm enough to convey his need for me.

"Now, touch me here," I say, moving his hand lower, slowly down my abdomen until I can feel the tips of his fingers slide just under the waistband of my underwear. "Kiss my neck, too."

His chin rests in the crook where my shoulder meets the nape of my neck, and I feel his warm breath speed up as he settles in behind me, nestling his hard body—chest, abs, and lower—into mine. I turn on my back to make myself, my body, more available. It's too dark for me to see him, but I can feel the stubble on his face. The perfect combination of rough and soft, sexy in one, perfect texture. He leans in and kisses me deeply. His tongue tastes like strawberries, and his scent is familiar. His hair is longer now, lightly brushing my face as he continues to make love to me with his mouth. I feel safe—aroused, wanting more, but safe.

One of his hands fondles my breasts, and he moves downward and kisses the side of one breast. He then slides his tongue over my nipple, making it perk up while the other slides my underwear past my hips. Down, down, off. He toys with me, one finger, then two, sliding deliciously across my clit, and a soft moan escapes my lips.

"Mmmm, I could do this all night," he says in a low, sexy voice. He sounds different, but it must be that we haven't spoken in a while. I've forgotten how he sounds when he's turned on. "Touch me," he continues in a gruff whisper, taking one of my hands to his erection. "Feel what you do to me."

The feel of him—firm, almost throbbing—inside of my hand sends satisfaction rippling through me. "I do that to you?"

"It's not that big of a surprise, is it?"

"It's not a surprise, but it is . . . big," I say, laughing.

"You want my body, huh?" he asks, sounding pleased.

"Yes."

"I'll give you that and more."

"More?" I ask.

"I can give you all kinds of things in life, Sarah," he whispers.

I pull at his heavy body. "I want you," I say. He starts to crawl on top of me.

"No," I say.

"No?"

I push him onto his back and move to straddle him, beginning to rub myself up against him.

"I want to be on top," I say.

"You like it up there on top, don't you?" he says and smacks my ass.

It's different than usual. But I like it.

I take his hard cock in my hands and run my hand up and down the length of it a few times. He's hard. He's ready. So am I. Positioning myself over his erection, I slide gently down on him, and I feel him fill me.

As he pushes into me, a moan escapes my lips before I can temper it. He is tender but insistent, hungry for more. I sit up and place one hand on his hard abs to balance myself while he kneads one of my breasts and grips me possessively on my waist, working with me to create the perfect rhythm.

All the while, he tells me in strained tones how sexy I am, how much he wants me.

"You're so amazing. I feel like I'm dreaming," he says.

"Maybe you are," I reply, and we continue to rock back and forth, bringing each other closer to orgasm with each thrust. "Maybe you are . . . Maybe you are . . ."

But then, I'm awake. Sunlight is streaming in through the curtains I left open last night, and I wince at the brightness. As I wake more fully, I take stock of my body. My face feels tight, traces of salt from the tears I cried last night still on my cheeks. And my stomach feels heavy, but it's not the weight of sadness or guilt. It's the unmistakable warmth and pulsing of arousal. I realize my underwear is low on my hips, and the fingertips of my right hand are still on the soft skin of my inner thighs, just millimeters from . . . well. That dream? Nothing short of amazing, but something feels off.

It was too dark to see his face, but his voice was different. His hands had felt different. Specifically, his hands *on me*—rougher, unable to restrain himself and his desire for me.

"*You like it up there on top.*" He said it in the dream and one other time. The familiar timbre of his voice echoes in my head, and to my dismay—my shame—I know exactly when I last heard it. "Sweet dreams," he said to me just before leaving me for the night. *Or so I had thought.*

There's an anvil on my chest as I stare at my guilty hand—the one I must have been pleasuring myself with moments before while dreaming. I take a deep breath. So much for starting the day with a clear mind. The man I fucked unabashedly last night in my dreams? Well, I'll be seeing him in the boardroom this morning.

CLOSED WON

SARAH

I drag myself out of bed, get dressed, and apply some light makeup. I'm usually completely non-functional before a cup of hot coffee in the morning, but my realization about who starred in my dreams last night has done more to get my adrenaline pumping than any espresso ever could.

I check my appearance in the bathroom mirror and snap a quick selfie. I look professional. I look good. I even feel good—not good enough to face Carter this morning, though. He's likely expecting to share an Uber this morning, but I'm not quite ready to face him after last night—both the dream and the real experiences. I text him my plans.

> **Me:** Good morning!
> **Carter:** Good morning, Sunshine. Hope you had good dreams.

No comment.

> **Me:** <smiley face emoji> I need to run through what I'm presenting today, so I'm gonna take an Uber now. I'll meet you there, okay?
> **Carter:** <thumbs up emoji> See you there.

Thirty minutes later, I walk into the LightVerse conference room, and I'm surprised to see Kevin already situated at the table.

"Hey, what are you doing here?" I ask, beelining over to give him a hug. It lasts longer than is probably appropriate for a corporate boardroom, but I can't help myself. Seeing him—like an extension of Nathan—shakes me. Kevin hugs me back and laughs at how I'm not letting go.

"Happy to see me? I thought maybe you'd try to steal my part of the presentation," he teases.

"Of course I'm glad to see you." *Very glad.* I don't know what exactly he knows about what's going on with me and Nathan—I didn't tell him when I saw him earlier this week—but he's Nathan's best friend. Since Kevin's been in Seattle, there's a very good chance he talked to him.

He tells me that he flew in on a red-eye—and honestly, he looks like it.

"How's your sister?" I ask.

"Doing okay. She told me to come. She didn't want me to miss such a big professional opportunity."

"I'm *really* glad you're here," I say quietly. I glance toward the front of the room, and he sees where my eyes have landed. Danica—perfect hair, makeup, and clothes, as always.

"Don't worry," he responds in a low tone. "It'll be fine. I don't think she even knows that Nathan chose you over her."

As soon as he says it, he grits his teeth, which tells me all I need to know about whether Nathan has filled him in on our situation.

"I'm sorry, by the way," he whispers.

I shake my head, dismissing the heavy expression on his face.

"I'll be okay," I reply with as much confidence as I can muster. I don't have a choice. I—we—have big things happening today.

"You will. You're going to do great."

I glance back over at Danica, who's deep in conversation with Carter.

"She doesn't know, Sarah," Kevin reassures me.

"She's a woman, Kev. She definitely knows."

"Anyway, it's fine. I'm sure Carter's sung your praises to all of them already."

I clench my jaw at the mention of his name. He certainly sang my praises last night, I think, guiltily.

Kevin begins to unpack his bag, and I discreetly watch Danica's body language as she speaks with Carter. She laughs at something he says and touches his arm frequently. When she turns to greet someone else who has arrived, he looks up and notices me staring at them.

"Good morning," he mouths at me.

I nod politely and lean down to unpack my computer from my bag, opening it quickly as if I'm super busy and important and have emails from the president to check. If I let myself even think back to that dream and the things we did to each other, I'll be utterly wrecked for this presentation today. I sit down at the conference table next to Kevin, who is clicking through his slides for the presentation.

"You need some coffee?" I ask.

He nods. "That would be great. Didn't get a lot of sleep last night."

I walk over to the coffee table and take two mugs—one for myself and one for Kevin. While I'm adding cream to my own mug, Carter comes up next to me.

"You ready for today?"

I noticed him walking over out of the corner of my eye, but I still find it jarring to hear his voice in real life this morning. The last time he spoke to me—in my dream—he was murmuring something about how hot and—*Focus, Sarah.*

"I hope I don't forget anything important," I reply. Cheeks aching from the fake smile currently plastered on my face, I take a sip of my coffee.

"Don't worry. You always end up on top."

My eyes go wide, remembering for a split second just how on top of him—er, things—I was last night. "I guess I do, don't I?" I manage to mutter.

Intending to escape, I grab Kevin's mug of coffee too forcefully, and the coffee sloshes onto my fingers. I set it down and shake the hot liquid off my fingers.

"You need some ice?" Carter takes my hand and inspects it.

"I'm fine," I choke out, snatching my hand back. I grab the two mugs and carry them back to the table, and as I take my seat, Danica stands and pulls up the agenda for the day on the large monitor at the front of the room.

"Good morning, everyone. I'm Danica Drummond, and I have the distinct pleasure of driving the meeting today."

As she runs through the agenda and intro slides, I'm impressed by her confidence and speaking abilities. I don't know if she came up with the numbers, the pitch, or the messaging, but she presents it well. At times, instead of watching Danica, I observe Carter listening to her. He has what seems like a carefully crafted look of interest on his face and occasionally asks a question, but the only time he smiles the whole morning is when he catches my eyes on him and graces me with one.

We break for lunch, and Kevin and I opt out of the catered lunch with the group in lieu of some one-on-one time together at a nearby sandwich spot.

"So, you talked?" I ask as he takes a bite of his sandwich.

Mouth full, he smiles at me until he can finish chewing. "With Nate?" he finally asks. "Yeah, we talked."

"And?"

"We didn't have much time, but I told him he should be supporting you at work. He doesn't disagree, but he's . . . going through some shit."

"Well, he hasn't reached out. I don't know—"

"Let's not talk about it now. We will, or we can, but you need to focus. You've got important things to do today. You *are* important . . . to a lot of people."

I notice his poor, tired—yet kind—eyes. *When did this guy become my friend? When did I start to matter to him?*

Returning to LightVerse, we begin our presentation. It's supposed to take around two hours, allowing for questions and discussion. Carter introduces us and talks about the purpose of our presentation today. From there, Kevin jumps in to talk about his goals in founding Instinqt and how, through careful planning and "meticulous execution." We lock eyes when he says that since he and I both know how early startups operate and the term "chaos monkeys" comes to mind. The company achieved what it did in a relatively short period of time and caught LightVerse's eye.

Kevin walks back to his seat next to me and winks as he sits. *I'm up.* I take over the story right about the time LightVerse acquired Instinqt and address how we've spent the past few months conceptualizing a combined roadmap for Instinqt's products that aligns with and complements—even catapults—a number of existing LightVerse products.

One of the board members stops to ask me how long I worked at Instinqt before the exit. I look to Kevin for support, and he half-nods at me as if to say, "Tell him."

"I was only there for four months, but . . . well, I'm just the type of person who jumps in the deep end and starts to swim."

"Sarah doesn't know the words 'that's too hard,'" Carter says, bolstering my confidence. "She . . ." He stops for a moment to smile in my direction. "She figures things out and has contributed immensely to our knowledge about the value of Instinqt. A lot of the ideas we're presenting today on integrating and leveraging Instinqt technology at LightVerse are hers."

"Well, 'Speak your mind' *is* one of LightVerse's company values," the board member replies. "So, tell us. Where do you think Instinqt-as-Light-Verse could be in three years?"

"Look, Kevin," I say in his direction. "They're asking for my pitch."

He smiles.

I return my attention to the man who asked the question. "Well, we all know how much machine learning techniques have progressed in recent years and how central ML has been in improving user content recommendations. After all, LightVerse is *one* of the leading forces in this field. But LightVerse acquired Instinqt due to its cutting-edge and *patented* use of a specific ML algorithm. Integrating this technology into LightVerse's legacy systems—or maybe even replacing those legacy systems with a better-architected platform—will make LightVerse *the* leader.

"We've worked with our internal analysts to do some basic financial analysis, and as you can see right here"—I pause to click forward a few slides—"based on highly-accurate user content recommendations and a conservative goal conversion rate of 18 percent, you're looking at a revenue increase of around $300 million per year."

I take a deep breath and smile. "That's . . . well, that's a lot of money."

Out of the corner of my eye, I notice Kevin—fighting to maintain his composure—silently tapping his thumb on the side of his leg. I can tell by his fidgeting and pleased expression he's holding in a "Hell yeah."

Carter, on the other hand, isn't holding in anything. He's beaming at me, and confirms quietly, "Indeed, it is."

We nailed it. I can feel it. I'm glad I have on long sleeves because I get goosebumps on my arms. Time to wrap it up. "I might be new to LightVerse, but I do know processes. And laser focus on the right goal here, combined with efficient execution, will take this straight to the moon."

A few people in the boardroom are nodding their heads in agreement and exchanging pleased expressions. Even Danica seems to have lost some of her skepticism. It's exhilarating knowing that we came here with a specific goal—impressing upon the LightVerse board just how central Instinqt and its team will be in the LightVerse product roadmap in the years to come. And we just might have done it.

"Kevin and Sarah," Carter says, pausing to glance in our direction, "have done an amazing job bringing me into their world. We knew when we acquired Instinqt that it had a lot of potential, but they've convinced me beyond all doubt that they have something really special to offer us."

He's talking about the product—of course he is—but I can't help but hear the meaning behind his words.

There are questions—many, many questions. They didn't fly us out here to be spoon-fed a fairytale, and they challenge us. But we answer them to the best of our abilities, and they seem mostly pleased with our responses.

By late afternoon, we're all spent. When we finish the meeting, Kevin turns to me and nods his head at me with a wide smile plastered on his face.

I laugh softly. "What?"

He bumps my shoulder with his own. "I'm proud of you," he says quietly. "Thank you. This is the next stage, and you played a huge part."

I've gotten glimpses of this softer, sweeter side of Kevin over the last few months, but it feels like we've leveled up in our friendship.

"Of course," I say, trying not to get too emotional here in the middle of a boardroom. "Thanks for letting me help you."

"I wouldn't choose anybody else," he says.

My body is buzzing with energy. Over the last few months, when something went well at work, my natural instinct was to share my success with Nathan. I suppress the urge to shoot him a quick text. That isn't a viable option right now. My happiness—my sense of accomplishment—is dampened by that fact, but I won't let it bring me down.

As everyone gathers their things and prepares to leave, Danica, looking beautiful and not at all fatigued by the long hours of discussion, appears next to me.

"Great job, guys," she tells me and Kevin.

"Sarah," she continues, taking a second to not-so-subtly take in my appearance up close, "very impressed."

Carter asks if we'd like to join some LightVerse colleagues for dinner. I turn to Kevin to see what he thinks.

"I've got to shower and take a power nap, bro," Kevin tells Carter.

"Of course," Carter replies.

I'm feeling drained as well and could benefit from some quiet time and a change of clothes. I consider bowing out, just staying in for the night at the hotel—to avoid any potential uneasiness—but it's my last night here. After our win this afternoon, it'll be fun to go out and maybe have a few drinks with Kevin. The apprehension I was feeling this morning toward Carter has dissipated throughout the day. Seeing him present today helped me focus on his professional persona, but the remnants of last night's dream are still swirling under the surface.

"Why don't we go back to the hotel, and then we'll meet you guys in a bit?" I suggest.

"Sure," Carter says. "I'll text you the address."

When Kevin and I arrive at the hotel, I leave him at the reception desk to get checked in. "I'll meet you here in half an hour."

I head upstairs, and the first thing I do is take off my heels and roll my ankles around. I stretch my whole body. I could use a massage for my stiff muscles, but just the thought of such activities reminds me of my dream last night. I quickly change my train of thought.

I need a shower. A *cold one*, a voice in the back of my head comments. But I reach for the hot water faucet and turn it on, waiting a moment before stepping in. It'll be hard to hear over the water running, but I put on some music anyway. I scroll through my music and settle on Kid Cudi. The beat and low tones are exactly what I need to relax and reset. I step into the hot spray and let it engulf me while I stretch my neck and massage my lower back. I consider doing something else to relax. The last time Nathan and I had sex was a couple weeks ago, and it's been a week since our FaceTime call. I've felt tightly wound since the dream last night, too. *It's okay to release some tension.* I'll feel more relaxed when I head out tonight with people who rile me up. Danica, for obvious reasons, and Carter, for reasons I'm finding harder and harder to ignore with each day that passes.

I brace my left hand on the wall as the warm shower spray hits me on my chest and let my right hand fall lower, beginning to stroke myself. I shouldn't, but in my head, my thoughts wander back to my dream, when someone else was touching me. I try to picture Nathan's face—after all, my dream started with him—but Carter's face keeps flowing in, replacing it. I think about him today, in the boardroom with the pinstriped button-down shirt he was wearing, slightly open at the collar, and imagine myself touching his neck, kissing just below his ears, then going down on my knees to explore other areas of his body. Imagining him naked doesn't actually take that much imagination at all. I've seen him climb, and we've been . . . close before. It doesn't take long for me to start to feel good—very good. *This is just what I needed.* I'm likely moments away from an orgasm when I'm distracted by the message sound from my phone. I try to get back into the right mind space, but find I can't. *Just as well.*

I forgo shampooing my hair and wash my face and body quickly before finishing up my shower.

When I get out, I check my phone and see a text from Kevin.

Kevin: I'll be down in 5.

I realize it's been longer than I thought. I'll need to hurry.

Me: I'll be down soon.

I dry off and choose a gauzy sundress due to the heat. I grab a light cardigan to cover my shoulders. A pair of strappy sandals and some light makeup later, I head downstairs carrying a small bag to meet Kevin.

I only have a minute while I wait for the elevator to arrive, but I need to do it. I pull my phone out of my bag and text Nathan.

Me: Can we talk when we both get back?

I scroll up and read the last text I sent him despite vowing not to be the first one to break the silence between us.

Me: I don't understand what happened.

It went unanswered, and it's still true. I don't *entirely* understand what's happened, but I want him to open up and talk to me. The elevator arrives, and I press *L* for lobby.

When I meet Kevin in the lobby, he looks like a new man after a shower and a change of clothes.

"Damn girl, you look great," he says. "That only took thirty minutes?"

I shrug. "Thirty-five. Amazing what a shower can do," I say, thinking back to what I was doing a few minutes ago.

"Your cheeks are pink."

"Hot shower, I guess."

He gives me a strange look, then checks his phone. "They're all at Lambert's barbecue restaurant," he says in his best Texan accent. I smile and roll my eyes. *What a dork.*

As we head out to the front of the hotel to wait for an Uber, I think about what awaits me tomorrow with Nathan. First, though, I need to get through tonight. *I'll keep my distance.* I have one more day to go. Then I'll be back in San Jose. *Nathan will be back. We'll talk. We'll figure it out. I know we can.*

And so, I set out for dinner and drinks with my ex-boyfriend's best friend, my ex-boyfriend's ex, and the guy who—if his recent behavior is any indication—wants to sleep with me. What could possibly go wrong?

FIREDRILL

SARAH

"Doesn't look like you're going to find much here, Sarah," Kevin says after scanning the menu at Lambert's while we wait for the hostess. "Oh, look, a salad. How exciting!"

"I'll manage," I reply. The knots in my stomach from today's presentation abated sometime on my way back to the hotel. They've been replaced by a churning due to an altogether different source of stress, namely tonight's dinner company. My appetite is currently non-existent.

The hostess greets us and takes us to the table where twelve or so LightVerse people are sitting, enjoying cocktails and chatting.

There are two open spots, one right next to Carter at one end of the table and another next to Danica at the other end. Though it's the exact opposite of my plan for tonight—Operation Distance Myself from Hot Coworker Who Obviously Digs Me and about Whom I recently Had an Erotic Dream—I choose the lesser of two evils and sit next to Carter. Kevin heads in Danica's direction.

"Hey, glad you made it," Carter says. "We already ordered, if you want to take a look at the menu. They don't have many vegetarian options, but I asked the server, and she said they can do any of the salads vegetarian or with grilled salmon if you eat fish."

"Oh, thanks," I reply. He remembered. I survey the menu quickly and place my order when the server reaches our end of the table.

After she leaves, Carter leans in and whispers, "You really kicked ass today. I knew you would, but I think you even surpassed my high expectations."

"Well, I owe you—"

"You don't owe me anything. It's all you."

I feel his eyes on me and look up at him through my eyelashes to find him smiling a bit shyly.

"You look . . . really beautiful tonight. Must be the glow of success."

"You, too. That color really suits you," I say. He has changed into a dark green short-sleeved Henley shirt, and the color makes his blue eyes seem even brighter. I force myself to look away.

As I do, my purse, which I've hooked on the back of the chair, slides to the floor, and Carter leans down, coming closer to me to help me pick it up. I allow him to, knowing that we have a bit of a history of bumping into each other while fishing for fallen items. As he pulls back up and leans closer to me to place my purse on the back of my chair, I catch a scent of him.

"Wow, you smell great." *Perfect, Sarah.*

"Um, thanks," he says, his mouth twitching.

Hoping to save myself with a joke, I continue, "Not at all like a mountain goat."

At this, he laughs out loud. He sniffs the air around me in a playful manner. "And you . . . smell like barbecue."

I laugh. "That's the worst possible compliment you can give a vegetarian."

"Well, if it makes you feel any better, I'm a big fan of barbecue, but I've chosen something vegetarian tonight. I figured we might end up sitting together, and I didn't want to gross you out."

Well, then.

Some of the people around us are discussing a big music festival happening next weekend, and Carter turns to chat with me. Luckily, he changes the subject and focuses on work.

"So, a couple of people asked me after the meeting this afternoon about you. Where you worked before and where you went to school."

"Nothing impressive on either front."

"Well, I guess some stars just shine bright on their own merits." He narrows his eyes and looks like he's contemplating saying more.

"What?"

"Well, I don't want to sound patronizing or anything, so . . ."

"Just say it."

"Fine. I think you're too modest for your own good. It's okay to take a compliment—without blushing—and to be proud of yourself for a job well done."

You might be smooth, C.H., but not as smooth as you think you are.

I'm not naive. I know he's helping me professionally, and I know he wants to sleep with me. I just haven't quite figured out whether the former is a means to accomplish the latter.

I catch his eye—it's hard not to with him looking directly at me—and notice his eyes track down for the slightest of a moment to take in my outfit. He coughs to cover the slip, and I press my lips together to keep myself from smiling.

"In that case, thank you for the kind words—and for the opportunity. Really. Things have moved fast for me the last few months, but it's nice to have someone looking out for me."

I glance down the table. Kevin is talking with Danica and another woman. We meet eyes, and he raises an eyebrow. I raise my eyebrow back at him. *What are you trying to say, Mr. Wong?*

"So, is Nate still going strong on the startup?" Carter asks.

Why is he bringing up Nathan when he knows we just broke up?

"Things are starting to shape up, I guess. He'd be really happy to find funding for it this year so it can actually become something. Um . . ."

I don't want to talk about Nathan right now, and I glance away. Carter seems to get the hint and says in a not-entirely-convincing tone, "I hope it works out for him."

Our food arrives, and we eat our meals while chatting with the other people around us. Things eventually wrap up, and as we start to leave the restaurant, Kevin pulls me aside and asks if I'd like to go out for a drink.

"Sure. You know any good places?"

"Some guy I was sitting with told me Cedar Door. We could try that," he says, opening up his phone to look it up.

Just then, Danica exits the restaurant with Carter and overhears us. "That's a great place. Awesome patio outside. Let's do it."

I'm facing away from Danica and try to SOS Kevin with my eyes. He grins and mouths at me, "It's okay."

"So," I ask, "are we walking or driving?"

"It's close by. We can walk," Danica says. She's wearing heels, but she must be used to them because she walks fast. We all try to keep up. I smile to myself, remembering my conversation with Carter last night about how Danica is "intense." Her speedy Friday-night bar-crawl pace is just one good example.

While Kevin and Carter lag behind discussing Austin real estate, Danica and I walk ahead. She surprises me and links her arm to mine, leaning in to talk with me. "Sarah, I told you before, but you did a really good job today. Not every woman can hold her own in a group of senior male colleagues, but you were confident and well-spoken. Good for you."

A *compliment? From the villainess?* And now I know which feminist girlfriend Carter was referring to. I noticed her paying attention while I spoke during today's meeting, but she didn't ask me any questions. We haven't actually spoken all that much beyond pleasantries and tight smiles.

"Thanks for the kind words, Danica." *Maybe she's not so bad after all.*

"So, I heard that you and Nate Goldman are dating," she says. *Well, that didn't take long.* I glance at Kevin, who has overheard the conversation, and give him an "I told you so" look. He grimaces comically back at me.

"Yes, we are," I say. There's more to the story, of course. At this point, she and I could be having a Nathan Goldman exes retreat, but I'm not disclosing any Nathan-related information to her.

I consider changing the subject, but before I even have a chance, she asks, "How long have you been together?"

I shrug nonchalantly and give a noncommittal "not very long" answer. We arrive at the bar and head inside. I hold Kevin's arm to stay back and tell him I'm going to need his help tonight with Danica.

"I don't want to get into this with her. The whole ex-girlfriend, and well ...." I trail off. I guess that I, too, am an ex now, but it's hard to think of myself that way.

"I got you, girl," Kevin says with a wink. He's an unlikely rom-com sidekick, but under duress, I'll take what I can get.

Just as I'm about to follow Kevin and Danica—who is unsurprisingly leading the way—out to the patio, though, Carter touches my arm to get my attention.

"Intense?" he whispers in my ear.

I laugh. "Yeah, something like that."

"Don't let her intimidate you. She doesn't have anything on you. Professionally or otherwise."

He grabs my hand to lead me out to the patio. It's a little uncomfortable for me—the only person's hand I've held in six months is Nathan's. When we join Kevin and Danica at the table outside, I note the overly interested look on her face, and I slip my hand out of his. Carter doesn't seem to notice since at that moment, the server comes to our table and asks what we'd like to drink.

Kevin is sitting next to Danica, and Carter has taken a seat, which leaves only one option—sitting next to Carter across from Kevin.

"Sangria?" Danica asks us.

"Tequila!" Kevin says.

"Sangria, please," I tell the server. "A pitcher."

"Kevin, we're not in college anymore. The last time I saw you drink tequila? Well, we won't talk about what ensued," Danica says.

Carter and I burst out laughing, and Kevin comically holds up a "shh" finger to his lips.

"The last time I saw *you* drink tequila—" he begins to say but then stops abruptly with a quick glance at me.

"Go on," I tell him. "Share with the class, Kev."

"It might not be an appropriate story in present company," he says, giving me a meaningful look. *Ah, it must involve Nathan.*

"Kevin and I—and Nate—just did a lot of dumb stuff in college," Danica explains. She says it in a way to suggest she knows things about Kevin—and Nathan—that I don't.

"Wait, I thought you guys knew each other from the Bay Area. You all went to college together?" Carter asks.

"Yeah," Danica, Kevin, and I all say.

Oh, shit. Does he not know that Danica used to date Nathan? Kevin and I meet each other's eyes. "Should we stop this or not?" is what I sense we're trying to telepathically ask each other.

It seems like Danica—ever cool and collected—is realizing she might've made a misstep. She swallows, but before she has to answer, the server returns with our pitcher of sangria.

"Oh, goodie," I say, feeling an illogical desire to help her out. What can I say? We bonded over feminism. "I love sangria." Danica shoots me what seems like a grateful look.

"Well, you like red wine," Carter says, and her expression instantly turns colder.

"I do," I say, matter-of-factly, but change the subject. "So, Danica. How's Austin?"

"I really like it. Definitely better weather than Washington, and I like it better than the Bay Area, too. It has tech, but there are also a lot of other things going on, unlike Silicon Valley." At that, she rolls her eyes. "Definitely better dating options here."

Damn, this girl is savage. I check Carter out of the side of my eye to see if he's listening. He's looking at his phone. I notice his mouth twitch as if amused, but he doesn't say anything. I think he heard her, but he's playing it cool.

Danica and Kevin begin to discuss the West Coast's finer points, including ski sites, and I drink my sangria, not having much to add. I hate cold weather and skiing. Carter types something on his phone and shows me the screen. "Intense." I press my lips together to avoid smiling.

The conversation flows, as does the sangria, and Carter—and his hands, his eyes—are hovering somewhere near the boundary of acceptability. I can feel the warmth of his body close to mine. He's had at least a few drinks between dinner and the bar, and I notice him glance down—I guess his willpower reserves have been depleted—from time to time at my bare arms and the short hem of my dress that shows off my legs. One of his hands rests on his thigh under the table, and his fingers brush my bare skin. *An accident?* He bites his lip, his eyes shift down again, and he moves his leg closer to mine—touching. No, *this man doesn't do anything by accident.*

"I need some water. I'm going to check what happened to our server," Kevin announces, jumping up.

"I'll come with you," Danica says. She's gotten a bit clingy with Kevin ever since we sat down, and it's none of my business. But knowing what I know about her, Kevin seems like he's playing with fire in more ways than one.

They head inside, and I turn to Carter. He's quiet, purposely—playfully—avoiding my gaze, and I break the silence. "That was rude, what she said before."

He meets my eyes. "About dating options?"

"Yeah, you two must've met out in California, right?"

He nods.

"She doesn't know what she's talking about," I say.

"I agree, but . . ." He narrows his eyes. "What do *you* mean?"

"I mean that . . . you're a perfectly nice guy."

"What a glowing recommendation," he says, his eyes dancing and a sexy smile replacing his serious expression. "That's the best you can do?"

"Competent manager . . . invested in my . . . professional development?"

"True. But is that really it?"

He waits patiently to see if—or what—I'll answer.

"Carter," I say, hesitating for just a moment. "You know what you are."

"What am I?"

I quickly glance down from his eyes to his mouth, hoping he doesn't notice. "You're . . . a great guy. Smart, successful, athletic . . ."

A smug look crosses his face, so I change my tack.

"But so ugly. Really horrendous," I tease.

He cracks a smile, enjoying this game. "You find me ugly, huh?" He turns toward me, placing his hand behind my back—close to my butt—on the chair.

"*Super* ugly," I retort. I can play this game, too.

"That's good news," he says, leaning in further.

"And why is that?" I ask, too eagerly to convincingly maintain my quickly crumbling facade of composure.

"Because the way you look right now—your lips and the way your hair's falling onto your shoulders, not to mention those legs of yours . . ." He places a large hand just above my knee and massages my leg.

Gazing directly into my eyes now, he presses his lips together. Those lips and his thumb tracing lightly over my quad muscle are making it very hard for me to focus.

"You know," he whispers in my ear, "I can barely even look at you without wanting to . . ."

"Yes?" I ask in a whisper.

"Run away screaming," he says and pinches my leg.

"What?" I say, surprised. I even giggle, and it sounds flirty—embarrassingly so—to my ears. I look away momentarily from his piercing gaze, but then I feel him turn my head back with a soft hand on my chin.

"But it also makes me want to do other things." His eyes move to my lips. "Seeing you today, so confident and in your element, it was . . . very hot. I've just been thinking about you, and wanting to be near you, close enough to touch you, to kiss you."

He moves his hand up my leg, and in a split second, I can imagine what it would be like to have his hands all over me. I take a sharp breath in. He seems to notice and moves closer, sliding his hand further up my thigh. He's squeezing it and moving it up, ever so slowly, after each squeeze, closer to my butt.

"You're a smart . . ." *Squeeze.* "Decisive." *Higher.* "Woman." He's about two inches from my lace underwear. Does he know how nervous I am? How turned on I am? "And I think." *Wicked grin.* "You. Know. What. You. Want."

His hand has crept up as far as my position will let it, and his pointer finger is lazily tracing the edge of the lace over my butt.

I can barely breathe at this point but manage to choke out, "And what exactly do you think I want?"

He closes the remaining gap between us and whispers in my ear, "I think you want to wrap those strong legs of yours around me while I make you come up against a hotel room wall."

Good god. In addition to everything else he's good at, he also knows how to talk dirty.

My legs feel weak, and if I were standing, I'd collapse for sure. He glances down at my breasts, and I wonder just how obvious it is that I'm aroused. As his eyes meet mine, the curled-up corners of his mouth indicate he knows exactly where things stand on my side.

Then he leans back. "Or maybe you'd rather I bend you over and bite your neck—"

"Stop," I say weakly.

"Stop? I thought you'd like that kind of talk."

I do.

He's moved his hand just the tiniest bit closer to the gap between my legs. He *must* be able to feel my heat there. And I gasp softly.

"Mmmm. I guessed right. You *do*," he says, the gleam in his eye unmistakable. "Sarah, did you stop breathing?"

Maybe. No, definitely.

"I should probably check for signs of life."

And then his lips are on mine. They are soft and taste of sangria, and as they gently but skillfully explore my mouth, I melt into him. *Fuck, this man knows how to kiss.*

It's hot—correction, scorching—and I'm more than primed for it after last night, my time in the hotel shower earlier, and the way he's been looking at me and talking to me tonight.

One of his arms slips around the back of my neck as he angles my head back. His other hand—previously on my ass—moves to my waist. His hands are large, and I'm overly aware of his thumb tracing over my ribs, just under my breast.

I use one hand to balance myself as the other begins to explore the pec muscle partially exposed in the open V-neck of his shirt.

I can't seem to pull myself away. His hands on me—his lips on mine—are a fire about to consume me. I'm vaguely aware that we're in a public place, but I can't seem to make myself care enough to pull away. He smells good, he tastes even better, and he's making me feel goddamn terrific. All of it is almost enough to make me forget the terrible week I've had. And the thought of why exactly I've felt so bad, but more so what I'm risking by doing this—a chance, albeit small, but still a chance with Nathan—makes me jerk away.

I pull back and inhale quickly.

"Carter," I say, exhaling his name, trying to catch my breath. "We can't do this."

I turn to check if Kevin and Danica have come back. *No, thank god.*

"Why not?" he asks, sounding confused. Reading my mind, he says, "Sarah, you need to be with someone who deserves you. He doesn't know how lucky he was, and . . . I overheard what you told Erin at the office one day—about him giving you a hard time about work. Some guys can't handle being with a woman who's successful."

I'm shaking my head. I'm not sure why exactly, but this is all wrong.

He continues, almost desperately, "I'm not that guy. I'm the opposite of that guy. I think I'm proving it, no?"

"It's . . . it's not that. It's—" Wrong. Despite feeling really, *really* right, it's wrong.

"What then?"

It's not like it is with Nathan.

That's the standard, apparently. The problematic but obviously very real standard—how Nathan makes me feel. Not just what he does for my body, but what he does to my heart.

Fuck. I'm messed up.

Carter's eyes are trained on me. He waits for me to say something, but before I can even begin to answer, Kevin comes back to the table, holding a pitcher of sangria and a bowl of tortilla chips.

"Success!" Kevin declares, setting everything down on the table.

"Where's Danica?" I ask in an attempt to talk about literally anything other than what just happened.

"Oh, I think she went to the restroom," he says. He pours a few glasses of sangria and raises his glass for a toast. "To mergers and acquisitions!"

At this point, Danica comes back and wraps her perfectly manicured fingers around her glass of sangria. "To new friends, too," she says, raising her glass at me and Carter with a sly smile. But then she turns her attention to Kevin, putting her arm around his shoulder. "Can you believe it? Still having fun after all these years, huh?"

Kevin's smile doesn't reach his eyes, which are focused on me. I stand up, mutter an excuse about needing the restroom, and head inside. But instead of walking to the restroom, I flee, bursting through the front door of the bar onto the sidewalk, almost running into a few people.

"Hey!" they yell at me, surprised.

I ignore them and wander down the sidewalk a store or two, and lean up against a brick wall.

What have I done? My breathing is labored, and I'm beginning to freak out. I'm leaning against the wall, replaying everything that just happened in my head, when I notice Kevin jogging over to me.

"Hey, you okay?"

I look down, trying to hide my face—my eyes are tearing up—when Kevin's comical but kind expression pops up in my line of sight, currently directed at the ground.

"What's going on?" he asks, using one hand to lift my chin, forcing me to look at him.

Judging by the expression on his face, I must look terrible. "Shit, what happened?"

I press my lips together and fight the urge to run away. I don't say anything. I can't.

He narrows his eyes at me. "Are you sick?"

I shake my head.

"What. Happened?" he asks again.

I run my hands through my hair. "I did something careless. Like, really reckless."

He places a gentle hand on my arm.

"Carter," I say.

Kevin's eyes lock on mine. Then he starts to nod like he suddenly understands everything without me saying a word.

"What happened, Sarah? Do you want me to go kick his ass?"

The thought of Kevin, fit but lithe Kevin, trying to kick Carter's ass is laughable, but man, do I appreciate the sentiment. He starts to stalk off back toward the bar, but then he doubles back and looks at me. He can't seem to decide if he wants to go after Carter—for whatever he thinks Carter did to me—or come back to make sure I'm alright.

The expressions on his face flicker back and forth between anger, confusion, and concern, and if I weren't utterly distraught, I might find it funny.

"Kev, he didn't hurt me. He . . . kissed me." *And a few other things. And I let him.*

"What? Did you tell him to stop?"

I hesitate. "Something like that." *Liar.*

"Motherfucker."

"I think I want to go."

"Of course. I'll go with you. We can head back to the hotel."

"Kev?"

"Yeah?"

"Thanks for being such a good friend."

"Of course," he says and pulls me into a sideways hug. "Let's get out of here, just in case our friends come out to find us."

"Good idea."

***

On our walk back, Kevin's usual humor is on overdrive. I realize he's quite drunk, but he was holding it together while I was telling him what happened earlier.

We arrive at the hotel, and he trips on the way in, but then does a funny sideways glance left-to-right, and says, "We cool, we cool," which sends us into fits of laughter. I'm drowning, but he's somehow keeping me afloat.

It's a nice hotel, and our boisterous arrival earns us a warning glance from the stern-looking doorman. When we get to the elevator, I ask him which floor he's on.

He shrugs. "I'm so tired, I can barely see straight. And the last four drinks I've had"—he holds up his fingers to count—"aren't helping."

"Okay, give me your key," I say.

"Okay, it's right—" he stops and puts his hand on his back pocket. "Shit, in my other pants."

"No worries. We'll go ask for another one," I say, but there's nobody working the reception desk when we walk over there.

We wait for a few minutes before the doorman informs us that the receptionist went on her break.

"Alright, um, let's leave them a note—" I begin to say.

"256."

"Huh?"

"256. My room number. Two to the eighth power."

"Okay," I reply, once again amazed at how these programmer brains work. I write a note for the receptionist that we need a new key and to please call up to my room when she's back for us to come down to retrieve it.

"You're such a good project manager, Sarah."

I snort. "Thanks, I guess. You want to come up to my room until she gets back? We can call down in a bit or wait for her to call me and then come get the key."

"Sure."

In my room, I offer Kevin a bottle of water. He cracks the cap seal and guzzles it.

"How can you drink so much and still be thirsty?" he ponders, sticking his tongue out. *How did I not know what a goofball he can be?*

Just then, my phone buzzes, and I check the text that came in.

"We should talk."

No, Carter. We shouldn't. We should probably never talk again. But then I notice the text right above it, the one I sent to Nathan earlier tonight.

It's not Carter. It's Nathan responding to me with a message so vague I don't know how to feel about it. Is it "We should talk" with an implied "So we can work things out?" Or is it more "We should talk" followed by an unspoken, "So we can end things properly?"

I glance up to find Kevin, currently seated on a chair near the window, looking at me curiously.

"From Nathan," I tell him.

"The plot thickens . . ."

"Kevin, please," I plead, collapsing in a heap on the bed and stuffing my phone underneath a pillow.

His teasing expression softens. "So, what happened with you and Carter, huh?"

I press my lips together, not answering.

"Sarah, listen. Shit happens, you know? Did *you* initiate the kiss?"

"No," I reply quickly.

"But you just didn't stop it quite as quickly as you should have?"

"How did you know? Did you see us?"

"Nah, but . . . let's just say I've seen stuff like that happen." He gives me a knowing look. I understand, without further explanation, exactly what he's referring to. He was there the night Danica started making out with Nathan, and Nathan took, well, more than a few seconds to come to his senses and stop it.

"It's okay. I won't tell Nate."

"I don't want you to lie for me, Kev."

"I'm not going to. I'm just . . . Well, I'm just gonna hold my tongue . . . better than you—or Nate—know how to," he says and starts cracking up. "Oh my god. I'm so tired. And sooooo drunk. Where is Mrs. Reception?"

"Want to call down there?"

"Would you hate me if I just slept on the extra bed? I can barely move."

His body has been sliding, almost oozing, down the chair little by little. His cheeks are pink, and even his usually perfect hair is mussed.

"Let me pull down the covers," I say, getting up. "I'll even tuck you in."

His shoes are already off, so I hold the covers open for him to slide in. He does, but he's a little off-balance and grabs my arm, pulling me to a sitting position on the bed next to him.

"Sarah?" he says softly. He looks intently into my eyes, and I notice for the first time ever how genuine—god, tender—his dark brown eyes are.

"Yeah?"

"You know you're great, right?"

He's acting strange, but I give him the benefit of the doubt, considering I've said and done a few of my own dumb things tonight.

"Who knew you're such a sweet guy?" I tease.

"I want to tell you something," he says earnestly.

In an equally serious tone, I reply, "Okay."

"You know the first night you met Nate? At the bar?"

I know exactly which night he means. The night of my one-night stand with Nathan. The night I thought would fade into my dating history. One I'd look back on years from now with a twinkle in my eye. And yet, it has shaped the last six months of my life and seems destined to do so for a while.

"Yeah?"

"I pointed you out to him. I knew you were a great girl, even from fifty feet away."

"Really?"

"I noticed Cam. Then I saw you, and I knew you were special." He touches my face gently. It's awkward—he'll probably die of embarrassment if I mention it to him in the morning—but after the rough night I've had, his kind touch soothes my fragile soul.

"Thank you," I say, squeezing his forearm.

"Nate didn't realize how lucky he got with you. He might be stupid, but I'm not."

Seems like a common sentiment tonight. But what is he trying to say?

But before I can ask him, he closes his eyes. The poor guy is completely worn out. I gently pull the blanket up over his shoulders and let him sleep.

***

Despite the exhausting day, I'm wide awake. I start my bedtime skincare routine in the bathroom, hoping that going through the usual motions might trick my mind into sleepiness. While I wash my face, all sorts of thoughts flit through my mind. *What did Nathan mean? "We should talk."*

There's a niggling feeling in my stomach, something a bit uncomfortable about Kevin spending the night in my room. I trust him—not to mention he's dead to the world right now—but I'm already on thin ice with Nathan. Once I tell him what happened with Carter—I *have* to tell him—telling him I spent the night with his best friend certainly won't help my case. I need to get Kevin's key. If I succeed in chasing down the wayward receptionist, maybe I'll just go crash in his room. I close the door softly behind me, and as I make my way down the dimly lit hallway to the elevator, I think back on this shit show of a night.

"You need to be with someone who deserves you . . . Some guys can't handle being with a woman who's successful," Carter had said. *"I'm the opposite of that guy. I think I'm proving it."*

In some ways, he's everything Nathan isn't—a little too cocky for his own good, so damn sure of himself, and god, he knows how to kiss—and touch—a woman. He's right. He's done so much to help me professionally since I've known him, which forces me to consider, yet again, a painful question. *Why did Nathan try to block me?* Carter—that cocky son of a bitch, who just as easily could have hit on me without offering me any professional opportunities—has supported me and encouraged me to dream. I was right when I told Nathan that Carter was a key for me.

I want to get back together with Nathan, don't I? Yet, as I make my way down to the lobby, thoughts of Carter—his hands on my skin, his lips on mine, his tongue in my mouth—begin to push any of the positive feelings I have for Nathan out of my mind.

I find the receptionist, a woman with tired-but-kind eyes, back at her post and consider how miserable it must be to work overnight.

"How are you doing?" I ask.

"Tired, actually. Pulling a double today. I must've been taking my cat nap earlier when you came by for your key. This is your note, right?" she asks, holding up the post-it we left on her computer monitor earlier.

"Yep. Can I get another key?"

"Sure, sweetie. Which room is it?"

That would be pertinent information, but I find myself at a loss. "Um, can you look it up by account that paid for it? LightVerse?"

"Let me see," she replies, clacking away on the keyboard. After a moment of searching, she declares "1024" triumphantly.

It sounds familiar and jogs my memory about something Kevin said earlier. I press the button on my phone. "Siri, is 1,024 a power of two?"

"1,024 is a power of two. Two to the tenth power," Siri responds.

I smile at the receptionist. "Perfect."

She laughs. "Mathematician?"

"Computer programmer," I respond wryly.

She clicks around on the computer and runs a key card through a scanner. "Here you go," she says and hands me the key. "You should get to bed. It's late."

"Yeah, it's been a long night."

"I saw you with a guy earlier. You make a cute couple."

I smile, thinking of Kevin, tucked in tight and asleep in my extra bed right now. She must have seen us when we headed out to dinner earlier tonight.

"Have a good night," I tell her.

As the elevator doors open and I step inside, I remember taking the elevator with Carter two nights ago. He'd held the door for me, touching my back as I'd gotten on. An older couple had stepped on, and the woman had remarked, "What a cute couple." The receptionist using those same words now must have jogged the sudden memory. Two nights ago, I'd simply smiled back at the couple and not corrected them. Carter had glanced at me and told them, "Thank you," with a playful smirk thrown my direction afterward. Nothing more on the topic was said, and they had gotten off at the second floor. I had exited at the third floor, and Carter had continued on to the tenth—to 1024. That's why it sounded familiar a few minutes ago.

I stare at the seemingly innocent plastic card in my hand right now and realize with a start that the key I'm holding isn't Kevin's. It's Carter's.

DISASTER RECOVERY PLAN

NATHAN

Nathan trudges to the bathroom and sticks his head under the faucet to drink some water. He's been up at least three times since laying down in bed earlier. Thoughts of Sarah—her face, her voice, her laugh—are keeping him from settling down and falling asleep.

It's been a week since he broke it off with her, and at least ten times a day, he questions whether it was the right thing to do. When they last talked, he could have shared with her that he had just gotten awful news. He could have waited until he had calmed down before they talked. But it all came at him at once. The news about LightVerse stealing his idea and finding out that the asshole behind it was whisking Sarah off to Austin.

He only wanted to protect what they were building together, but months of frustration and doubt had fueled the conversation, resulting in angry words and accusations. It all had gone so, so wrong. *Could he have saved it? If they'd been sitting together in the same room, would they have communicated better? Would she have gotten so angry? Would he?*

In the time they haven't spoken, he hasn't learned much more about the LightVerse project that sounds suspiciously similar to his, but he's somewhat reassured that he has the provisional patent application in place. He doesn't know when or if LightVerse might have filed its own, but he hopes he beat them to the punch.

He's also spent hours thinking about how LightVerse got information about his startup in the first place. There's no way Sarah could've accidentally leaked sufficient information to Carter or to anybody else there. She's smart, but she hasn't been in the code like Nathan has. And he's certain she wouldn't do something so careless or dishonest. He's privately ashamed his mind even went there in the first place.

He opens his phone and reads the text Kevin sent him earlier today.

Kevin: Your girl knocked it out of the park today.

She's not my girl, he thinks sadly.

He's not surprised at all that she did an amazing job. He almost texted her "congratulations," but after asking her to forgo what might very well end up being her big break, he knew it wouldn't be welcome.

But then he'd gotten a text from her. `Can we talk when we both get back?`

So, he texted her back. `We should talk.`

Hearing her voice would make him feel better right now, but what he really needs is to see her, to be in the same room as her. He's sure if they can just talk—together, close to one another—they'll be able to figure it out.

PIVOT

He feels warm. Someone is hugging him from behind. Even now, in his dreams, he somehow knows it's been a long day, a long night, and the touch feels comforting. Then it feels much more than comforting. He's turned on. Not very surprising with the dreams he's been having lately.

He moves his hand down to adjust himself and realizes that he is awake and that he's not alone.

"What?"

"Hey, there," she whispers. He doesn't even need to turn over to see who it is. It's completely dark in the room, but he knows her voice. He dreams of it.

"Wh-What are you doing?" he asks.

"I thought I'd join you."

"Oh." *Oh.* He turns over and touches her face, then her shoulder, feeling his way. "Are you . . . sure?"

"I thought about what you said."

"And?" he asks.

"Well, you do quite the sales pitch, and you convinced me . . . that I'm special."

"And you want to be with me?"

"Yeah, I think I do," she replies. He can hear the smile in her voice, but he wants to be sure.

"Even with—"

"Quit talking now," she warns. "Use your mouth for more important things."

He laughs. "I love a bossy woman."

"In that case, kiss me," she orders. "Now."

She doesn't have to ask twice, and he kisses her hungrily, his mouth crushing into hers. When he comes up for air, he asks her, "Am I dreaming?"

"No," she says, taking his hand, which is resting on her waist, and moving it up her body to the side of her breast. "But I had a dream about you last night."

"You did?" he asks, surprised but slowly beginning to understand that this is actually happening.

She caresses his bare shoulder with her soft hands before leaning in to kiss his chest. He takes advantage of the angle and slides his hand down to her sweet, sexy ass and realizes she's only wearing a bra and lacy underwear.

"And what exactly did we do in your dream?"

"Well, I could tell you, or I could show you," she whispers, sliding a hand between his legs and curling her hand around him.

"*Definitely* show me."

She laughs. "That's what I thought you'd say. Maybe we'll turn on the light. I want to see you the first time."

He reaches over to turn on the lamp. "I can't believe this is happening."

"You mentioned that already." She slides her hands down his chest and hooks her fingers into the front of his boxer briefs. "Take them off."

"Okay," he says, licking his lips lightly. But before he does, he leans up and undoes the front clasp of her bra, and he's greeted by a sight that makes him even harder than he was already. He takes in the view of her amazing body as she helps him out of his boxers.

She gently pushes him back onto the bed, lying down, and straddles him. "Where am I allowed to put my mouth on you, lover?" she asks.

"Anywhere you fucking want, baby."

She readjusts herself between his legs. "Let's start here, then." As she slides down, he can feel her breasts—her hard nipples—rub lightly over his thighs. She meets his eyes and smiles when she sees the effect she's having on him and lightly grips him, but just as she's about to put her mouth on him, he puts his hand on her face, stopping her.

"No. I need you first."

"You need me?"

He nods and leans up so he can reach her and pull her toward him. He pushes her to lay on her side and lifts one leg up. He bites the inside of one thigh, and she inhales sharply.

"You like that?" he asks.

She nods, not uttering a word.

He pushes her further back, so now she's on her back. He hovers above her. "Take them off. I want access."

"Access?" she asks, laughing.

In lieu of a verbal response, he simply tugs the waist of her sexy underwear down and traces kisses down her stomach.

"Oh, that's nice," she says, exhaling, satisfied.

He palms both of her breasts now.

"I knew they would be amazing, but . . . damn."

He parts her legs and begins to kiss her in the space between her belly button and where he's headed next.

"Do you want this?" he asks. He can tell she does, but he wants to hear her say it.

"I want someone who makes me feel good, and *you* make me feel good."

"I can definitely make you feel good," he replies in a low voice.

Parting her with a gentle touch, he leans into her and slips his tongue onto her clit, and she responds with a satisfied whimper. He kisses, licks, sucks—he loses track—because he's been dreaming of her, her taste, for too long, and it's all finally happening. It's a blur of his tongue on her, his fingers inside of her, her hands in his hair, and one of his hands on himself—because he simply can't help himself—while she cries out his name.

When her breath finally steadies, she pulls him up to her and tells him in a low voice, "Come here. Come . . . in me."

He crawls on top of her, bracing himself with his arms, and positions himself between her legs, leaning down to whisper in her ear, "I think I've wanted you since the moment I saw you."

"Good things come to those who wait?"

"Well, we waited a while. You ready for more?"

"Hell, yes."

"Right answer," he says. All of a sudden, he seems to realize he has no idea where a condom is.

"Don't worry. I came prepared," she says and twists her body to grab a small package from the nightstand.

"Damn, you're good."

"I bet I can make you say that again," she says, snickering.

"I don't doubt it," he replies, taking the small foil packet from her.

After rolling the condom on, he slides into her. "You feel . . . so fucking good."

Her only response is a satisfied moan. After a few minutes of concentrated effort and whispered mentions of how good it is—how many more times they need to do this tonight—they both finish.

Lying spent on the bed, he asks her, "Was that at all like your dream?" He hopes she'll say "yes."

"Even better." She snuggles into him, and he falls asleep, his hand resting on her rib cage, thinking of one thing and one thing only. She's finally his.

Zero-Day Attack

NATHAN

They're about twenty minutes from touching down in San Jose, and Nathan is staring out the plane window, trying to recognize any of the landmarks thousands of feet below on the ground. Since moving here from Illinois a year ago, a lot has happened. Up until a few weeks ago, he would've said it was mostly good, but he's scared to think that this afternoon will likely have a big impact on how he looks back on his first year in the Bay Area. A raging success with a startup exit and a solid, loving relationship? Or a complete disaster should his attempts at founding a startup and building a relationship with Sarah both fail?

Maybe Sarah's text last night about wanting to talk will be a step in the right direction. *What should I do now? Go back and wait for her at her place or go back to my place downtown?* Her flight is supposed to land in an hour, so he settles on her place. She won't kick him out. At least, he doesn't *think* she will.

When the plane lands, he switches off airplane mode on his phone to check his messages, and he notices something that surprises him. A few months ago, messages from "Dan," a.k.a. Danica, were common. She was helping them connect with the right people at LightVerse before the exit, but he hasn't gotten anything from her in a while. *What's this all about?* She's in Austin now, and he wonders if maybe she met Sarah in the office. He braces himself and opens it.

Danica: Hey Nate - it's been a while. We should really catch up.

No, *thanks.*

Danica: Met your girl in Austin this week. We all went out last night. Had some drinks. Thought you might like to see some pics.

It looks like she has sent a photo, but it's still loading. He hopes it's not some unsolicited selfie of her half-dressed like the one Sarah intercepted last spring. That's the last thing he needs right now.

People are getting off the plane around him, so he gathers his bag from the floor and heads toward the exit. He walks through the terminal toward the ride-share pickup area, and his phone vibrates in his hand while a few more emails and texts load now that he has better cell service. He glances down. The screen with Danica's text is still open, and the photo has loaded.

It's dark, and it takes him a minute to register what he's looking at. What he *thinks* he's looking at is the back of Sarah's head. He notes the dress she's wearing more than her hair, but he knows it's her. And she's kissing someone. It's clear because someone's hand is on the back of her neck, and her head is tilted the same way as when she kisses him, Nathan.

For a second, it all doesn't compute. The only thing he can think is that this is some cruel joke from the universe. "Look, dummy, your worst nightmare! Photographic evidence!"

He's stopped in the middle of the concourse, just staring at his phone, and people are flowing around him like he's a stone lodged in the middle of a river.

For a split second only, the question "Who is she kissing?" comes to mind, but he doesn't need to ask because he knows. Carter. If it weren't clear already, he zooms in on the image and sees the fucking tattoo on the arm around Sarah.

The world seems to stop revolving and explode all at the same time, like some apocalyptic mushroom cloud at the end of a Cold War-era movie. His eyes fall shut. Seeing—just being—is too much right now. Then he feels someone lightly touch his arm.

"Are you alright, young man?" an older woman asks him.

He looks straight into her kind eyes and struggles to find his voice. "No, definitely not."

She gives him a bewildered look, and he stalks off, ducking into a nearby restroom to splash his face with water.

He doesn't know what to do, but he can't stay in the bathroom forever. He pulls his phone from his pocket, scared to even unlock it, but he does so quickly, taps on the Uber app, and enters Sarah's address.

P0 Incident

SARAH

I texted Cam earlier to see if she could pick me up at the airport, but she hasn't answered. It's been a wild few days—I'm completely drained—and I just want to go home and rest. But I have to talk to Nathan.

When? Where? How? I don't know, but we certainly have a lot to talk about. He's been saying for a while that Carter wants something more from me, and I always told him that things were fine. I thought I could handle it. *Or did* I? That's what plagues me the most, that I might have walked knowingly into the whole situation.

He'll be angry, and he deserves to be. My mom always says that in a relationship, you can't avoid the hard conversations because the problems will always catch up with you at some point. She's right. I owe him the truth, no matter how painful it all is. Even if it means our relationship is over.

I check Nathan's location on Find My Friends, and he's already at our place. I guess it's *my* place now? I order an Uber and head out into the dry San Jose heat to meet my destiny.

NATHAN

Nathan is sitting on the couch when he hears Sarah's key in the door.

"Hey, there," she says, giving him a hesitant smile and setting her things down.

"Hey," he says.

She takes off her shoes and gives him an uneasy look. He can understand why. He's feeling pretty grim and probably looks it, too. She walks into the kitchen to wash her hands. *Is she stalling?* Then she comes back to the living room and sits on the chair at a right angle to where he's sitting on the couch.

"I—" she begins to say.

"How could you?" he blurts out, interrupting her.

She sighs. "You're right."

"So, you know what I'm talking about?"

"What *are* you talking about?"

"Don't make me say it," he says, anger boiling up in his stomach. "How could you not tell me what happened? Do I mean *nothing* to you?"

"I *wanted* to tell you today, in person. But . . . I guess this means someone already told you?" She sounds confused, but he doesn't have the patience for a lengthy explanation.

He notices her leg is twitching, a sure-fire Sarah sign of anxiety.

Good, let her be anxious. Let her feel as shitty as I do.

He picks up his phone sitting next to him on the couch and hands it to her, not meeting her eyes. Sarah glances at the screen, and her eyes widen. She takes a deep breath, then sets the phone face down on the coffee table.

"Where did you get that picture?"

"Does it matter?" he asks, picking up the phone and shoving it into his backpack at his feet.

"No, I guess it doesn't."

He narrows his eyes at her.

"I-I'm terrible. Is that what you want to hear?" she asks in a strained voice. He can see the tears filling her eyes, but not yet falling, as she almost whispers, "I'm sorry it happened. But you . . . fucking broke up with me. And . . . you're allowed to be mad and—"

"Of course I'm mad," he interrupts her. And to think he was coming back here today to say *he's* sorry to her, to try to make up. He gets up and strides toward the window.

SARAH

I knew Nathan would be upset when he found out, but I thought it was going to be on my terms. I didn't know I was walking into an ambush in my own home. I can see the veins of his forearm popping out, his hands braced on the window sill while he stares out the window.

I take a deep breath, trying to calm myself. One of us has to maintain control here.

"Can you look at me?" I ask, standing up and moving closer to him.

He refuses to turn around, and I won't force him into anything.

"Fine, don't look at me. But at least listen. We all went out, and I drank a little too much. We all did. We were all hanging out. And it was late—"

He turns to look at me. "I don't want to hear anymore. I don't *need* to hear anymore."

My surprise must show on my face. He stares at me coldly. "It's not like I can believe you anyway," he says in a harsh tone he's never used with me before.

"What?"

"You've been keeping things from me."

I close my eyes to keep tears from streaming down my face.

"Am I wrong?" he demands, and I snap them open.

Yes. No. *I don't know.*

"Show me your texts with him. Show me I'm wrong. Please." His voice cracks on the last word.

"What?" I ask. I'm confused, overwhelmed.

He picks up my phone and glances at the lock screen. He could open it. He knows my passcode the same way I know his. But we have an agreement. We don't check each other's phones.

He hands it to me and shrugs his shoulders. "If you've been honest with me, just show me."

I open it with my thumbprint. He can look. There's nothing there. I hand the phone back to him, and he begins to scroll through my texts, looking for a thread with Carter, surely. And then I remember. *The selfie.* The selfie meant for Nathan that I accidentally sent to Carter instead. *Did I delete it or not? Oh, no. Fuck, fuck, fuck.*

He looks at the thread, mostly stuff about where we were meeting for dinner last night. After I fled from the bar last night, thankfully, there were no texts asking what happened. He and I both know I let things go too far.

Nathan scrolls up a few times, skimming, but just as he's about to hand it back to me, his eyes narrow. And as if in slow motion, I see his finger touch the screen and scroll up one more time. He's looking at the drunk selfie of me and the accompanying text I sent Carter, "Wish you were here tonight."

He clenches his jaw and tosses my phone on the couch.

"Right."

"Nathan, it was a mistake. I didn't mean to send that to him. It was supposed to be—"

"Sarah. Enough. Just—"

"What?"

"Stop."

The muscle in his jaw pulses as he clenches it, and his beautiful brown eyes—usually full of curiosity or warmth—hold only resentment now. The acid rises in my throat, and my heart feels like it's being crushed. I want to look away—to hide from the pain—but I force myself to look at him. *I've done this. Me.*

I open my mouth, but nothing comes out, and in the split second my brain tries to generate words to verbalize something, anything, Nathan's brain must be working faster because—still as a stone a moment before—he runs his hands roughly through his hair and stalks toward the door to leave.

"Na—" I start to say.

"I'm leaving," he says, cutting me off. "I can't do . . ." His eyes scan the apartment, then finally land on me. "This," he finally mutters, shaking his head sadly. "I can't do this." His meaning is crystal clear. "This" means "us." Our grand attempt to fall in love and start a life together is over.

He grabs his roller bag and shoves his feet into his shoes. I don't have enough time. He's leaving, and the words begin to spill from my mouth. "Nathan, please don't go. Don't leave. I didn't mean for it to happen. I messed up. All of this—work, us—it was all so new and . . . I got confused."

"Confused?" he scoffs. "About who you love?"

That's not what I mean. It's all coming out wrong. But before I can clarify, he spits out, "I've never been confused. I love—" He winces. "Loved you."

My breath catches in my throat.

Past tense. No.

He stalks out the door, and I find myself unable to say or do anything. The click of the lock brings me out of my trance as the tears run down my face.

What have I done? And what the hell do I do now?

Null

It's late Sunday morning, and I'm still lying in bed. After Nathan stormed out yesterday, the first thing I did was break down and cry for an hour. I sat on the floor and replayed everything that's happened, not just in the most recent act in this play, but the past few months. *Did I gaslight him?* He knew that Carter was into me. So did I. And yet, I told him, again and again, "Everything is fine."

But it's not fine. It's lost. Our relationship—our past, our present, our future—are lost. I'm sure of it now. He broke up with me, and then he did it all over again a week later.

My phone buzzes somewhere in my pile of blankets, and I rifle through them in search of it. I open it to find a text from Erin.

> **Erin:** You're back, right? Brunch?
> **Sarah:** I'm back, but I'm not in the mood for brunch.
> **Erin:** Really?! Are you sick?
> **Sarah:** Something like that.
> **Erin:** Is it the rona?

Leave it to Erin to make me laugh when I feel like the living dead. I don't feel like talking about what happened, but I'll likely feel better if Erin's around.

Sarah: No. But I need to talk. You wanna come over?

Erin: <smiley face emoji> Yes, I'll bring brunch to you.

Forty-five minutes later, there's a knock at the door. In the meantime, I've managed to get out of bed and wash my face, though I'm still looking pretty rough. That much shows on Erin's face when I open the door and find her holding a bag of bagels and a tray with two coffees.

"Oh, honey," she says and sets everything down on the dining room table.

She comes and hugs me. She doesn't ask what's the matter.

"Erin—" I say and begin to cry again.

"I know, sweetheart. I know. It's going to be okay," she says and gestures for me to sit at the table with her.

"You know?"

Word travels fast. I assume Nathan told Kevin, and, well, I don't know why Kevin would tell Erin, but there it is. She knows. At least a few people know, and even though I didn't think it was possible, it makes me feel even worse. When I feel like I can breathe normally again, I tell her the story.

Erin knows that it didn't just start this week, that all of this has been building for a while. But as I pour out my heart to her, it becomes clearer to me just how many challenges Nathan and I have been facing—individually and also as a couple.

"It sounds like he's been having a really hard time with his work. It must be a big blow to his confidence to struggle when he knows he's capable but can't seem to pull it all together."

"Yeah, I always told him it would work out. I tried to encourage him. But I couldn't solve it for him. I don't know how."

"Sometimes people don't need someone to solve it for them. They just need them to listen."

I asked, but did I listen—really listen—to what he was saying? What he was too scared to say?

She sees the expression on my face. "Sarah, you're twenty-seven years old. Nobody expects you to be perfect. Not to mention, you also were dealing with a ton of new things at once. A change in your role, moving in with a new boyfriend, and . . . a *few* different kinds of pressure at work."

I nod, and the tears begin to roll down my face again. Erin pulls me into a hug and lets me cry as long as I need to.

"It's new. Raw," she says. "He's hurting, too. Give it some time. It takes guys some time to process their emotions."

There isn't enough time in the world to fix what I've done.

I shake my head and stare at my hands clasped in my lap. Not listening carefully to Nathan could maybe be forgiven, but what happened in Austin? No. "Carter started it, but I didn't stop him. And I enjoyed it. What's wrong with me?"

"Well, not to show my age, but I think Ross from *Friends* would have something to say about this one."

"Huh?"

She smiles. "Oh, I forgot. You were, like, a toddler when that show was on. I'm just saying that technically, you *were* 'on a break,' but it's still a pretty big fuck-up, especially since you still have feelings for Nathan."

My face drops.

"But you know that," she says.

"I know that," I concur.

"But," she says, "shit happens. And people recover. Relationships re-cover . . . when there's something worth recovering."

"He'll never forgive me. You didn't see the way he looked at me." My face crumples again. "Or the picture. If there hadn't been a picture, he would've known—I would've told him—but the picture—" I stop abruptly, suddenly realizing something. Who sent him the picture? There were only two other people with us. Kevin and Danica. Kevin would never hurt me this way . . . "God damn it."

"What?"

"It was Danica. She sent him the picture."

Erin's mouth forms an O.

"She's an evil genius. Oh my god. She was acting friendly with me like she wanted to be all buddy-buddy, working women. The whole time she was just waiting for me to screw up. Probably so she could go after Nathan again."

"You really think?"

"Well, she also used to date Carter, so there's that."

"You sure know how to make an enemy."

"Oh my god, Erin. What's wrong with me?"

"You behaved badly, but there's nothing wrong with you. Finish your coffee, eat a bagel, and then we're walking to the Rose Garden."

I groan.

"Up," she says. "Everyone knows that caffeine, carbs, and fresh air are the trifecta for getting over a breakup."

"I thought the third one was wine," I reply, as she grabs my hand and pulls me toward the door.

She winks at me. "You've whined enough, baby. Time to get moving."

BROKEN BUILD

NATHAN

Nathan returns the free weights he's been lifting to the rack and catches sight of himself in the mirrored walls of the small gym. He looks like shit. He considers going back upstairs and returning to the hermit state he's been in since Saturday—playing video games and eating carbs—but he promised his mom earlier that he'd get out of the house today. He made it down to the building's gym. *Counts for something.*

He steps on the treadmill and begins to jog. After a few minutes, he zones out. Running is usually therapeutic for him, but today, thoughts of Sarah plague him. He increases the incline, then bumps up the speed, hoping through simple physical exertion he'll be able to stop the endless loop of pointless questions playing in his mind. *How could Sarah do this to me? How could she be so callous?* Most importantly. *How did I read her so, so wrong?*

After twenty minutes, he powers down the treadmill and sits to stretch. As he wipes his face on his gym towel, memories from earlier in the year pop into his head. Specifically, Sarah coming to Seattle after they fought. She came because she knew his dad was in the hospital and he needed support. *It doesn't matter. One good deed doesn't cancel out what happened.* Deep down, he knows it's unhealthy to fixate on her shortcomings, but as long as he does that, he won't have to think about his own mistakes. The list is long. He should have expressed more interest in her successes at work. He should have shown more patience and communicated better.

He tried to tell her to distance herself from Carter, but maybe he should have simply been the type of man she wanted to come home to, someone she *wanted* to give her whole heart to. *Why wasn't I enough?*

He pulls himself to standing and heads upstairs. Only after he's inside the shower does he realize that he forgot *again* to buy shampoo. One more thing he left at Sarah's that he needs to replace. Has she thrown it out yet, or is she tripping over his belongings, wishing they were gone? Does she think of him when she sees his favorite coffee mug in the cabinet? Because he sure as hell thinks of her when he catches sight of her beloved bean bag near the picture window.

He leans his forearms against the shower wall as the scorching water flows down his back. It stings, but he relishes the pain. It distracts him momentarily from the weight in his chest.

After a long shower, he pads into his room to grab some clean clothes and finds Sarah's green t-shirt crumpled up on the floor of the closet, the only evidence of his meltdown yesterday. He found it tucked under the blanket near the foot of the bed. *Forgotten. Just like him.* He'd looked at it and, he's embarrassed to admit, sniffed it, hoping to find her scent still on it. Luckily or not, the faint, but still recognizable fragrance of *her* remained.

Just thinking about it now pisses him off, and he snatches it from the floor and balls it up to toss it in the garbage can. At the last second, he changes his mind and shoves it into the back of the closet. Still wrapped in a towel, he falls back onto his bed and stares at the ceiling. *I have to fucking get past this.*

Tomorrow, he promises himself. Tomorrow is the day. He will wake up, act like a human being again, and get to work.

It takes more than one day, though. "Tomorrow" turns into at least a few tomorrows. By the end of the week, he's nowhere near past it, but he's starting to feel a little lighter. He's actually beginning to make some progress with the startup. Kevin connected him with a friend of a friend who secured him a Zoom call with Redwood Capital, the holy grail of medical investment venture capitals. The call this morning went well, and this afternoon, he received a follow-up email informing him that if he can get his proof of concept and business model nailed down soon, he has an invitation to present to the venture capital in October. There's no guarantee they would fund a seed round—allowing him to hire some engineers to build out a more robust product—but it's a tangible sign of progress.

Still, he's painfully aware that he's on his own with no co-founder in sight. He can go it alone. He's technical, and he's been the Chief Product Officer at a successful startup, but there's something missing on the operations and business side of things. He has some feelers out in his own network and Kevin's, but no bites yet.

I have a chance to pitch and a great idea. It will just have to be enough. He opens a new spreadsheet and begins to make a list of all the things he'll need to do in the next couple months. Just seeing it all laid out is overwhelming. It's going to take a lot of hard work and a lot of time. *No job. No girlfriend. I've got nothing but time,* he thinks wryly. And so, he gets to work.

DATA TRANSFER

SARAH

It's Thursday morning, and I'm at my desk searching in Jira for a project I'm supposed to help kick off. All I can remember is that it starts with an "M," so I start my hunt for the project on the alphabetical search page. As I scroll through the different "M" options, trying to jog my memory, I notice something called Project Meteor. Projects at LightVerse have all kinds of strange—often astronomy or sci-fi related—code names. For some reason, this one piques my interest, and I scroll through the product backlog, interested to see what kinds of new features another team is developing.

MET-101: MVP User Interface for Test Results Display
MET-113: V2 Dashboard for Medical Professionals

Huh. That sounds . . . familiar.

I click into a few of the user stories to check the product requirements, and my stomach drops. A good 75 percent of what I'm looking at sounds exactly like Nathan's startup idea. *What the hell is going on here?*

Who can I talk to about this? It's not even a question. I text Kevin on WhatsApp instead of using the company messaging system:

Me: Have you heard of Project Meteor?

No response.

Me: Take a look in Jira when you're alone.

Just as I finish my text, Carter walks over to my desk. I shut my laptop and stand up.

"Hey, I haven't seen you in the office all week," he says. His hands are stuffed in his pockets, and he gives me—what I'm ashamed to admit is—a most adorable smile. "Want to get some coffee and catch up?"

Part of me is tempted to go with him. There are definitely things we'll have to sort out at some point. Pretending nothing happened isn't exactly the adult way of handling . . . whatever is going on between us. But who said I have to act like an adult anyway?

"I actually have to run. I'll see you soon?"

"Um, sure," he says, stepping back out of my way as I pack my bag. As I turn the corner to walk toward the elevator, I glance back and meet his eyes. He gives me a sad smile and turns to go.

Division by Zero

NATHAN

Nathan's sitting at his kitchen table, just staring at the computer screen when his phone buzzes.

> **Kevin:** I'm coming to get you. B-ball. You and me.
> **Nathan:** I'm busy.
> **Kevin:** Like shit you are. You're probably just staring at your laptop and not getting anything done.

How does he do that?

> **Kevin:** Meet me downstairs in 15.

Nathan knows that there's no arguing with Kevin when he's in CEO mode, so he relents.

> **Nathan:** Fine. See you soon.

He's waiting downstairs in front of the building, dressed to play basketball, when Kevin shows up twenty minutes later and rolls down the passenger window.

In lieu of a hello, Nathan asks, "Aren't you supposed to be working?"

"I took the day off," Kevin replies as Nathan gets into the passenger seat. "I thought you needed to get out of the house. You've been a little . . . mopey."

"Mopey?"

"You heard me," Kevin says.

Nathan stares out the window. "How's Kara doing?"

Kevin snorts. He's likely quite aware Nathan's changing the subject. "Good. How's your dad?"

"He's okay."

Familial inquiries covered, they ride in silence the rest of the way. When they reach the gym, they head inside and start by just shooting some hoops. Ball in hand, Nathan is grateful to have something else—besides Sarah, besides the startup—to focus on. A couple of guys join them for a pick-up game, and they play for about thirty minutes before taking a water break.

"It's good to be out with people, huh? Not awake at night, acting like a zombie," Kevin comments.

"How do you know when I sleep?" Nathan asks.

"Saw some of your commits on GitHub."

"Now you're stalking me on GitHub?"

"Well, I just happened to see that Python logger library project. Why are you wasting time on that? You need to be working on your own code."

"I *am* working on it, but when I'm stuck, I just check out some open-source projects. It helps me get the creative juices flowing."

Kevin nods. The other guys are going back on the court, and Nathan turns to join them.

"Wait a sec," Kevin says.

"Yeah?"

"You heard from Sarah lately?"

"I'm not talking to her. I don't want to talk *about* her."

"Well, I *am* talking to her, and I need to tell you something important."

"That's a pretty grave look on your face. If it's about Carter, I don't want to hear it. I can't believe she kissed that asshole while she was in Austin. Come to think of it. Where were you when all this was happening?"

"Well, if it happened when I think it did, then I was probably inside getting a pitcher of sangria with Danica."

This information while not the most pertinent detail of the situation, adds insult to injury.

"So, you hang out with Danica now?" Nathan challenges him.

"I wouldn't say we hang out. We *all* went out. Not very exciting," Kevin replies.

"Seems like it was pretty exciting for certain people."

"Sarah didn't kiss him," Kevin says.

"Looked like it from the picture."

"You have video? You saw *her* lean in and kiss *him*?"

"Same thing."

"You know better than anybody what it's like when you're feeling a little weak and someone acts first. Sound familiar, man, or you need me to refresh your memory?"

Nathan does *not* need a refresher. He remembers all too well what happened with Danica a few short months ago. She had taken matters concerning Nathan into her own hands—and lips—and he hadn't stopped her right away. He's fortunate that nobody had taken a picture to share with Sarah.

"No, that won't be needed." But he can't shake the feeling that something else might have happened *after* that moment, the one memorialized forever in that photo still sitting in his texts. "How do I know what happened after that? Maybe they spent the night together?"

"They didn't," Kevin says.

"How do *you* know?"

"She definitely didn't spend the night with Carter, dude."

"You seem to be avoiding my question," Nathan says, his voice harsh. "*How* do you know?"

Kevin considers him for a moment. Then he takes a deep breath and says, "I know she didn't spend the night with Carter because she spent most of it with me."

Nathan stands. Kevin seems to think his explanation has settled things and stands, too. Unfortunately for Kevin, this makes it that much easier for Nathan to lunge at him and shove him to the ground. Kevin is smaller than Nathan but not one to take a blow without fighting back. He stands up quickly and responds in kind. They're wrestling each other, not entirely unlike how they used to in college, but those times were in jest. Now they're both angry, and the adrenaline is pumping, testosterone pushing them forward.

Nathan elbows Kevin in the face, and blood spurts from his nose. The guys playing basketball on the court run over and try to break up the fight when Nathan suddenly pulls away. He takes in Kevin sprawled on the floor, now holding his face.

"Just . . . fuck off," Nathan spits out. He grabs his phone from the bench and stalks out of the gym, slamming the door open on his way out.

As the door closes, Kevin yells, "What the fuck's your problem, man?" But Nathan just keeps going.

GOING PUBLIC

ENCRYPTED

As they lay in his bed with the waning light of the day filtering through the sheer curtains, he glides his fingertips over her bare back.

"Stop," she says, giggling. "You're giving me goosebumps." She snuggles closer to him, and thinking he can get away with it, he grabs her ass and pulls her in closer.

"That time was really good," she says, kissing his neck and resting her head on his chest.

"It's always really good," he says, defending his honor.

"Well, yes, but this time was really, really good."

Yeah, she's right. This time was really, really good.

"I guess sometimes these things are worth the wait. Build up the suspense. A little sexual tension, huh?"

"I should've known you'd be good in bed," she admits with a rueful smile on her face, likely knowing how much satisfaction he'll get from hearing her say so.

He presses his lips together, trying to hide a smile, and she snickers. While he lays there, with her in his arms, he thinks. And while he thinks, he lazily twirls a lock of her hair in his fingers and breathes in her scent—shampoo mixed with a bit of sweat from the hot day and their recent activities.

"Are you sniffing me?" she asks, laughing.

"What if I am?" he replies, pinching her side. Her laugh does things to his heart—his body—he didn't even know were possible. *I could stay in bed with this woman forever.*

But the real world awaits, and begrudgingly, he shifts the mood by whispering to her, "We have to tell people."

"People?"

"Nate, specifically."

He can feel her tense under his hand. "No. Really?"

"It's time for him to understand what's going on. He needs to know the truth."

She sighs. "*I'll* tell him."

"That would probably be best, all things considered," he says.

"It'll work out." She stretches to kiss him on the lips. "I'll talk to him soon. You want to rest?" Her hand trails down his lower abdomen and begins to head further south.

"Why? You want another round?"

"I want what you did to me in Austin. If you think you have it in you ..."

"For you, beautiful? Anything," he replies, yanking the sheet from her body and pulling her on top of him.

RETROSPECTIVE

NATHAN

Nathan leans back in his chair on the patio of the coffee shop while he waits. He was more than a bit surprised to get the text from her last night, about eight hours after he lost his last shred of hope and physically attacked his best friend. Maybe ex best friend. He doesn't quite know yet.

It's only a few places down from Decades, and he glances over there, allowing himself a moment to remember the night in January when he and Kevin had ended up there to grab a drink. The night he met Sarah for the first time.

She arrives and notices where he's looking. "A lot has happened since January, huh?"

Yeah, it sure has.

"Thanks for coming to meet me," she says as she sits and takes off her sunglasses. She looks pretty today—bright eyes and some shimmery type of lipstick. The waiter comes over, and she orders an iced latte.

"How are you?" she asks, narrowing her eyes at him.

"Not great."

"Yeah, I know."

What does that mean?

"So, it all started a few months ago," she says.

"A few months ago?" he asks, and his throat tightens.

She narrows her eyes at him like she's trying to understand what he's asking. Something isn't adding up for her. It's not adding up for him, either.

"Kev and me."

"Kev and *you*?"

"It's been going on for a few months. And now . . . we're together."

He blinks, then looks down, trying to work something out. Then he turns and looks at her, and it all becomes clear.

Why didn't Kev just come out and say it?

"Yessss?" she asks.

Elbows on the table, he looks down and pinches the bridge of his nose with one hand and exhales through his mouth.

"Are you okay?" she asks.

He's been angry for the last eighteen hours—his muscles taut, his stomach churning. Like an ice statue thawing in the sun, he feels the tension drain from his body. He's beginning to feel like himself again, no longer controlled by anger and disappointment. He looks up and sees her watching him warily, probably trying to understand his reaction.

He smiles at her. "I'm okay. That's amazing news, Cam."

She smiles broadly and blushes.

"I've always liked you. Kev's a lucky guy. You on the other hand ..." he says, smiling at her ruefully.

"Yeah, I know," she says, joining in on his amusement. "But he makes me laugh."

"Shit," Nathan says. It hits him like an unexpected aftershock—the memory of him tackling Kevin in a fit of rage at the gym yesterday and the nasty sound Kevin's nose made when he had him on the ground. All because he had some fleeting, misguided notion that Kevin had made a move on Sarah. Because he'd spent the night in a hotel with Nathan's girlfriend—ex-girlfriend—and failed to mention it for a month. Because in the deep, dark recesses of Nathan's mind, he'd imagined they both could have been fucking him over—either romantically or with the startup.

What the hell was I thinking?

"Oh my god." He looks away, embarrassed to meet her in the eye.

Stoic as always, Camila simply remarks, "It's not broken. But he does have a black eye. It makes him look kind of tough, though."

When he raises his eyes to look at her, she has a warm expression on her face, and she's waiting for him to respond. Her eyes—the openness in them—they're like a lifeline, a bridge back from the dangerous, murky space in which his mind has dwelled the last day, even longer.

He takes it and gives a smile, hesitant at first. "I really messed up, Cam."

"Yeah, you did," she admits, but there's no anger in her voice. "At least you didn't use a frying pan?"

"Oh, god."

"Nate, sweetie, what was going through your head yesterday? This angry, aggressive guy . . . it's not you. Sarah wouldn't have fallen in—" She stops mid-sentence.

He looks at her, feeling even more lost than before. She gets up, sits in the chair next to him, and puts a hand on his shoulder.

"Is Kev home?" he asks.

"That's where I left him."

"I have some apologies to make."

"You do," she agrees, standing up. He stands, too, and pulls her into a hug.

"Cam?" he asks, still holding her. It's not the same as holding Sarah. He doesn't know if he'll ever have the chance to do that again, but right now, he just needs a fucking hug. It feels good in a totally platonic way.

"Yeah, Nate?" she says, pulling back slightly and peering up at him but not letting go.

"Thanks for talking to me. Things have been . . . kinda bad for me lately. And it means a lot that you're a . . ."

"Friend," she says, completing his sentence. "We're friends, Nate. Now, go talk to Kevin, and maybe . . ."

"What?" he says, finally letting go and grabbing his bag to get ready to leave.

"Don't be afraid to really talk."

***

Nathan parks his car in front of Kevin's house and surveys the situation. Cam said he's here, but he doesn't see Kevin's car. It could be in the garage, but he'd like to know either way what awaits him. Is Kevin inside plotting his revenge on his supposed best friend who almost broke his nose for no reason? Or maybe he's out buying a shovel to bury Nathan's body after he drowns him in his perfectly maintained sparkling pool?

In any case, despite the twenty-minute drive over, during which Nathan tried to figure out what the hell he's going to say to Kevin, he still doesn't feel ready. He leaves his car at the house and goes on a walk to clear his mind.

He walks around the neighborhood for about fifteen minutes. Then out of the corner of his eye, he sees Kevin's car. *Teslas just sneak up on you. Quiet motherfuckers.* He *does* hear the window roll down, and Kevin pulls up ahead of Nathan and parks the car on the side of the road, blocking a delivery truck.

"What the hell are *you* doing here?" Kevin growls at him. His face looks, well, like someone strong attacked him, actually. *Shit.*

Nathan's at a loss for words. Sorry would be a good start, but before he can say anything, Kevin's yelling at him from inside the car.

"Hey, asshole, I don't even understand you. Did you think I slept with Sarah or something? I'm your fucking best friend."

The delivery truck driver honks. "Hey, asshole, you're blocking me in."

Well, they're both right. He *has* been acting like an asshole.

"No," Nathan says, coming closer to the car and talking to Kevin through the window. "I know you didn't sleep with Sarah. I'm sorry for . . . everything."

Kevin exhales loudly and makes a pissed-off sound. "Get in the fucking car, Goldman," he says resignedly.

Nathan glances at the delivery truck driver, wondering if it might be best for there to be a witness to his murder, but opens the door and gets in. He sits down and buckles his seatbelt.

"I should've just run over your ass."

"Kev?" Nathan says, staring out the window and feeling completely defeated. "I'm sorry, man."

Kevin huffs out, rolls his eyes, and begins to drive to his place.

"I know you're super pissed at me, but . . . can we, like, hang out? I'm kind of fucked up, man."

Kevin studies him, with a cocked head and a furrowed brow. After a moment, he looks down and shakes his head, to himself. *He thinks I've completely lost my mind.* "Yeah," Kevin finally says. "We can hang out. But you acted like a fucking lunatic, in case that's not clear."

"I know, man."

"I'm trying to start something with Camila."

"We talked."

"Good."

"I'm really happy for you. Cam's awesome."

"She is," Kevin says, suddenly warming up. He has a truly happy smile. "Smart, funny, hot. The whole package."

Nathan nods.

"Bro, I'd never fuck you over with Sarah. Or anything else. How could your mind even go there?"

He remembers what Cam told him. *Don't be afraid to really talk.* "I've been . . . really mixed up the last few months. After I calmed down yesterday, I guess I knew nothing happened between you and Sarah. I just . . . so much stuff has been happening behind my back. Carter trying to steal my . . . Sarah, and LightVerse trying to steal my idea. And then you told me yesterday one more thing I had no fucking clue about and . . ."

Kevin slaps him on the back. "I get it. I mean, you're still an asshole, but I get it."

Damn. He *must* be his best friend because what other person would let you take out a month's worth of aggression on their face and then take you back the next day?

"Kev, I'm so fucking sorry."

"Well, I should've told you before now that I slept in her room that night. Things were just wild that night. Then you guys broke up—again—and things have been a mess." He gives him an "I screwed up look," then winces.

"I think you might need some ice on your face."

"You're about twenty-four hours too late." Kevin looks in the rearview mirror. "You know, I'd probably sue you if I didn't already have a whole lot more money than you."

Nathan gives him a pitiful laugh, leans his head back in the passenger seat, and closes his eyes as Kevin steers them onto his street and parks his car in the driveway.

They head inside, and Nathan tells Kevin to go chill by the pool. "I'll bring you some ice and a beer. It's the least I can do."

"That's more like it," Kevin quips and opens the patio door.

"What do you think about frozen peas?" Nathan says once he's rounded up the supplies and joined Kevin outside. He tosses Kevin the cold plastic bag and cracks open a beer for him.

Kevin takes a swig of the beer, positions the bag over his nose and eye area, and leans back on the lounge chair. "Dude, I'll forgive you this one time but don't screw with me again. I might be smaller than you, but if you ever punch me again, I'm going to come at you like Ryu in Street Fighter. Uppercut straight to the jaw."

Nathan glances at him uneasily.

"I might wait until you're asleep, actually. I knew you'd been working out the last few years, but damn. I still feel like my head is gonna explode."

"You want something stronger?" Nathan asks.

"Yeah, this is a night that calls for bourbon."

"I don't know. Last time I drank that *with you*, I got in trouble with Sarah."

"Well, maybe you'll come full circle," Kevin says, "and get yourself *out* of trouble with Sarah."

His logic doesn't make any sense, but Nathan goes into the house to grab the bottle and some glasses from Kevin's kitchen cabinet. He comes back to the patio and hands Kevin the bottle. Kevin pours generously for both of them, then suggests they order take-out.

By the time the food arrives, Nathan is feeling much more relaxed. He's feeling . . . well, closer to good than he has in a while.

"So, you and Cam?" Nathan asks, curious how it all went down.

"Yeah, can you believe it? She's amazing. Super smart and feisty. God, what a woman," Kevin says dreamily.

Nathan smiles to himself. As long as he's known Kevin, he's talked about women, but this time, he sounds *different*.

"So, about *your* woman," Kevin continues. "Sarah—"

"Sarah's not my woman. You keep saying that, but—"

"You going to talk to her?"

"I don't know. I need to think about what I'd say."

"Maybe you just need to listen," Kevin says.

"I need to think about it."

"Why don't you *think* about passing me a chicken wing because I'm hungry?"

While they've been talking and eating, it's gotten dark and a bit cold. Kevin lights the gas firepit and heads inside to get something.

Nathan leans back in the lounge chair near the fire and just watches the flames, feeling more relaxed than he has in a while. The chilly evening, the fire, and a feeling that something—someone—is missing must be what conjures the memory now of the camping trip he went on with Sarah a couple of months ago in the Santa Cruz Mountains. Like an aura off the flames, the whole day arises in his mind.

They're hiking in the woods, and it's a hot day. He's wearing a t-shirt but Sarah, always cold in the morning, started out with a fleece, long since removed and stuffed into his backpack. Her skin is flushed, and her tank top is stuck to her lower back.

She's walking fast, and here and there, he has to scamper over large rocks to keep up with her. He can tell she's trying to beat him to, well, he's not sure where because she hasn't stated explicitly that they're in a race. But she's breathing hard, and he can almost feel the energy emanating off of her in waves.

"Are you running away from me?" he playfully calls out to her.

"Is that what losers say to demoralize the person beating them in a race?" she calls back from ten feet ahead of him.

"You're gonna regret that," he says and speeds up to catch her.

He could catch up easily, if he really wanted to, but he's enjoying the game—the banter back-and-forth, the playful trash-talk. He can tell she is, too. It's a nice break from the heaviness he's been feeling lately.

It's hot out here—and it's a hiking trail—but what he'd really like right now is to make out with her. Watching her walk ahead of him for the last forty-five minutes, gradually stripping off layer after layer, has given him ideas.

He decides that this has gone on long enough and breaks into a run. As he races past her, he smacks her on the butt, and she cries out in surprise. Her footsteps speed up to chase after him, but then she calls out as she trips and falls.

He heads down to check on her. Her hands are scraped, and it looks like she has smashed her knee into a rock. "Are you okay?"

He runs his hand up her leg and carefully raises her pants above her knee, testing the area around her bloody knee carefully with his thumb. He pulls out some wipes and a bandage from his backpack, and she watches him closely as he works to gently clean her leg and bandage it.

"What?" he asks, looking up at her.

"You have beautiful hands," she says, and he smiles.

"Good for coding . . . and bandaging beautiful, injured hikers."

She laughs and dusts off her hands on her pants.

"You'll be just fine," he says, giving her a peck on the forehead.

"I'm already 'just fine,'" she replies, placing her hand on his and moving it further up her leg toward her butt.

"You know," he says, testing the waters. "We haven't seen a soul out here the whole day."

"I guess we took the road less traveled," she says, narrowing her eyes at him, trying to figure out what his intentions are.

"There are some distinct advantages to being alone in the woods," he explains.

"Getting eaten by a wolf?" she jokes.

"I'm no wolf. But I wouldn't mind taking a bite out of you," he says, leaning down and nipping her neck with his teeth.

"So corny, yet so hot," she jokes back. "What if someone comes by?" Very practical.

He can be practical, too. He surveys the woods around them and sees the perfect spot. Down the side of the mountain–about fifty feet away–is a giant redwood, hollowed out and surrounded by boulders. Luck and nature are on his side today.

He stands and offers her a hand. "Can you stand?"

"I could pretend it still hurts and let you carry me down the mountain," she says, giving him an evil smile as she takes his hand and stands. She's referring to Danica, of course, but she doesn't seem to want to linger on that memory, and neither does he. She does a little dance to test her knee, gives him a thumbs up, and winks. "I'm fine."

They make their way down the steep trail to the redwood. When they get there, they explore, crouching down to peer into the partially hollowed-out tree. Nathan finds a cozy nook in the lower part of one of the large rocks, shady and hidden from any potential passersby.

"It's no elevator," he says, "but ever had sex in a redwood?"

"Of course. Hasn't everyone?" she says, laughing at him and his imaginative ideas.

"In that case, there's a second time for everything," he says. He sits down, leaning up against a rock, and pulls her gently down onto his lap.

"Are we seriously going to make out here?"

"Why not?"

She considers his question for a moment. "Yeah, why not?" She rubs her hands over his shoulders and biceps, leaving a few traces of the dirt on her hands.

"Why are you always in such a rush, huh? Racing me up the mountain like that?" he asks, kissing her neck and pulling her in closer. She's damp from sweat, but he doesn't care. If anything, the taste of the salt on her skin is turning him on even more.

"I just like to get places fast."

"Oh, I can take you places," he says, laughing, looking pointedly at where her tank top has ridden down, revealing the lacey trim of her bra and tracing his finger around the curve of the side of her breast.

They start to kiss and are really getting into it when she suddenly stops. "Nathan, our hikes are really fun," she says in a breathless voice. It's the voice that has the ability to make his heart race yet somehow also bring a veil of calm down over him. "But I really don't think we should have sex here."

He laughs. "Next, you're going to tell me you've never had sex in an elevator, either," he says, pouting at her.

She giggles.

"You know that I love you?" he asks.

"Yeah, I know that," she replies, then slides off of him and sits with her legs draped over his lap. He wraps his arm around her, letting her lean into him. They just sit and listen to the sounds of nature around them. Mostly, animals scamper here and there, and occasionally there's the call of a bird. It's peaceful, quiet, and nothing really needs to be said.

Things are tough with the startup. He feels lost sometimes, unsure of whether he should even continue pursuing it or give up now and just find a corporate job. But here, with Sarah, things feel whole, certain. She always encourages him—sometimes explicitly, with a pep talk, and sometimes just with her presence. Like a stamp of approval telling him he's worthy, good enough for her, and therefore good enough to achieve his lofty goals.

He runs his fingers through her ponytail with one hand while she traces the delicate bones on the back of his other hand resting on his knee. "You ready to go back to the car and get the camping stuff?" he asks, drawing her out of some meditative state she seems to have gone into.

She meets his eyes and nods, and they walk back quietly at a much slower pace than on the way there.

Later that night, after setting up camp and eating a simple dinner, they crawl into the small tent and slip into their respective sleeping bags. As hot as the day has been, it's considerably cooler now. They lay on their sides, facing each other.

"It's so dark. I can't even see you," Sarah says, reaching out and almost poking him in the eye.

"Be careful, you nut," he says, taking her hand and kissing it.

"Nathan, you know that I love you?" she asks, repeating to him the question he asked her earlier in the day.

"I do know," he answers.

And it's the perfect segue into a long and eventually sleepy conversation. They talk about all sorts of things—from hopes and fears to their favorite childhood movies and snacks. Out here in the wilderness, away from everything and everybody, he doesn't feel any pressure about the startup. Lying down so close to her, any worries he has about her and her feelings for him are gone. They're here, together, and they can just . . . be.

Nathan must drift off at some point because one minute Sarah is explaining to him why exactly she and Camila have seen Mean Girls so many times, and the next thing he knows, he's coming out of a sleepy haze to the sound of a zipper—Sarah unzipping his sleeping bag.

"I'm cold," she whispers as she slips in beside him and twists her body to zip up the bag behind her. Her close proximity to him and the position would give him quite the view if there were any light to speak of. But his other senses—smell, touch, sound—are on overdrive. He inhales her scent, a combination of her freshly laundered hoodie and the clean smell of the freezing creek water, where she took a quick dip earlier. She snuggles into his body until it feels as if there's no way for them to possibly be any closer. She dressed warmly for bed, but he can feel her shivering.

"My poor little popsicle," he says, laughing softly. "I'll warm you up."

"I might melt." She kisses him on his nose.

"Is that a threat or a promise?"

She giggles, and he uses one hand to pull down the zipper of her hoodie while the other settles on the curve of her ass.

"Thank goodness for cool nights," he says, kissing her on the lips and seeing whether she joined him only because it's a chilly night or whether she might like to pick up where they left off earlier in the day, near the giant redwood.

Her hands answer his unasked question as they creep up both the front and the back of his shirt simultaneously. Her cold fingers explore the muscles of his back and his abs. He tenses for a second, then murmurs in

*her ear that he loves her. He doesn't care if her hands are cold. Her touch is
everything to him. Her breath, the taste of her on his tongue.*

Thinking about it now, his chest tightens. He . . . just misses her . . . so
much. The way she would casually touch his shoulder or run her fingers
through his hair as she passed by him working on his laptop at the kitchen
table. The sound of her voice as she sang along to songs in the car or while
she cooked in the kitchen. More than anything, how she made him feel
like he could do anything he put his mind to. *How did it all go so wrong?*

He opens his eyes and sees Kevin has returned and is watching him.
"You should call her now."

Even in his current less-than-sober state, Nathan knows it's a bad idea.

"How will it help anything?" Nathan says doubtfully. "Knowing even
more details about what happened? That picture—" His jaw clenches,
matching the sudden tension in the rest of his body. "It doesn't leave
much to the imagination."

"I *think* you imagined way too much. Carter . . . Wait, you promise not
to tackle me again?"

Nathan cocks his head. "Depends on what you're about to tell me."

"Seriously?"

"I'm joking, okay? My reflexes are slow tonight. You're in luck."

Kevin side-eyes him and decides to speak up. "It's more about what
I should have told you earlier. I noticed some stuff over the past few
months. I think Carter had his eye on Sarah, but he was also helping
her so much professionally, and I didn't want to get in the way of that.
I mean, the opportunity to present to LightVerse board members is not
something most program managers get, right?"

"Right," Nathan says gravely, a gnawing feeling in the pit of his stomach.
Guilt, stupid. After all, he had asked her not to go on the trip. *Don't forget
selfish.* He ended up being *right*, his ego reminds him. Carter *did* make
a move on her, but surely he could have found a better way to handle
the whole thing. He could have encouraged Sarah to go after what she
wanted but communicated to her more clearly what his worries were.

"I never wanted to block her success. You know that, right? I just . . . I was insecure. Things don't go well in one area of life, and you begin to wonder if you're not enough in other areas."

"Nate, man. You're enough for this startup shit. For a relationship, too," Kevin says and then snickers.

"What?"

"I'm talking like we're in some cheesy romantic movie. Maybe the happy ending is you and me falling in love."

Nathan chuckles, then his expression sobers. "So, if you shared a room with her that night in Austin, then she wasn't with Carter."

"Nope. That night, afterward, she told me what happened—"

"You knew *when* it happened? So, why didn't you tell me?"

"She was going to tell you herself. You know she would have when she came back, if Danica hadn't sent that picture first. She wouldn't keep something like that from you, not after—"

"Don't even say it," Nathan warns, standing up and beginning to pace to avoid looking Kevin in the eye.

"I think you're in a unique position here to listen to Sarah and to really understand what it's like. You know how . . . *things* can happen. When you're overwhelmed by a situation, by a person, when . . ."

Nathan feels like Kevin's talking on a few different levels at once—what happened with Danica earlier this year, what Kevin felt about Camila, but more than anything, Sarah and himself. Since the moment Nathan met Sarah, he felt overwhelmed by her. Their first night together was the direct result of him feeling like he was under her spell from the moment he saw her smile.

He turns around, looking at Kevin. "You mean . . ." Nathan starts but pauses. There's a part of him that would love to dig into his feelings of betrayal, twist what Kevin's saying to suit his mood, and spit out something like "When someone breaks your trust or cheats on you." But he's so damn tired of feeling alone, sad, and angry. His heart and mind can't take it anymore, and what comes out of his mouth is much more generous and understanding than he intended, "You mean . . . when that other person makes a move, and it takes a minute to react?"

Kevin nods. "Have some experience with something like that?"

Nathan shoots him a look, indicating he should probably quit while he's ahead.

"You don't have to call her tonight, but you should go over there and listen. Soon. And if you're ready to listen to what I was trying to tell you yesterday. . ."

"Yeah?"

"When you attacked me?" Kevin clarifies.

"Yes, I remember. I'm an asshole, and you're my undeserving victim."

"Exactly." Kevin picks up his phone from the table, taps a few times, and scrolls, then holds his phone out to Nathan. There's a string of WhatsApp messages from Sarah to Kevin from yesterday morning, a few hours before Nathan tried to break Kevin's nose.

> **Sarah:** Have you heard of Project Meteor?
> **Sarah:** Look in Jira. When you're alone.
> **Kevin:** What's going on?
> **Sarah:** It's Nathan's. His startup idea. Most of the user stories are things he talked about with me.
> **Kevin:** I'll take a look.
> **Sarah:** I don't think you have access. I asked for admin access recently and I guess I can see all the projects.
> **Sarah:** Can you talk?
> **Kevin:** Yeah.

"What did she say when you talked?" Nathan asks.

"She called me, and then she screenshotted some of it. I deleted them from our thread—just in case—but they're in my Dropbox. It was a big risk for her to do it, but she wanted me to see it. She wanted me to tell you.

"She had heard that LightVerse had something that sounded *like* your project, but when she saw that, she knew something weird was going on. We talked today and exchanged notes on things Carter had said to her and to me. She has a theory."

"What?"

"She thinks Carter is not only the spokesperson for Project M, but the person who *somehow* got all the information about your project himself. She said it all came together when she saw this stuff. He would ask her questions about how you were progressing."

Damn. If Nathan ever needed any proof that it wasn't Sarah who leaked the information, he certainly has it now.

He's still holding Kevin's phone in his hand and glances down at the messages. He's about to scroll to see if there's anything else, but he stops himself.

Kevin seems to read his mind. "Go ahead, you won't find anything suspicious. Just us talking about how you never even gave her a chance to tell her side of things."

Mr. Kevin Wong, folks. Master of subtlety.

"Unbelievable," Nathan says, more out of wonder than anger. But it makes total sense. The only people who know about his startup who have connections to LightVerse are Sarah, Kevin, and Carter. Sarah and Kevin are, well, he knows now, they're loyal. But Carter. *How does he know?*

"Fine. I'll go talk to her. Tomorrow. I'll listen to her, but I'm not making out—"

Kevin snorts.

"Making *up* with her. I miss her, but the fact remains that she kissed another guy. One week after we broke up."

"After you broke up with her," Kevin corrects him, glaring at him. "After you told her not to go on a potentially career-changing business trip."

Nathan considers what he's saying.

"I might've kissed him, too, if I were in the same situation," Kevin says bluntly.

Nathan rolls his eyes at him, at first annoyed, but he can't help but crack a smile.

"What? The guy's good-looking," Kevin jokes.

"Dude, shut the hell up."

"I get it, man. Just listen to her, though. Don't throw away the love of your life over a stupid kiss," Kevin says.

"I don't know that she's the love of my life."

"Well, it's pretty fucking obvious to everyone else," Kevin replies, and he leaves it at that.

One-on-One

NATHAN

The next day, Nathan wakes up even later than usual. His head might as well be glued to the pillow, and his eyelids are moving in slow motion.

What the hell happened last night?

Then he remembers Kevin shoving him into an Uber around 2:30 a.m. Somehow, he made it up to his apartment and into bed. His pants are off—*okay*—but he's still in the shirt he wore yesterday.

His phone buzzes near his head, and he picks it up. It's a string of texts from Kevin, starting five minutes ago:

> **Kevin:** Sleep well?
> **Kevin:** I almost forgot you tried to kill me, but then I woke up and looked in the mirror.
> **Kevin:** Asshole.
> **Kevin:** If anybody asks, we were at Krav Maga class.

And finally:

> **Kevin:** You heading over to S today?

Oh, right.

S. For Sarah. For sex. For sex *with* Sarah. *That's* what he was dreaming about when the texts started coming in and woke him. Like most of the dreams he has, a moment after he wakes, it's almost gone, but he wills himself to remember, knowing it will be torture but doing it anyway. He closes his eyes, and faint images return. Fuzzy but they're there.

Sarah was sitting on his lap, legs to one side, her arms around his neck.

"*I miss cooking with you,*" *she says.*

"*What else?*"

"*I miss falling asleep on the couch next to you while we watch TV together.*"

"*Anything else?*"

"*A lot else,*" *she says, shifting her weight a bit.* "*Am I hurting you?*"

"*Never.*"

"*I did hurt you.*"

"*Yeah, you did, but I think I hurt you, too.*"

"*You did,*" *she replies.*

"*I don't want to hurt you again. I only want to make you feel good.*"

"*Massage my shoulders for me?*" *she asks, her lips curling up into the smallest of smiles.*

"*Come here,*" *he tells her, spreading his legs so she can sit between them. She slips her butt between his thighs and leans back on his chest. He laughs and tells her he can't get to her shoulders if she's so close.*

She turns her head to look back at him coquettishly and asks what he can reach. "*There are other things that make me feel good, and you said that's what you wanted to do, right?*"

A challenge.

"*I can reach right here,*" *he says, gently brushing the outside of his fingers down the side of her neck. She leans to one side, and without meaning to, his finger slips under her loose collar. It's where a bra strap should be, but there isn't one.*

"*Mmmm,*" *he says, without meaning to.*

"*Can you reach any lower?*" *she asks huskily.*

For the moment, he leaves his hand where it is on her collarbone, tracing it softly with one finger, and takes his other hand and touches her waist, just under the waistband of her pants, his fingertips brushing her warm, soft skin.

She puts her hand over his and guides it inside her pants but outside her underwear to a point even lower. He can feel her heat through the thin underwear, and he can barely keep a moan of approval from escaping his lips.

"That would make me feel good," she says.

"It would make me feel good, too," he admits and leans forward. His lips are almost to her throat.

"So, let's feel good instead of bad?"

"I want to," he tells her.

"So, do it," she says, pulling his hand out of her pants and slowly turning around to straddle him. A dare.

He slips both of his hands to the curve of her waist and waits for her to make the next move. He wants this, but he has to be absolutely sure that she does, too. And she does. She unbuttons her pants and slips them down further, below her hips. She's wearing the sexy black lace underwear he loves. He feels his own face curling into a smile despite his best intentions not to show too much emotion. He feels bare—so exposed—and he doesn't want to get hurt again.

"Nathan, will you kiss me? It's been so long." She leans in, parting her lips slightly, readying herself for his mouth. He hesitates because, in his head, he sees her kissing someone else. He can't un-see it. But he can do more for her. He knows her, he knows her body, and he can do more—be more—for her. In an instant, he decides that he will. He has to. He moves her off of his lap and lays her back on his couch.

"What're you doing?" she asks, surprised by the change in position.

"Kissing you," he says. "Somewhere else." The delight on her face makes him burn, and he begins to tug her pants down. Understanding his intention, she helps him, and soon, she's bare, open to him, and he crawls toward her, caressing her smooth, strong legs. They begin to wrap around his back as he gets close to his target. He touches her first with his thumb, and she shivers.

"I want you to feel good, Sarah," he says as he begins kissing her most intimate places.

"I do. That feels so, so . . . good." She can barely get the words out.

He slips his tongue into a place he knows will make her melt, and it doesn't disappoint.

"Fuck, Nathan. It's so good. You are so good. I've missed you. So much." Her voice betrays her emotions—relief, ecstasy, longing.

He stops for a second, replacing his mouth with his hands, and slides up her body. "Is it because I know how to make you come?" he asks, in a voice thick with desire—and the tiniest bit of fear. He's sure she can tell. Because the same way that he knows her, she knows him.

"No," she answers. "It's because, without you, there's just no way to feel good at all."

She reaches down to touch him through his pants. "Don't you understand? I want you to feel good, too."

And it was as she began to touch him with her gentle but sure hands, to make sure that he was as ready for the next step as she was, that he had woken up.

***

Great. He remembers all the pertinent details of his hot dream, and now he's frustrated as hell. He drags himself out of bed to start the day. It's either that or wallow in disappointment or go—well—take care of things in the shower. The latter feels just a little too desperate, so he makes himself some coffee and begins to work down his Sunday to-do list. The one task *not* on his list—talk to Sarah—occupies his thoughts throughout the day, and around six o'clock, he finally admits to himself that he's been stalling.

Do it already, Goldman.

He calls Sarah, and it rings. One. Two. Three. *She doesn't want to talk to me.* Four. He slides his thumb over to press "end," and she answers.

"Hello? Nathan?" She's breathing hard, panting. There is traffic in the background, and he realizes she must be on a run. *But she answered.*

"Sarah," he says on an exhale. "Um . . ." His words escape him.

"Yeah?"

"Are you on a run?" he asks.

"Just finishing up. What's going on?"

"Could I come over?"

"Oh," she says, sounding surprised. "Sure. Um, just give me thirty minutes to get back home and shower."

"See you then."

He walks to her place instead of driving to burn some time and maybe some of his nervous energy. While it usually takes twenty minutes, he makes it in fourteen, and he's sitting in the courtyard when she returns. In short, tight black running shorts and a sports bra, she's a sweaty—god-damn, sexy—mess. *This is going to be harder than I thought.*

"You're early," she says, wiping her forehead with the back of her hand.

"Sorry. I can wait down here while you get ready."

"It's okay. You can come up."

They ride the elevator up together in silence. He stares at the floor but can see out of the corner of his eye that she's examining him. He lifts his head and ventures a tentative smile. She doesn't smile back. *Funny what a few weeks and the silent treatment can do to destroy a relationship.*

She opens the door to her apartment and heads to the shower while he waits in the living room. A few of his things—a book he was in the middle of reading, the missing charger cable for his watch—are sitting out. *What does that mean?* He should have spoken to her—or at least come to get his things—but he wasn't ready to admit that things were over.

She finishes her shower and joins him in the living room but stands near the wall. Even from across the room, her familiar pleasant scent reaches him—her coconut body wash, some flowery concoction she uses on her soft, brown hair. Is it longer than before? A lighter color? It's only been four weeks.

"It's been a while. Three, no, four . . . long weeks," she comments pointedly.

"I'm ready to talk now," he says, trying to sound conciliatory.

He's not sure if *he* should be apologizing or if she should, but he's here. That's a start. He stands. If she won't come to him, then he'll go to her. She seems to understand his intent and sits down—near him, but not next to him. He returns to his spot on the couch. His first instinct is to pull her into a hug, but they haven't talked in a month. Their last conversation was anything but friendly.

He reaches out for her hand, and after a moment of hesitation, she places her hand in his. He pulls her closer to him and tries to hug her, but her body is tense under his hands. It's not the same as before. Not at all.

SMOKE TEST

SARAH

"I need some water," I say, pulling away gently from his hug. "Do you want some?"

He shakes his head, and I get up and go to the kitchen. I *am* thirsty, but I mostly need the space. We've needed to clear the air, but I feel unprepared. I'm not nervous. No, I'm angry. I take a gulp of water and head back into the living room.

By way of greeting, I simply say, "Why are you here now? You didn't let me explain anything the last time we talked, but now, all of a sudden, you're interested?" I set my glass of water down and begin to pace back and forth like a prowling tiger waiting to attack.

Despite the aggressive energy emanating from me in waves, he holds my gaze. "I don't know what changed, but I'm ready to listen now."

But am I ready to talk about it? Just when I'm starting to feel normal again, like I might someday recover?

I sit, rubbing my hands up and down my thighs rhythmically, and focus on the copy of *Wild* I left on the table last night. It was a gift from Nathan when we moved in together, and I wish I'd had the chance to put away the book. That stray thought isn't enough to distract me, though, from the indignation I feel bubbling up inside of me.

Half-angry, half-desperate, I spit out, "Do you have any idea what it's like to be a twenties-something woman working in high-tech? In engineering? With 90 percent men?" I train my eyes on him. I get the feeling he would rather look away, but he simply blinks and waits for me to continue. "It's intimidating. I told you I don't feel like I know what I'm doing half the time, and yeah, maybe I liked the attention Carter was giving me, but it felt supportive. It . . . *was* supportive. Despite the fact that . . . well, he obviously had some other motives."

"That's putting it lightly," he says boldly, and I narrow my eyes at him.

I take a deep breath to calm myself. "You're right, okay? I should've been smarter—stronger—but it's hard when professional opportunities are being dangled in front of you and . . ."

"And what?"

"You feel vulnerable. You feel like a fake. You feel like . . . maybe the person who's supposed to be your biggest advocate . . . isn't as interested in you as he used to be."

He looks down, not saying anything, then locks eyes with me. *Is the pain in his eyes his, or is it a mirror of my own?*

"Will you tell me what happened?" he asks.

I don't feel ready for this. I'm not even sure what, or if, I should tell him, but I stand up and walk over to the window.

Fine, he asked for it.

"Well, we can start with what went well," I say. "I was there, in Austin, despite you not wanting me to go—"

"Sarah—"

"No, you asked, so I'm going to tell you in my own way."

He nods.

"I did a great job, Nathan. I'm sorry that things—between you and me—turned out the way they did after what happened on that trip, but part of me is glad I went. I did a great job on the presentation. I totally kicked ass."

"I know," he says. "Kev told me how amazing you were."

Of course he did.

"We all went out afterward. Kevin and I showed up late to dinner, and the only spot open was next to Carter, so I sat near him. Well, there was *one* other spot. Next to . . . Danica."

I give him a rueful smile, and his mouth twitches, despite the tension still swirling in the room.

"We had some drinks, and then after dinner, Kevin wanted to go out, and Danica and Carter joined us. I was . . . tense. Danica was asking me about you, and Carter was, what can I say? He was interested in more than just a professional relationship. And I was exhausted and nervous ... and sad and desperate."

His expression falls.

I push forward. It's hard, but I have to say it. "And Carter kissed me. And I . . . let him."

He avoids my eyes.

"You don't want to hear it, but I have to say it—for me. It wasn't fair of you to ask me not to go."

"I know."

He does?

"But I wasn't fair with you either," I say. "I should've been more careful long before that night. I should've tried to listen to your concerns."

I'm through the hard part now, and I sit down on the chair near him but not on the couch with him.

"Right after that, I left. Kevin and I went back to the hotel. And he couldn't find his key, and the receptionist was MIA. It was late, and it had been a long night, a long week. And we ended up in my room, and Kev talked a lot and fell asleep."

"You spent the rest of the night with Kevin?" he asks.

"Yeah, I did. He 'spent the night,' I guess, but we slept in separate beds. I mean, by the time I woke up at 6:00 a.m., he was gone. I guess he got up in the night and somehow made it back to his room."

He nods but stays silent, taking it all in.

"I barely slept that night. But I certainly didn't sleep with Carter ... or Kevin, for that matter, just in case you'd considered that strange scenario."

Something strange flickers in his eyes. Then he glances away.

"So that's it. A week after we broke up, I kissed another guy. It might not mean much, but when I came back here on Saturday, I was going to tell you everything. I didn't get the chance."

Nathan looks at me, then down at his hands. He's working his jaw, likely trying to figure out what to say now. Has he heard enough? Can he leave, feeling better, knowing that I kissed Carter but that I didn't sleep with him? Knowing that I might've done something irreparable to our relationship, but at least I didn't give myself completely to a guy he hates, a guy who stole his ideas, his dreams?

"Danica—" I start to say. He looks up at me and shakes his head. "Enough," his expression seems to say.

He holds out his hand. *God, those strong, capable hands.* If only . . . Well, we're past all that. I probably won't feel them on my waist again. I place my hand in his, and he pulls me to sit next to him.

"Just so it's clear," he says, "I'm not . . . okay . . . with what happened. But if I'm being honest, I was imagining much worse."

"You really thought that I slept with him?" I ask, unbelieving.

He winces. "I've been in a pretty dark place."

And I helped put you there.

"But I'd be a hypocrite if I didn't at least forgive you—try to let it go."

He's calm but not smiling. This is as far as he can go. I've already given up hope on being able to repair things between us. If only there were time machines. I nod at him and give him a sad smile.

"So, I am," he says. "I'm letting go."

I don't know what I wanted him to say, but it definitely wasn't that. He's letting go—of his anger, but also of me. I look away so he won't see the tears threatening to spill over the edges of my eyes.

He turns my head gently with his hand and brushes away a lock of hair that has fallen into my misty eyes. I feel my heart crack in two because he always used to do that right before he kissed me. Step One in the Nathan Goldman Two-Step Guide to Kissing Sarah.

I take a shallow breath and close my eyes, trying to steady myself and not let the tears fall. It must only take a second. I don't want to be dramatic. Just keep myself in one piece. But I'm shocked to find his lips on mine. They're hesitant, like a first kiss, asking permission, "Is *this* okay?"

Step Two? Here? Now?

It's not, in any world, okay. Not at all. The last few months have been so dramatic—so utterly filled with action, emotion, passion, falling in love, and then betrayal—that it's probably the worst idea in the world to respond to this kiss, but my body does indeed respond. But not in kind. Where Nathan's lips are gentle, exploring reluctantly, mine crush against his, part them, and demand more.

Any second now, he'll realize what he's done or explain to me that it was just one last parting kiss, and he'll get up to leave, but he doesn't. As my tongue, without my mind's permission, traces the opening of his mouth, he opens it, welcoming me in. And all at once, I'm filled to the brim and utterly empty, frozen in time and ready to burst into flames.

Our hands move at the same time to each other's faces, necks, and shoulders, and we seek peace and shelter from the storm the last couple months have been.

"I'm not sure—"

"You don't need to be—"

"I don't think—"

"Don't think. Just, just—"

But neither of us can finish a sentence because, ultimately, we don't want to. What we need from each other can't be expressed in words. We need each other's touch. Each of us, in equal measure, needs the other.

He leans me back on the pillow-covered armrest and snuggles into me, his hair tickling my chin. I tilt my head down to take in the scent of his shampoo and thread my fingers softly through his thick hair. He sighs, and I feel his breath on my bare arm.

"I hear your heart beating," he says softly.

"Is it fast?"

He lifts his eyes to mine and nods.

That's what you do to me.

After my shower earlier, I threw on a light summer dress. He takes advantage of it now, tracing one of my nipples with his thumb over the thin fabric.

"I love the way your body responds to me," he says.

I respond, "I guess it just knows what it likes."

I can't reach with my hand the part of his anatomy responding to *me* in this position, so I gently rub my bare foot over it.

"Mine, too," he admits, begrudgingly but not bitterly.

He looks into my eyes. "What do you want, Sarah?"

I wish he was asking me about life. *What do I want?* I want to go back in time. I want to have met Nathan before I ever met my ex and before he ever got involved with Danica again. I would have wanted us to work at different places so we could meet and get to know each other with a clean slate—no issues, no drama, no problems. We could have simply dated, met each other's families, and fallen in love. Marriage, children, a long and happy life together.

But he's not asking that, surely. He's asking me what I want now? And the only thing he's probably ready to give me tonight is something that will just have to be enough.

So, I lean up and begin to undo his pants. I kiss his neck, squeeze my eyes together so the tears can't escape, and lie to him in a whisper, "I want one last night, Nathan. Give me your body tonight."

I want more, but I don't deserve it. "Give me another chance with your heart" is on the tip of my tongue, but I don't have the courage to say it.

He breathes in—a ragged sound—and I wonder if it's regret. Will he pull back, stand up, and leave? But then he rakes his eyes down my body and meets my eyes before leaning up to pull his shirt off over his head. He stands and yanks off his pants and boxers. Then he sits back down close to me, slips the thin straps of my dress off my shoulders, and kisses my neck. His warm hands travel down my shoulder blades, he undoes the clasp of my bra, and his mouth drops to my now bare breasts. Pleasure is not the word. After all this time, ecstasy is closer. I pull down my underwear, pull his hips to mine, and he enters me without hesitation.

I want him in me. I don't want to wait, but my body is not quite ready. He pulls out. "Let me help," he says and settles next to me, where he can put his mouth on my nipples and use his hands on me at the same time.

He dips his fingers into me, stroking my clit with his thumb. "Oh my god, you're so hot, your cu—" he cuts himself off.

"Were you gonna say the C word?" I whisper, amusement likely evident in my voice. He looks up and licks his lips before breaking into a sheepish grin. I purse my lips, then run my fingers through his hair and gently tug.

He hesitates for only a second before replying in a teasing voice. "No, I was gonna say 'your . . . couch.'"

"My couch, huh?" I say, interrupting him. "Is that a euphemism?"

"Your couch ..." he pauses, "isn't very comfortable."

"Mmm. I hope you're talking about my real couch then."

"Of course I am. Your other 'couch,'" he says, starting to laugh, "is very, very comfortable. Trust me."

I giggle, and he begins to laugh, too, despite the goddamn complete and utter inappropriateness of the timing. With this admission, he pulls me up and off toward the bedroom. We reach the bed, and he pulls me to face him. He is completely naked at this point, but I'm still somewhat dressed. My dress straps are caught on my arms, keeping it from falling off of me. He kisses me roughly on the mouth, and I return every bit of his energy. I hold my arms above my head, and he pulls my dress over my head. I sit, then slither up the bed and wait for him to make his move.

He's only mine for tonight. That realization alone is enough to make my heart break open, but I'll take what I can get. There's a small voice whispering in my ear that we shouldn't, but there's a much louder voice somewhere in my head telling me not to give up this chance, one last time with Nathan.

He crawls onto the bed toward me, positions himself between my legs, and kisses me on the mouth.

"What were you going to say before, Nathan?" I ask, wrapping my legs around him.

"You're gonna make me say it, huh?"

"I'm not going to make you do anything," I say. I look into his eyes and wait for him to respond. When he stays silent, I move my hands to his cock to see if that will elicit a response. He closes his eyes and exhales in satisfaction, then leans down and whispers in my ear the words I want to hear.

I look up at him, satisfied. "You didn't."

"I did. And it's soft . . . and warm . . . and so fucking perfect. You push me over the edge."

I wrap my legs around him, aligning our bodies, and pull him inside of me with ease as if his body was created for the sole purpose of fitting mine.

"Take me over the edge with you," I say, in a tone somewhere between a whisper and a cry.

It might not be smart, logical, or helpful to the situation we're in, but right now, I'm exactly where I want to be.

***

I'm cold. That's my first thought as I wake. I was so, so warm last night, curled together in the bed with Nathan shortly after we finished making love. I had faced the window, and he had cuddled up behind me, holding me until I fell asleep. I'm not sure when he left, but I know he did. I don't even need to check to know that he's not in bed with me anymore. If he were, I simply wouldn't be cold.

It's still mostly dark in my room, but my level of tiredness and a very faint lightening of the sliver of sky I can see through the part in my curtains suggests it's very early morning. The clock on the nightstand reads 5:55. The only time Nathan's ever been awake before me, and it was in order to leave me.

What happened last night wasn't a dream, but it seems like it. I've woken up plenty of mornings the last few weeks, imagining Nathan's hand has just left my waist or that I can smell his clean, pleasant scent. But dreams are just that—dreams. They're certainly not a sign of what's to come. If anything, only what has been or—even worse—what *might* have been.

I roll over to find my favorite blanket *of his* resting, neatly folded, on the pillow next to me with a small note placed on it. I grab my phone and use the light from the screen to read it.

S, I took most of my things, so they won't be in your way anymore. But you should keep the blanket. I know you love it. It'll keep you warm. -N

I wish you were here, keeping me warm. There's no way I can fall back to sleep now, so I wrap the blanket around my shoulders to head into the kitchen to make coffee and start the day.

FOCUS TIME

He pours cream into his second—no, third—cup of coffee of the day and watches it swirl into the dark liquid. At least while he was coding, he wasn't thinking about her.

"What do you want, Sarah?" The words escaped his mouth a few nights ago, an involuntary response to being near her, from spending so many months wanting to please her physically—sexually. He would ask, "What do you want?" and she would tell him—with or without words—what she wanted, what she needed. When he asked her the other night, he thought he was asking about sex, but who the hell knows?

She had answered that she wanted his body. And he had wanted hers, too. Giving in to their physical desires was a mistake—a fleeting, ephemeral fix to a bad situation. But he couldn't say "no." His body—one part of him or all parts of him—wanted her too much.

When he woke in the middle of the night after a short but deep sleep cuddled up against her, reality set in. Upon realizing it was the last night he would ever spend with her, his chest tightened in sadness—regret for so many things—and he rolled out of bed quietly to search for his clothes and gather the few things he'd be able to carry back to this apartment. He was willing to be the asshole to save them both any embarrassment or pain in the morning.

Listening to her side of the story had proven to him what he already knew—Sarah had messed up. But . . . so had he. He might be able to admit that to himself, but he wouldn't be able to look her in the eye and say it to her. So, like a coward, he left before she woke up.

It's been three days, and he can't shake one thought. What if she had answered his question differently? What if, when he had asked her what she wanted, she would have told him she wanted *all* of him? That she wanted to try again?

He sighs and takes a sip of his drink, burning his lips, and he's jolted back to the present. It doesn't matter. It's over.

***

"What's up, bro?" David asks.

It's almost noon, and Nathan is still in the clothes he slept in last night. He knew David was going to FaceTime him, so he should have made an effort. He didn't, and now he's paying the price.

David shoots him a disdainful expression. "Dude. Pull yourself together."

"I'm pulled together just fine," Nathan replies.

"Alexa?" David asks. Alexa chimes in response. "What's the name of this song?"

A disembodied voice from David's side declares: "This is the song 'Better Now' by Post Malone."

"Really? *This* is your breakup music?" David asks sardonically.

"You know, next time, I'm not answering your call."

"Fine. Dad told me the VC meeting is a few weeks out. How's the prep going?"

Nathan sighs. *From one lighthearted topic to the next.* "You want the answer I gave Dad or the real answer?"

"Real."

"It sucks, and I have no fucking clue how I'm supposed to get this ready in time for the meeting."

"Sorry, man. Is there, I don't know, anything *I* can help with?"

"Not unless you recently became a programmer or business major?"

"Nope. Still in advertising."

"Tangentially related, I guess, but I don't think you can help."

"Doesn't sound like it. So . . ."

"Yeah?"

"I'm not supposed to tell you this, but I'm calling to check in on you. Making sure you're, how did Mom put it, 'emotionally healthy and mentally stable?'"

"Well, you've already told me to get dressed and change my music so you can arrive at your own conclusions."

"Yeah."

"I knew Mom told you to call. You *never* call," Nathan says.

"I *do* call."

"When mom tells you to," Nathan replies.

"I guess you're right," David admits. "We're brothers. That's normal."

"You don't have to tell *me*. Anyways, the answer to your question is 'somewhat.'"

"Meaning?"

"Meaning, I didn't think I'd be doing this entirely alone," Nathan replies.

"Pitching to a VC?"

"That, and I guess, other things, too."

"Sarah?" David asks.

Nathan makes a sort of low noise, indicating his brother has hit the nail on the head.

"Any chance you guys might patch things up? It wasn't that long ago that I drove you to the airport to meet her in Park City."

"I'm not sure we can fix what we broke."

"We?"

"Both of us. Me, too," Nathan admits.

"Sorry, man. I know you thought she might be . . . well, your person."

"Yeah, I did," Nathan says a lump forming in his throat. "I, uh, need to go, okay? Get back to work."

"Sure. Uh. . ."

"Yeah?"

"I know brothers don't really call each other," David says, with a small smile. "But you can always call me. Or text me, and I'll call you."

"Thanks, man."

He ends the call and notices a new text from Kevin. It's yet another link to a YouTube playlist. "Essential Breakup Songs: The 90s."

What an asshole.

Nathan snickers. Kevin's an asshole, but he's glad—not for the first time—that he's his asshole.

> **Kevin:** Let me know if you wanna run through the slides, okay? You doin' ok?
> **Nathan:** <thumbs up emoji>
> **Kevin:** Dinner tonight with me and Cam?
> **Nathan:** Nah. Gonna keep jammin' on this. Gotta hit the release date. Gotta ship it. Sound familiar?

He smiles to himself, remembering how many times he heard Kevin say "ship it" to the engineers at Instinqt.

> **Kevin:** Fuck off, dude. I hope one day you have the privilege of being a CEO who has to answer to a board about quarterly numbers. Then you'll understand.
> **Nathan:** Just joking, man.
> **Kevin:** I know. Get back to work, asshole.

He clicks on the YouTube playlist—"Don't Speak" by No Doubt begins to play—and sits back down at his desk. Time to get to work.

REFACTOR

SARAH

I'm just grabbing some *afternoon* gummy bears—Erin has laid down some ground rules on when exactly we're allowed to partake in LightVerse's endless snack options—when Kevin comes up behind me in the office kitchen.

"Want to go for a walk?" he asks.

"Sure. I have a free hour now."

When we leave the building, we head down a tree-lined street in search of shade in the July afternoon heat.

"What's up?" I ask.

"So, your boy Nate—"

Well, that didn't take long.

"He's not my boy, Kev."

I don't know what Nathan told Kevin about us, but I sincerely hope he didn't mention our little "slip-up" last week.

Kevin shoots me a subtle but clearly knowing grin that I can only suspect means he knows more than he's letting on. "Well, whether or not he's your boy, I thought you should know—since he might not tell you himself—that he's in crunch time right now." He pauses, thinking. "I think you—and me—should check in on him from time to time."

"Is he alright?" What does he mean by crunch time?

"He's probably in over his head with the startup. He still doesn't have a co-founder, and it would be better if he didn't have to go it alone, especially since he's prepping for a VC meeting."

"He has a VC meeting?" I ask.

Kevin nods and smiles. "At Redwood Capital in a couple weeks. And it's stressing him out. He's been holed up at home working the last week."

I can imagine. I was stressed about the board meeting presentation, and I had two seasoned veterans helping me prepare. Nathan's doing this mostly on his own. *Damn.*

Kevin stops and leans up against a large bay laurel tree. "It would be better if he had a partner, but I'm not worried about it. The second he gets funding—*if* he gets funding—he'll be able to find some non-technical co-founder. But maybe you could send him a text to check in?"

"Yeah, definitely." I haven't heard from him since our last night together, but I didn't really expect to. He crept out in the night, so he obviously didn't want to talk about it. I wonder how he must feel now, preparing for one of the biggest opportunities of his professional life.

Kevin's voice pulls me away from my thoughts. "Maybe you don't want to hear this, but ..."

"Spit it out, Wong."

He snickers, but then his expression becomes more serious. "He misses you."

"He said that?" I ask, doubtful.

"He didn't say it, but it's obvious. He barely leaves the house."

"You just said yourself he's busy working."

"Trust me. I've known the guy for ten years."

"Kev . . . I'm not so sure. Even if he does miss me, he said he's forgiven me, but I don't think he really has—or can."

He huffs out his breath in a frustrated manner and studies me for a moment. "Sarah?"

"Kevin?"

He rolls his eyes, and a reluctant smile comes to his face. "Give it some time, but don't give up."

I open my mouth to speak, but before I can say a word, he walks off, leaving me to wonder what exactly he meant.

***

"Real talk?" Cam's saying. "You're an idiot."

"Where the hell did that come from?" I ask. But I know where it came from. We're having brunch on the patio of Café Rosalena, and she's on her third mimosa.

"I've been on the dating market the past year, and I can tell you from experience that Nathan was a jewel in a forest of imbecilic monkeys."

Odd description, sure, but she's piqued my interest. "Where are you going with this?"

She leans back in her chair and crosses one leg over the other, letting a sandal-clad foot dangle back and forth. I move my shin to avoid getting injured by her substantial platform heel. "I've thought about your situation, and I don't get how you could risk someone as great as him. I mean, he's smart, he's so good-looking, he's kind, he was in love, like *really* in love, with you."

"Are you *trying* to make me feel like shit?"

She taps her fingers on the table, and I note her bright fuchsia nails, perfectly matched to her flower-print dress. *Why is she so dressed up this morning?*

"I'm trying to galvanize *you* into action," she replies curtly.

"Why?"

She sighs. "I saw Nathan the other day. Downtown. Having coffee with—"

"With?" I interrupt her.

"I don't really know. Some blond woman."

My mind immediately goes to Danica.

"What did she look like?"

"I don't know. Pretty? Fit?"

I open my phone, search for Danica's picture on LinkedIn, and hold it out to Cam.

"Was it her?"

She leans in to look, then raises her sunglasses and squints. "No."

"No, definitely not? Or no, I don't *think* so?"

"Definitely not."

"Shit."

"I thought you wouldn't *want* it to be her."

"I don't. But this means he's going on dates with *other* pretty blond women. That's not good either."

"Oh, it's not?"

I shoot her a dirty look. "Of course it's not."

"So you *do* care?"

"Of course I care!"

"Well then, you're ready for the second part of my speech. The 'it's time to go win him back' part."

"No, I'm not actually. I need a minute." I get up and head to the restroom. While washing my hands, I notice my lackluster reflection. I'm thinner than I should be, with dark circles under my eyes from sleeping poorly. I gather my strength to go tell Cam that fate has likely spoken and that what I thought I had with Nathan just wasn't meant to be, as sad as I am to admit it. But when I get back, she's on her phone texting someone, smiling from ear-to-ear, which makes me smile.

"Who are you sexting, Ms. Hernandez?" I joke.

Just then, I get a text from Kevin.

Kevin: Did she tell you yet?

I look back and forth from my phone to Cam a couple times.

"What?" she asks.

"Youuuuuuu. Kevvvvvvvin."

Her brown eyes go wide.

"You. Are. Hooking. Up. With. Kevin."

She looks up at me, and I can tell from the surprised expression on her face that I've hit the mark.

"Oh my god, you are!" I shriek.

"Shhhh, you're screaming," she says, getting up and dragging me into my seat.

"I can't believe it. Well, actually, I can. No, I can't. It's too cute. You two are so cute. Have you guys had sex?" I whisper the last part.

I'm rambling. Words are flying out of my mouth. And she's looking at me like I'm deranged.

"How long? How long have you been hooking up? Why didn't you tell me?" I demand.

"Um, well, for a few weeks, but we matched up on an app a few months ago. It was a mistake—well, maybe not a mistake, but a mix-up. We didn't realize we'd swiped right on each other. And it took us a while, well, mostly *me*, to think it wasn't such a bad idea."

"That is so freaking cute."

"Sarah, I . . . I came to Austin."

"*What?*"

"The last night you guys were there, I took a late flight, showed up at his hotel room, and surprised him."

"No way, Cam. That is so fucking crazy and awesome. How did you think of an idea like that?"

"Uh, you," she replies.

"Huh?"

"Sarah, it's what you did with Nate when you flew up to Seattle to make things right with him."

My mouth drops open. "You're right. I did go there to make things right with him."

"You do a lot of dumb things—"

"Hey!" I say.

"But you're also really brave. At work and with your heart." She smiles lovingly at me. "You really live life. And I decided that's something I could learn from you."

"Cam," I say, feeling tears spring to my eyes. "That's so sweet." I reach out and take her hand. "Wait. Who else knows? Oh my god. You have to tell Nathan."

She scrunches up her face. "He already knows."

"WTF, Cam?"

"We had to. I'll explain later. But I promise I was going to tell you today. But Kev jumped the gun."

"Fine," I say. I am somewhat peeved—I'm her best friend, after all—but the news is actually too exciting for me to stay annoyed. It has somehow managed to lift my spirits from the bad news she delivered earlier about seeing Nathan on a date with a beautiful woman.

Suddenly, so many things Kevin has said or tried to say to me over the last couple of months make sense.

"Cam, I think Kevin almost told me the same night you came to Austin. Oh, geez. He spent part of the night in my room. Sorry. I mean, of course, nothing happened. He was drunk and couldn't find his key. Then he fell asleep."

"I know. He told me. He woke up and found his key inside his wallet in all the *unexpected* places." She rolls her eyes. "And then he stumbled back to his own room."

"I actually tried to get a new key for him, but the receptionist accidentally gave me . . . Carter's."

"What the what?" Cam says, eyes wide.

"I . . ." I begin to say, but I hesitate. Cam and I have been friends since high school, and she's been there for me through everything. Still, I don't want her to think less of me. She hooks her pointer finger in mine, something we used to do when we were teenagers. Our secret handshake of sorts.

Confession time. "When I realized whose key I had, I thought about taking advantage of it. I know he would've invited me in, and I know where things would've gone."

She waits patiently for me to continue.

"Nathan had broken up with me, and I was thinking about everything Carter said about me. How I was meant to succeed. How Nathan should be supporting me, not keeping me from opportunities. It was late, and I was so sad. I just wanted to forget about all the shit I was going through with Nathan."

Cam nods.

I bite my lip. "There was a split second I considered using it. Just slipping into his room and forgetting about all my troubles back here in California. Just surprising him in bed, naked or something."

I notice her blush.

"Oh, shit. Is *that* what you did with Kevin?" We both start to laugh, mine mixed with tears. "You little minx!"

When we calm down, she looks at me with a kind smile.

"But you didn't," she says. It's not even a question. She knows me.

I shake my head, confirming that she's right, and grab a napkin off the table to wipe my eyes. "I didn't. I messed up, but I could never do that to Nathan."

"I know you wouldn't."

I give her a small, sad smile. "I kept thinking—hoping, I guess—that he'd forgive me, that maybe we could get back together, so I just, uh, 'lost' Carter's key and headed back to my room."

"Sare-Bear?"

I half-gasp, half-laugh. It's been a while since I've been called that. The first time Camila heard my dad call me by my childhood nickname, she had cracked up. Fifteen years old at the time, I was mortified, but Camila had loved it. It had remained a source of amusement for her throughout our high school years. *Why now?*

As if answering my unasked question, she shrugs. "You made some mistakes, S.B., but you've always been a good person, and you still are. Don't forget that, okay?"

I nod.

"Listen," she says, "I'm sorry for not telling you sooner about me and Kevin. I just needed to figure it out on my own, no pressure. I'm not sure why it took me so long to finally accept that maybe he's a good guy. Maybe the money intimidated me. Or maybe he's such a . . ."

"Goofball?" I offer.

She laughs. "For sure, but I like being around him. I think he could be good for me."

"It's okay. I get it. And you know, you could make it up to me if you tell me one thing," I say, giving her a mischievous look.

"Oh, god. What?"

I lean in. "Is he good in bed?"

She blushes and nods. I might just be exhausted or have had one too many mimosas, but I feel like I'm about to swoon from happiness for her. I get up suddenly to give her a hug, then flop back into my chair.

"So, why all the talk about imbeciles? Kevin's awesome. I mean, he's a character sometimes, but he's, well, a legit good guy. Hang on to him."

She smiles. "Speaking of legit good guys ..." she begins to say.

"It's too late, Cam."

"It's not too late. I'm telling you. Kev agrees with me," she says. And I think back to what he told me earlier this week. *Don't give up.*

"Have you guys been playing us?"

"Wouldn't *you* like to know?" she replies.

"It's nice of you both, but it's not going to work."

"Rejected."

"What?"

"'It's not going to work.' You"—she stops and points at me—"must do everything you can to get him back. Grovel on your knees if you have to, give the guy a BJ while you're down there so he remembers exactly what's at stake, and beg for forgiveness."

"I don't think it would work. The night he came over to talk . . . what happened, it was a mistake. He left. He left me . . . the same way I left him that first night. I don't think he's interested in trying again. I mean, you saw it. He was out with someone else."

She looks at me, silent.

"That night, it was a mistake," I reiterate, hoping she'll get the point.

"No, that might be the only thing you've done right the past couple of months where it concerns him."

"I don't know. Kevin said he's really busy now, trying to prep for a big VC presentation. He's stressed because he's going it alone and—"

I stop talking.

"What?" she says.

I have an idea forming. I stare at my empty mimosa glass for a second while I think. Then it comes to me. "I know what I need to do."

"Butt stuff?" she whispers.

"No, Cam. Jesus!" I explode into laughter so loudly that the people at the next table stop their conversation and stare at us.

"Well, first, I need to tell him I'm sorry for a few things . . . but I also need to help him get that seed money."

She narrows her eyes at me, trying to understand.

"I have to help him. He needs a co-founder. I'm not a co-founder, but I can pitch it *with* him. I pitched our ideas to LightVerse, and they loved me. I can make those guys love me, too."

"Well, if the past few months are any indication, I don't doubt your abilities to get men to love you," she says.

I roll my eyes in exasperation, and a wry smile crosses her face.

I can do it. I'm *going* to do it. I'm going to get Nathan back.

***

Before walking over to Nathan's, I take a shower and choose an outfit I know he likes on me. I know he's at home because I checked with Kevin. When I arrive at this building, I take off the flats I wore on the walk over and slip on the heels I have in my bag. I steel myself and ring the bell.

"Who is it?" he says through the small speaker over the bell.

"Buzz me up?"

"Sarah?"

Why is he asking? He can see me on the app on his phone, probably looking uncertain, chewing on my lip. *Right, he can see me.* I plaster what I hope looks like a confident smile on my face and face the little doorbell camera.

"Yeah. Let me in?"

It takes a minute for him to respond. *I hope he doesn't have some-one—someone blond—over.* But then I hear the buzz and open the building door. I take the elevator up, and when I arrive at his floor, I find him waiting with his apartment door already open.

"What are you doing here?" he asks directly but not unkindly. He's leaning on the door frame, and I take in his outfit—some workout shorts and his beloved threadbare high-school cross-country t-shirt. He's never looked better. No, that's not entirely true. He looks tired.

I close the distance between us and stand in front of him. He's barefoot, I'm in heels, and there's still a six-inch height difference.

"Can we talk?" I ask him.

"Sarah, if this is about . . . us," he says, working his jaw and looking uncomfortable, "I'm really busy right now. I have a lot of stuff to get ready for this pitch I'm doing at a VC and—"

"I know," I say gently. I look at him as directly, as honestly, as I can and try to say with my eyes what I haven't yet found the confidence to say with my mouth. *Here goes nothing.* "That's why I'm here."

His brow knits in confusion.

"To help. If you'll let me?"

He hesitates for a second, then steps out of the doorway and lets me in. The dining room table, one of his favorite places to work, is strewn with post-it notes and a couple coffee mugs. I smile.

"You need a co-founder, right?"

"Does Kevin just go straight to you and tell you everything?"

"Well, a lot of things," I admit.

He rolls his eyes, but a smile crops up on his face.

"We both know I'm not a co-founder, but I can help you prep the deck or pitch or . . . really anything that will help you out."

"You don't have to do this. I didn't ask you."

"Do you have a better option?"

He seems to understand that while on the face of it, I'm asking about the startup, I'm also asking something else.

"No," he says, not breaking eye contact with me. "There's no one else."

I wait a moment to see if he'll elaborate. I'm curious, but I'll be damned if I let on that I know he went out with someone. I push it from my mind. This isn't about her, whoever she is. It's about Nathan—and me, I hope.

I move closer to him. I want to take his hands in mine, but I lock my arms at my sides.

"Nathan, I know we're not . . . what we used to be, but I was there when you came up with your startup idea. I want to help you get the money you need to develop it and turn it into something real. The economy is awful, but you have to try. And I have to help you. Please let me," I say, the doubt in my voice evident even to my own ears.

He looks at me, undecided.

"Is it so different than it was a month ago? Two months ago?" I plead.

"*Are we?*" is my unspoken question to him.

"Things have changed," he says, answering both my spoken and unspoken questions.

No. *Please don't say that.*

He takes a moment. His mind is working behind his thoughtful brown eyes, and I can see the millisecond he comes to a decision. "But there are some important things that haven't," he says, "I think we can work with that."

I give him a relieved smile.

"There's a lot to do to make it work," he continues, considering me carefully. I feel exposed.

"That's what I'm here for," I say softly.

And so, we get to work.

ATTENTION IS ALL YOU NEED

The next two weeks are exhausting. I'm either at work in Mountain View, working from home, or preparing for the upcoming pitch with Nathan in the evenings at his place. One night, as we take a break for a quick dinner, I suddenly realize Nathan has been at this for five months.

"You're incredible," I tell him.

"What do you mean?"

"I mean that you've built something amazing, and you've worked your ass off, and you did it all . . . alone." I think about all the times I went into work, and he stayed by himself and worked. All the times I worked from home, I was on meetings, collaborating with other people, and again, he was doing it all alone.

"It did feel pretty lonely sometimes," he says with a sad smile.

"I'm sorry."

"For what?"

"I . . . should've been more supportive. Asked more. Made sure you knew I was there for you."

"Well, I could've done the same for you, too."

I give him a curious look.

"You told me how you felt out of place sometimes in the engineering organization or how you thought you were unqualified for what you were doing, and I brushed it under the rug. I mean, I didn't do it from a bad place. It's just I know you're really smart and I know you can handle anything. I didn't understand then that even Superwoman needs reassurance sometimes."

"I guess we both could've done better, huh?"

He bites his lip and nods.

"We should get back to work," I tell him, and we clear the dishes from the table to open up our laptops.

The intensity of working together reminds me of cramming for finals during college. At times, it feels never-ending, but we manage to accomplish a lot in a short amount of time. Nathan fixes bugs and polishes the application he's built out—a prototype that shows a preliminary workflow and user interface. He finalizes all the slides related to the system architecture, which outlines the different data sources being pulled into the model he's conceptualized. The goal is to provide users—hospitals, doctors, labs, and perhaps the patients themselves—clear, accurate analyses of their lab results and biomarkers for specific diseases. I, on the other hand, design the deck and work on the messaging and talk track—what I've been calling "the easy part."

"It's not the easy part," he corrects me late one night. He squeezes my hand. "You shouldn't discount your efforts, your abilities."

I glance down at his hand holding mine, and he slowly balls his hand into a fist and returns it to his lap, giving me a self-conscious smile.

Oh, my. "I just mean the part I'm helping with is stuff most people can understand," I reply. "The stuff you've done? I don't even know how your brain works to be able to come up with something so . . . complex, intricate . . . I'm not sure what the right word is."

"Genius?" he offers up, grinning.

"Sure, genius," I agree. *God, he looks so cute right now.* We've been working for a couple of hours. Every time he stopped typing for a minute, he would put his elbows on the table and stare at the computer screen, running his hands through his hair. It's standing on end, and I want to touch it so badly, smooth it down for him. But that's a girlfriend thing to do, and that's not me anymore.

"You okay?" he asks.

My mind, wandering somewhere between Memory Lane and What Might Have Been Boulevard, returns to the present.

"Yeah, I'm fine." I'm about to dive back into the slide I was working on when his phone sounds a "good night" reminder, and he glances at the wall clock. It's a quarter to midnight.

"I need to head home," I say.

He nods and stands up. "I'll walk you down to your car."

I begin to pack my laptop into my bag. "You don't have to."

"I know, but I want to make sure you're safe."

We walk to his front door, and he stops. "Wait, you almost forgot your leftovers." He heads back to the kitchen. The refrigerator opens, and he comes back with a brown paper Trader Joe's bag. "Here you go. Make sure you eat it all," he says, winking.

As we make our way down to the parking garage, I dig in my bag for my car keys, all the while muttering that I'm sure I put them in there. When I look up, he's fighting to hide a smile.

"I'll never understand how at work you're so organized in everything, like, frustratingly so, but you can't keep track of your car keys."

"Hey, I'm tired," I reply, shooting him a fake pout.

"That's my fault." He twists his mouth, looking guilty.

"No, I offered to help you, and I'm enjoying myself. It's a different type of challenge."

The elevator doors open to the dim parking garage, and I realize I do feel better having him here with me. On the walk to my car, I shake my bag, listening for my keys. Nathan is behind me, and I feel a tug on my jeans as he plucks something from my back pocket.

He jingles them in front of me. "Missing something?"

"Are you kidding me?" I take the keys from him and roll my eyes at my own forgetfulness. I turn to open my car door but then turn back and lean against the car. "I need to tell you something."

"What?"

"That selfie you saw on my phone that I sent to Carter?"

His eyes seem to cloud, and the muscle in his jaw tightens. I reach out and touch his arm, hoping he won't pull away. He doesn't, but he doesn't respond either.

"I was trying to send it to *you*, but I—"

His mouth falls open just the slightest.

"It was the night I went out with Cam, and we had too much to drink. I missed you. It was the same night we, you know, on FaceTime?"

I can see the second it dawns on him—what I was feeling that night, what we *did* that night, and how I might've made a mistake after having a few drinks on an empty stomach.

"Oh. Shit."

His eyes go a bit glassy. *Is he remembering that night?*

"Can I ask you something?" For some reason, here in the almost-dark, I feel the courage to finally ask him who the blond woman was.

"I didn't send anybody half-naked selfies," he quips.

I smirk at him.

"Ask away," he says, putting his hand on the roof of my car and leaning on it. My heart begins to race from his sudden closeness.

"A couple weeks ago, someone . . . well, it was Cam . . . she saw you at a coffee shop downtown."

"Okayyy?" he says, tilting his head, confused.

"And you were there with someone. On a date."

"Huh?"

"Someone pretty. Blond."

He thinks for a moment, then smiles. "She *is* pretty."

No.

"And she *is* blond."

My heart drops. All this time, the last few weeks, we've been working together, and I thought we were building a bridge, coming together, but maybe not. Maybe the nights I'm not at his place, she is. I turn to get into the car, but he touches my arm.

"Sarah, it was my ex, Alena. She was out here on a business trip, and we met up."

Nathan and his exes. Correction. Nathan and his beautiful, blond exes.

"You, uh, seem to have a thing for blonds," I say resignedly. Danica. Alena. *Fuck my life.*

"Actually, I think I prefer brunettes." He lightly touches the ends of my hair.

Excuse me?

"She invited me to have coffee, and she told me she's getting married soon."

"Oh."

"I'm happy for her."

"Me, too," I blurt out. His mouth twitches.

He leans down and opens the car door, holding it open for me while I get in and place the bag of leftovers on the passenger seat. I start the car and realize that he hasn't walked away yet, so I roll down the window to say goodbye. As he leans in, I realize with a stab of sadness that a few months ago, this would have been the precursor to a goodbye kiss. Tonight, he simply touches my shoulder, and I have to fight myself not to grab onto his hand and never let go.

"Thanks for all your help. Drive safely, okay?"

"Good night," I whisper before rolling up the window and pulling out of the garage to head home.

When I get to my apartment, I'm dead tired, but I need to put the leftovers in the refrigerator. I open the bag and find two containers—one with what we had for dinner and another filled with blueberry muffins. On it, Nathan has placed a yellow Post-it Note: *Chihuahua or muffin?* He's also drawn a small cartoon dog with heart eyes. I think back to the first time he left me a container of muffins at work before we'd started dating. I'm not sure whether to cry or smile, so I do a little of both.

***

It's late Sunday afternoon, the day before the meeting at Redwood Capital. Nathan and I have been practicing for the pitch tomorrow, and neither of us has the energy to even look at a computer anymore.

"Nathan, I could do this pitch in my sleep. I could do it underwater. I could do it in a race car. I could do it—"

"In an elevator?" he suggests.

"Huh?"

"Maybe in a redwood?" His eyes glitter with mischief.

What in the world?

"All the places you could have sex," he elaborates. "Sorry, was that not what you were talking about?" He grins at me.

I look at him, unable to respond. "Folks," he announces to the imaginary audience in the room, "I've done the impossible—stunned Sarah Hoffman into speechlessness. Is that a real word?"

I burst into laughter and shove him, wanting to leave my hand on his muscular arm—wondering if I did, if he'd pull away or take my hand in his—but I ball my hand into a fist and put it in my lap.

He narrows his eyes at me. "I think we're done. Do you need to head out, or would you want to hang out?"

"You mean not crouched over our laptops? Let me see if my back still works properly." I stretch my arms overhead. Then I arch my back. He's very obviously watching me while trying to act as if he's not. *Well, then.*

Realizing I've caught him, he coughs and turns to close my computer and place it into my backpack.

"So, what should we do?" I ask.

"We could go for a walk or just talk."

"Not about the pitch, though," I add.

"Not about the pitch," he agrees. "Wine?"

"That would be heaven."

I call to him in the kitchen, "You want to look out the picture window and imagine what's going on downstairs like we used to?"

"Sure," he calls back.

I flop down on the bean bag chair near the window, the one I considered my early-morning "perch." When I used to spend the night with him, I'd sit here with a cup of coffee and admire the view.

He hands me a glass of wine when he comes back from the kitchen. "Cabernet Sauvignon."

My favorite.

"From Picchetti."

I smile, remembering the last time we hiked at the winery, followed by a lazy afternoon, enjoying a picnic and each other's conversation on their lawn.

He sits on the floor, facing me, his back against the window, and picks up his phone. "Music?"

I nod, suddenly realizing we've been working mostly in silence these last few weeks.

He puts on "alone time" by lovelytheband. It's perfect. *Did he do it on purpose?* A distant memory of us bumping into each other on the street and him holding up one of my AirPods and this song playing on it flickers into my mind and is gone just as quickly.

"You're going to have a hard time looking out the window facing this direction," I say quietly.

"My view's alright from here," he replies, letting his gaze wander lazily from my face to my body and back up. His lips curl up in a small smile, and I feel my skin heat up.

"Shall we toast to . . . collaboration?" I ask.

"Nah, too stuffy."

"To chihuahuas?" I tease.

He shakes his head. "Too silly."

"You come up with an idea, then. I want to drink already!"

He laughs. "How about to learning and helping and—"

"Forgiveness?" I suggest, hopefully.

His beautiful brown eyes meet mine, and I feel bare—the dark corners of my heart in desperate need of the light only Nathan can give me, completely exposed.

"Yes," he whispers, his eyes still trained on mine. "To forgiveness."

We clink glasses, and each take a sip.

"You know, all this time, I've been trying to debug what happened," he says.

"With the code? The app?"

"With us, Sarah," he says softly.

I give myself a moment to figure out what I need to say, but it doesn't take me long because it's actually pretty simple. "It was me, Nathan."

"No, it wasn't just you." His tone is obstinate, surprising me. Then, he touches my hand. "It was us. Me, too," he says in almost a whisper.

He dips his head. "I mean, when I broke up with you, I'd just found out from Kevin that something about the startup had been leaked, and there was a small part of me that thought you'd told someone at Light-Verse—Carter, maybe—"

"I'd never do that."

"I know you wouldn't—definitely not on purpose—and the more I thought about it, I knew you were too smart to even do it accidentally. When we both got back—me from Seattle and you from Austin—I wanted to talk, to see if . . . well, I don't know. But then I got that . . ."

"That." That photo. Me in Carter's embrace, kissing him. Evidence, in Nathan's mind, of how little he means to me. I stare into my wineglass unable to meet his eyes. *What must he have felt when he worried that I'd given away his secrets?* I'm beginning to understand why a seemingly simple conversation had ended in a breakup. I set my glass down and offer him my hand. My skin all but sizzles as his fingertips touch mine.

"Your fingers are warm," he remarks, his eyes trained on mine.

"So's my heart," I say in a silly tone, trying to break the tension. I'm exhausted—physically and mentally—right now, and I don't know where this conversation could lead. Somewhere good? Maybe. But potentially somewhere terrible, too.

"Nathan, all that stuff is over. I'm here now."

He opens his mouth to say something, but I'm scared, and before any words can leave his mouth, I jump in. "I should go home. We've both been working hard, and we need to be fresh for tomorrow."

"I'll walk you down," he says.

"You don't have to. It's early. I'll text you when I get home."

"Okay," he says. He walks me to his front door, and as I open the door to head out, he says my name.

I turn back, hand on the door handle. "Yeah?"

He puts his hand over mine.

"Thanks for helping me. And . . . for coming back."

I look down at his hand, covering my own. I force myself to look up, and I find his eyes searching my face.

"Nathan, I . . . I don't think I ever really left."

One edge of his mouth raises, the smallest smile imaginable, but it makes my heart pound. Before he can say anything else, I slip my hand out from under his and pull my bag up on my shoulder.

"Try to get a good night's sleep tonight," I say. "You have a big day tomorrow."

***

I want to make sure I'm ready for tomorrow, so I look one last time at the different outfits I've pulled out of my closet, determined to make a decision. I settle on the dark green silk blouse and black dress pants I wore for the presentation to the LightVerse board in Austin. Plenty of things might have crashed and burned on that trip, but the presentation was the peak of my professional career up to this point in my life, and I know I'll feel confident, competent, and impressive wearing it for the pitch. I stare at the tall black heels I wore in Austin and text Nathan.

> **Me:** You think heels are too much?
> **Nathan:** I'm already pretty tall, though.
> **Me:** <laughing emoji> On me, you nerd.
> **Nathan:** Oh, right. Well, YOU look great in everything. Do what makes you feel good.

You make me feel good. I just wish I could tell you.

> **Me:** Okay, but don't wear taller heels than me tomorrow. <winky emoji>
> **Nathan:** I promise. Sweet dreams.

I crawl into bed with a smile on my face and have very sweet dreams indeed.

Pitch It

NATHAN

Nathan is picking up Sarah at noon to drive together to the venture capital offices in Palo Alto. Though not a co-founder or official participant, Kevin will attend as an "adviser." He knows someone who knows someone at the VC. He still won't tell them who, hoping to shield them from any claims of insider information or unfairness, but Nathan's guess is that he wants to show his face and give the impression that Nathan "knows people" and that he's well-connected.

He arrives a few minutes early and texts Sarah that he's downstairs. She walks out the front door of the building. *Wow. Those heels were the right choice.* When she gets in the car, her eyes fall on his outfit: a cream-colored polo shirt and dark blue chinos.

"Not nice enough?" he asks.

"Way more than 'nice enough,'" she says, blushing a bit and attempting to hide her smile. "You look great. Just the part."

"And you . . ." he starts to say, taking in her appearance from up close. He stops himself just short of reaching out to touch her smooth hair.

"Well, would you give me a million dollars?"

"I'd give you everything," he blurts out and then laughs. "Like, ever."

She blushes a bit, then asks, "You ready?"

"As ready as I'm going to be."

On the way, they run through the key points of the presentation one last time. When they arrive thirty minutes later, Kevin is waiting in his car, texting someone.

"Camila," he and Sarah say at the same time and laugh.

"I couldn't believe it when she told me," Nathan says.

"I think they're actually a good match."

"Me, too."

He thinks he feels prepared, but as he steps out of the car, he notices the tightness in his jaw. Sarah walks over to his side of the car and reaches up both of her hands to massage the tense area just below his ears. She looks him straight in the eye and says, "Try to relax. It's going to be great."

He nods, trying to believe her. He's nervous enough about the pitch that he can *almost* ignore the other butterflies in his stomach, the ones fluttering around due to her familiar, comforting touch.

"I believe in you and your idea," she says. *Thank you.* "Are you ready to go kick some ass, Goldman?"

A small laugh escapes his mouth. "Yeah, let's go kick some ass, Hoffman."

***

Nathan came in feeling on edge, but in the interim, he has forgotten to feel nervous. After some short introductions to the four people they're meeting today, Sarah launched into the intro of their presentation, and he's listening to her intently, wondering how she's making everything they've worked on together the last couple weeks—everything he's been pouring his days and nights into the last six months—sound so amazing. Her command of these people's attention is undeniable. She moves gracefully and uses her hands to good effect, gesturing at the slides she's referencing when it makes sense and even doing a peace sign at some point. *Wait, what?* He missed it, but whatever she did worked. The men listening to her chuckle, and she's smiling back at them.

"Before I pass it off to my esteemed colleague, Nathan, I would just like to thank you for your time. We know that the current economy creates many challenges that didn't exist a few years ago, which makes your decision harder. Not to mention that you likely have many startup founders asking for your support. But let's be honest, we're the best." Her joke hits home, and he sees a few of them smile at her and at each other.

Sarah raises her eyebrow slightly at him to indicate it's his turn. He nods and glances at Kevin, who's sitting at his side. He hears Kevin whisper "LFG" as he stands to take Sarah's place at the front of the room.

He's talked about his idea and its proposed implementation at least a thousand times, so it's not hard for him to do it time 1,001. This time, though, is the one that matters. *Make it count.* And he does. He can tell by the expressions on Sarah's and Kevin's faces that he's doing a good job. He can tell by the partners' faces that they like what he's saying.

When he finishes, Kevin jumps into the conversation and positions it all in the perfect way. "What you have here is a founder with a PhD, who not only knows technology but has also been the Chief Product Officer of a successful startup—one that had an exit earlier this year. He knows business. He knows how customers think, but also how to build what customers want."

Nathan smiles and tries to look confident. It's still weird to hear people talk about him so highly while he's present. He notices Sarah beaming next to Kevin, and as he finishes talking, she looks to Nathan, waiting for him to continue.

Time to wrap up. At least that's what he tries to do when there's another question. A man who has been mostly silent during their pitch asks a question. "What you've presented is very impressive, especially considering the short amount of time you've been working on it, but I'd like to know how you expect to compete with larger companies who are better set up to handle business partnerships, the necessary infrastructure for the massive amounts of data streaming, and the like? In July, LightVerse issued a press release about something that sounds *very* similar. How can you compete with a giant company that has endless resources?"

Nathan's stomach drops. "Well," he begins, but he falters. Should he tell them what really happened? That somehow they have his intellectual property in their hands? Why would these people even believe him?

The room is silent, and he glances at Sarah. She nods a fraction of an inch, indicating he should answer. This week, he, Kevin, and Sarah had talked about what to do should the LightVerse press release come up.

"Focus on your patent application," Kevin had advised.

"Then emphasize the speed startups can move, their lack of bureaucracy, and their ability to sign deals quickly," Sarah had added.

"You can do this," her eyes are saying now.

But in the millisecond of time he's interpreting her expression, he notices Kevin's hand move, and he catches Kevin's eye. They've been friends for ten years, and he understands that Kevin's saying, "I got this shit."

Kevin speaks up. "I could probably get fired for sharing this, so I would appreciate some discretion here?" Everyone nods, and he smiles a smooth, cocky smile back at them and continues. "Nathan applied for a provisional patent, and LightVerse didn't. They issued a press release as a predatory action meant to block Nathan and his product or take advantage of him in the future. They didn't anticipate that he'd be smart enough to file the provisional patent application before them."

The man who asked the question nods, considering what Kevin has said.

But Kevin's not done. "I know for a fact that the LightVerse project isn't even moving. It only has half an engineer's time on it, and he doesn't even know what he's doing. They don't have anything except an idea—an idea that doesn't belong to them."

A few of the partners exchange what seems like positive glances, and he *thinks* they're in agreement that the LightVerse project doesn't seem like much competition. They're about to finish off when one of the men, someone whom Nathan knows from the introductions has a good twenty-five years of technical experience, chimes in with a question about an article he read recently.

"So, all of this reminds me of an approach I heard mentioned at a conference earlier this year. It must've been SC '21, but I'm not able to find it on my phone right now. Maybe you know the paper?"

He can't be serious. Nathan waits for more clarification from the person asking the question, but when one doesn't come, he simply says, "I do happen to know which paper you're talking about, and we'll definitely be taking some of those approaches while developing this technology."

"Maybe you should talk to the researcher."

"Well, I'm actually well-acquainted with him, and I can say that the approach is very well-researched and, uh, I one hundred percent support that scholarship. In fact, I'd say that guy's a genius."

"And why is that?"

"Well, because he's me. That's my research."

He sees Sarah and Kevin exchange almost identical expressions of surprise. Several people start to laugh good-naturedly.

"Thank you for the compliment," Nathan says graciously, catching the eye of the man who asked the question, who nods back at him and smiles.

"Well, folks, unless we have any more questions, I think we'll wrap it up," one of the partners says.

Nathan is feeling on top of the world as he sits back down next to Sarah and Kevin.

As they begin to pack up their bags and head out, the partners thank them for their time. "You'll hear from us soon," one of them tells them.

"That was epic," Kevin says as they walk through the parking lot filled with Teslas, Audis, and even a McLaren or two. He's patting Nathan *hard* on the back.

"What do you think they'll say?" Sarah asks Kevin. Nathan, too, hopes that maybe he'll have some guidance.

"I'm not sure, but I'd guess you'll get some indication—one way or another—pretty soon," Kevin replies.

"How are we going to wait for an answer?" Sarah asks.

"Just go home and . . . try to keep yourselves busy," he says, giving Nathan a look that couldn't be more obvious in its meaning. "Anyways, great job. I gotta go. Have to do some work before my date with Cam later."

Kevin heads to his car, and they get in Nathan's car to drive back to San Jose.

"We need to celebrate," Nathan says, glancing over at Sarah, who has taken off her high heels and curled her feet up in the passenger seat, massaging her pinky toes. He used to love rubbing her feet, hearing the pleased sounds she made as he hit just the right spot.

"What should we do?" she asks, bringing him back to the present. "It's not every day you pitch to a VC, right?"

"I know it's only 3:30, but honestly, I'm exhausted," he admits.

She laughs. "Me, too. I didn't sleep well last night."

"Me, either. I had too much nervous energy."

"What could you possibly have been nervous about?" she teases.

Only . . . everything.

He looks at her, thinking. "Would you want to order takeout and watch a movie? I know it's lame, but—"

She interrupts him. "That sounds perfect."

"My place or yours?"

"Well, we've been at your place for the last few weeks, and I'm pretty sure my mind now associates it with slide presentations and spreadsheets on anticipated profit margins. You want to come over to . . . my place?"

The word "my" hangs in the air for a second. Once—for a short time—it was *their* place.

"Let's go."

On the drive back via the highway, Sarah scans through the DoorDash app on her phone, and they discuss their takeout options. Nathan is in favor of Thai, but she's in the mood for Ethiopian.

"We could get both," he suggests.

"No, it's okay. I can compromise."

He sighs. "You shouldn't ever have to compromise."

She looks up from her phone, a confused expression on her face. "On takeout?"

"On . . . life, Sarah."

"Go on."

"And I . . ." he starts to say but then stops.

"And you what?"

I never should have broken up with you.

But he can't just come out and say it. She's waiting for him to answer, though, so he shares something else he's been thinking about. "I'm really glad things are going well for you at work. You've come so far in less than a year."

"Well, Cam predicted it."

"What do you mean?"

"The night we went out in January. The night . . . you and I met. She said I'd be running the place in a year."

He smiles in response.

"I'm not exactly running LightVerse, but I'm doing okay in life, I suppose."

"You're doing better than okay," he says.

But the look she gives him—a cross between yearning and uncertainty—makes him think otherwise. "No. Just okay," she reiterates.

Traffic is heavy heading south on 101, and a car stops unexpectedly in front of them. As he brakes, he shoots his arm out in front of her, brushing her chest.

"Sorry," he says when he realizes where his hand is and quickly returns it to the steering wheel.

They both laugh a bit nervously.

"What were you going to say before?" she asks quietly.

It's go time. He glances sidelong at her and braces his arms on the steering wheel. "I shouldn't have asked you not to go to Austin."

"Well, you ended up being right, didn't you?" she replies in a sad, soft voice. "Everything you thought could happen *did* happen."

Yeah, the worst self-fulfilling prophecy of my life. He notices her hands are clasped in her lap. What he wouldn't do to take her hand in his own, to trace his thumb over her delicate fingers, to try to communicate—through touch—how much he regrets. Touch he can do.

Words are harder, but he has to try.

"We could have figured everything out together. We could have thought of a way for you to get everything you're trying to achieve career-wise but also . . . do what it takes to stay together."

She looks up. "Maybe."

"I've missed you." The words leave his lips in a rush. He couldn't have held them back if he had tried.

"I'm right here," she says, reaching out to lightly touch his arm, and he hopes his quick intake of breath isn't too obvious. With both of his hands on the steering wheel, Sarah settles for the crook of his elbow.

"The past few weeks have been—"

"Hell," she says, interrupting.

"Heaven," he says at the same time.

He smirks at her, then focuses back on the road, where traffic has stopped in front of them. "The work has been hard, but having you there with me, I knew we'd get it done."

"I *am* an excellent project manager," she jokes.

"True. But that's not what I mean."

She smiles.

"I missed you," he says again. "So much. After we broke up, when I didn't talk to you for a few weeks . . . God, we ended up sleeping together because I just . . . just touching your face that night, it—you—set me on fire. I couldn't stop myself. I didn't *want* to."

She looks at him for a moment, not uttering a word. *What is she thinking?*

He takes a deep breath. "When I was prepping for the pitch by myself, every time I'd run into a problem, I'd ask myself, 'What would Sarah say about this?' You were helping me long before you showed up at my place looking . . . well, before you showed up and offered to help."

He reaches out and squeezes her hand, then returns his own to the steering wheel. They ride in silence for the next fifteen minutes. Both apparently lost in their own thoughts.

When they arrive at Sarah's place, she blurts out, "We didn't choose. Thai or Ethiopian?"

"Neither," he replies. "Let's make dinner together."

In Sarah's kitchen, Nathan opens the refrigerator and then turns to her. "There's barely any food here. How are you even surviving without me cooking for you?"

"I haven't wasted away yet," she says, defending herself.

He sticks his head back into the refrigerator before allowing his lips to crack into a smile.

"Don't think I don't know you're smiling. I'm doing perfectly fine," she says, pinching his side in a sneak attack, causing him to flinch and bang his head on the refrigerator.

He straightens up, a scowl on his face, and hands her eggs and tortillas. "Breakfast burritos?" he suggests.

"Brinner of champions," she replies, taking the ingredients from him and lightly running her fingers over his sore head.

The simple dinner they make together—breakfast burritos and sliced Persian cucumbers—is the most delicious meal he's had in weeks. It's not the food. It's the person with whom he's sharing it.

After the meal, they wash the few dishes together. As she dries her hands on a daisy-print dishtowel, he reaches for it and sets it on the counter. He hesitates only a second before taking her hand in his and stroking the back of her wrist with his thumb.

"Sarah, I was a jerk this summer. I know I was. Everything felt really . . . out of control sometimes. And I tried to control the one thing I shouldn't. You. Us."

"We don't need to talk about it now," she says softly.

"I feel like I need to?"

"Okay," she says. "Go on."

"I was alone with the startup, and it felt like you were pulling away—"

"I wasn't pulling away, but . . ."

"Yeah?"

"But I understand why you felt that way, because . . . I wasn't always who I should have been for you. For us."

He winces. "Don't say that. You did what you needed to do for you to accomplish your goals. And I shouldn't have made you feel bad for that. I should've trusted you. And I should've supported you."

"I was so—" they both begin to say at the time. They look at each other wide-eyed.

"What were you going to say?" he asks.

"Stupid. Careless. You?"

"Stupid. Self-centered." He tilts his head to one side and does his best impression of a remorseful puppy.

His expression has the desired effect because she cracks a small smile. "We both made mistakes. We're both just . . . human."

He pulls her into a hug, and she wraps her arms around his waist, resting her cheek on his chest.

"That we are," he replies quietly. He waits a moment—maybe she needs the closeness as much as he does—but then holds her out at arm's length and sizes her up. "It's getting kinda heavy in here for what's supposed to be a celebration. You still want to watch a show?"

"Definitely."

They settle on the couch, and the remote is nowhere to be found. He digs in the cushions and finds it hiding there. He playfully rolls his eyes at her, and she hides her grin behind her hands.

"Don't worry," he says. "I'm not going to give you a hard time about losing the remote. I'm a changed man."

She coughs, covering the word "Sure," and giggles.

"Wait, do you know where your keys are?" he challenges her.

"Yes, I do," she declares triumphantly.

"If you say so," he teases. "So, what're you in the mood for?"

"Whatever you want," she says, and he shoots her a knowing look. After ten minutes of exploring different trailers, Sarah chooses *Outlander. Of course.* They sit on the couch, not touching at first, but it's hard not to fall back into old patterns, comfortable patterns, and soon, without even realizing it, she's curled up next to him, clutching a giant pillow, her head resting on his shoulder like she used to. And little by little, she ends up pretty much laying on him while he drapes his arm across the back of the couch.

During one of the spicy scenes, she suddenly twists her head up and looks at him, then pulls away. "Sorry," she stammers. "I didn't realize I was using you as a recliner."

"It's okay," he says, moving his hand from the back of the couch to her shoulders and gently pulling her closer.

Unsure at first, she slowly relaxes into him, and her hair brushes his chin. Scenes of Scottish highlanders sword-fighting flicker in front of his unfocused eyes, and he simply allows himself to enjoy the feeling of her weight—her warmth—on him. He's thought a lot about what's happened with Sarah since January, starting with their one-night stand, their "will-they-won't-they?" spring, and their summer—first honeymoon-like and later, more soap opera in nature. The one constant—despite the drama, the peaks and valleys, the challenges—has been an unshakable feeling that Sarah is the one for him, the piece that completes his puzzle. Despite her flaws, and his, *because* of who she is and who she helps him become in this life, he wants to—has to—be with her. *But does she feel the same?*

Sarah eventually falls asleep, and around ten o'clock, he gets a text from Kevin.

> **Kevin:** Have some news for you. You awake?
> **Nathan:** I am, but Sarah's asleep.
> **Kevin:** Nice. Where are you?
> **Nathan:** Her place.
> **Kevin:** Can I come over?
> **Nathan:** Yeah, I'll come down.
> **Kevin:** Be there in 5.

When Nathan goes downstairs, Kevin is already waiting for him in the courtyard. "Having a good night, bro?" he asks Nathan with a questioning smile.

"I am, actually. So, what's going on?"

"Well, I got a text from my contact. He spoke with his friend at the VC."

"And?"

"And they said they're gonna fund this seed round. It'll give you enough for a good dev team until you can build things out more and get a few beta customers. Then they're likely to put in a very nice sum for Series A."

"Are you kidding me? That's awesome."

"Well, they had a condition," Kevin says. "They want Sarah."

He smiles. *Of course they do. Who doesn't?*

"They want her to sign on as a co-founder," Kevin explains. "They liked you—a lot, in fact—according to my source, but, well, they *loved* her. *And* they want more startups on their roster with women founders."

Nathan nods, thinking. Sarah has his back. If he ever had a doubt, the support she's given him over the last few weeks and her bowling them over with her presentation has made it clear beyond all doubt. But he *doesn't* know if she wants to be an official founder. Whenever they've discussed the startup, she's always referred to it as *his* dream, not hers.

"You okay with that?" Kevin asks.

"Of course *I'm* okay with that. But . . . I need to talk to her," Nathan says. "I'll call you later." He turns to go upstairs but looks back. "Hey, Kev?"

"Yeah?"

"Thanks for everything, asshole."

Kevin snickers. "Always, asshole."

When Nathan comes into the apartment, he doesn't find Sarah where he left her on the couch, so he checks the bedroom and sees her in bed under the covers. The shape of her silhouette—the curve of her hip, the dip of her waist, lit up by the moonlight coming in the window—is the stuff of dreams. She stirs a bit. She must not be fully asleep.

He wants to talk to her, but it can wait. It *should* wait until morning. He has some things to think about. He kneels down next to her, and she turns over.

"Oh, hey, I'm asleep."

He smiles to himself. She's adorable when she's half-asleep and tries to have a conversation.

"I'm going to head home. Let's talk tomorrow. Can you take the morning off tomorrow?"

"I think so," she responds.

"Okay, sweet dreams," he says and kisses her on the forehead.

"You too, my love," she says sleepily and closes her eyes.

BINARY DECISION

For the first time in a long time, I sleep well, waking only when my phone alarm goes off for work at 7:01 a.m. I check my calendar for the day. With only a few one-on-ones planned, I move them to later in the week and mark myself "out of office" on my calendar. I vaguely remember Nathan asking me if I can take the morning off, but I decide that pitching to a venture capital is an accomplishment that warrants me a full day of PTO.

I lie in bed for a bit, thinking about the pitch. It went well, but what do I know? It's a new world for me—the first time I've done something of that nature—so there's no way for me to know whether we were successful or not. Sorting that item into the "pending" column in my brain, I move to the next item on my mental checklist—Nathan.

Where do we stand? Will he be willing to give us another chance? I can't pretend, even to myself, that I won't be crushed if the answer is "no." Cooking dinner with him last night, falling asleep in his arms on the couch and even presenting to the venture capital yesterday—achieving something together—were all reminders of just how much I miss him. How much I need him in my corner.

I'm pulled from my thoughts when my phone buzzes with a text message. I'm surprised to see it's from Nathan at this hour.

Nathan: Awake yet?
Me: Of course.

Nathan: Right <smiley emoji> Were you able to clear your calendar? Maybe til 12 or 1?
Me: Still tired from yesterday, so I took the whole day off.
Nathan: Perfect. Too tired to hike?

I am tired, but being out in nature after the past few weeks hunched over a computer for endless hours sounds like paradise.

Me: Let's do it.
Nathan: I'll pick you up in 30?
Me: I'll be ready.

It'll only take me twenty minutes to get ready, which means I have ten minutes to text Erin and Camila in our group thread.

Me: Guys, I'm going on a hike with N today.
Erin: What?!
Camila: Wear something cute!
Me: We hung out last night, and I'm taking the day off. He asked me to.
Erin: Are you getting back together?
Me: I don't know!
Camila: Lip gloss. High ponytail.
Erin: This sounds promising <heart eyes emoji>
Camila: And tight leggings. (Thong!) He loves your butt.
Me: Cam!
Camila: Sarah!
Erin: Guys! Stop. OMG. We're gonna need real-time updates.
Me: Not happening. Out in nature. No cell service.
Camila: Also lots of privacy. OMG. THIS IS HAPPENING.

I try to check the time on my phone, but I can barely see it due to the plethora of celebration and sex-related emojis both Erin and Camila are sending me.

I smile, feeling a bit giddy myself. Taking Cam's advice, I choose a cute but practical outfit and head downstairs to meet Nathan. He's just pulling up, and a sudden wave of nervousness washes over me as I open the passenger door and get in.

"Good morning," I say shyly. *What is going on with me?* Nothing major is going to happen today. If things go well, it will take time for us to get back to where we were, and this is exactly what I want. A few hours alone with Nathan to have a good, honest conversation on whether he's willing to give me—us—another chance.

"Good morning," he says, a bright smile on his face. "So, I had an idea for a hike, but you said you're a bit tired." He twists his mouth, thinking. "It's a forty-five-minute drive. You could rest on the way?"

He looks hopeful. I'm going to say "yes," of course. I'd say "yes," even if he told me the plan was to hike on the moon today. "Do you have a good playlist?"

"I do," he replies.

"I'm in."

We begin the drive south to Uvas Canyon, and Nathan's playlist *is* good. I glance at his phone, sitting on the console between us, and see it's called "P0." *Priority level zero? Interesting.* I don't know what it refers to, but it's hard to ignore the common theme of the songs—love, mistakes, second chances. I look out the window and purse my lips to hide the smile that comes to my face after the fifth or sixth song in a row that seems to indicate that maybe, just maybe, I'm not imagining things. There's still something between us.

Nathan focuses on driving, so I close my eyes a bit and lean my head against the window to "rest." I'm actually surreptitiously checking him out.

"I suspect you're not actually resting," he says.

Guess it wasn't that surreptitious after all. "Maybe I'm not as tired as I thought. Or, I am, but . . ." I trail off.

"But what?"

I'm hesitant to share what I was thinking, but . . . *What the hell?* "I don't want to waste my time with you sleeping."

He snickers.

Oops.

"I didn't mean it that way," I protest, joining in his laughter. "I meant . . . that I enjoy spending time with you. And talking to you and . . ."

"I know. It's okay." He glances at the GPS. "We're almost there."

We wind our way up into the hills and arrive at the state park a few minutes later. When we get out of the car, I comment, "I should've brought a fleece." In my rush to look cute this morning, I must have forgotten the cardinal rule of Northern California outings—always bring a sweatshirt.

Nathan sets his backpack down and pulls his sweatshirt off. "Here, take mine."

"No. Then *you'll* be cold."

"I'll warm up when we start walking." He hands me the sweatshirt, and as I take it, our fingers brush against each other. Mine linger on his an obvious second too long, and he glances at our hands.

I pull the soft, cozy sweatshirt over my head and bask in the scent of him. He must notice because, when I pop my head through the collar, he has an amused smile on his face. I look away and smile to myself as I head off toward the trailhead to start our hike.

Uvas was a good choice. We find hordes of ladybugs and a few banana slugs as we hike up the path that follows the river. There are a ton of trails out here. Today is a weekday, so we have the place pretty much to ourselves, coming across a stray hiker or runner only once every half hour or so.

It has been at least six months since the last rain, but there's still a bit of water flowing. We come across a small waterfall and plenty of gurgling creeks. After the last few weeks—no, months—of stress, it's soothing. The sounds of water, the physical exertion, the closeness to Nathan. Out here, without the pressures of the world—my job, the startup, other people distracting us from what's important, our connection—being together feels right.

The path is wide, so we mostly walk side-by-side and talk about all kinds of things—recent layoffs at the big tech companies, interesting books we've both read recently and even how we both missed that Kevin and Camila were into each other.

"Yeah, like, what the hell? Why didn't they say something?" I ask.

"To us?"

"Well, that, too, but also to each other? Some people just don't know how to be direct, you know?"

"And others are really direct," he replies. "What did you say our first night together? 'Wanna bang, sexy man I just met in a bar?'"

I giggle, and an easy smile graces those soft, downright kissable lips of his. He starts down a steep side path to hike to the creek below, then turns back, offering me his hand. I take it and edge my way down. Though I'd be happy to hold hands with him the rest of the hike, when we reach a small bridge, I gently pull it away and lean on the railing.

"For the record," I say, "I think it was more along the lines of 'I want you. Now. Here on your couch.'"

He leans on the railing next to me and then looks at me intently. "And do you?"

"Do I what?"

"Do you want me?" he asks.

My fingers tighten on the wooden railing of the bridge. *I want you. So. Damn. Much.* But I can't make the words come out. He places his hand over mine but doesn't say anything right away. I hear only two sounds—the stream flowing under us and the beating of my own heart in my ears. After a moment, he inclines his head toward mine and taps it softly on my own, making me turn to him and smile at the playful move.

"So," he says, "last night, after you fell asleep, Kevin came over. I went downstairs to talk to him. He has his 'source,' you know—and the VC partners said they really liked our idea, us."

"What? Why didn't you wake me up or tell me on the drive here?"

"Because you were exhausted last night, and you looked so sweet with your eyes closed, pretending to rest on the way here." He touches my face, and I have to consciously try not to lean my cheek into his open palm.

"And, I . . . needed to get my thoughts together, and I have, which is why I'm telling you now."

"So, what did they say?" I ask impatiently.

"What were Kevin's words? They *liked* me, but they *loved* you," he says, laughing a bit. "Which makes sense because so do I."

I look away for a second and try to calm myself. The day is warming up, but despite the exertion from the hike, it's not quite hot enough for me to be sweating. Nevertheless, a drop of sweat trickles down my back. I meet his eyes and find the courage to whisper, "You do?"

"I do," he says simply.

My stomach clenches.

"But you broke up with me," I protest.

"I did," he admits sadly.

"Twice!"

He scrunches his face and looks down at the ground.

"Nathan, please be real with me. What do you mean? What do you want?"

He looks up and takes a deep breath. *What exactly is he steeling himself for?*

"I have two questions for you," he says, "and the answer to one doesn't affect the other. I mean them both, and no matter what you say, I want you to do the right thing for *you*."

"Spit it out already, Goldman."

"Okay. One: Will you be my co-founder?" he asks.

My eyes go wide. "And two?" I ask.

"Will you marry me?"

At the second question, my mouth drops. He laughs at my expression. I consciously make an effort to close my mouth.

"They seem to think that you being a co-founder will help ensure our success," he says. "And they want to support women in tech, so they want you on board. But you don't have to say 'yes' if you don't want to. I know that maybe this isn't the path you'd choose for yourself."

That's what he decided to explain? Why I should found a company with him?

"But you're asking me to *marry* you?"

"Yeah, I am," he says.

"But why?" I ask.

"Because you and I are an amazing fucking team," he says bluntly.

"That sounds like a reason for me to start a company with you, but to be together, to get married? We can't seem to get it right. We've both made so many mistakes in such a short amount of time. Nathan—"

"Sarah, I know you couldn't keep your eyes off me while we drove here . . ." He pauses and smirks. He knows *exactly* how much I was checking him out. "But maybe you were also paying attention to the playlist I put together?"

I nod.

"For you," he clarifies.

For me.

"Love songs. Sad ones," I say, starting to recall some of the less-than-stellar moments we've experienced together this year. "About mistakes and breaking up and—"

"They're not sad," he tells me. "Yeah, they're about making mistakes but also *learning* from them. They're about second chances and hope."

"But I'm so . . . broken sometimes."

He looks at me with so much love in his eyes I feel my chest tighten. "You're not broken, baby."

Baby? It's out of character for him, but that tiny term of endearment might as well be a crowbar prying open that dark, scary box deep inside of me, the one filled with my guilt and my fears. His large hand touches my face so, so gently, and I look into his eyes. *My weakness. Those eyes. This man.* After everything I've put him through, he calls me "baby." And all at once, my insecurities, my regrets, my dashed hopes for the shared future I had given up on—everything inside that damn box begins to pour out of me.

"I didn't tell you, but I got in touch with my therapist again. The one I talked to after my dad died. I was drowning in . . . guilt about what happened between us. I kept asking myself how—why—I hid things from you . . ."

He looks at me, waiting for me to continue.

"I-I'm sorry. I had gotten so used to doing it with Blake to . . . avoid criticism, to protect myself, and I guess old, awful habits die hard. How—" My voice cracks. "How can you want all this . . . with *me*?"

His face falls, and he brushes a lock of hair out of my eyes. "We're all a little bit broken. You. Me. But I found my glue," he says.

"Your glue?" I ask, smiling through tears at the unexpected analogy.

He gives me a sheepish smile. "I know it's kind of corny, but that's how I think about you. When I was breaking—with family stuff, and now with work—you were there. Any imperfections or cracks you might have *here*," he says, placing his hand on my heart, "those are the things that make you, you."

"And who am I, to you?" I ask.

"Easy. You're imperfect Sarah, who's perfect for me."

His hand is still over my heart, and I place my hand over his. I have a visceral need to touch him, but I also need to steady myself.

"You're the glue that held me together when I needed it, and I'm here for you, too. Sarah, neither of us is perfect, completely whole. We're just . . . real. You and me, our connection, our story—it's not perfect, but it's real."

I turn and rest my hands on the bridge railing and take a deep breath. *Real. Not perfect, but real. Me. Him. Us.*

Out of the corner of my eye, I notice him fishing in his pocket for something. It takes a few seconds before he looks up at me smiling, a ring—no box, no bag, just a ring—between his thumb and forefinger.

"Sarah, I love you . . . so much. Let me be your left-hand man, your husband, and your partner in everything. It won't always be perfect, but I know it'll be damn good, and it'll be real."

He's right. What we had, what we could have, it's real.

Looking into his eyes—so honest and vulnerable—I feel my heart open up. "We're really good together, aren't we?"

He nods. "I mean, we convinced some rich guys to give us a million dollars, if that's any indication."

"We did?"

"You never get lucky with the first VC you pitch to," he says. "But . . . we did. They're giving us what we asked for."

"Wow," I exhale. I begin to comprehend just how much we've done and how much we *can* do together in this life. "And you're absolutely sure your life wouldn't be simpler without me and all my . . ." I wave my hands around to indicate there's a lot to deal with—with me. *Drama. Flaws. Mistakes. Baggage.* It hurts to verbalize my fear, but I need one last reassurance that he knows what he's getting into.

He shakes his head. "Sarah, not to be a total nerd—"

I laugh softly.

"But you're a part of my codebase now. If I take out your line, the program—my life—just doesn't work. There's only life *with* you in *my* head. Quit trying to tell me why I shouldn't love you. I do. It really is that simple."

I bite my bottom lip and look up toward the tall redwood trees, trying to stem a new round of tears, and I contemplate the man whose hand is currently resting near my own, patiently waiting for me to collect myself.

"Hey, girl," he says softly.

Is he really trying to Ryan Gosling me out of my self-doubt and uncertainty?

He wipes a stray tear from my cheek with his thumb, and I lift my eyes to his.

"My smart, beautiful business ninja, are you happy about this or not?" I feel the corners of my lips turn up a bit. He blinks at me and waits for me to answer.

I manage to find my voice. "I'm happy. It's just a little unexpected. But I guess this whole year has been—meeting each other in the way we did and everything that came after. But it's a . . . welcome development."

"'A welcome development,'" he says as he pantomimes, clutching his heart. "So romantic." He's teasing me, trying to get me to loosen up.

"Well, are you asking about the startup or ..." I swallow. "The other thing?"

"I don't even know anymore," he says, squaring his body against mine and bracing his arms on the railing behind me. "I love you, and I want to be around you. If it has to only be at work at first, it'll be hard, but I'm pretty sure I can win you over sooner or later."

I laugh. His acceptance of whatever our fate may be, but his confidence that in the end we'll be together, heartens me.

"In that case ..." I start to say. And then, I leap—a leap of faith, of love—"Yes."

He leans his head down and kisses me. The warmth of his mouth, the familiar, sweet taste of his lips, the sensation of his tongue on mine—there are no words for how much I have missed this with him.

He breaks away and looks down at me. "Yes to what?"

"Yes to both." I pull him down close enough that my lips brush his as I whisper, "My heart, my body, my brain, whatever you might need it for—it's all yours."

He embraces me, and I hug him just as tightly, wrapping my much smaller arms around his middle. He pulls back and holds up his hand. The ring is on his pinky, just past the top knuckle, patiently waiting for its intended recipient to agree.

"May I?" he asks.

I hold out my hand, and he slips it on my ring finger. So *that's what this feels like.*

The smile on his face is huge. "What do we do now?"

I shrug.

"Well," he says, "I think we should find a place with cell phone reception and call the VC and tell them you're in. No, *we're* in."

I raise an eyebrow. "Really?"

"Uh, no. Wrong answer. First, we call our parents and tell them we're engaged?"

I nod.

"Should we head back? I mean, I brought you a sandwich."

Of course he did.

"What kind?"

"Your favorite," he says, pulling a sandwich out of his bag and offering it to me.

I take it from him and begin to unwrap it. "You could've saved money on the ring and given me this. I would've said 'yes' right away."

I offer him half the sandwich. "You want to sit here to eat?"

"No, let's eat while we hike back. I can't wait to get home. There are a few, uh, things I want to do."

I catch his drift, shove the rest of the sandwich in my mouth, and take off running. He chases after me and the promise of what's to come means the way back only takes us half the time. Some things, after all, are more important than a meal.

PERFORMANCE REVIEW

On the way back to San Jose, we call our families. My mom starts to cry on the phone. I manage to calm her down with a promise that we'll come visit soon so we can celebrate together. Noah and Claire, I notice, are happy but seem less surprised by the news.

After we hang up, I ask Nathan, "Did they know?"

"Yeah."

"Since when?"

"I told them last night I was planning on proposing."

"They're not mad at me about everything that happened?"

"You showed your true colors when you visited us in Seattle. They know you're a good person."

"They said that?"

He nods. "They also told me that relationships are hard work, but if you have the right partner, then the hard work is worth it."

With parents like that, it's no wonder he's such a good guy.

"And well, I agree," he says. We're nearing San Jose, and he asks, "Your place or mine?"

"*Our* place, maybe?"

"Yeah, I'd like that. I've missed my blanket."

"Well, it's on the bed now. I sleep with it and think about you," I say.

"I'd rather you sleep with me and think about the blanket," he replies, and I snort.

"I've missed your snorts. All your other noises, too."

"I don't make 'noises.'"

"Sure, you do. You snort sometimes when you laugh. You talk in your sleep occasionally. And, uh, when you come . . ."

"Oh, god, here we go," I say, starting to blush.

"When you come, it's the best sound my ears have ever heard. That first night . . ." He sucks in his breath through his teeth. "I'm getting turned on just thinking about it."

I reach over and begin to rub his thigh. "How far are we from home?"

He looks at me with hungry eyes. I'm still wearing his sweatshirt, and I lift it over my head and throw it in the backseat. Then I return my hand to his leg and begin to stroke the inside of his thigh. With the other, I flick one of the spaghetti straps of my tank top off of my shoulder and give him a mock-innocent look, "Oops."

"In about sixty seconds, you're going to pay for teasing me," he says as he pulls into the parking lot of my building.

"Is that a threat or a promise?"

He shakes his head at me and laughs a genuine, joyful laugh. God, it feels good to hear it. It all just feels good.

When we get on the elevator, Nathan's hands are all over me in an instant. He presses me up against the wall and slips his hand up my shirt, palming my breast. His tongue is in my mouth, and I kiss him back, desperate for more. I grab his ass and pull him closer to me.

The elevator dings when we reach the fourth floor, snapping us out of our quick-but-heavy make-out session, and we both race out of the door toward my place. As soon as we're inside my apartment, he pushes me up against the door I just closed behind me and leans in to kiss me, hard and needy.

One of his hands is at the back of my neck, his fingers threading up through my hair, and the other is on my breast. He begins to knead it slowly and moans. "Oh my god, I have missed this so much."

"This? This one breast?" I joke. I take the hand that's in my hair and move it down to my other breast. "What about this one?"

He laughs. "Give me a break, woman. I can't be held accountable for anything stupid I say right now. All the blood in my body has left my brain and gone elsewhere."

I reach down to check his assertion. "You might be right. We should probably take off your pants and confirm."

He pulls off his shirt before I can say another word.

"Mmmm," I say, taking in his bare torso.

"What?"

"You're so fucking hot, Nathan. I want you all over me."

"Did you just say you want me to come all over you?"

My eyes widen in shock. "Um," I choke out. "No, but, uh . . . well, we can make that happen if . . ."

"Shit, I want you so much right now, I'm imagining things. I didn't mean that," he says and kisses me softly on the lips.

"Wait a second. I mean, I didn't *say* that, but, uh, I'm open to . . . ideas."

His eyes narrow, likely to check if I'm messing with him. Then he crushes my lips with his own, parting them roughly with his tongue and kissing me deeply. He stops for just long enough to pull my tank top over my head and sees the sexy bra that I—*thank god*—had the prescience to put on this morning.

"Lace, huh? Did someone think something might happen today?" he asks, fingering the decorative straps. Then he traces his pointer finger over the lace flowers, finally arriving at my nipple.

"I didn't think what happened," I hold up my now ring-clad hand, "would happen. But I guess you can never be too sure."

He rubs his thumb over one nipple and palms my other breast with his other hand, all while leaning down to kiss me sensuously, slowly. He finds the front clasp and snaps it open, and the straps fall from my shoulders. As I reach down to begin to unbutton his pants, my bra falls to the ground. I slide the waistband of his pants over his hips, and he steps out of them quickly, impatiently.

"I'd happily have sex with you up against this door right now, but let's go to the bedroom. This is going to take a while, and I want you to be comfortable," he says, biting his bottom lip and appreciating my naked breasts.

I nod and lick my lips, letting my glance fall over his muscular, beautiful body. I lightly rake my fingers over his pecs and down his abs. He smiles, pleased at how much I'm enjoying his body, and then turns, presumably to walk to the bedroom. I hop on his back, and even though he's surprised, he manages to catch me.

"What are you doing?" he asks, laughing.

"Getting a ride."

"Oh, you're *about* to get a ride," he says, laughing. Holding me tightly, he runs into the bedroom and swings me around to drop me on the bed. He sheds his boxers in a move worthy of a strip show, then grabs at my legs to help me pull off my pants. He doesn't need to do much because I'm right there with him, scooting my underwear and pants off my hips as quickly as I can. When they're off, he climbs onto the bed to lie next to me. We face each other—both of us on our sides—and he begins to rub his hands up and down my body, starting from my shoulders and down to my hips. I lean in to kiss him and press my chest into his hard body. He rolls onto his back, taking me with him, and I straddle him, sitting up a bit. I roll my hips over him and watch his face.

"That feels so good," he says in a strained voice. He reaches up with one hand and massages one of my breasts while the other begins to stroke my clit as I rub myself on him.

"Yes, it . . . ah . . . definitely does," I agree.

His strokes become faster, and I can feel myself getting more aroused. Where there was only heat before, there's now a slickness from both of us being ready—far beyond ready—for this.

"Sarah, baby," he says. *There it is again.* "Fuck me hard."

I'm a bit surprised, but not at all put off by his directness. If anything, it makes my pulse race even more.

"Tell me again. What do you want?" I say in a low, needy voice.

"I want you to fuck me. And I want you to come hard. I need it. I need . . . you."

I caress his face and feel the slight roughness of his stubble. He looks up at me, and his deep brown eyes draw me in before he turns his head to kiss the inside of my wrist. I pull my hand back, bracing myself on his hip to lift myself up a bit, and slide down onto him, taking him inside of me.

"Ahhhh, yes," he breathes out. "I've wanted to tell you—"

"Tell me. I'm listening."

"Just that I need you. So fucking simple. I didn't want to be weak, to admit it, but I need you."

I'm rocking back and forth on him, and he's lifting his hips and grabbing my ass, pulling me into him hard and slick. He's hitting a perfect spot in my body, but it's more than that now.

So, I tell him, knowing that he needs to hear it. "It's not weakness, baby. It's love. And I need you, too. So. Much."

We move in sync until I peak, and knowing he's given me what I need, he lets go and shudders inside of me.

Somehow, we fall asleep. It's late afternoon, but I think we're both exhausted from the pitch and all the recent emotional upheaval. When I wake up from my nap, I open my eyes to find Nathan looking at me.

"You're beautiful when you're asleep," he says softly.

"And quiet," I joke.

"True, but I like our conversations."

"In that case," I say, curling up closer to him, "I have a question."

"Shoot."

"Since when do you like dirty talk?"

"Dirty talk?"

"Yeah, all that 'fuck me hard' stuff?"

He gives me a shy smile, but then his smile widens. "I've always liked it," he admits. "I was just holding back a bit."

"Mmmm, don't hold back. You know I like it."

"Well, I've done a lot of thinking. And some of what happened is due to me not communicating that well, so I'll make myself tell you what I need, what I'm thinking."

I reach out and trace my pointer finger down his jawline to his chin. "That's . . . really good. Thank you."

"Should I start now?"

"Start what?"

"Telling you what I want?" he says, giving me a naughty smile, tracing his fingers over one of my exposed breasts.

"I'm all ears."

He leans in to whisper something, and my eyes widen in surprise.

"Mmmmm, I like the way you think."

"Do you want to now?"

I nod. "But first, shower with me."

He jumps up and pulls at my hand, urging me to come with him.

I drag myself out of bed, and when I make it to the bathroom, he's already standing in the shower waiting for me. "Come hither," he gestures with his pointer finger, and I join him under the warm spray. I face him, and he soaps me up. Then, I do the same for him, enjoying the feel of his hard muscles beneath the bubbles I've created with my coconut bath wash.

"Mmm, that feels so good," he says, kissing my forehead.

He moves his hands to my waist and turns me to face the wall, pressing his front to my back. His fingers trail down, and he begins to stroke me with fingers that know all too well what I like.

A soft moan escapes my lips. "In a rush?"

He nips the side of my neck with his teeth. "We have to make up for lost time."

I know if I suggested it, he'd be perfectly happy to go another round in the shower, but I want to do what he suggested in bed a few minutes ago. I disentangle myself from him and quickly rinse off all the remaining soap while batting away his hands that are still trying to touch me anywhere they can. I open the shower curtain, and he takes a break from his efforts so we can step out of the shower and dry off a bit. He heads back into the bedroom, and I tell him I'll be a second. I cup my hands to drink some water from the faucet and notice the glint of the ring on my finger. *What a day.*

When I come back to the bedroom, he's already lying in bed, waiting for me on his side, propped up on his elbow.

"Alexa, let's get it on," he says with a barely restrained grin on his face.

"What?"

Then I hear the first strains of Charlie Puth singing "Marvin Gaye."

I start to crack up. "You didn't."

"I totally did."

"When?"

"After you fell asleep last night."

I make my way to the bed and sit next to him on my knees. He places a warm hand on my thigh. "I've missed being close to you," he says. "I mean, *this* is a fucking blast, but all those times, when we were working together and I couldn't touch you—I don't mean having sex, just wanting run my fingers through your hair or touch your hand—it was torture."

"I know what you mean." I remember what it was like wanting to reach out but forcing myself not to. I don't want to think about that now, though. I want to look ahead. I lightly run my fingertips over the back of his hand and notice the muscles in his forearm tighten. I pull his hand to my own—my *other* hand, the one I'm lazily using to stroke myself. His eyes shift downward, and his mouth twitches.

"If you want, you can touch my hand now," I say and smile. "I mean, I *know* it's not about the sex because that's *definitely* not what you meant."

He laughs and begins to gently rub his thumb over the two fingers I'm using to massage my clit. He takes his other hand and grabs a handful of my ass. "Why are you trying to ruin my sweet moment, huh?"

"Well, you told me ten minutes ago that something else of mine was very sweet and you wanted to taste it. In fact, you said, and I quote, 'I want your pretty little—'"

"Yessss?" he replies, looking extremely pleased with himself.

I lean down and whisper in his ear. He laughs and reaches out his hand to touch the spot I just mentioned, and I part my legs to give him better access.

"Go on," he says.

"In your mouth."

"I do. And what else did I say?"

"That you're gonna—"

"I'm going to work on you so long and so hard, you won't know the difference between coming . . . " he says, slipping a finger just inside of me.

"Ah."

"And going."

Yes. Please.

He leans up and moves both of his hands to my waist, dragging me over to him. He lays back down, and I crawl on top of him. "How do you want to do this, huh?"

In lieu of a verbal reply, he simply grabs my hips, hauling me forward until I'm straddling his shoulders. I can feel his breath just above my groin.

He's looking up at me eagerly, and I lean back, bracing myself with my arms behind me, pressing against his lower torso. He begins to kiss me and lick me, sucking me in and flicking me with his tongue.

It's . . . well, it's fucking amazing. It's not the first time he's given me oral, not by far, but never in this position. Spreading myself to him like this—it's vulnerability and power, all wrapped up into one. I hear him take a deep breath and worry he can't breathe.

"I'm not suffocating you, am I?"

"Don't worry. I'll die a happy man."

I laugh. He licks me again and hums his satisfaction into my clit.

"Oh, god." I look down at him, and he's grinning at me like a loon.

"In fact, if I don't make it, just make sure you tweet from my account that I died pleasing the woman I love."

"Stop it."

"'He was found with a perma-boner, and his casket had to be specially made.'"

I crack up, and I can feel him shaking under me as he begins to laugh, too.

"Donations can be made in his memory to Silicon Valley Food Bank—"

"And Cunnilingus Addicts Anonymous." I have tears in my eyes from the laughter. He grips my hips and scoots me down his chest—still astride him—presumably for him to get some air.

"You know, this isn't how it's supposed to go," he says.

"What?" I caress his face, and he looks up at me—god—adoringly.

"I'm supposed to be rocking your world right now, and instead, we're laughing."

I force myself to stop laughing. And he looks at me, silent, waiting.

"That's the way I like it," I admit.

He reaches up and touches my face. "That's the way I like it, too. But . . . maybe you'll just let me make you feel good now?"

"Yeah, make me feel good." I slide back up to my previous position.

He resumes his previous efforts, parting me, just so, with his skillful tongue while grabbing my ass and tweaking my nipples as it suits. I moan and grab the headboard for support. I rock my hips into his face, his mouth, and I hear—*feel*—him moan into me, and it pushes me over the edge.

"Ahhhh, yes. Oh, fuck, like that, Nathan. Yes. Yes." I explode, and he gives me about three seconds to recover before flipping me over like I weigh nothing and laying me face-down on the bed, his arm under me, pulling me close to his chest. I angle my hips just so, and he quickly slides into me. When I moan, and he knows I'm ready, he begins to thrust fast and hard, moaning.

"Sarah, you . . . are so . . . fucking . . . hot. I wanna do this . . . with you . . . every . . . night. Oh, my sweet . . . amazing . . . beautiful . . ." He's saying anything and everything that's coming to mind, which means he's getting close. I'm laughing from happiness and moaning from pleasure, and the physical movement, but his weight on my back and his strong arm clutching me are making me feel like I need more oxygen.

"Nathan, I can barely breathe. I need to turn over."

"Huh?" he asks, panting. "Oh, yeah, of course." He stops for just long enough to flip me back over, and we end up sideways on the bed. I lean up to wrap my arms around his neck and pull him back down to me, and he enters me once again. I bite his ear lobe and whisper how much I need him. As I do, I catch an amazing live-action show in my mirrored closet doors—Nathan's strong, large body simply ravishing me.

"Fuck me, baby, hard." My words have an immediate response, and he thrusts into me harder, and it doesn't take long before he lets himself go completely. He moans in pleasure as he comes inside of me and leans down to kiss me once more before rolling off of me.

After at least two minutes of silence, during which we try to recover our breath and our sanity, I turn onto my side and look at him.

He gives me a broad, exhausted smile. "You didn't toss out my shampoo."

"Huh?"

"While I've been gone. You kept it. You even kept it *in* the shower."

"Sometimes I'd open it up and sniff it when I missed you," I admit, my lip jutted out in embarrassment.

He breaks into a shy smile. "Sometimes I did the same thing with the green t-shirt you left at my place."

"I've been looking for that shirt like crazy!" I say, swatting him.

"*Maybe* I'll give it back to you now that you're going to be my wife," he teases.

"Don't forget co-founder," I whisper, pecking him on his sweaty forehead.

"Yeah. But we probably shouldn't do *this* at work, right?"

"Only on slow days."

He snickers. But then his face stills, and he leans close to my ear to whisper. "Beautiful, I can't wait to do life with you."

PATCH

SARAH

The next couple of months are a whirlwind. Between planning a wedding and formalizing all the things related to the founding of a company, Nathan and I are busy, to say the least. *"Oh-my-god-are-we-completely-nuts?"* runs through my head at least three times a day as I juggle emails, texts, and calls with different vendors for the wedding and real estate agents, lawyers, and accountants for setting up the new company.

Kevin is serving as an informal adviser, so we talk at least a few times a day. Until we officially found the company and can hire for some general administration roles, I'm a sort of combo CEO/COO, while Nathan has taken on the role of CTO. He's combing LinkedIn to find software engineers who might like to join a startup during an economic crisis and the tail-end of a pandemic.

"They'll be junior," he keeps warning me. "Shit, this is gonna be hard."

"It'll be okay," Kevin and I take turns responding when Nathan's doubts get to be too many.

As soon as the papers guaranteeing funding were signed with the venture capital firm, I gave my notice at LightVerse. Telling Erin was hard, but now I have to tell Carter. Just before I open the door to the meeting room—my first one-on-one meeting with him since Austin—I receive a Slack message:

Carter: Can we go for a walk? Meet me downstairs?

After dropping my things at my desk, I take the elevator down to the ground floor, where Carter is waiting outside the glass entrance doors. The fall day has warmed up considerably since the chilly morning, and my skin turns clammy as I walk outside. *Is it the weather or my nerves?*

"Hey," I say, running the back of my hand over my damp brow, hoping it's not obvious but knowing Carter's eagle eyes never miss a thing.

"Hey."

"So, I guess you know?" I say to him as we start to walk.

He nods.

"Carter—"

"Sarah—"

We both start to say and then smile.

"You first," I say.

"Okay. I owe you an apology."

What? There were a few things I could have expected from this conversation, but his apologizing to me was not one of them.

"For what, exactly?"

"Probably not what you think."

I *thought* he was about to apologize for kissing me in Austin.

"I won't apologize for kissing you unless you tell me I need to because, as far as I knew, you weren't anybody's girlfriend when it happened. And, if it's all the same to you, I'll take it as a small comfort that it wasn't one-sided. At least it didn't seem that way to me."

I level a stare at him while the gears of my mind turn, trying to figure out where he's going with this. I nod, but I won't say more on the topic. I'll surrender that small acknowledgment that, no, he hadn't been imagining things.

"What are you apologizing for, then?" I ask, my voice raspy to my own ears.

"Well, I don't know Nathan very well, but I have a feeling it's almost as bad—maybe worse—than kissing his girlfriend."

He pauses, and I look at him. I cock my head, and just like that, everything falls into place. I feel sick to my stomach. I'd held out hope until this moment, hoping that somehow, he was innocent, unaware of what exactly was going on. But him apologizing now—mentioning that it's worse to Nathan than him kissing me—it's worse than I feared.

"You did it, didn't you?" He narrows his eyes at me, maybe trying to figure out what exactly I'm accusing him of. "I thought—I *wanted* to believe that maybe you didn't know, but of course you knew." All the questions about Nathan's progress on the startup, always checking in and telling me he'll never get funding in this economy.

"I thought maybe they just threw your name on there, wanted you to be the spokesperson for the project, but you stole his idea. You started the same fucking project here, didn't you?" My voice is getting louder the longer I talk, and he reaches out his arm to calm me. He quickly draws it back when he sees the furious look on my face.

God damn it. How could I have done this to Nathan? Despite the progress we've made, the relationship we're rebuilding, it takes me back in an instant to what happened and how Nathan must have felt. I run my hands through my hair and look across the street, knowing that if I look at him, I'll likely slap him.

"No," he says loudly. "That's not how things went down."

I roll my eyes at him and turn on my heel, beginning to stalk back in the direction of the office.

"Sarah," he calls out, and the desperation in his tone makes me turn around. He strides quickly toward me. "I knew about it, but I didn't start it. When I realized what was going on, I tried to slow it down. I put every roadblock I could think of into that project to give Nate time to get his shit together and get funding. I . . . fuck it . . . I *wanted* him to win. I wanted *me* to win . . . *you.*"

My mouth drops open in surprise.

"But I wanted him to win . . . with the startup."

He crumples to a seated position on a low concrete wall near the sidewalk, resting his elbows on his knees, his head in his hands.

I exhale a surprised, "What?"

As he slowly raises his head, I note the look of anguish on his face. "This guy—it's not important—he knows some guy that Nate talked to a few months ago. It was early days for Nate, and he—stupidly, by the way—shared some early-stage slide deck of his that had an appendix of some sort. He must've forgotten it was there when he sent it. And this guy, being a smarmy asshole, sent it to his buddy in product here. They started brainstorming and scoping it out and realized it was really fucking good."

"That's where he got the user stories? That little shit!" I begin to pace. "So, you knew?"

"I knew. I found out. But things have been busy, and we couldn't be slowed down. We had to prepare for the pitch."

"I heard it went well."

"Kev told you?"

"Someone I know . . . he works at the VC. He asked me what I thought when he realized you're the Sarah I told him about—the Sarah I work with."

The Sarah you told him about. Wow.

"And what did you say?"

He presses his lips together, then locks eyes with me. Usually the color of the sea, today, they remind me of storm clouds. "I told him not funding your startup would be a huge mistake. It's an amazing idea."

I smile a bit.

"And with you and Nate working on it together, there's no chance it wouldn't succeed."

Now, it's my turn to sit down. I couldn't stand right now if I wanted to. "You did that for us?"

"I did it for *you*, Sarah. I told you; you deserve to shine. You *will*," he says. He reaches over and pulls me up to stand.

We walk in silence for a few minutes back in the direction of the office. I understand all of a sudden, like a ton of bricks hitting me, the reason Kevin kept his "source" a secret all this time. *Fuck me.*

Carter stops, and I look at him. It's clear he wants to say something.

"I wasn't perfect," he admits. "I probably should've backed off and not caused you any trouble with Nate. He's a good guy. And you know, the person who told me some less-than-stellar things about him . . . I should've taken into consideration the source."

Danica.

"I should've known it might be wrong," he says. "But I just wanted to do the right thing in the end."

I take in his grim expression. He looks miserable. I understand. I wish I could crawl into bed right now—curtains drawn, lights off—to give myself time to process everything I've learned in the last ten minutes. But we've arrived at the office, and in a minute, we'll go our separate ways—for the day and soon, forever.

I reach out but pull my hand back before touching his forearm. "You did the right thing," I assure him.

He nods, his eyes clearly sad. "I advised them to shut down Project M. When I told them about its origins, they were worried about a lawsuit."

"Right."

"Anyways, congrats on your engagement," he says.

I nod and smile. I can't help it. I've been on the moon since Nathan and I got back together.

"Carter?"

"Yeah?"

"Thanks for helping me succeed."

"You just needed someone to show you the door. You stepped through it and did all the work."

He *has* been a key, exactly like I told Nathan, and I'm grateful. But what I want, what I need, is not a key to open doors with opportunities waiting behind them. What—who—I need is someone to hold my hand and walk through those doors with me. Hell, to help me build the whole damn house and everything in it. It took me too much time and some wrong turns along the way, but I know now *that* person is Nathan.

"I have to go," I say. I mean that I have another meeting soon, but I'm also talking about leaving LightVerse. I mean that we won't be in touch anymore.

He smiles. "Will you still remember me when you're on Forbes 30 Under 30?"

"I'll invite you to the party," I say, laughing.

"I'll hold you to it." Then, he scans his work badge and enters the building.

As I watch him walk through the lobby to the elevator bank, I replay his words in my head. "I wanted *me* to win . . . *you*." If only he knew how close he had actually come. Even thinking about it, my skin prickles. I told Cam that I'd momentarily contemplated going to Carter's hotel room, but only I know just how close I was to ruining everything I had—or could have—with Nathan.

I exit the hotel elevator and look at the room numbers. 1008. Only a few rooms away. As I walk down the hallway, images flicker in and out of my mind. Carter's mouth on mine, only a few hours before, and his hand running up my thigh. My last phone call with Nathan, him telling me he needs a break from me.

I continue walking down the hall, but my pace has slowed. I rub the slick surface of the key between my fingers. I stop and take a deep breath.

Now or nothing, I think to myself, standing in front of Carter's door. And suddenly, an unexpected memory comes to mind—the night I spent with Nathan in Seattle. We'd talked for hours, just lying on his bed together, and I'd felt for the first time in my dating life that I had maybe found someone I could spend my life with.

Standing in front of this hotel room door on the verge of slipping the key into the lock and slipping myself into Carter's arms, I realize that what I want isn't behind this door. I deeply need someone who will be there for me, and I still believe that Nathan could be that person for me.

I turn and walk quickly back to the elevator. As I step on and the doors close, I kneel down and slip the key card to Carter's room into the crack between the elevator and the door. I messed up earlier, but maybe, just maybe, there's still hope.

Through the glass entrance to the building, I see that Carter has been held back by one of the engineering managers. The elevator opens, but before he gets on, he glances out the front doors and sees me. He tips his head and smiles at me one last time.

PUSH TO PRODUCTION

NATHAN

It's 7:00 in the morning. Nathan can't believe he's up this early, especially with how little sleep he got last night. He's in Kevin's kitchen, contemplating why a PhD in computer science isn't sufficient to figure out Kevin's fancy coffee machine when his best friend stumbles in, half-asleep.

"Dude, go back to bed," Kevin mumbles.

"Can't. Big day."

Kevin shuffles over and presses a series of six or seven buttons, and like magic, it starts. The aroma of coffee is already hitting his nose.

"You nervous?" Kevin asks.

He thinks for a second. *No. I'm not.* He shakes his head.

"Good. You shouldn't be. You found a girl who loves you, *and* she knows how to pitch to a VC. Every computer nerd's dream."

Nathan smiles. He grabs his cup of coffee and tells Kevin he's going to go take a shower. "We'll leave at nine?"

"We can leave at ten," Kevin replies. "Guys have it easy. No makeup. Cam said she'll be up at 7:30 for hair and makeup."

Sarah and Cam spent the night last night with Sarah's mother in Santa Cruz since it's closer to the bed-and-breakfast in Capitola where the wedding ceremony and reception are taking place. Nathan and Sarah decided they wouldn't spend the night before the wedding together, and Kev had suggested that he and Nathan stay at his place and drive down to Capitola to the wedding location today.

Nathan looks at his phone. He'll text her. They also decided on no phone calls and only essential texts, but this feels essential.

> **Nathan:** My soon-to-be wife, I hope you slept better than I did last night. I missed having you close. I can't wait to see you today in your dress and touch your soft skin. I love you.

As he presses send, he feels a presence behind him. Kevin snooping.

"What a romantic," Kevin teases.

"I've seen some of the stuff you text Cam, so shut up," he replies.

A few hours later, they're on their way to Capitola, and Kevin's driving. Nathan doesn't know whether it's Kevin taking the turns on Highway 17 at 50 mph or the fact that he's getting married in a few hours, but he's starting to feel a little nauseous.

"I feel like Dueling Banjos should be playing in the background at the speed you're going," Nathan remarks.

"I'm not going to be the guy who brings the groom late and gets murdered by the bride," Kevin replies.

Just then, Nathan gets a text. Sarah responding. *Finally.*

> **Sarah:** Got my phone back from Cam! She wouldn't let me have it! She thought I'd send you a selfie <devil emoji>

He sees a message come through with a photo. He laughs and tries to cover it with a cough.

"What're you looking at?" Kevin asks.

"A picture of Sarah."

"Can I see?"

"Definitely not."

Technically, it's a selfie. But it's not of her face or her hair, so he supposes she followed the rules. And he's definitely not letting Kevin see a photo of Sarah in what he guesses is her wedding lingerie.

A string of text messages comes in.

Sarah: Nobody tells me what I can and can't send to my future husband <winky face>
Sarah: But on a serious note . . .
Sarah: My soon-to-be husband, I didn't sleep any better than you last night. I can't believe I get to spend the rest of my life with you. I love you so much and can't wait to put my lips (and other body parts) on yours.
Sarah: I am here, waiting for you. I love you.

When they pull into the driveway of the bed-and-breakfast fifteen minutes later, Kevin parks the car and asks him, "You ready?"

"I'm ready."

"Let's fucking go, man."

***

Having an outside wedding in December was a gamble, but it seems to have paid off. It's a crisp and clear early December day. Sarah texted him earlier that the view of the bay from the cliff-side gardens is magical. As he looks out at the wedding guests and beyond to the water, he has to agree.

The ceremony begins, and he watches his mother and father walk down the aisle and wait under the wedding canopy. Kevin and Camila flank Sarah's mother, one on each of her arms, and they all join his parents, waiting for Sarah and Nathan to come.

Sarah has been waiting in a room off to the side and steps out, almost shyly, to the vestibule where he's standing. His breath catches in his throat. He saw her less than an hour ago when they came together with the rabbi and their families to sign the ketubah, the Jewish marriage contract, but the business nature of it all didn't allow him the quiet and the peace that this moment—between the two of them, alone—affords. In a pale cream silk dress with lace sleeves, she looks like . . . well, it doesn't make any sense, but what comes to mind is a distant star out in the galaxy.

He leans in to whisper in her ear, "You, my love, are beautiful." His desire to kiss her is overwhelming, but he restrains himself. Her hair is loose, cascading down her back in soft waves, and he touches the ends, quickly twirling a tendril of hair around his fingers. She gazes up at him lovingly, and he momentarily gets lost in her hazel eyes.

"Are you ready?" he asks, holding out his hand.

She takes it in hers and brings it up to her lips. "So ready."

They begin to stroll hand-in-hand toward their families, waiting for them under the marriage canopy. When they're halfway down the aisle, Sarah halts her pace so abruptly it takes him a second to notice, and he pulls her forward a step or two.

"Nathan," she whispers.

He turns to her. "Hey, you okay?" Then he notices where her eyes are focused, on the canopy itself. The *chuppah* is made up of two prayer shawls—one is his own father's, and the other belonged to Sarah's father.

"I'm . . . I'm sorry," he says quietly, pulling her close. "It was my idea. I thought you'd like it, but it was a mistake, I guess. I'm—"

"No," she replies. "Don't be."

"But you're starting to cry."

"Tears of joy, I promise."

"Do you need a moment?" he asks. "We can leave and come back out again when you're ready." She's shivering, and he wraps his arms around her, pulling her in close.

They stand in the middle of the aisle as the music continues to play, and he turns toward their families, who wait patiently but curiously for them to continue up the aisle. Sarah's mom, Lynn, is studying her daughter while his own mother holds her hand and leans in to whisper something in her ear. Lynn listens to his mom but keeps her eyes on Sarah and gives her a soft, reassuring smile. He recognizes it because it's the same one Sarah gives him when he's in need of reassurance—peace. Lynn takes a noticeable deep breath and exhales, her mouth forming an O. Sarah watches her, then does the same.

After she inhales and exhales several times, she trains her eyes on Nathan's. "Baby, you're my glue, too. You help me stay together. You fill in the cracks," she says. *Well, then.* "Thank you for thinking of a way to bring him here."

He shifts his eyes from side to side. All the guests are looking at them expectantly. "So, what do we do now?" he whispers.

And she whispers back, "I think we're supposed to get married?"

He laughs, and she surprises him by pulling him roughly up to where their families are waiting, eliciting soft laughter from their guests. When they're standing under the canopy, his brother leans in and asks if he is trying to run away.

He looks at Sarah as he answers him. "No point in trying. She'd catch me." Nathan grins.

They face the rabbi and wait for her to pour the wine for the first blessing, and Sarah leans in to whisper in his ear, "It's hard not having him here, but I'm happy."

"I know you are," he whispers back. "You can be happy and sad and thankful and sorrowful all at once sometimes."

"When did you get so wise?" she asks.

"I'm not. Just good at choosing someone who helps me be a better person."

"Yeah," she says, smiling up at him with tears still in her eyes, "Me, too."

***

Things are busy for the next couple of hours. The ceremony, the dinner, the party. But despite the copious amounts of food, he hasn't seen Sarah eat once. Right after the ceremony, when he stepped on the glass, they had had about seven minutes together, away from everyone else. They were meant to eat—hell, given eight minutes, he might've gone for the other things he was thinking about—but they mostly drank water and talked and prepared themselves to face the throng of wedding guests waiting for them. Between greeting each table of guests, hand-in-hand with Sarah, and receiving their congratulations, *he* had managed to stuff a crepe in his mouth. Every ten minutes or so, Kevin and other friends had been handing him shots, and he knew he needed to get some food into his stomach.

He'll make sure Sarah eats something when he goes back out, he thinks, as he changes his shirt in a side room. Thank goodness someone gave him that advice. "Take an extra shirt." He decides to forgo a dress shirt and chooses a casual one instead. Then he steps out to rejoin the party. He hears one of his and Sarah's favorite songs playing, and he glances around. Camila is dancing with his dad. He smiles.

Then his eyes alight on Sarah dancing with none other than Carter Michaels. *Are you kidding me?* Then he remembers who Sarah just married, who she's going on a honeymoon with, who she's decided to build a life and a company with, and he forces himself to relax.

He was annoyed when Sarah told him she'd accidentally invited him. For a split second he'd thought it couldn't be a mistake, but then he'd seen that he came right before Chetan on the invitees email list. What are the odds of something like that happening twice? Apparently, it's pretty high.

"I can't un-invite him now," she had said six weeks ago when the mistake had been discovered. "I know you guys . . . don't like each other—"

"Sarah, I don't like asparagus. My feelings for *him* are much stronger."

"I told you what he said to the VC. I mean, we can feed the guy dinner, and . . . who knows? Maybe he'll meet someone at the wedding?"

He'd given her a look like, "*You can't be serious,*" but Kevin and Camila had been around. Kevin, overhearing the conversation, invited him to go on a walk, and that had settled it. "He might be a dick who tried to take your girl for a hot second, but he also took out the competition and helped you get VC money."

Nathan must still have a sour look on his face because when Sarah glances up and notices him, her brow furrows. She whispers something to Carter and starts to walk over. She looks a tad unstable in the tall heels she's wearing—the same ones she wore the night they met—and when she's about a foot from where he's standing, she stops, sways, and faints.

MODEL CONVERGENCE

SARAH

Something soft—gentle—is touching my face. I hear waves and a wind chime. I open my eyes and see Nathan. *Why is he over me?*

"Have you eaten today?" he asks.

"Why do you ask?" I'm a bit confused.

"Because I'm currently holding you up after you fainted."

"Oh, right," I say plainly. "I got really hot, and these shoes are killing me. It's probably that." *And the memory that flitted through my mind right before I started feeling the anxiety creep in.*

Dancing with Carter must have brought back my memory of that night in Austin. The night I almost made the worst mistake of my life.

Nathan's looking down at me, trying to understand if I'm okay. "I didn't do it, though," I say stupidly. From the look on his face, I suspect I'm not making a lot of sense.

"Are you okay, beautiful?" Nathan touches my face softly, and I can see the concern in his eyes as he leans in closer to examine me. "Do you need to rest?"

"Nathan, I chose—I choose you. You know that, right? I'll keep choosing you every day for the rest of my life."

A flicker of understanding crosses his face. He leans in and kisses me softly on the lips, and I hear a few people say, "Awww." *Oh no, people are watching us.*

"I choose you, too, my love," he whispers in my ear. "Want to take off your shoes and drink some water? Maybe eat something?"

I nod.

"And then . . . I want to dance with you if you're up to it," he says.

"I'm up to it, but first, I need another kiss and a . . . brownie. Yeah, a brownie."

"I can make that happen."

One kiss, a brownie, and a bottle of water later, Nathan and I are standing in the middle of the dance floor. "Did you choose a song for us to dance to?" he asks.

"I tried to, but I couldn't narrow it down. Did you?"

"Yes. You do so much. I figured it was the least that I could do."

"What is it?"

"Just ignore the part about the sandy blond hair?"

I give him a stern look. We both know blond women are a sore spot. "I thought you told me you prefer brunettes."

"One brunette, in particular."

"You sure I'm your type?" I tease.

"Well, I have my whole life to figure it out now," he jokes back. "As for the song, your other option is me singing 'My Universe' to you."

"You wouldn't," I say in fake-shock.

"Erin's on standby to sing the Korean parts. Try me."

"In that case, I can ignore a reference to blond hair."

He tips his head in the direction of the DJ, signaling that he should start.

Within the first few strums of the guitar, I recognize the song "I'm With You." I still feel weak in the knees, but Nathan's embrace, as we sway to the music, makes me feel safe. Resting my head on his chest, I close my eyes for a moment, taking in the lyrics as he strokes my hair. Everything—for this short moment in time—is perfect.

"Sarah?" he says, and I tilt my head up to look at him. He takes advantage of the moment to kiss me softly on the lips. "I love you," he whispers, his mouth still close to mine. Then he deepens his kiss.

I smile and pull back. "Nathan, we can't make out on the dance floor."

"Why not? It's our wedding."

"But my grandma is here."

"Your *bubbe* definitely knows how to get down. How do you think you got here?"

I giggle. He twirls me around, and I catch my mother's smile before he pulls me back into him.

"I don't think we discussed it," I say to him softly, "but I'm staying Hoffman."

"I would expect nothing else," he replies. "We could both hyphenate if you want."

"Goldman-Hoffman?" I scrunch my nose. "No way."

But before he can respond, I hear the first notes of "My Universe" come on. "You wouldn't!"

"No, I wouldn't," he says, enjoying my shock. "But we can dance to it."

Everyone begins to join us on the dance floor—Camila, Kevin, Erin, Ryan, Zoey, and all our friends—and I feel Nathan's hands around my waist. I look at him—then around us—and I can't believe where this year has taken us.

Later that night, we say goodbye to the last of the guests. Cam and Kevin are taking my mom and Nathan's parents back to Santa Cruz, where they'll stay for a few days. Nathan and I are left standing in the bed-and-breakfast driveway in the dark, truly by ourselves for the first time all day, and Nathan tells me he'll be right up to the room we're staying in for the night.

"I just want to make sure Elaine's all set, okay?"

We're donating all of the unserved food to the food bank in Santa Cruz, and he arranged for the donations coordinator to pick up everything.

I lean to whisper seductively in his ear, "Just don't take too long, okay?"

I'm close enough that I can feel his jaw turn up in a smile. "Anxious to get the honeymoon started?"

"Yes," I say. "But I also slept, like, three hours last night, and I might very well fall asleep before you get back."

"Why don't you run a warm bath and get in, and I'll join you in a few minutes?"

"That sounds amazing, but I thought you might want to, uh, see what I shared in this morning's selfie in real-time?"

"Intriguing." He slides the fabric on the shoulder of my dress over, presumably to get a glimpse of the sexy lingerie underneath. "Well, your choice, baby, but just know that given hot-wife-in-sexy-lingerie and hot-wife-wearing-only-bath-bubbles . . ."

"In that case, I'll take a bath, but hurry up."

He salutes me comically and jogs off.

I head to the room and see our luggage already there. It's a sizable amount—more than for just one night—since we're planning to leave for our honeymoon tomorrow. I take off my dress and lay it over the back of a chair. It's freezing in the room, and I turn on the heater on the way to the bathroom, where I begin to run a bath in the oversized bathtub, adding some of the lavender bubble bath from the bottle on the ledge.

In an attempt to tease Nathan for missing the show, I hang my sexy bra and thong on the doorknob on the outside of the bathroom door. I close it, slide into the warm bath, and finally allow myself to relax.

It's not long before the front door to the room clicks open, and I hear Nathan's familiar footsteps. He reaches the bathroom door and chuckles—likely at the sight of my underwear—and then he peeks into the bathroom, finding me in the tub, water and bubbles almost up to my neck.

"Dream. Come. True."

"You have too many clothes on," I tell him.

"I couldn't agree more," he says, beginning to pull his shirt over his head and unzipping his pants.

I watch him, murmuring in delight as each piece of clothing falls to the floor. Then he's naked, standing next to the tub, trying to figure out the best way to get in without falling on top of me.

"I'll slip in behind you," he suggests.

I lean up to make room, and he carefully gets in, filling up the tub significantly more than with just me in there. He wraps his arms around me and, in short order, cups my breasts.

"Ohhhh, yes," he says and kisses the back of my neck.

"You don't waste any time."

"Hell, no. I dreamed about you last night and have been wanting to do this since 4:00 a.m. when I woke up with a hard-on."

I turn to kiss his jaw.

"So, what do you think, Mrs. Hoffman-Goldman?"

"About what Mr. Goldman-Hoffman?"

"About today? About tomorrow? About life?"

"I think I'm very happy that I'm doing life with you," I say.

"Me, too." He kisses the side of my neck, and I turn to make my mouth more available.

Things heat up, and I'm enjoying myself but can't truly relax. "This is great, but I feel like I might drown at any second."

"You didn't know? I'm also a trained lifeguard."

"In that case, save me from these dangerous waters and take me to bed."

"Can I give you mouth-to-mouth there? Maybe mouth-to-something else?"

I stifle a laugh. We get out, and he wraps me in a fluffy towel before grabbing one for himself. He takes me by my hand and leads me into the living room area of the room. "I promise to make tender, sweet love to you later, but right now, I just want to be inside of you and make you scream."

"That sounds like a very good idea." I push him down on the couch and sit on his lap, straddling him.

He has opened his towel, and I begin to rub myself on him as he cups my breasts in his hands. "Is this what married life will be like?" he asks. He hungrily kisses my mouth, then moves down to alternately nip and lightly suck on my neck.

"I certainly hope so," I say, arching my back so my breasts are closer to his face.

"In that case, I should've proposed to you the first night I met you."

I lift up on my knees for a moment, and he grips his hard shaft so I can slide down onto him.

"Ohhhhh, yessss . . ."

"If it's any consolation," I say, beginning to move up and down on him, "I think I knew then."

"Knew what?"

"That your Python is amazing, and I'd have to marry you for it."

He grimaces but then starts to laugh. "Are you seriously making a programming language joke while I'm fucking you silly?"

"Well, you can't exactly escape, can you?"

"I wouldn't want to, even with that bad joke." He grabs my hips and pulls me into him harder, thrusting and making me gasp in pleasure.

"How long have you been waiting to make that terrible joke?" he says, the strain in his voice quite evident.

"Since Seattle," I reply, breathlessly.

"Six months?"

"I had to convince you to marry me first. Now your Python is mine for life," I say and arch my back, begin to ride him harder.

"Fuck, Sarah. Stop it. I can't concentrate while I'm laughing."

"So just fuck me, baby."

His eyes flash with arousal, and all of a sudden, we're serious. Eyes locked on each other's.

"Yeah, but I changed my mind. I want to do it differently."

"How?" I ask. I slow my rhythm and slip off of him.

He takes my hand and leads me to the bedroom, where the covers are partially turned down.

"Get in, and let me make love to you, my beautiful wife."

I slip under the soft sheets, and he crawls on top of me. I open myself to him, and he slides in—smooth, hard, perfect.

"No jokes?" I ask, giving him as genuine a look as I can so he knows I'm as inside this moment—this feeling—as he is.

"No jokes, baby. Just you . . . and me. Always." He kisses me on my mouth, my neck, my earlobes, everywhere, somehow, it seems, all at once.

And as we come together, physically, for the first time as a married couple, I whisper something simple—something I realize now I must have felt the first time we ever made love. "You're the only one for me, Nathan."

DEFINITION OF DONE

SARAH

We're relaxing around the pool of a house in Maui for our honey-moon—Kevin's generous wedding gift. He didn't plan on joining us, but since we like hanging out with him and Camila, we invited them along. The view from the deck of turquoise water is heavenly, and I snuggle back into Nathan and take a sip of my mai tai.

"This is really strong," I whisper to Nathan. He steals the straw and leans down to taste it.

"Camila might need to work on her recipe," he says and smiles.

"I think she has other things to deal with right now," I comment, gesturing with my head in the direction of the pool, where Kevin just told Camila that he can buy a car for her.

"I don't want your money," she says.

"I'm just trying to sweeten the deal," Kevin says.

"You're already sweet enough," she replies, kissing him on the cheek.

Nathan rolls his eyes good-naturedly, and I snicker.

"I could tell all that hitting on girls stuff was an act," Camila says, pinching Kevin's arm.

"It was *not* an act. You should know that I do like women very much, Cam."

"Oh, that I believe. Someone who doesn't like girls as much wouldn't write an app in college to date them."

"You know about that?" Kevin asks. He shoots Nathan a dirty look.

"Girls talk Kev," she says and slips into the pool, pulling him in after her.

Girls *do* talk. For example, I know, thanks to a girls' wine and cheese night hosted by Camila this fall, that Kevin's swollen nose and black eye a few months ago was not, in fact, a Krav Maga injury, but I haven't brought it up with Nathan or Kevin—choosing to let them both keep their pride.

"You guys want to go out tonight?" Nathan asks. He's looking at his phone.

"Is anybody here sober enough after Cammy's mai tais to drive us?" Kevin jokes. She sneers at him, but it quickly morphs into a flirty smile. She love-hates that Kev has a cutesy nickname for her.

"I'm fine. I can drive . . . if Nathan will let me have the keys," I joke. He's been guarding the keys for our rental car the whole trip.

"You can drive, but I'm holding the keys. You always lose them."

"Sometimes keys *need* to get lost," I say without thinking, and Cam catches my eye.

"What?" he asks.

"Don't worry about it," I say and lay back in the giant lounge chair that I'm sharing with him. He scoots closer to cuddle with me.

"Maybe we'll just go tomorrow night? I'm kinda tired," I say.

Nathan leans in and whispers in my ear, "That's code for something else."

He's right.

It's code for "*Let's just stay in bed all night enjoying each other's company with occasional breaks for sustenance.*"

"So what if it is?"

"You could just tell me I'm irresistible, and you need more of my cock," he says in a low voice.

"When did you get so naughty?"

"Come join me in the bedroom, and I'll show you naughty."

Sitting there in his swimsuit, shirt off—tanned from our vacation—I don't need much convincing.

We make our way inside our room, and I stroll nonchalantly to the picture window overlooking the water and remove the sarong over my bikini. I hear his intake of breath.

"I am a very lucky man."

I take him in, my new husband, sitting on the bed, muscular legs spread wide and leaning back on his elbows—abs tensed and evidence of his appreciation for my body quite obvious. I'd say I am a very lucky woman. I bite my bottom lip and very obviously let my eyes rake up and down his body.

"Nathan?"

"Yes?"

"You're irresistible, and I need more of your cock."

"Then come join me on the bed where the magic happens, baby."

I shake my head and begin to laugh.

"Get over here already. I want to spend some quality time with my smokin' hot wife."

"That's CEO to you." I sashay over to within arm's reach.

"Damn right, it is," he says, suddenly grabbing me by the waist and pulling me down on the bed with him. "If it's okay with you, Madam CEO, I think it's time for a little executive one-on-one."

Indie Authors Just Love Reviews

If you enjoyed *Pitch It*, please take a moment to leave a review on Goodreads, Amazon, or any other bookish sites. Shout-outs on Instagram, Tiktok, and other social media are always welcome!

ACKNOWLEDGMENTS

First and foremost, I must thank my amazing husband. Your patience while I go on and on (and on) about my story ideas and characters and plot lines is admirable. Your poor heart almost couldn't take all the drama and angst of *Pitch It*, but you made it through! Thank you for always being by my side and giving me helpful feedback on the way men think, the statistical probability of some of the events in my book, and other—*ahem*—important topics.

To my early readers who gave me their eyeballs, brains, and time (and carefully worded opinions): Linda Till, Avital Samet, Sara Dean, Kacie Douglas Leicher, Suzy Schneider, Heather Worden, Allie Goldberg, Kelly Schaplowsky, and Kendra Tarbrake. Thank you for your helpful critiques and your willingness to help me brainstorm when it came time for book taglines. Don't worry! I'm saving some of the spicier ones for a rainy day!

To all of my family and friends who continue to support me and ask me how "the writing thing" is going: Thank you for your encouragement and showing up to my book events and liking my posts on social media.

To my daughters (to whom I've promised I will one day write a book they're allowed to read): Thank you for your support and interest in this creative side of your mom.

To Nimo Rotem and Matt Jaeh, the guys who gave me a crash course on the venture capital world. If I got anything wrong, I apologize. I am but a humble romance writer.

To Jen Boles, for her heroic editing efforts and positive attitude. Thank you for helping me become a better writer and for laughing at my corny jokes.

To Maxine Higginbotham, for helping me believe in myself enough to embark on this indie author path to begin with and for proofreading 1,000,000 words. I might've added an extra zero, but surely, you'll catch it.

To Harriet and Robin at Books Inc., an amazing indie bookstore. Thank you for supporting me on my author journey this year. I promise that one day my events will bring the masses. (I'm doing my best!)

To my fellow indie authors fighting that "good fight" (i.e., writing on the side, trying to figure out what the hell we're doing, and working to make our dreams come true), I see you. Keep writing and kicking ass, Lexie Sloane, S.L. Astor, and Samantha Renee—just to name a few!

To the Queens Library, an awesome Facebook group for indie authors and readers. Your positivity and the support and opportunities you give indie authors cannot be overstated. You rock. And if you're a reader who wants to join a group of lovely ladies talking bookish book stuff, check them out!

To my colleagues in the high-tech world, who are some of the coolest cats out there. There is *never* a dull day at work in a startup, and sharing the insanity with people who know how to keep perspective on life and have a sense of humor (and know how to play mini-golf one-handed, while holding a sangria) makes it all a lot more fun.

To Chelsea S., for sharing your knowledge and experience in the mental and emotional health world. People faced a lot of challenges during and following the Covid pandemic. Thank you for helping me, a layperson, understand these challenges. It enriched my understanding of my characters and their experiences.

Thanks to Rachel for her knowledge of Austin geography and hot spots!

And to the reviewer of my first book who said, "Nerds deserve love, too!" You're damn right! (Your words made it into this book.)

About the Author

Evie grew up on the beautiful Florida Gulf Coast and has been an avid reader her entire life. After finishing her bachelor's degree, she decided to explore the world and ended up moving to Israel, where she lived for almost a decade. While there, she earned a master's degree in political science, worked in academia, founded her own translation and editing business, and married a pretty awesome guy.

Their path led them to the San Francisco Bay Area, and Evie found her way into the world of high-tech. She has helped found and grow a hardware startup, been part of a successful software startup exit, and participated in an IPO.

The pandemic gave her plenty of time—and reason—to want to escape reality, and she read approximately a million romance novels, including the entire *Outlander* series . . . twice. Evie tried her hand at writing contemporary romance and published *Ship It*—a fun, (somewhat) realistic love story set in a Silicon Valley high-tech startup—in 2022. So many readers were curious to know the rest of Sarah and Nathan's story that Evie set out to discover it herself. *Pitch It* is the culmination of that journey.

Evie always has some project in the works, so look for more—something different—come 2024. Find her online at www.evieblum.com or @evieblumauthor on TikTok and Instagram.